Ace of
Hearts

BARBARA METZGER

A SIGNET ECLIPSE BOOK

SIGNET ECLIPSE
Published by New American Library, a division of
Penguin Group (USA) Inc., 375 Hudson Street,
New York, New York 10014, USA
Penguin Group (Canada), 90 Eglinton Avenue East, Suite 700, Toronto,
Ontario M4P 2Y3, Canada (a division of Pearson Penguin Canada Inc.)
Penguin Books Ltd., 80 Strand, London WC2R 0RL, England
Penguin Ireland, 25 St. Stephen's Green, Dublin 2,
Ireland (a division of Penguin Books Ltd.)
Penguin Group (Australia), 250 Camberwell Road, Camberwell, Victoria 3124,
Australia (a division of Pearson Australia Group Pty. Ltd.)
Penguin Books India Pvt. Ltd., 11 Community Centre, Panchsheel Park,
New Delhi - 110 017, India
Penguin Group (NZ), cnr Airborne and Rosedale Roads, Albany,
Auckland 1310, New Zealand (a division of Pearson New Zealand Ltd.)
Penguin Books (South Africa) (Pty.) Ltd., 24 Sturdee Avenue,
Rosebank, Johannesburg 2196, South Africa

Penguin Books Ltd., Registered Offices:
80 Strand, London WC2R 0RL, England

First published by Signet Eclipse, an imprint of New American Library,
a division of Penguin Group (USA) Inc.

First Printing, September 2005
10 9 8 7 6 5 4 3 2 1

To Mrs. Eleanor Brennan

Prologue

The Earl of Carde was dying. Part of him had already died when he lost his beloved young wife and baby daughter in the coaching accident. Dearest Lizbeth had taken little Lottie north to her family's home on the coast, near Hull, but the carriage had toppled over a cliff on the way home. Lizbeth had died instantly, they told him later, along with her maid, the driver, a groom, and the horses. Missing from the carnage, though, was the newly hired replacement guard—and Lottie.

Lord Carde had rushed north through the rain and snow and icy winter weather, but too late, of course. He searched for Lottie anyway, leading the shepherds and drovers, the shopkeepers and the sheriff, the entire community, through the cold. No trace was found of either the child or the guard, only a child's bonnet and some bloodstains, quickly washed away by the freezing rain. The locals said the man must have run off, fearing he'd be blamed. The child would have been carried away by wild dogs, they whispered, or found by Gypsies, or else the three-year-old had wandered toward the chill waters. She would never be seen again.

Broken in body and spirit, the earl returned home to Cardington to bury his beautiful young second wife in his family crypt at Carde Hall on another sleet-shrouded day. The congestion in his lungs turned putrid, and the fevers stole what strength he had left. He called for his sons.

The earl was proud of his boys, products of his first marriage. His heir, Alexander Chalfont Endicott, was fourteen, a serious, bespectacled lad, tall and wiry. Nicknamed Ace by his school friends because of his initials and the Carde connection, Viscount Endicott would make a good earl. Lord Carde was not worried about the succession.

His second son, the Honorable Jonathan Endicott, was eleven, but still boyishly rounded. He was no scholar, the masters at Eton reported, but the earl knew Jack, as they called him, was pluck to the backbone, horse-mad and athletic. He'd do.

Both boys were dark-haired like their mother, but with the earl's own aquiline nose. They were the fulfillment of his duty to king and country, his legacy to the world, the future of his house and name and family honor. Yes, they made him proud.

But they never made him laugh with dimpled smiles, high-pitched giggles, and pleas for one more horsey-ride on Papa's back. They never climbed next to him in his library chair for tickling, or curled on his lap like a sleeping blond angel. Sons were all well and good, the earl thought, looking at the two somber boys at the foot of his bed, manfully trying to hide their fears. But they weren't his precious baby girl.

He raised one trembling hand to wipe a tear from

his eyes and beckoned the boys closer, so he could whisper to them, all the voice left to him.

"You will take my place, Alexander, and do a fine job of it. Your uncle will help."

Viscount Endicott nodded, a lock of black hair falling into his eyes. He brushed it away, or a tear of his own. "Yes, Father. I shall do my best."

"I know you will, lad. And you, Jack. Help your brother. Being earl is no easy task."

"But Ace is only a schoolboy," the younger boy complained, not ready for the truth he saw in the doctors' and servants' eyes. "And you are the earl!"

Lord Carde tried to take a deep breath, and they could all hear the rasping sound of it in his throat. "So I am, and so Alexander will be. You will be his right hand."

"But—" Jack began, but Alexander kicked him. "Yes, Father."

The earl took another breath. "Good. Now I want another promise from you, lads."

"Anything, Father," Alexander said and Jack nodded.

"Find your sister."

Jack was sniffling, and his brother handed him a handkerchief, frowning. "But you looked everywhere, Father."

"And hired men to keep looking. But none of them will care as much as you. I know she is alive somewhere, needing you." The earl took Alexander's hand and placed it on his own steadily weakening heart. "I know it, here."

"But we are only boys, sir, like Jack said."

"You are my boys, though. Endicotts. 'Ever True.' Don't forget that, our motto, and do not let anyone else forget to keep looking. Promise me."

"I swear, Father, to keep searching for Lottie until she is home with us."

"Me, too."

The earl sighed and closed his eyes, his eldest son's hand still in his. Alexander reached his other hand out to his brother, who grasped it firmly.

"Father," Jack whispered, despite the doctors' frowns. The earl's eyelids fluttered half open.

"Will you see Lottie's mother in Heaven?"

The earl's dry lips twitched to a smile. "I . . . hope so, lad."

"Tell her we'll try. But Father . . ."

Moments went by while they waited for the earl to find another breath. "Yes?"

"Will you see our mother, too?"

Lord Carde reached out his other hand to his younger son, who climbed onto the high bed at his brother's nod, to take it. "I'll see your mother too . . . and thank her . . . for the fine . . . young men she . . ."

CHAPTER ONE

The Earl of Carde was engaged. Affianced. Promised. He was thrice betrothed, thrice accursed. Bad enough he was parson-pledged—but to three different women? He was regally, royally, ridiculously damned, done in, and ditched. How, by all that was holy and a great deal that was not, had such a nightmare befallen him?

Alexander Chalfont Endicott, Carde to most, Alex to a few, Ace to his closest intimates and the gleeful London gossip columnists, took off his glasses and poured himself another glass of brandy, despite the early morning hour. He preferred the fog of his poor eyesight and the fog of inebriation. If he drank enough, perhaps he could forget this past week. If he smashed his spectacles to smithereens, perhaps he could ignore the scandal sheets.

Ace of Hearts, they were calling him, with cartoons depicting the winning hand, a stacked deck, three of a kind. Every blasted joke about his title and rumors of his situation were spread out on his desk, and on breakfast tables and in boudoirs throughout London, if not all of England, he supposed. Alex cursed, shoved the newspapers and his glasses to the floor, and tried to let the brandy bring him solace.

An hour later, he still had three hopeful brides, but now he had a headache, too. He rubbed the bridge of his somewhat beakish nose, yet another legacy from his father, along with the title and fortune that made him a prize on the marriage market.

He cursed his nose, his headache, the avaricious, ambitious, velvet-draped vultures of the *ton*, and Fate. Mostly, he cursed himself for being a fool. How had this mess happened? He'd shown three women respect and admiration, that was how. He'd forgotten that the so-called frail sex had no sense of fair play. Honor was not in their vocabularies, nor in their blood. Hell, any man who turned his back on a female deserved a knife stuck in it. But three times? Alex groaned at the injustice, and the headache.

After all, he was not a rake. He'd sown his wild oats as a young buck, of course. What man worth his salt didn't? Later, when he first came into his majority and control of his own fortune, perhaps he had cut too wide a swath through the *demimonde,* the gambling dens and the opera dancers. He outgrew that nonsense soon enough, when he realized the full weight of the earldom and the extent of his responsibilities. Between his estates and investments, his seat in Parliament, his reform committees, and social commitments, the young lord barely had time for reading a book, much less carousing all night.

Whatever his personal inclinations, Alex never forgot what was due his name and his legions of dependents. He took his responsibilities to heart. No half measures for the Earl of Carde.

He laughed now, but without humor. Half measures,

indeed. Who else found three fiancées when he set out to fill his nursery?

Again setting his personal desires aside, Alex had decided it was time for him to take a bride and beget heirs for the earldom. After all, he was twenty-seven and his only brother was in the army. Who knew what dangers that daredevil was riding into on the Peninsula, if he would return a hero, or not at all? Alex sorely missed Jack, his best friend and confidante, and worried over him constantly, but Jack was a man now too, and had made his own choices. So Alex had set out to find a suitable countess. His first mistake was mentioning his intentions to a few of his acquaintances at White's Club. As soon as rumors started circulating that the Earl of Carde was contemplating wedlock, Alex was a dead man. His second mistake was not shooting himself and being done with the misery.

First, his mistress decided that they were engaged. His mistress, by Harry! A man didn't marry his mistress, not even if she was well-born and beautiful, a wealthy old baron's widow. He was not even keeping Mona, Lady Monroe, under his protection, for heaven's sake, and for a modicum of propriety. The richly—and lushly—endowed widow had her own house and horses and servants. He merely bought the occasional expensive bauble to show his appreciation.

Alex couldn't imagine where Mona got the notion in her gorgeous red head that he'd take another man's wife as his countess, and a lustful, licentious woman at that. Somehow she must have plucked the idea from the morass of her social-climbing mind.

"Darling," she'd said when he was drifting off in satiated slumber one recent night, "we really should talk about the wedding."

"Hm? Were we invited to someone's wedding,

then?" He'd rolled over, pulling the blankets around her. "Remind me in the morning."

"Our wedding, silly."

That had him wide awake, in a hurry. The blankets and sheets were on the floor, as was the earl, barefoot and bare-assed, scrambling for his spectacles. "Our wedding?" He practically leaped into his inexpressibles. "We have no wedding plans that I am aware of," he said out loud. "Or ever shall," he muttered under his breath, pulling his shirt over his head.

"Oh, but you asked me," Mona said with a purr and a pout that she must have thought adorable. He thought it predatory. "Last week, after Lady Carrisbrooke's birthday party."

He remembered the dinner party, and all the champagne served afterward. He might have lost count of how many glasses he'd swallowed, but surely he would recall losing his mind? He vowed never to go near the stuff again. "Refresh my memory."

"We came home, here, afterward. And we were, ah, making love."

What they did was *not* making love. It was fornicating, plain and simple. What else was their relationship about? "Go on. We were in bed." Or so he assumed. Mona had a fondness for the fur rug in front of the fireplace. "And . . . ?"

"And you said 'I wish this could last forever.' I said it could, and you said yes. In fact you shouted 'yes' so loudly that I feared my maid might come running."

Now he remembered. He remembered where her luscious red lips were at the time, what she was doing with her tongue and her hands, and precisely what he wished to last forever. "Great gods, you could not have taken that for a proposal of marriage! Why, a man would promise you the moon, if he was soaring toward the stars. He'd offer you his heart on a silver platter if he thought you might stop otherwise."

"You promised me a ring."

"And I bought you that emerald, didn't I?" He looked at the huge stone on her finger, flashing in the candlelight. He draped his neck cloth over his collar and said, "That was not the Carde engagement diamond." Which was here, in town, in case he found the lady of his choice. Mona, Lady Monroe, was not and never would be his choice for the Countess of Carde. "The emerald was a gift, nothing more. Consider it a parting gift, in fact."

"I think not. You nearly begged for forever, then you bought me a ring. What else was a woman to think but that you were offering marriage?"

"That I was grateful for a good f—" Alex couldn't say it, not even in his anger. Whatever else she was, Mona was a female, and he was a gentleman—a gentleman on his way out the door as soon as he located his shoes.

"I have to be thinking of my future, you know," she said, raising one knee in a suggestive pose.

To hell with his shoes. Alex would walk barefoot, through hot coals, to get out of here. He did, however, need his coat, with his keys and purse, to hire a hackney. "You can't have gone through Monroe's fortune so fast. Hire yourself a good man of business."

He was searching under the dressing table when she said, "But I want respectability."

Alex looked around the room with its flickering candles, the scent of sex mixed with her heavy perfume, the pink satin bedcovers in a heap on the floor next to her filmy red robe. "You should have thought of that sooner, then."

Mona brushed that aside with a flick of her long nails. "I want a title."

Ah, there was his coat, under the bed. "Well, this one is not for hire, madam. The earls of Carde have always married for love, nothing else. And I never, ever said I loved you."

"Ah, but you will come to, after the wedding."

His hand was on the doorknob. "There will be no wedding, Mona. Not soon, not later."

"But they say you are looking for a bride."

A pure, innocent bride, not a harlot who knew a hundred ways to pleasure a man—and might have a hundred men before the wedding lines were dry. A man might dream of a wife with the skills of a seductress, the lustiness of a light skirt, but he wanted to be the one to teach her. Alex's Lady Carde was going to be just that, a lady, through and through. "I am still looking."

"Oh, I think you will stop your search when my solicitor threatens you with breach of promise."

Now Alex had to smile. A man in the extremities of ecstasy could not be held accountable for any promises, pledges, or pleas. If there wasn't already a law to that effect, he'd bring one up at the next session of Parliament. "Any barrister with balls under his robe will laugh at any such lawsuit."

"Not my former brother-in-law, the new baron, who craves respectability as much as I do. He would not like the scandal. Nor would you, I think."

Mona was right. Alex did not like the scandal—and there were only rumors so far, fanned by Lady Lucinda, his next lapse in judgment.

Lady Lucinda Applegate was a leading light of London. She might have been considered an old maid at the advanced age of twenty-five, firmly on the shelf, except that she was a duke's daughter. Instead of being called a spinster, she was called particular. Lud knew she'd had offers aplenty, and turned them all down. Despite the fact that her father was a gamester and had wagered away most of his fortune and her dowry, the lady was still much sought after in the beau monde. Lady Lucinda was a tall, stunning, raven-haired incomparable, whose beauty was marred only by a nose matching Alex's own in aristocratic dimension. So elevated was her beak, so haughty her attitude, that Lady Lucinda Applegate was labeled Close-the-Gate by the same would-be wits who called him Ace.

She could have looked as high as she wished for a husband. Perhaps she was tired of looking, or perhaps an earl was high enough, for she smiled at Lord Carde at one of the social gatherings they both attended. Talk about his own search for a bride must have reached her ears, for the woman had ignored Alex's existence when he was merely another cheerful, contented bachelor. He'd smiled back. The lady would certainly be an excellent match for him, bred to the position, poised and polished, educated and accepted everywhere. So what if her dowry was negligible? Alex had no need for a wealthy bride. So what if her father gambled? Alex could afford to make a few loans. So what if their children would resemble baby elephants? Now that thought gave him pause. Still, if Lady Lucinda was being friendly, the least he could do was return the courtesy, to see if they might suit.

They danced well together, he found, and conversed easily on a variety of topics. She was an excellent rider, he discovered the following afternoon. At the end of a fortnight, however, Alex realized he knew the young woman no better than he did scores of other polished diamonds of the *ton*. They glittered, they sparkled, but they gave off no warmth.

Naturally a virtuous female did not act the wanton in public, not if she wished to make a respectable match, but Alex was hoping for a hint of passion in the woman he would marry. He was not a celibate man. He never had been, never desired to be, never saw a reason to be. Neither did he believe in adultery. He was not about to keep a mistress while he had a wife, like so many other men of his circle. After all, the reason for wedding in the first place was the begetting of heirs, and Alex intended to take earthly pleasure in that heaven-sent duty. His countess would, too.

He was surprised, then, but both curious and delighted, when Lady Lucinda indicated that he was to follow her out to the balcony at the Carstaires' ball. He took off his spectacles and wiped them clean, to make certain he had interpreted her gesture correctly. Yes, that was a come-hither glance if he had ever seen one. Before thithering, he looked around to locate Lady Lucinda's chaperone, asleep on a gilt chair in a corner of the ballroom. He already knew her father was in the game room, for Alex had just left the duke with another losing hand. He casually strolled toward the balcony, as if seeking fresh air.

From the balcony, Alex could see couples strolling down the stairs to the lantern-lit gardens, and a few stepping behind trees for more privacy. Lady Lucinda was waiting near the steps, fanning herself for the view of anyone passing by. He joined her, seemingly by accident, still cautious of her intentions.

No accident caused her to take his arm and lead him down the stairs, and no accident made her head in the direction of an unlighted path through the shrubbery. So the Ice Maiden had an ember of passion in her after all. Ah.

They made idle conversation as they walked, the type of small, social prattle they were both so practiced at, until they reached a spot not quite as isolated as Alex could have wished, but away from any other couples that Alex could see. Alex began to express his pleasure in getting to know her better over the past few weeks.

With an exasperated *tsk,* Lady Lucinda pulled him closer and planted her lips against his. Actually, their noses got in the way at first, then his spectacles, but Alex managed to position them correctly for a proper kiss.

It was just that: proper. She never softened her lips under his, never nestled her body against his, never sighed or murmured. She was not even breathing hard when she stepped back and said, "There, now you will have to marry me."

Not that Alex's blood was heated either, but her words were an icy bath. "What?" was all he could yelp, then he looked around to make sure no one could hear. "What the devil are you talking about?" he shouted in a whisper.

"Everyone knows you are looking for a bride, and none too soon, either, with your rackety ways. You cannot find a more fitting spouse, nor one who will grace your table more elegantly."

"What about my bed?" he muttered. "I fancied a wife who liked my kisses."

"Do not be vulgar."

Vulgar, was it, when she had tossed herself at him, and now tossed a metaphorical noose over his neck? "I shall not offend your ears with what I think of your assumptions and aspirations, but we are not going to be wed!" Alex no longer cared who heard them. At that point he did not care if Lady Lucinda followed him back toward the stairs or not, either.

"But you have compromised me. Everyone knows we left the ball together."

"One kiss"—one extremely unsatisfactory kiss, although Alex was too much the gentleman to say so—"does not make for a compromising situation. Nor are you some fledgling debutante seduced into indiscretion. Besides, your chaperone is fast asleep, and I doubt anyone else noticed, in this crowd."

"I could tear my gown!"

"And I could toss you in the decorative fountain we are passing and leave you there. We still would not be marrying."

"My father will insist."

"Your father? He is too busy losing more of your dowry at cards to notice if you return to the ballroom with your hair mussed, your stockings around your ankles, and your skirts stained with grass. None of which will happen," he stated in a firm voice, jerking his head toward the fountain in unspoken threat.

Lady Lucinda raised her nose higher still. "He will call you out for dishonoring me."

"First of all, madam, I have not dishonored you. Your own pride gives you whatever insult you imagine. Second, your father owes me a large sum of money. He is not about to challenge me to a duel if I offer to return his vowels. And third, he is an old man who would not have a chance in hell against my skill with a pistol."

"Oh, you'd have to take off your ugly spectacles to make it an even match."

His spectacles were ugly? Alex made a growling noise in his throat that had the lady stepping farther from his grasp, and the fountain. "Your ambitions know no bounds, do they? You would sacrifice your own father, or the man you hoped to marry, to pursue your connivances."

They were almost back on the balcony. Lady Lucinda was almost out of breath, hurrying after Alex. "It was never going to come to that," she said toward his back. "Your sense of honor would never permit it."

"A sense you are sadly lacking, my lady. I bid you good evening, and better hunting next time."

"We'll see, won't we, after the announcement reaches the newspapers."

Damn, she was right. He'd be a cad to renounce an engagement once it was made public. The scandal and speculation alone would destroy his chances of finding a suitable bride, but the duke's daughter would be ruined. That almost seemed worth the disgrace. "You would not dare send in the notice without my permission."

Lady Lucinda opened her fan as they neared the ballroom, as if she'd been doing nothing more than cooling herself between dances. She merely smiled at him as she floated across the ballroom toward where her next partner, the poor fool, was waiting.

Would she do it, make an engagement announcement? A fox in a trap would gnaw off its own leg. Lady Lucinda seemed no less desperate or determined.

Then there was Daphne.

Miss Daphne Branford was too young, too silly, too much the little girl he'd seen grow up on the neighboring estate in Northampton. Her father was the magistrate for the area of Cardington Village, the local squire, and Alex's deceased father's good friend. Mrs.

Squire Branford had befriended the orphaned Endicott boys after the earl's funeral, and for years afterward she had them over for Sunday dinner whenever
they were home from school.

Alex owed them.

When Squire wrote that his ladies were coming to
town without him for the Season, what could Alex do
but offer to make them welcome, ease their way
among the *ton*, and see that little Daphne's come-out
went off without a hitch? He opened avenues that
would have been closed to ordinary country gentry,
and he made introductions to important hostesses who
would have turned their backs on his undistinguished
neighbors. His very presence at their table, at Daphne's
side at the theater, riding alongside their coach in the
park, ensured her success. Young gentlemen looked
to follow where the Earl of Carde led, and he led
them straight to Daphne's door. He made certain no
fribbles, fortune-hunters, or rakes came near Daphne.
Only respectable young gentlemen were presented to
her as dance partners, an occasional baronet, and an
officer or two home on leave. Any one of them would
have made the chit a comfortable match, but she
showed no inclination to choose. Maybe she was hoping for a love match, Alex mused, when he considered
the matter at all.

He should have been paying more attention. Lud,
he should have dragged the squire to town by his ear,
away from his sheep and his hogs, to play escort to his
own womenfolk. He should have asked little Daphne's
intentions as soon as she came to London.

Little Daphne intended to wed him, Alexander
Chalfont Endicott, the Earl of Carde. Hell.

Strolling in the park one day, he asked about her

suitors, and which she preferred. "Shall I speak to anyone, bring him up to scratch?"

She giggled. "Don't tease, Carde. I am going to marry you, of course."

Alex tripped. When he recovered his balance, if not his temper, he said, "Explain yourself," as well as he could through gritted teeth. "And where you got that preposterous idea."

Daphne's lip started to tremble.

"And do not start crying. Tears might work with your father, but they will not affect me in the least," he lied, looking away so he did not have to see her eyes turn red and her cheeks go splotchy. "What the deuce are you speaking about?"

She sniffled until he handed over his handkerchief. Only after blowing her nose—as loudly as a goose, Alex noted—did the silly wigeon say, "Everyone knows we are going to get married. Our fathers planned it when we were children."

"The devil! That's the first I ever heard of any such arrangement. My trustees would have mentioned it anytime this past decade had such a match been formalized. That's rubbish, and you know it!"

Daphne tried to hand him back his sodden handkerchief but he shook his head. "How could you even think of such a thing?"

A drip forming at the end of her nose, Daphne whined, "Papa says you have too much honor to renege on your father's pledge. He's merely waiting for word from us to send the announcement to the newspapers."

What, another notice in the journals? Alex used his fingers to straighten his disordered hair rather than pulling it out. He took a deep breath and tried for a rational conversation. "My father died when I was fourteen. You would have been, what? Five years old?" She had sniveled then, too, he remembered. "No one could hold two adults to such a vague, distant, unwritten, and unsanctified agreement, likely made when our sires were in their cups."

"Are you accusing my papa of being a drunk? Or lying?" She started hitting Alex over the head with her reticule, which was dangling from her wrist by its drawstrings.

Good lord, if anyone saw the chit making a public scene like a spoiled brat, her reputation would be ruined. She would never receive another invitation, never meet an eligible gentleman, never make a suitable match. Alex would be honor-bound to— No! Honor only went so far. Not as far as the altar.

He left the park so fast no one could see Daphne's reddened eyes, or his reddened cheek from the flying purse. He had Daphne home before another drop dripped from her nose, before she could remind him of their fathers' friendship.

Then Alex Chalfont Endicott, the Earl of Carde, did what any self-respecting, honorable gentleman, red-blooded or blue-blooded, would do when faced with such a conflict of conscience, a dilemma of duty, a mares' nest of marriage proposals: He ran like hell.

CHAPTER TWO

"Pack," he ordered his valet.

"Cancel my appointments," he ordered his secretary.

"Get to every single newspaper, journal, and scandal sheet in town," he ordered his solicitor. "Tell them to print no engagement announcement without my signature and seal, or face charges of slander, sedition, whatever. You'll know."

"Spring 'em," he ordered his coachman.

The farther the carriage traveled from London, the easier Alex breathed. Relief outweighed any thoughts of cowardice or conduct unbecoming a gentleman. How could it be craven to avoid a trap? How could it be unchivalrous to save a woman from an unhappy marriage based on trickery and lies and deceit? No, he was doing them all favors by leaving town. Daphne, Mona, and Lady Lucinda should be thanking him, the unscrupulous, underhanded, unlovable shrews.

He drowsed as the coach made its way north to his family seat at Cardington, not even getting out when they stopped to change the horses. Who knew if some desperate daughter of the aristocracy would pounce on him as soon as he gave his name to the innkeeper? Lord Carde? Let's see if we cannot pull an ace out of our sleeve and win the pot. No, he would not expose himself to another female's machinations. The problem was, no matter how much he thought about it as the carriage made its steady way north, Alex could not figure how he was to beget heirs without getting leg-shackled.

For that matter, perhaps the women had a point, though, for no man in his right mind would step into a parson's mousetrap without being forced into it. If Alex never saw another young, unmarried female— He'd be deuced frustrated, that's what.

Very well, he thought, women were good for something besides bearing children. Damned if he could think of a third reason to have one around.

He dredged his mind for examples of wedded bliss. A few of his friends, most particularly those newest wed, were still in the euphoric honeymoon state, deliriously— and tediously for everyone else—enraptured with their brides. One would think the vicar had glued them together rather than merely bound their mortal souls. Ah, but give them a few more months or a year or two, and give them good evening when you passed them at Harriett Wilson's or some other high-class bordello. The glue was dried up, and so was the rapture. At least half the older married men he knew in town had mistresses in keeping or visited their favorite houses of accommodation, likely because their wives were not—accommodating, that is. Chances were the other half did too, but were more discreet about their philandering. Then there were the couples who, having produced the requisite progeny, maintained separate residences altogether. Perhaps they had the happiest marriages.

Alex was not finding many recommendations for wedlock among his acquaintances, so he examined his own parents' marriage. His mother had died in childbirth when his brother Jack was still a toddler, so at least they were sharing a bed after the heirs were secured. But had the earl and his first countess been happy together? Alex had spent most of his time in the nursery with nannies and nursemaids, far away from any tears and shouts, if such occurred. His father had been drunk for days after her funeral, and had always spoken highly of her.

He missed her so much that he married as soon as one year of mourning was passed.

Alex knew he was not being fair to his deceased father. How could he know how lonely the previous earl had been, or how much enthralled by his beautiful, new, young bride? And what about Lizbeth, Alex's stepmother for so brief a time? Was she a scheming jade, marrying an old man for his money and position? Alex did not think so. She was as lovely in character as she was in looks, he recalled, remembering her fair beauty far better than he remembered his own mother's dark-haired, elegant appearance. Everyone loved Lizbeth: the servants, the neighbors, her stepsons when they were home from school. Why wouldn't the earl, her husband?

According to Alex's aunt, his father had loved Lizbeth so much that he died of a broken heart when Lizbeth was killed.

See where love got a man?

Hell and damnation. If Alex wanted a marriage without love, he could have his pick of the marriage mart. And a miserable future.

He sighed, starting to feel stiff in the confines of his carriage, no matter how well padded the seats and how good the springs. Maybe his thoughts were making his joints ache, like cold fingers prodding at his mind and body both. And maybe he could convince Jack to sell his commission and come home, saving him by providing the heirs.

Hah. Alex knew there was small chance of that. What was rescuing one brother, when the clunch was busy saving the world? Why should Jack trade his independence for a ball and chain?

For an instant Alex was jealous of his younger brother's freedom. Jack could go his own way, choosing directions Alex could not, not with the weight of the earldom on his shoulders, dragging him back to duty. Jack did not envy Alex the responsibilities, and Alex had long since stopped resenting his brother's carefree ways.

His first glimpse of Carde Hall reminded him why.

And why he had to find a wife.

Here was his home, his sense of self, mingled with centuries of pride. Here past glories and future hopes were embedded in the brown bricks and mortar, just as they were embedded in his blood and bones. This land, this earldom, this heritage was his, and he belonged no less to it.

The first thing he did, after greeting his staff, who were understandably appalled to find their lord and master at their doorstep without notice, was write to his brother, giving Jack his new location. Alex felt better knowing Jack could reach him in case of emergency. He also knew how much his letters meant to his brother, so far away from home. What a laugh Jack would have over Alex's matrimonial morass, so some good could come of the mess. Alex just hoped his sibling wouldn't share the joke with all of his fellow officers.

Lord, he missed having Jack nearby, more so when here at their boyhood home than in London. They'd been constant companions at Cardington, fishing, hunting, hiking, learning their lessons together, and learning how to flirt with the dairy maids together. Right now Alex missed having his brother around to debate the imponderables of life, such as if love could grow after marriage, and if it mattered. Then again, what did Jack know, serving in the army?

The second thing Alex did at home, after exchanging his perfectly fitted and elegantly tailored London clothes for old, comfortable garments that he did not need his valet to help him into, was ride his acres. He had trustworthy stewards and land agents, but these fields were his and everyone who worked the land or tended the livestock were his people, no one else's.

The third thing he did, when he'd run out of excuses not to, was visit his neighbor, Squire Branford, Daphne's father.

He walked to Branfield, Squire's estate, because that would take longer than riding. The hike also explained why his mouth was dry. Strangely enough, though, a glass of his neighbor's home-brewed ale did not loosen his tongue.

Alex studied his glass so long that Branford finally said, "Heard you were here, my boy. Funny, after all these years I still cannot get used to calling you Carde."

"No matter. I sometimes have a hard time believing it too; it's as if people are speaking of my father."

"Good man, your father. A great loss to us all."

They both drank to the late earl. Then Branford

offered Alex another glass, a platter of bread and ham and cheese, a pipe. As long as he didn't offer his daughter, Squire could offer rat poison.

Alex ate, rather than bring up the awkward subject on both their minds. The food tasted like sawdust.

"Actually," Squire said around the stem of his pipe, "I expected you here sooner, to ask a particular question." He looked over at Alex and winked.

Alex put his plate down on a nearby table. "I thought we settled that boundary issue before I left for town. I have already hired workers to drain the swamp."

"That's the way of it, is it?"

"Of course I came to ask after your health, as soon as I took care of some business at the hall."

"Nothing else? No other question you wanted to put to me?" Squire raised a bushy eyebrow.

Alex had plenty of questions. Like, had Squire Branford considered sending his buffle-headed daughter to Bedlam. But the chess game was over. Check, but not quite mated. "Actually there was a minor issue I was hoping you could clarify. Miss Branford mentioned some faradiddle about an arrangement you and my father might have made. Silly, of course, but I wonder if you know where she got such a goose-ish notion?"

"No moonshine or make-believe, if that's what you are thinking. The earl and I shook hands on the deal."

Selling a horse was a deal. Selling off your eldest son was slavery. "My solicitor had no such instructions."

The older man shrugged his beefy shoulders. "Who needs lawyers and such between two old friends?"

"Was there any record somewhere else, then? Your family Bible or such?"

"No, we didn't want to make it so official back then. You see, after my Daphne was born, the physicians said Mrs. Branford would have no more children. I wanted my lands secured, my little girl's future provided for. Your father wanted to add my acres to his."

That sounded like Alex's father, unfortunately.

"But what if the quacks were wrong?" Squire went on. "What if I had a son? God forbid, but what if I lost my wife and took another, the way your father did? Then my boy would have the estate."

"And Daphne, Miss Branford, would have a merely modest dowry." Unspoken was the fact that without her father's vast unentailed property, Daphne was not a fit bride for the future earl.

"I see. My father would have looked to make a different dynastic match. But why was I never informed about the possible connection between our two families?"

"What, talk about marriage settlements with a boy?"

"What about later, when my father died? You could have spoken of this matter to my guardians, or my man of business."

"What, and have them think I was scavenging on the poor earl's body, with him not cold in the grave? Besides, my wife was still young. We might still have had a son."

"Very well, then when I came down from university, or reached my majority. You never had that boy child, and were no longer likely to. Why did you never discuss Daphne's future with me, since I was so intimately"— he winced at the poor choice of words—"involved."

"I suppose I should have, but there never seemed to be time, and she was just a wee lass still. Mostly, though, you were a rackety young sprig loose on the town. I didn't want my baby tied to any here-and-thereian, or my lands to go to someone who might gamble them away. Then you settled down, just as you ought. Your father'd be proud."

His father could go to Hades, Alex thought, for landing him in this mess. If he ever had sons, Alex swore, he'd stay out of their lives and their affairs. Of course, if he ever had daughters, he'd be as careful and as crafty as Squire Branford. Which was all academic, as he had no intentions of having children, sons or daughters, in the foreseeable future. Not without a wife.

He cleared his throat. "I do not love your daughter, sir, and I cannot like having my hand forced," Alex said.

"No man does, my boy, no man does. Have you ever met the chap yet who was eager to put on leg shackles? But it comes to all of us, in time."

Now was not Alex's time. Daphne was not Alex's future countess. "I regret, sir, that I do not consider your handshake with my father to be binding on my future."

The older man's bushy eyebrows met in the middle of his forehead. "Dash it, man, then why did you raise expectations? You acted as the gal's escort, bought her bouquets. M'wife wrote how attentive you were."

"I wished to make your daughter's come-out a success, that was all. I acted as a friend, a neighbor, a caring older brother, if you will. Nothing more."

Squire was still scowling.

Alex went on: "You and your lady have always been kind to me, so I thought to repay your generosity." Which went to prove that no good deed went unpunished. Hell would freeze over before Alex did another good turn for anyone with a marriageable daughter. Or niece, sister-in-law, second cousin.

"Well, I thought a man's handshake was his bond."

Now Alex frowned, that this gentleman farmer with hair sprouting out of his ears might be impugning Alex's honor. "No one shook mine, sir. Yes, I know, I was a mere stripling at the time. I am no longer a child, however, and I shall not permit anyone to make crucial decisions for me."

"Hmph. I thought Jonathan was the headstrong brother."

"Jack is headstrong. I am the Earl of Carde."

They were a few words, but they held a world of unmistakable meaning, especially matched to the earl's broad, squared shoulders and the direct, brown-eyed gaze over a hawklike nose.

"Very well. I concede. You have a day or two to think how you're going to explain all this to my poppet. Don't look to me—I wash my hands of the argle-bargle. I'll let you two work things out. Who knows, you might even change your mind."

Alex shook his head. "I don't think I'll be going back to town until after the summer." And he was not going to change his mind.

"Oh, there's no need for you to jaunt to London. I sent a messenger off as soon as I heard you were in residence here. My womenfolk will be home tomorrow or the next day at the latest. We'll have supper, right?"

In his haste, Alex tripped over a footstool on the way out. He did not offer Squire his hand in farewell. Look where that other handshake had gotten him.

"Pack," he ordered his valet, who had just finished putting away his lordship's London wardrobe.

"Cancel my appointments," he ordered his butler, who didn't know that the earl had any plans in the neighborhood. He'd tell Cook to cancel dinner instead.

"Saddle my horse," he ordered his coachman. The carriage and baggage could follow. This time Alex was riding. It was faster.

CHAPTER THREE

"**I** do."

A promise. A pledge. An oath. They were mere words, but what was a man without the strength of his word? A cheat, a liar, a villain.

What was the world without honor? No debts would be paid, no boundaries would be safe, no transactions could be completed, no peace would be kept. And there would be no weddings. Why bother if oaths were meant to be broken?

"I do."

They were mere words that kept repeating in Alex's ears in time with his rough-gaited hired horse's hoofbeats. Most men he knew did not honor their sacred wedding vows—perhaps their wives did not, either. Certainly Alex had received enough invitations from married ladies, and not just for tea. He fully intended to honor his own vows, though. He believed with every tired inch of his jostled and jolted body that promises were to be kept. His family's very motto, "Ever true," spoke of honor and loyalty. The Endicotts had always been true to their king and true to their country. They were true to their word. So was Alex.

"I do," he repeated to the gelding. "I do know where I am going."

So much for scruples. He was already lying to a dumb horse. No, Alex told himself, that was not precisely a lie. He knew where he was going, he just didn't know where he was at this moment. The directions at the last inn had been so confusing and conflicting that he swore he'd passed the same split oak twice, once from the right, once from the left. Either he was going in circles, or there was a great deal of lightning damage here in Humber, near Hull. He was looking for the village of Kingston Upon Hull, which was either around the next curve or three miles back and across the river, depending on which drayman or drover he asked.

The reason he was here, lost, was yet another promise, this one thirteen years old and as yet unfulfilled. Alex had sworn an oath to his dying father to locate little Lottie, his half-sister. He had not done so.

There was nothing much a boy of fourteen—or sixteen, or nineteen—could do from his schoolroom about solving the disappearance. Alex had insisted more men be hired to investigate the accident that had killed his stepmother, and he had demanded copies of all their reports. When his trustees would have given up the search, claiming it was a futile effort, a waste of money to keep men on the payroll when there was nothing more to be found, Alex made them hire more experienced trackers, more professional thief-takers. If Lottie was dead, her body would be somewhere. If she had been kidnapped, someone, somewhere, had to know by whom, and why no ransom was ever de-

manded. If a blond cherub had been taken in by anyone, Alex wanted to know about it, or if she had been
laid to rest in an unmarked grave. Surely there was a
record of her death somewhere, or a celebration of
her rescue.

Alex's father had believed the child still lived. That
was enough. That was thirteen years ago, however.

Alex still received quarterly reports from a solicitor
in Hull, who was brother-in-law to the constable,
whose cousin had helped arrest a highwayman, who
had kissed the magistrate's daughter. In other words,
Alex was paying a lot of men to do nothing but waste
his money. Now seemed like a good time for him to
make final inquiries for himself, to put the riddle of
Lottie's loss to rest once and for all. He might never
get another opportunity—or the freedom—to travel
about the country like this, on the spur of the moment,
without an entourage or fanfare. Even now, hundreds
of matters demanded his attention, from business affairs to political, from social obligations to charities,
from scientific advances in agriculture to the latest in
literature. Once he was married— No, that did not
bear thinking on. Suffice it to say he would not be
lost in the shires on some fool's quest when he had a
wife and children waiting for him at home.

Alex had scant hope of finding anything his paid
minions hadn't, not after all these years. If Lottie had
survived the coach accident, which was not at all certain except in his father's dying heart, then she could
have succumbed to any number of perils. Or she could
have found safe haven somewhere with a new family
who chose to ignore the reward posters. She would
have a new life and a new name, and heaven alone
knew where or what.

Alex doubted if he would ever have any answers to the questions, but he had to make one last effort to find them, here at the source of the tragedy.

He might not fulfill the promise to his dying father to bring the child home, but, by god, he would have tried. *Ever true.*

Alex had picked a good time to turn footloose. Most importantly, the flaming rumors of his mingle-mangle engagements would quickly burn out as soon as another scandal occurred, which was every other day in the bored London social circles.

In addition, England was at her prettiest in springtime. The weather was comfortable, the roads were passable, the scenery had to gladden even the hardest winter-cold heart. Alex found himself whistling for the first time in years, as if he had no cares but finding the next landmark on his journey.

He was traveling incognito, giving his name, Alexander Endicott, instead of his title. He wanted no reports of his whereabouts trickling back to London, and no tales of his narrow escape made public.

Besides, he was not running away. He was taking care of urgent family business. Thirteen years later.

After his first day on the road, when he'd had to leave his spent Thoroughbred at a stable and hire the first of many indifferent mounts, Alex did not look like an earl. Innkeepers and stablemen saw a dusty man in country clothes, a bit taller than most, seemingly well built but in loose, worn garments of unfashionable tailoring and boots that were made for hard use, not promenading in the park. The spectacles and the dark, wind-tousled hair gave him an abstracted, studious air. He might have been a cleric or a clerk, they thought, a gentleman by his educated accent, although of modest means. They did not doubt he could pay his bills; they did not believe he could leave generous vails for exemplary service. So he did not receive it—good service, that is.

Whatever food was ready in the kitchens was slapped in front of him, whatever horse was nearest the stable door was saddled for him, whatever cramped room was available was assigned to him.

He did not rate a hot bath, only a basin and some tepid water, with flannel cloths so dingy they would have added dirt to his face rather than wiped it away. As for the sheets, well, the insects could have the bed to themselves. Alex decided to spend the night in the room's only chair, with his riding coat as cover.

Before blowing out the single candle, Alex penned a letter to his brother. He would be home at Cardington or back in London long before his brother received the note, but Alex felt better telling Jack where he was going and why. He'd vowed to himself when his brother left England to make sure Jack could always find him. If Jack was injured in battle, Alex would not leave him to languish in a plague-ridden field hospital. If he fell to the enemy's swords or cannons, then Alex would bring him home to lie with their parents on the English soil he had died to protect. God forbid.

So he wrote, joking that Jack had received all the courage in the family, which was fine, since Alex had all the brains. He was hoping to use some of that wit, he added, to solve the mystery of their sister's disappearance, or to resolve that it would stay a riddle forever, simply one of those questions that had no answer, like the nature of stars and the source of inspirations. Alex intended to interview the constable, the magistrate, the solicitor, and the paid investigator, but he was also going to speak with anyone he could find who had been in the vicinity that winter: the servants, the neighbors, the vicar, the village washerwomen who knew everyone's business. He was going to start at Ambeaux Cottage outside Kingston Upon Hull—if he ever found it—where his late stepmother's father had settled after leaving France before Lizbeth's birth.

Both of Lizbeth's parents were dead now. She had been traveling home after attending her father's funeral, in fact, on that tragic day over a decade ago. Her husband, the earl, had not been able to escort her north because of a crucial vote in Parliament, but Lizbeth insisted on going anyway, and taking their baby daughter to ease her own mother's grief. Besides, Lizbeth could not bear to be parted from her child that long.

The countess's frail mother was delighted with her granddaughter and the visit from her only child, but she did not long survive their loss. It was too much, Alex was told, atop the death of her husband. Her heart gave out when news of the accident was brought back to the cottage.

Lizbeth's aunt, Azeline Ambeaux—her father's sister—still resided there. Aunt Hazel, as she was known to the family, had left France as a girl of eighteen, leaving behind a fiancé in the army, André. When André died in battle, Azeline rejected her French tongue and her status as a mademoiselle. According to the reports, the elderly lady now believed that all of her deceased loved ones walked the halls of Ambeaux Cottage, her brother and sister-in-law, her beloved niece Lizbeth, and her dearest André. No matter that her lost lover had died in France without ever seeing the place, he was with Madame Ambeaux now. The villagers did not believe the crazy old woman's rantings, the solicitor had written, scoffing at the notion of ghosts and midnight meanderings. Nor did they seek employment at the isolated estate, however, unless they could return to their own beds at night.

Alex doubted he would find any help from Madame Ambeaux.

Lizbeth had two cousins from her mother's side, however. Orphaned as children, they had been taken in by Lizbeth's parents and raised as her siblings. Phelan Sloane still lived at the cottage, looking after the estate and the small shipyard founded by Lizbeth's father in Hull. Phelan Sloane should be about forty years of age now, and had never married—at least, no mention of a wife and children had made it into the solicitor's reports that Alex could recall.

Phelan had a sister, or perhaps a half-sister, who was much younger. The solicitor's reports were sparse about Miss Sloane, too, except that she had been sent away to school following her aunt's death. Alex supposed she had grown up, wed, and moved away. He could find her direction easily enough once he arrived at her childhood home, but he did not suppose she would have any answers for him either, since she could not have been more than twelve years of age at the time of Lizbeth's death.

Alex vaguely remembered both of the Sloanes from the wedding. Phelan was dour and distant, with no time or patience for the earl's young sons or his own little sister. The girl was shy and skittish, Alex recalled, and no wonder, an orphan thrust into a houseful of strangers, relegated to the nursery with Alex and Jack, two rambunctious boys. She was spindly, too, with huge blue eyes the color of Lizbeth's—and little Lottie's, later—and fair hair like her older cousin. While Lizbeth was beautiful, a golden fairy princess in the besotted boys' opinions, Eleanor Sloane was a pale, fragile-looking wraith.

Alex could not imagine a man wedding a female such as that. What dowry could she have to sweeten the deal? He doubted her own parents had left a legacy. He decided to call upon her if she still lived in the neighborhood, out of sheer curiosity.

Meantime, he was lost. And traveling incognito was not all it was cracked up to be. He had cuts on his face from shaving himself, scuffs on his boots that no polish could repair, and a horse under him that would have been laughed out of Hyde Park. The late afternoon was coming on to rain, and he was hungry besides.

Luncheon had been a wedge of cheese and a loaf of bread purchased at the last village he passed, hours ago. He'd been lost ever since. At least he'd found a stream to fill his flask and water his horse. The stream, thank goodness, eventually led to a lone farmhouse just as a pelting rain started to fall. Now Alex was happy enough to sit through the storm in a warm kitchen, sharing a rough wooden bench with a one-eyed hound and a bushel of potatoes. He gladly ate the pigeon pie the farmer's wife provided, laughing to himself that the lofty Lord Carde was taking his meal off a plank table in the kitchen for the first time since he was a boy begging snacks from the cook at Cardington Hall.

Alex paid far more than the humble fare was worth, but learned that he was no more than three miles from his destination, that Miss Eleanor Sloane kept house for her brother, that the aunt was tetched, and that no one talked of the long-ago tragedy, not if they wanted to work at Ambeaux Cottage or do business with the estate. Since the farmer sold his produce there on occasion, he chewed his tobacco and glared his loose-tongued wife into silence. He sent the stranger on his way as soon as the rain let up, before Alex could ask another question or, sadly, for another slice of his wife's excellent apple pie, hot from the oven.

It was almost dark when Alex finally reached Kingston Upon Hull, with Ambeaux Cottage supposedly another mile or so past the little village down a dirt track. Alex decided not to call on his distant relations that evening, uninvited, in all his dirt. Instead he took a room at the only inn in the town, The King's Arms, where his valet and baggage would catch up with him in a few days. He gave his name and his title, along with his haughtiest stare and aristocratic mien. The landlord recognized Quality, despite the shaving cuts on that raised chin. Mr. Ritter also recognized gold when the earl handed over a fistful of coins, so gave his new guest the best rooms in the inn, which he would have anyway. The Queen's Suite, which Ritter's wife, Sarah, insisted the connecting rooms be called, was too costly for the usual traders and wool merchants.

More coins changed hands. A copper tub was carried to the dressing room, and a steady stream of steaming-hot water cans were carried up the stairs. The clothes Lord Carde wore and the soiled ones in his saddlebags were carried off to be sponged and ironed, his boots to be shined. His letter to Jack was carried away to be sent on to London for the military dispatch bag, and his calling card was carried toward Ambeaux Cottage, requesting permission to call in the morning, at Mr. Phelan Sloane's convenience.

Alex leaned back in the tub with a bar of sweet-smelling French milled soap in one hand and a glass of aged French wine in the other. This close to the coast, the bottle had likely never seen an excise tax, but for once Alex would not complain that the smugglers were putting money into French hands, which put bullets into French rifles, which were aimed at British soldiers. He sighed with pleasure instead of asking the innkeeper or his staff questions. He had already discovered that no one in the village answered questions about Lizbeth's family, so why would they speak of contraband?

After drying from his bath with thick, snowy towels, Alex was offered his choice of beef or lamb or ham. He said yes to all of them, plus a sampling of soup, vegetables, fruits, and sweets. When the earl had eaten his fill—for the first time in a week, it seemed—his host presented a tray with a decanter of brandy and a glass, cigars, a London newspaper a mere three days old, and a jar of snuff. Ritter also proudly pointed out the shelf of books in the sitting room, the stacks of extra blankets, the plate of biscuits his wife had made specially. His lordship was to have every comfort and convenience the inn could provide. If it was company the earl sought, there was always a game of cards or darts below stairs in the common room. If Lord Carde wished another kind of company, Ritter said with a wink, one of the waitresses was willing to serve above stairs, once the straitlaced Mrs. Ritter had gone to sleep.

Alex declined both offers. Tonight he only desired his bed, his clean, comfortable, lavender-scented bed, alone. He thought of joining the locals, thinking a few rounds of ale might loosen some tongues, but he was far too tired to begin his investigation, and far too content to dredge up unpleasant topics.

The only thing he wanted, which the innkeeper could not provide, was a response to his note to Ambeaux Cottage.

"The lad came back while you were at supper, my lord. But he did not have any message for you."

"He waited?"

"Just the way you told me to tell him. But he never did get a reply, nor a coin for his troubles, neither."

"I'll take care of it tomorrow. I suppose Sloane intends to call on me here in the morning."

The landlord looked dubious, but he bowed himself out of the room before Alex could ask any more questions or the reason for his doubts. No notes, no messages, no gossip; they were a closemouthed group, here in Humberside.

There were no visitors in the morning, and no invitation to call at Ambeaux Cottage either. Alex thought of calling on the solicitor, Mr. Silbiger, who kept an office in Upper Kingston, an hour away, but somehow that felt insulting to Lizbeth's cousins, speaking about them to strangers before speaking with them face-to-face, discussing family affairs with employees rather than with the family itself. Alex had few enough relatives and was halfway leaning toward considering the Sloanes as kin, except for their lack of hospitality. If nothing else, they should have shown his title the courtesy of a reply if not the respect of an interview. Hell, he would have thought they'd be curious as to why he'd come to this godforsaken place at all.

"To whom did you give my card?" he asked the boy who ran errands for the innkeeper, finding him in the stables, mucking out stalls. Alex handed him another coin for his trouble, and for his cooperation.

"T' the butler, m'lord, Mr. Redfern. Just like Mr. Ritter bade me."

"And what did he do with the card?"

"He read it, a' course. Then he went off t' give it t' Mr. Sloane."

"Sloane was at home?"

The boy shrugged. "I din't see him, if that's what you mean. But Mr. Redfern, he went down the hall all right."

"And then?"

"Then Mr. Redfern never come back. It was long past supper time and my mum'd be worried. And it were dark." That seemed to speak volumes to the youngster.

It did not say much to Lord Carde. "Surely you had a lantern? Ritter would not have sent you up a dirt track without one."

The boy looked over his shoulder to make certain no one was listening. "Lights don't matter." He lowered his voice. "The place is haunted."

"Nonsense. There are no such things as ghosts."

"Then how come nobody stays out there after dark, not the cook or the maids or the footmen? The grooms sleep over the stables, out of sight of the house through the trees, so they don't count."

"What about Redfern? The butler must stay at the house overnight."

"My mum says he's one of them."

Another relation? "A Sloane? An Ambeaux?"

"A ghost."

CHAPTER FOUR

Something was wrong.

Something was always wrong, so Nell had learned not to get excited or upset when a new maid went flying off in hysterics, a window shattered for no apparent reason, or three hens flew into the ornamental fountain and drowned. She lived with Aunt Hazel's ghosts and her brother's moods, so only an earthquake could shake her now.

"You are leaving this minute, before dinner is served?" she asked Phelan.

He did not bother replying as he set down his valise and donned his driving coat while waiting for his carriage to be brought around to the front of the house.

He was obviously leaving. Another cook would likely hand in her notice. "What could be so important that you have to leave now?" Nell had only been gone an hour or so, helping the church guild ladies pack baskets for the poorhouse.

"Nothing that needs disturb you, missy," he told her. "I invited you to come along, anyway."

"Yes, but you know I promised to sit with Mrs.

Mahoney tomorrow so her daughter can go to the tooth drawer, after I start the maids on wash day. And I do teach the drawing class at the school in the afternoon. Besides, you know I cannot like leaving Aunt Hazel alone." Although Aunt Hazel never thought she was alone. "It is far too short notice to change my plans and make other arrangements."

"Suit yourself," Phelan said as he drew on his gloves. "But swear to me you will not talk to strangers."

Her older brother always had odd notions about people he did not know, and for him to demand such an oath was no more peculiar than usual. Nell tried to reassure him with a smile. "Strangers? There has not been a stranger in Kingston Upon Hull in ages."

He did not answer, but placed his beaver hat at the perfect angle on his thinning locks to hide the receding hairline. "I heard about him somewhere. I do not want you taken in by any rakehell."

"A rake, here in the village?" Now that was something far out of the ordinary. If it were not so late in the day Nell would have hurried into the village to hear the gossip for herself and perhaps get a glimpse of this rare bird.

"I am serious, Nell. He might be dangerous to an innocent such as you."

Nell smiled. To think that Phelan worried about any sly seducer taking an interest in her was touching. Foolish, but nevertheless touching. Nell supposed she would always and forever be Phelan's little sister, but Miss Eleanor Sloane of Ambeaux Cottage, at her advanced age of twenty-five, in her plain and serviceable gowns, with no great beauty and no fortune or prospects, could not possibly attract a discerning libertine. The chances were worse if he was staying at The

King's Arms, as seemed likely. Kitty Johnstone waited on tables at the inn, and waited for Mrs. Ritter to look the other way for more profitable employment. Compared to Kitty's lush charms, Nell was a broomstick of a female. Why, she would have to dance naked on the bar top to get a man's attention, and then he'd likely toss her his coat to hide the offending sight.

"I do not think you have to concern yourself," Nell told Phelan.

"I trust your morals," he said, mistaking her meaning, "but he might be a smooth-talking swell."

"A gentleman, is he?" Kitty Johnstone would definitely be waiting on the man's doorstep, or on his counterpane.

Phelan's face darkened until Nell regretted asking. When Phelan was determined on a course, there was no stopping him; when he was angry, there was no placating him. She had learned years ago to lower her head and nod her agreement with whatever he said. She might go her own way afterward, but she did not like to stir his temper. No one did. "Of course I will not speak to any strangers. I have been brought up as a lady, you know. You must, for you paid for my education at Mrs. Merton's Select Academy. Matron's favorite rules were that a young lady never noticed a gentleman without a formal introduction and never remained in a gentleman's presence without a chaperone."

Nell had never had much opportunity to practice Mrs. Merton's strictures. Since leaving the academy, she had met a mere handful of gentlemen at the assemblies in Hull, once in Scarborough when she could convince Phelan to permit her to go. None of her dance partners, after the proper introduction, of course, had shown any interest in luring her off for a private rendezvous. Her lack of dowry, her lackluster family name, and her lamentably peculiar relations discouraged any would-be suitors that her beanpole figure did not.

"You will not speak with him," Phelan persisted. "In fact, I think you should not go into the village at all tomorrow or the next day. No, that will not do. The cursed fellow might call here. He is dangerous, I say."

"Here? Why would a stranger call on Ambeaux Cottage?"

Phelan did not answer. "You had better come with me, after all. If we are gone for a few days, he will travel on."

"Fine. I shall tell Aunt Hazel to pack her bag. You know I cannot be without a chaperone at a hotel in the city." She assumed the nearest, Hull. "That would be far more dangerous than giving good day to a passing stranger on the high street of Kingston Upon Hull."

Phelan despised Aunt Hazel and her spectral sightings. He refused to claim her as a relative at all, much less be seen with her in the larger town where he did business and socialized. He adjusted his hat lower. "Quite right. Then you shall have to keep busy here. After sitting with Mrs. Mahoney, check the stable. Make sure it is properly swept. The men are lax if no one is watchful, and grow lazier by the day. Then call on the tenant farms. I do not want to hear any excuses about late rentals this quarter. Warn them, each and every one of the lazy oafs. Then go into Upper Kingston and order my blend of snuff. I am running low." He pulled out his purse and withdrew a few folded bank notes. "And buy something pretty for yourself."

What for, if she was not to impress any wicked

strangers? Still, Nell tucked the money away as her brother drove off. It would join the small cache of savings she kept in a hat box with her best bonnet. She seldom wore the bonnet, and seldom spent her cash. They were for her future, if she ever had one.

Without a dowry, marriage was nearly impossible. Even the local men wanted a sturdy wife to help with the crops and livestock or to take a turn at the wool looms to bring in money, not an educated, well-mannered miss with no practical skills. Landed gentlemen were as rare as hens' teeth around here, and could have their pick of the daughters of wealthy mill-owners, shipbuilders, prosperous farmers, or other idle gentry.

Phelan's estate was not prosperous, he said, barely staying self-sufficient, especially if the rents were late. The small shipyard was always losing money, he told her, because they could not compete with the larger companies in price or speed of production or latest design. So there was never enough extra to set aside for a marriage portion for Nell.

Now it was almost too late as she came nearer and nearer to her thirtieth birthday. Five more years and she would be a hopeless spinster. She still had a glimmer of a dream left, but it was fading fast.

Nell thought that she might go off to be a governess. Who knew what opportunities might come her way? If none did, if the life of an upper servant was as dull and as hard as keeping house for her brother, how much worse off could she be? She had the education, the breeding, and the experience, since she taught drawing classes, Sunday school lessons, and reading to the servants who stayed long enough to learn. But then she would have to leave Aunt Hazel here at Ambeaux Cottage on her own.

Phelan swore their uncle Ambeaux had not made provision for his sister in his will, so he would have the right to toss her out, into the poorhouse, most likely, or an asylum for the insane. He threatened it often enough, when Aunt Hazel reported chatting with their cousin Lizbeth. No one spoke of poor Lizbeth, not in Ambeaux Cottage, not in Phelan's hearing.

He'd been close to their cousin, close in age and close in affection. Nearly fifteen years younger, Nell had admired their beautiful relative and was happy for her in finding the earl, in having her beautiful baby daughter.

They were gone and times went on, except in Phelan's memory. He was the other reason Nell could not leave Kingston Upon Hull. Her older brother was difficult, demanding, and parsimonious, but he was her brother. He'd stood by her when they were children, and he'd paid for her education. Even now, he never failed to bring Nell a pack of ribbons or a pretty pin or a new book when he came back from business trips to Hull. How could she leave him in his grief and loneliness?

Aunt Hazel looked at the array of dishes on the table. "Oh, good, company for supper. The vicar?"

"No, a new cook, trying to impress Phelan." Nell picked up her fork, determined to do the meal justice, in hopes of placating the woman. Aunt Hazel ate like a bird, and she herself was never very hungry. She thought of asking Redfern to sit at the table with her and her aunt, but the butler would have had apoplexy.

"So where is that sour-faced sibling of yours?" Aunt Hazel wanted to know, taking a sip of her asparagus soup before setting the bowl aside.

"In Hull, I think. Some crisis or other."

"Hah. Most likely his ladybird sent him a billet-doux. I saw a boy come up from the village."

Aunt Hazel was of the firm belief that Phelan kept a mistress in Scarborough, farther away than Hull. Of course, Aunt Hazel was of the firm belief that her long-dead lover André visited her during the night too. Nell could never ask her brother, of course, but a woman under his protection might explain why Phelan never had any money, and why he never took a wife.

"Be happy he visits her there instead of moving her into rooms in Kingston Upon Hull," Aunt Hazel went on, taking a forkful of veal before waving to Redfern to take the dish away.

Nell could not imagine what she would do if Phelan's light o' love resided in the same village. The residents of Ambeaux Cottage were already considered odd in the neighborhood. If not for doing business with Phelan, and being fearful of his threats, the local populace would shun them altogether or gossip unmercifully.

"Of course it could be worse." Aunt Hazel turned up her nose at the braised chicken in mushroom sauce. "He could install her here in the house."

Nell choked on the fricassee of beef. "You mean marry his mistress?"

Aunt Hazel gave a gallic shrug. "*N'est-ce-pas?* Who can say, *cherie*?"

Nell's appetite was gone. She could not stay in the house with a woman no better than she ought to be, wedding band on her finger or not. Besides, if Phelan took a wife, he would not need Nell to run his household. She told Redfern to take the dishes away. "And apologize to the cook. Everything was delicious. I shall speak with her tomorrow about changing the menus."

"If she is here tomorrow," the butler muttered, glaring at Madame Ambeaux. The two were mortal enemies. Redfern blamed Aunt Hazel for the problems with the staff. She blamed him for the chill English weather, the high price of coal, and the fall of the French aristocracy.

"Ask him," Aunt Hazel told Nell. "Ask him where Sloane has taken himself off to." She would not ask Redfern herself, since the two had not spoken since Redfern's arrival over a decade ago. No one knew why, and Nell doubted the elderly foes could remember.

"Did my brother state the nature of the emergency?" Nell dutifully asked the butler. "If there was a fire or an epidemic, we should prepare baskets for the afflicted."

Redfern's nostrils flared. "I am certain I do not ask my master's business. If Mr. Sloane wished you to know his affairs, he would have discussed them with you, Miss Eleanor."

Nell was embarrassed at the rebuke, but nodded. "Of course, Redfern. I regret asking."

"I'll wager he read the note that boy brought up from the village earlier," Aunt Hazel said when the servant had left, but before the door was shut tightly behind him. "The old snoop."

The dishes rattled on Redfern's tray, but he did not deign to answer.

Nell did. "You are only sorry Redfern beat you to the front door, or you would have read it too."

The old woman shrugged again. "Why not, *cherie*? Do you think I like having to wait for André to tell me everything?"

Before she even left the house the next morning, Nell heard tales about the stranger staying at The

King's Arms. According to the maids who came up from the village for wash day, he was a nabob, a peer, a spy asking questions. He was too stupid to find his way around, or devilishly clever, taking notes about the smuggling business as he meandered about the countryside looking for likely hiding spots or caravan tracks. He'd already sent a message back to the government offices in Whitehall Street.

Worse, and what branded him more suspicious to the little village, he had refused Kitty Johnstone's favors. No man who could afford her asking price had ever turned down the local *belle du* back room. They said Kitty was in a taking for not having partaken of his largesse. Kitty was claiming he was homely anyway, from her glimpse of the gentleman as he came to the inn's front door yesterday. Unkempt and ugly, with a big nose and thick spectacles, riding a horse no proper gentleman would mount. And he thought too much of himself to take a pint with the common folk in the taproom, Kitty was heard to grumble. A queer nabs, she told all and sundry, and likely a nonstarter at the gate.

When Nell went to sit with old Mrs. Mahoney, who was crippled by rheumatics and half deaf, she heard a different story.

"Sour grapes on Kitty's part," the old woman shouted to Nell after her daughter left for the tooth drawer. "I heard he's got all his bits and pieces." Mrs. Mahoney's neighbor's cook, it seemed, had a nephew who worked at the inn. He'd carried up cans of hot water and seen the gentleman at his bath. "You know what they say about a man with a big nose."

"He has big feet?"

Mrs. Mahoney cackled. "That and more."

"No!" Nell gasped, a hand over her mouth in mock

disapproval of the gossip and horror at the discussion of the stranger's attributes, or lack thereof. She wished she could see for herself. So did Mrs. Mahoney, slapping her bony thigh.

They shared a cup of tea and a giggle at the poor man's expense.

He was not a poor man, though. That much was undisputed. The water-bearer declared him polite and generous. Mr. Ritter at the inn was sporting a wide smile, and Timmy, who did odd jobs and ran errands there, had a crate of piglets to bring home to his mother, courtesy of the nob's coins.

The children at drawing lessons wanted to know if Nell had seen the stranger yet, and did she think he was an excise officer or an East India merchant come to buy up all the land? What she thought was the gentleman, whoever he was, was the most exciting thing to happen in Kingston Upon Hull since the previous vicar ran off to Canada with his curate's wife.

They were even talking about the unnamed visitor in Upper Kingston too, when Nell went to replenish her brother's snuff jar.

"Is it true you have a nobleman hiding out in the village?" the clerk asked her while he filled her order.

"I heard he's an earl," another customer put in.

"Nah, a duke." A toothless old man was sucking on the stem of a pipe. "They're a scurvy lot anyway. Didn't one kill his own valet?"

The clerk leaned over the counter toward Nell and whispered in dramatic fashion, "Word is, this one is trying to hire our Mr. Silbiger the solicitor to defend himself against charges."

The other customer added, "He sent a letter over from The King's Arms by special rider this morning."

"And I heard Mr. Silbiger sent a clerk to the magistrate's office," the pipe-gummer said.

The tobacconist scratched his head. "Though why he'd come here to hire hisself a lawyer is anyone's guess."

Nell could not begin to imagine, she told the smoke shop denizens, disappointing them further by admitting that she had not seen anything of the man. "But I hope to," she added in all honesty as she paid for her purchase and left the shop.

She truly wished to know the stranger's business in her tiny village. The coincidence of his arrival and her brother's departure at the same time was simply too suspicious. The so-called emergency note to Phelan had come from the village, after all, at the exact time the stranger would have been at his bath. Thank goodness Nell was out of the tobacco store, for she felt her cheeks grow warm at her wayward thought.

No, prominent nose and privates aside, there had to be a connection between the traveler and her brother. Not a happy one, either, or Phelan would have stayed to greet an old friend or acquaintance or business associate. Instead he had left suddenly, warning Nell to avoid the dangerous stranger.

Wouldn't a rake have sought out Kitty Johnstone?

On the other hand, the one picking out a length of lace for Aunt Hazel at the dry goods store, who knew what Phelan was up to on all those visits to Scarborough or Hull? Aunt Hazel assumed he was visiting a woman, but what if he were involved in espionage or smuggling or gambling or . . . or any number of things that might make him want to avoid a titled gentleman with deep pockets, connections in London, and correspondence with a local man of law?

Phelan was prickly, subject to bouts of melancholy and dark moods, but he was not a criminal, Nell would swear to it. He was abstemious and, frankly, too miserly to part with his money at games of chance. He could not be involved in skulduggery, she thought, loyally. Phelan was her brother, who looked after her and worried about her safety and well-being, who brought her trinkets and gifts whenever he was away from home, who refused to let her consider wedding a common working man. Phelan thought his baby sister was beautiful. For that alone, Nell would have loved him.

If Phelan thought the man was dangerous, therefore, then dangerous he must be. But not dangerous enough that Phelan had to stay to protect her. Nell could not help the niggling doubt that wormed its way into her thoughts as she made her slow way home from the neighboring village. Phelan had taken the carriage, naturally, so Nell had been left with the donkey cart and old Eager, who was anything but.

Since she was headed in that direction on her way home anyway, Nell decided to stop off at one of the tenant farms connected to Ambeaux. Phelan never encouraged her to visit the tenants' cottages, saying the men were too rough, the women too coarse. The farm wives were not welcoming, either. Nell was not one of them. She was not of their class, not born nearby, not of their limited learning. For all her education, she knew nothing of their interests: cooking, childbearing, making ends meet.

Often Nell had Aunt Hazel up beside her, and the countrywomen considered Madame Ambeaux akin to a witch, and a foreign one at that, despite Aunt Hazel's near half-century in England. Either way, alone on her errands or with her elderly companion, Nell was seldom invited into any of the farmsteads that provided Ambeaux its income, not even when she delivered baskets of food or the latest baby present.

The first cottage she came to, up a narrow dirt path that the donkey cart barely fit through, was empty, its roof falling in. Nell knew she had been here at Yuletime, with Boxing Day gifts she had paid for by scrimping with the housekeeping money. The farmer had thanked her without a smile, but he had touched his cap with respect and wished her good tidings. Now he was gone, with his young family? No other tenant had taken his place, not with the cottage in such disrepair. Yet Phelan had never told her?

Something was wrong, all right.

Nell had intended to go straight home, to make the rounds of the rest of the tenants tomorrow. Instead she took another path to another cottage, far out of her way, all thoughts of the stranger at The King's Arms flown from her mind.

The Doyles had been friendliest of all the farmers who paid rent to Ambeaux, and their little girl was one of Nell's Sunday school pupils. She expected a warmer welcome than a barking, snarling guard dog that no one came to call off, although she could see smoke from the chimney and wash hanging on the line. The house needed paint and the gardens were overgrown, but at least someone lived there still.

The donkey brayed its displeasure at the dog, the delay, and the distance from its dinner. The mongrel showed its teeth. Nell turned the cart without getting down to knock on the door.

She had time to go to one last farm, Nell decided, with the daylight lasting longer now, and Phelan away from home. Dinner for herself and her aunt would be ready when Nell fixed it, the new cook having departed this morning.

An immensely fat woman was tossing grain into a pen of geese when Nell arrived at the Poseners' place. No, that was Sophie Posener, immensely pregnant. Nell got down from the cart and asked, "Are you sure you should be out and lugging that pail of feed?"

Sophie glanced at her, pursed her lips, and went back to the honking flock. "And who else is supposed to feed them, I'd like to know."

"Where is your husband?"

"Laid up with the influenza, so I cannot ask you inside."

Nell could hear a horrible hacking cough coming from the house, even over the noisy geese. "I told Mr. Sloane, I did. Walked all the way to Ambeaux Cottage, too. So if you are here for the rent, I have not got it. I told him I would not. With my James laid low, there is no way of getting the geese to market in Scarborough or Hull. I cannot herd them that distance in my condition. Or leave my James so long."

"What about in crates, in a cart?"

"Th' horse died last year. We told Mr. Sloane that too."

Nell's head was aching, and her heart, too. "You told my brother, and he did nothing?"

"He said it weren't his problem, and we owed the rent no matter what. He said times was tough all over and we'd have to tighten our belts." She looked down and the mound of stomach in front of her, where no belt would fit. "Tell that to the babe."

"Are you, that is, do you have enough to eat?"

"Oh, we have plenty, if you like goose eggs, goose liver, roasted goose, and goose soup. The problem is, I'm running out of feed for the geese. Then they'll lose their weight and be worthless at market, if I can get them there." The woman's voice was quavering, but she looked away so Nell could not see her damp eyes, or the fear.

Heavens, and Nell had been worried about not having a dowry. She went back to the cart and took out the sack of peppermints she had bought at the apothecary while she was in town. "These might help your husband's cough. I don't have anything else, but— No, I do have something to help you now, until my brother gets home and I tell him of your plight."

Mrs. Posener took the sack, but shook her head. "He knows. He don't care."

"I will make him care," Nell said. "And even if he does not, I care."

"But I don't see what good you can do, miss, pardon me for saying. You can't be herding my geese to town."

Goodness, Nell could teach the squawking, flapping geese their ABCs sooner.

"And I have heard you don't have a shilling to call your own," Sophie went on, looking at Nell's plain gown and simple straw bonnet, her lack of jewelry beyond a pinchbeck locket. She shook her head.

"Yes, I do have a shilling. And more." Nell pulled out of her pocket the money Phelan had given her for fripperies, paltry as it was. She had taken it along on her errands instead of squirreling it away with the rest of her hoard, in case she found a need for something in Upper Kingston. The need was here. She only regretted spending some of her pin money on lace for Aunt Hazel. She held the coins out to the other woman.

"I can't take that, Miss Sloane. Why, you look like you don't get enough to eat, yourself."

"Of course I do. I just have a small appetite and a slender frame." While Sophie compared her own bulk to Nell's skin and bones, Nell thought of all the food wasted at Ambeaux Cottage. They had thrown out enough to feed a family for a week just last night. Phelan never stinted on his own comfort, foodstuffs, coal for the fireplaces, expensive candles, only everyone else's, it seemed. The geese might be aghast at fricasseed chicken, but Sophie and her husband could have had something but goose for dinner if only Nell had known.

She *should* have known. Her late aunt, Lizbeth's mother, would have known. Nell should never have listened to Phelan, never have let the cool welcomes discourage her from doing her duty. He had urged her to do her good works in the village, with the children or the church, and she had listened to him, ignoring the very people who depended on her. Guilt ate at Nell, despite the fact that she did spend most of her free hours trying to improve the lives of the schoolchildren and the cottage servants. At least she could do something about Sophie Posener's situation right now.

"You take the money to hire a horse and wagon in the village tomorrow. I would send you our coachman, but he is driving my brother on business." The nature of Phelan's business was debatable, but Mrs. Posener did not need to know that. "Find someone you can trust, someone who will take your geese to market and get you a fair price."

Sophie looked at the few lonely coins in Nell's hand and shook her head again.

"It is not enough?" Nell was thinking of her little nest egg at home. Sophie's need was far more urgent, with her egg about to hatch. "I could bring more tomorrow, when I deliver some extra foodstuffs and some cough elixir my aunt brews. And I can drive you into the village myself then." She gestured toward her cart, where Eager was asleep in the traces. "I doubt I could get the donkey to go anywhere but back to his stall this afternoon, but I could come first thing—"

Sophie was not much for book-learning, but she could add and subtract like a horse trader, or a goose monger. "Oh, your blunt is enough, and I thank you for the offer. I can use it to hire Dan. He's the man of all work we used to keep on, when we could afford him. He lost a leg in the war, which is why he cannot herd the birds to town on foot, but he can drive. He'll come out and fetch a few geese to sell in the village, to buy more feed. Then he could take the rest to the markets in return for a share, I suppose. But I cannot take your money. It wouldn't be right."

This was not the time or the place for pride, yet Sophie Posener, with her belly swollen with child, her husband ill in bed, her stupid geese soon starving, and her rent money owing, was refusing Nell's pitiful gift. "I know," Nell said. "I'll purchase one of your geese."

Nell was thinking of a wrapped parcel, all cleaned and plucked, one she could roast if Redfern had not hired a new cook yet. Instead, Sophie had a string around a live goose's neck and the fowl tied in the back of the donkey cart before Nell could say foie gras. With Sophie's tearful, heartfelt thanks and the goose's honks echoing in her ears, Nell finally headed for home.

Oh, yes, something was wrong, very wrong. Nell was being nibbled to death by guilt, suspicion . . . and a hungry goose. It was not the goose's neck she was thinking of wringing, only her brother's.

CHAPTER FIVE

Alex waited at the inn until afternoon. He enjoyed another fine meal of Mrs. Ritter's cooking and a quick trip through the handful of shops in Kingston Upon Hull's high street. Feeling as if he were on holiday, he purchased a new spotted kerchief in case his valet did not arrive soon with his trunks, a sack of licorice drops, and a book of poetry. He would have enjoyed himself more except that the townsfolk acted as if he had come from the moon, not London.

He was intrigued by what he heard from the local people about his Sloane connections and, more interestingly, about what he did not hear. "We do not talk about our betters here," said one matron selecting gloves at the haberdashery. As if she was not going to visit every house on her way home, discussing his peerage, his purchases, and his proboscis.

When he had used up the diversions the village had to offer, enlivening the locals' day too, he returned to the inn to see if any messages had arrived. None had. Turning down a card game, a mill, and a buxom barmaid, he hired a horse.

This time the earl had his pick of the stable's mounts, which was not saying a great deal. Not one of the nags would have been fit for his own stables, of course, but one or two would not shame him in front of his late stepmother's relations. Alex chose a good-looking gray the hostler said was a handful, because he was in the mood for a good challenge.

The ride to Ambeaux Cottage was just that, a battle of wills to see who would walk and who would trot. Alex was too busy to notice the countryside, trying not to land in it, but he guessed that Ambeaux Cottage would look like a moldering castle from some lurid Gothic novel. The innkeeper had been anxious about giving him directions; Ritter's wife had crossed herself; the hostler had spit tobacco juice dangerously close to Alex's freshly polished boots.

From the wary looks and head shakes Alex received as he made his way through the little village earlier, he'd imagined his destination was a crumbling ruin with vine-choked windows and spiderwebs for curtains. No, it would have arrow slits instead of windows, and a fetid moat where the accursed residents tossed the innards of unsuspecting, unexpected guests. No one he asked knew if Mr. Sloane was in residence or not. No one wanted to go out to the cottage to find out, including his horse, it seemed.

When they finally arrived there, sweating and blowing hard—that was the earl; the horse was still fresh and fractious—Alex wondered if he had come to the right place after all. Instead of being the forbidding fortress he had expected, Ambeaux Cottage was a gentleman's residence of respectable size, in excellent repair, with Grecian columns and twin porticos. It had a neat, colorful border garden filled with Holland bulbs and spring flowers, and carefully trimmed shrubbery. Ambeaux could not compete with Alex's own castlelike Carde Hall, but it was almost as large as his London town house, and nearly as handsome. What was the matter with the ignorant countryfolk hereabouts, that they spoke in hushed tones about such a pretty place?

No groom came to take his horse, and Alex did not see a stable, but there was a post nearby. He tied the gray and walked up the wide front steps, admiring the primroses in marble urns at either side of the door.

No one answered his rap. He knocked again, harder. Again, with no results. Smoke came from the chimneys, though, and the boy at the inn had reported giving his card to a butler, so Alex slammed the lionhead knocker as hard as he could.

This time the door opened. Before he could give his name, his card, or his opinion of servants who kept guests waiting, Alex realized why no one stayed at Ambeaux Cottage in the dark. They were right: The place was haunted. A specter stood there.

As soon as Alex's heart slid out of his throat and back to his chest where it belonged, he could see that the phantom was extremely tall, extremely thin, but well dressed in black butler garb. Cadaverous was the only word to describe him—well, that and ancient. His bones creaked as he bowed, unless he wore a corset, like Prinny. Worst of all, his complexion was as white as milk, his chalky skin stretched so tautly over sharp features that it was nearly translucent, with tiny red and blue tracery showing. His eyes were an odd pinkish gray.

The man was an albino, or close to it, Alex realized, in relief. Of course the superstitious villagers would distrust the unknown and unusual, considering a simple accident of nature to be freakish and frightening.

Alex only wondered why the old relic had not been pensioned off decades ago, instead of being left to frighten small children and unwary visitors. Surely Ambeaux Cottage could afford the cost of his bound-to-be-brief retirement. If he were not already a ghost, the skeletal servant definitely had one foot in the grave.

"Redfern?" he guessed.

"Lord Carde?" the butler guessed. He did not wait for Alex to state his business. "I regret the family is away from home. I shall inform them of your visit. Good day."

And he shut the door in Alex's face.

Alex could swear his hired horse was laughing. The Earl of Carde, turned away by a wraith! Well, he might be wearing a spotted kerchief instead of an intricately tied neck cloth, and he might be riding a hard-mouthed brute instead of one of his well-bred beauties, but Alex was every inch the aristocrat. He drew himself up to his full height—higher than the haunt, thank goodness—and hammered on the door with his fist.

Redfern opened the door an inch. "Yes?"

"No." Alex pushed the door open farther, forcing Redfern backward. "No, you shall not treat me like some itinerant peddler. I wish some answers and shall not leave without them. Do you understand?"

Redfern understood that the gentleman was far too young, strong, large, and angry for him to overpower. "Yes."

"Good. Now, is your master at home? I would have the truth, with no roundaboutation."

Looking over Alex's left shoulder, the butler bowed and said, "No."

"Shall he be later in the day?"

"No."

"Tomorrow?"

"I do not know."

"Where is he?"

"I am not at liberty to say."

Alex would address that matter later. "What of Miss Sloane? Is she at home?"

"No."

"Is she with her brother?"

"No."

"Then shall she be home later? Tomorrow? Or is she somewhere I might call?"

"I am not at liberty to say."

Alex started to tap his riding crop against his boot. He would try to hold his temper, simply because the butler was so old. "And Miss Azeline Ambeaux? Is she receiving?"

The butler's sharp nose twitched, the first sign of life Alex had seen. "Madame regularly receives communication from her deceased relatives."

"But is she in this deuced house, man?"

"No."

"And you are not going to tell me where she is, either, or what everyone is doing, or why no one responded to my message of yesterday?"

"No, my lord, I do not discuss my employers."

"Commendable, I am sure. But let us start over, then." He stepped past the butler into a wide hall, with baskets of flowers, shining woodwork, an ugly portrait, and two matching benches. "Perhaps you would care to sit? This might take awhile." His tone of voice brooked no argument, making it clear that he would follow Redfern to the kitchens, to the attics, to the ends of the earth to get his answers. Barring a blunderbuss, the butler had no choice: The earl was staying.

Redfern waited for Alex to take a seat, then he lowered his creaking body onto the other bench with a sigh that was more a moan. When Alex saw that the man was not going to keel over, he began. "Where does your salary come from, Redfern?"

The ancient's eyebrows lifted. "From the Ambeaux estate, of course, my lord."

"No, Redfern, your wages come from me. I own this place."

"Bloody hell. That is, like hell you do."

"Well, who inherited the estate after old Mr. Ambeaux died?"

"Why, his nephew, Mr. Sloane."

"No. I understand you came here later, but Mr. Ambeaux left it to his wife and daughter, who survived him, although not by much. The property was unentailed, and Phelan Sloane was no blood kin to Mr. Ambeaux anyway, being his wife's nephew."

"I see," said the butler, beginning to see far more than those peculiar rheumy eyes would have indicated. If it were possible for a colorless man to get even paler, Redfern did just that.

"Yes, and isn't it the law of the land that a husband takes possession of his wife's property?"

The butler gulped, and stood, teetering slightly. "Yes, my lord."

"And so the Earl of Carde, having wed the former Miss Ambeaux, would own this estate outright on the death of her mother? No need to answer. Nor do we need to consider the obvious: that on my father's unfortunate passing, so quickly after those other sad losses, I inherited the estate, its holdings, and its income. Now let me ask you again, Redfern, where does your salary come from?"

"From you, my lord," the butler said, bowing as low as his old bones would permit. "And may I be the first to welcome you to Ambeaux Cottage."

"Sit, man. I won't have you falling over until I get the information I came for."

"Oh, but if we had known—" Redfern began, sinking back to the bench, shaking his head.

"Sloane knew. He had to be at the reading of Mr. Ambeaux's will. I chose to ignore the situation, thinking that I would never evict my late stepmother's family anyway, and they would need the income to support themselves. I have no way of knowing if the women believe Sloane is the rightful heir or not."

"I would wager Miss Eleanor thinks he is, since your name is never mentioned. As for the Bedlamite witch, there's no telling what she thinks."

"Madame Ambeaux?"

"Aye, she'll tell you that her dead uncle predicts rain, or that her dead lover says the meat has gone off, or her sister says the maids have been slacking. The worst of it is, it usually rains, the meat usually smells bad the next day, and I find dust under the carpets."

"Well, let us forget about Madame Ambeaux and the afterlife for now. Do you know anything about the late Countess of Carde's tragic death?"

"Only what little is whispered in the village, my lord. Mr. Sloane does not like anyone to speak of it, and will not have her name mentioned in the house."

"That's what I heard too. So I shall have to speak to him. When do you expect him back?"

"I would say if I knew, my lord, I swear. But he

never tells me, nor where he is going. He has an address in Scarborough, however, and a set of rooms in Hull. Odd, though, that he left in a hurry as soon as he received your card. And told me not to admit you."

"Odd indeed. Perhaps he thought I was finally come to toss him out, bags and baggage. What of Miss Sloane?"

"She's out and about, deeding."

"Deeding? She works in real estate?"

"No, she does good deeds. A waste of time, if you ask me, for the kitchen maids do not need to read, and the schoolchildren do not need to draw. No one accepts her as one of theirs anyway, no matter how much she does, on account of her being away so long at that fancy academy for girls. That and the crazy aunt and how no one likes Mr. Sloane."

Alex looked at the amateurish portrait on the wall over Redfern's head. It depicted a thin blond-haired woman staring cross-eyed into the distance. He assumed the blue color of her eyes was real, the poor focus a product of poor artwork. "She looks somewhat as I remember her cousin Lizbeth."

"That is Miss Lizbeth. Lady Carde, that is. Mr. Sloane painted it himself, from a real portrait in the drawing room and his imagination. He has a number of them, hanging everywhere."

Now that was oddest yet.

With a great deal to think of before he spoke to the solicitor, Alex left. He'd return in the morning to see Miss Sloane. Redfern swore she would be there, if he had to tie her to a chair.

As he went to untie his horse, Alex thought he heard voices. Thinking perhaps Miss Sloane had returned home, he followed the sound around the house.

He found what promised to be a lovely rose garden in another few weeks, and one small old woman in a wide straw bonnet holding a conversation with . . .

Alex looked around. The lady was not speaking with anyone he could see, although she was quite animated in her side of the discussion. He coughed, out of politeness, to get her attention. "Madame Ambeaux?" For it could be no other. "I am Carde. The Earl of Carde."

She squinted at him. "Oh, no, you are not. He is a much older gentleman. I spoke with him just last week. He knows a great deal about roses."

Alex's father did—had done, that is. The rose gardens at Cardington Hall were renowned, thanks to his efforts. Alex did not have the same interest but he did see that the flower beds were carefully maintained. "I believe that was, ah, my father. He is deceased."

"Of course he is, else he wouldn't be speaking to me, would he?"

Alex did not know how to answer that question, so he said, "I believe we met many years ago, at your niece's wedding to my father." The old woman must have taken a tour of the grounds then, to remember the roses.

Lizbeth's aunt—which must make her Alex's stepaunt, more's the pity—took off her straw hat, revealing neatly braided, almost white hair. She stepped closer to Alex, peering up at him through faded blue eyes from a few inches away. She smelled of moldering decay. No, that was the trowel she held, filled with manure. He stepped back. Sane women had been known to throw things. Who knew what a crazy female would do? "I was Viscount Endicott then, Alexander."

"You have his look."

"Yes," he said, glad she recognized him.

"Poor boy."

Because his father was dead or because he resembled the prior earl? Devil take it, his nose was not all that homely! Especially not when his spectacles hid part of it.

Lizbeth's Aunt Hazel turned and went back to her gardening. "He's not here," she called over her shoulder as she knelt next to a small budding rose to work the manure into its roots.

"My father? I, ah, did not really expect him to be. I was hoping to see your nephew, Phelan Sloane."

"Not my nephew," she said. "Hand me that bucket, will you?" Once he did, wishing he had bought new gloves this morning, she added, "He was my sister-in-law's nephew, poor thing."

Her late in-law, or Phelan? Alex's head was spinning. He'd had a more meaningful conversation with the hired horse. He squatted down to her level, more to wipe his gloves on the grass than to be convivial. "Can you tell me about Phelan?"

"I just did. He's not here. Did you bring the licorice drops?"

Alex reached into his pocket without thinking, then paused. "How do you know about the licorice drops?"

"They were always Lizbeth's favorite, weren't they?"

Of course. Now he recalled how his father's new wife always had a jar of the sweets to share with two hungry boys. Perhaps being in her place of birth had brought back the memory, so he'd bought that particular treat. The old woman must be reliving the past, that was all. He handed her the twisted paper.

Aunt Hazel unwrapped the paper—leaving who knew what filth on it—took one, and handed it back.

"No, thank you. You keep them."

She placed the licorice drop in her mouth. "She said you'd be calling."

He frowned. "Redfern said Miss Sloane did not know of my arrival."

"Not Eleanor. Lizbeth."

"But Lizbeth is . . ." No, he would not bother with the truth as most people accepted it. Aunt Hazel spoke with her dead relatives, that was all. Otherwise she seemed as normal as half the matrons in London, and more interesting than the other half.

"Something about a promise," she said, licking her lips.

Alex stood up in a hurry. "How could Lizbeth— That is, how could you know about the promise?"

"She told me, of course. I cannot quite recall who it was she promised to keep company this morning, but that is where she went."

"Oh, your niece," he said, relieved.

"No, Eleanor. Lizbeth is dead, you know."

"Yes, I do know," he said, deciding to humor the addled auntie, "and my condolences. But I thought Miss Sloane called you Aunt Hazel all those years ago."

"Of course she does. But she cannot be my niece if Phelan is not my nevvy, now can she? I thought you were the smart one. Your father always says so, anyway, calling the other son a fool."

Alex did not feel very smart now. In fact, he'd change places with his brother in a flash, facing French cannons instead of one small crazy woman.

Trying to return the conversation to logic, and to the living, he asked, "Do you know where Mr. Sloane can be found? Phelan," he added, in case she spoke with some spectral Sloane too.

"No, he received an urgent message, he said, and

had to leave. He did not tell us where or why. Of course André might know."

"That would be a great help. Is André in the stables? Or working in one of the other gardens?" Alex looked around hopefully.

"Oh, André is dead." She patted her lips, then wiped at her eyes, leaving a trail of dirt and stickiness down her cheek. "Poor boy."

André or him?

Aunt Hazel offered to consult with André about Sloane's directions as she walked Alex back to the front of the house and his horse. She also offered to tell the old earl that his son was behaving just as he ought.

Alex thanked her for the thought, promised he would return in the morning to speak with Miss Sloane, and untied the gray's reins from the hitching post. Then Madame Ambeaux offered her hand to be kissed. With her foul, filthy glove still on it.

CHAPTER SIX

Nell was deep in a fog, despite the late afternoon sunshine. When she was not swatting at the goose to keep it from snatching her bonnet's ribbons or the fringe on her reticule, she was lost in thought. Luckily, Eager knew his way home.

Her brother's odd behavior, the arrival of the stranger, the conditions of the tenants all swirled in her head like a cyclone. Ugly debris, caught up in that maelstrom, smashed against the safe cocoon she had been living in, opening it to the elements, to the raging storm.

Had she been living such a sheltered life, then, protected from the truth by her own desires, her own fears of being left homeless, alone in the world? The only answer Nell could honestly give herself was yes. She had always known her brother was not liked in the village, but she had always accepted that as jealousy, as class distinction. She should have seen more, asked more, done more, by heaven. But he was her brother, with firm control over her life. If Phelan said she had to stay at school over the long holidays, what choice did she have? If he refused to let the local bachelors call at Ambeaux Cottage, what recourse did she have? If he said they had no extra funds for a season or a dowry or a trip to London where her schoolmates might have introduced her around, where was she to get the money? If he said he needed her at home, how could she leave?

Things would have been far different if Lizbeth had not died. Nell's beloved cousin would have seen her presented at court and to society, with a countess's backing. Lizbeth had promised all that in her letters, and again when she came for her father's funeral. She would find Miss Eleanor Sloane the most handsome, richest, kindest gentleman in all of London, see if she didn't. A few years more, that was all they needed for Nell to be of marriageable age. Dear Lizbeth was the one who ran out of time.

Nell's life might still have been far different if her Uncle Ambeaux had left her a dowry in his will, but he expected Lizbeth or Phelan to look after her interests. Phelan could not even look after a little girl, he was so grief-stricken at all the losses. A day after their Aunt Ambeaux's death, Nell was bundled off to school.

She should have been sent to a lesser academy, where daughters of the gentry were educated or girls from merchant families sent for polishing. The Select Academy Nell attended, where Lizbeth had gone, was for wealthy aristocratic females, all assured of successful seasons, suitable marriages. Nell had neither.

She had a quiet life instead, caring for Lizbeth's Aunt Hazel and keeping house for Phelan. Again, what choice did she have at eighteen years of age? She had learned to accept what she could not change, and to make the best of what she was given. She might have landed in the poorhouse if not for Ambeaux Cottage, so she looked after it as if it were her own. Now that she was of age and could leave Kingston Upon Hull, where could she go? Some of her old school friends wrote occasionally, but most had husbands and families. None invited her to their balls and betrothal parties. How could she ask them for a paid position in their households? And how could she leave her brother?

Phelan was different. He had been full of laughter and play, even after they lost their own parents and came to live here. He changed when Lizbeth wed. They all suffered, because glorious Lizbeth had been the very heart of Ambeaux Cottage, but to Phelan most of all. When she died, it was as if a part of him had been shattered in that horrible coach accident.

He should have grown resigned over the years, putting his grief behind him. Instead he had become bitter, morose, sunk in melancholy that only deepened with time. Now he seldom smiled, rarely spoke to anyone and went off by himself for days. When he was at home, he stayed in his library for endless hours with his brandy and the portrait of Lizbeth. Maybe he spoke with her, the way Aunt Hazel chatted with her lost loved ones. Nell did not know, and could never ask, not without sending Phelan into one of his rages.

She had accepted that too, telling herself he was working hard, he was worried about finances. She tiptoed around his moods and megrims like the rest of the cowering servants. Never could she admit that her brother was unbalanced, as peculiar in his ways as Aunt Hazel was in hers. Never could she admit that she was afraid of him, afraid of being tossed out, like those same servants.

Now, though, now she had no choice but to confront her brother. Surely he would have realized she'd find out about the tenants when he sent her to collect the rents. Surely he knew she would not let such injustice, such blatant uncaring cruelty go unchallenged. Nell was twenty-five and she had a tiny sum of money set aside. Aunt Hazel had a few bits and pieces of jewelry they might pawn if both of them had to leave. And leave they would, if Nell did not have answers.

Eager trotted right to the stable, ready for his oats. Nell was not quite so eager. While the new stable boy Christopher unhitched the donkey, Nell slowly untied the goose, stroking the soft feathers of its head, now that the wretched bird had stopped pecking at her. She thought she could lead it around to the kitchen garden and leave the thing there for whatever cook they managed to hire, but the goose had other ideas. It hopped over the low rabbit fence and followed at its new friend's heels.

"Won't Redfern be happy to see you at the front door?" Nell asked, not expecting any reply. The goose bobbed its head, though, and waddled along.

As she turned the corner toward the front of the house, Nell spotted a man and a horse, neither one familiar to her. The man was tall and broad and dressed casually, but with shining boots and a well-tailored coat. Here, obviously, was the stranger Nell had promised not to speak to, the dangerous rake she had sworn to avoid. How many other unknown gentlemen could arrive in the little town on the same day?

He was a scoundrel and a knave, all right, for there he was, wrestling with tiny Aunt Hazel, twisting her arm this way and that.

Nell did not stop to think what the gentleman could be about, mauling a batty old woman. She just ran. So did the goose.

* * *

Alex kept trying to shake Madame Ambeaux's hand rather than kissing it, but she kept raising her muddied paw toward his mouth. French manners or fastidiousness, which was it to be?

Then he heard a shout from behind him.

A slim woman in a drab, dun-colored gown with a paisley shawl over her shoulders was running his way with her pet . . . goose? Alex was so startled he dropped Aunt Hazel's hand. Then he was so busy defending himself from the squawking, flapping, pecking—and slapping, punching and pummeling—that he let go of the horse's reins.

The gray, not unexpectedly, took serious exception to the melee. He bucked and kicked, perilously close to the elderly Frenchwoman. Alex ducked the goose and the girl, and dove to push Madame Ambeaux out of danger. He rolled, taking the fall on his left shoulder rather than rolling onto the frail old woman. A hoof caught him a glancing blow he never noticed, not with the women, the horse, and the goose all screaming and jumping and getting in one another's way. He lurched to his feet and grabbed the younger woman's shawl to pull her to safety. Instead she struck him with her reticule, knocking his glasses off. He dragged her away anyway, despite the sharp kicks of wooden-heeled boots to his shins and a boney elbow to his midsection. Again he rolled onto his shoulder, which had no feeling in it anyway, to protect the hellcat from the horse's hooves. She scrambled away, unhurt, while he lay on his back, winded.

Things should have calmed down after that, except that the feather-brained fowl attacked the horse. If the fool horse had turned and run, it could have outdistanced the bird, but no, the stupid steed was fighting back. Alex was beyond caring what happened to any of them, least of all the suicidal goose. But the slim woman was wringing her hands and weeping, and Madame Ambeaux was shrieking in French. Alex could not help thinking, as he lay there in the dirt, that if the goose died and came back to chat with Lizbeth's lunatic relative, they could call it a poultry-geist. He shook his head and spit dirt and down and bad puns out of his mouth.

Then he got up to rescue a goddamn goose.

He caught the crazed horse's reins and hung on, hoping one of the women would have enough sense to chase the goose away. Hah. Together they must have had enough sense to fill a thimble, for the old lady was still screaming, and the younger one came to help him hold the rearing, bucking, berserk horse. Which meant Alex had to watch out for her instead of his own welfare. So of course he got kicked again.

He cursed and yelled at her to get the blasted bird, not the horse. Which she did, letting go of the rein so suddenly that, when the gray tossed its head, Alex was jerked off his feet. He landed, unfortunately, under the horse's.

The panicked beast bounced up and down a few times, crow-hopping, before it realized it was not goose-stepping a goose into the ground, but its former rider. Realizing its error, or fearing the consequences, or simply deciding to find its safe stall, the horse galloped off, landing Alex a mere glancing blow to the head this time.

"Talk to me, boy, talk to me," Aunt Hazel was yelling.

"Why, am I dead?" he answered, not daring to move, afraid he wouldn't be able to. He could not feel his legs, which was bad, but he was beginning to feel his shoulder, which he feared was dislocated, which was worse. It hurt more, at any rate.

"Don't move," the younger woman ordered, as if Alex had a choice.

She shooed the goose away from pecking at his brass buttons, and sent the older woman to find water, Redfern, and smelling salts. Then she knelt at his side, using her handkerchief to dab at the blood running down his forehead.

Alex looked up to see an angel and wondered if he were dead after all. She had creamy skin, golden curls that tumbled out of a bedraggled ribbon, and the bluest eyes he had ever seen. Of course, with his glasses lying some distance away, as broken as he was, everything was a blur. But Alex knew she was beautiful. He just did. She was soft anyway, with the gentlest of touches, and she smelled of peppermint. Could this be Lizbeth's little shadow, the skinny, pale waif he and his brother had teased so long ago? Lord, miracles did happen.

Nell looked down at a visage she had never forgotten. The Endicott nose, the thick dark hair, the spectacles—the stranger was no stranger at all. He was the gentle, serious boy who had taken her part all those years ago, the gallant youth who'd stopped the younger scamp from putting a snake down her back at Lizbeth's wedding. He'd looked out for her at the wedding breakfast too, bringing her the choicest delicacies, as if her thinness was an affront to the hospitality of his house. He'd possessed the dignity of a nobleman even then. Could this be her childhood idol all grown up, the Earl of Carde?

He had no dignity now, of course, flat on his back in the dirt, his left arm at an unnatural angle, blood

streaming from a gash on his forehead, his face con-
torted with pain, and his brown eyes squinting to see
without his glasses. He was still her champion, though.
He'd fearlessly saved her and her aunt and even the
goose. Now she prayed he was not as badly hurt as
he looked. Lord, miracles had better happen.

She dabbed at his face again, willing him to live.

"Nelly?"

"Ace?"

He smiled. Then he shut his eyes.

An old lady, an older butler, and a thin woman
could not get him into the house, much less up the
stairs to a bedroom. The stable boy Christopher would
have left for his own home as soon as he saw Eager
bedded down, and Phelan had taken the coachman
and groom with him.

Nell did not think the unconscious Lord Carde
ought to be moved yet anyway, not until they knew
the extent of his injuries. What if they hurt him worse?
She would never forgive herself.

"We need help."

That was an understatement if she ever heard one.
Redfern was shielding his pale eyes, even from the
late-afternoon sun, and Aunt Hazel was nearly as
white and wan as the colorless butler. Nell would have
to saddle Phelan's horse and ride into the village herself. The gelding had never carried a side-saddle, and
Nell had never ridden astride, but they would manage.
She hated to leave Lord Carde here, however, in the
carriage way. He might wake up, or he might be
bleeding inside. He could not die here in the dirt, with
no one beside him but an ancient servant and an
attics-to-let auntie. He could not!

So she rang the fire gong beside the front door. She

hit that brass circle as hard as she could swing its
mallet. She hit it again for good measure, and once
more for luck. Heaven knew they needed it.

Aunt Hazel clapped her hands over her ears and
Redfern staggered back.

Alex felt the sound through his whole body as the
ground shook. They were ringing the doomsday bells,
he thought in his befuddled, half-conscious state. He
was dead. But then he felt his head lifted into a soft
lap, so he did not mind half as much. He tried to smile
when he felt a tear land on his cheek. Angels should
not weep. Not for him.

Aunt Hazel knelt at his other side. "Good, *cherie*,"
she told Nell. "And he is awake. Now the tenant farmers will hear the gong and come running. They will
help move your earl and fetch the surgeon."

Who would come? Nell thought. Sophie Posener,
who was about to give birth, or her ailing husband?
The Doyles who would not open the door to their
landlord's sister? Or the Macalisters, who had left the
neighborhood altogether? None of them would come
to the aid of Ambeaux Cottage. She feared the other
tenants would stay away too, not caring that their
landlord's house burned down as long as the flames
stayed away from their homes. "I am hoping the stable
boy is not too far away yet. He can run to the village
for help."

Young Christopher did come back, out of breath
and fearful. The place had not been on fire ten minutes ago, so it must be under siege of the resident
ghosts. He was the only one relieved to see that the
emergency was only a half-dead stranger, not a long-
dead specter.

He set off again at a run—he could cover the mile

to the village on foot in half the time it would take
to harness and saddle Mr. Sloane's gelding—with Miss
Sloane's instructions ringing in his ears, along with the
reverberations of the fire gong.

There was no need. The earl's rented horse had
come back to the inn, lathered and wild-eyed, without
its rider. Mr. Ritter feared for his patron's life, and
his own unpaid bill, so he'd gathered a handful of his
hostlers. The fire gong had brought out half the village, curious, deliciously frightened, excited, almost
like it was a holiday. Now they were all on the dirt
path toward Ambeaux Cottage, many for the first time.
They carried a wooden door, in case the earl needed to
be carried, and a few of the men carried pistols in case—
Well, just in case. Some carried buckets, some shovels.
The blacksmith had his hammer, the surgeon had his
bag, Kitty Johnstone had her skirts hiked up, ostensi-
bly to make better time walking.

The vicar carried a cross and his bible, not that he
believed any of the ridiculous stories about the cottage
residents. He took tea there on occasion, and dinner
once a month. Miss Sloane was a decent, god-fearing
young woman who taught Sunday school. Mr. Sloane
never attended services, but that did not make him
more of a heathen than a lot of others in the hurrying
crowd. Redfern was an unfortunate soul, not a sign of
sin from on high. And Madame Ambeaux was a Papist, not a witch. No, the vicar was merely prepared
for the worst, he told himself, although praying for
the best as he puffed and panted his way up the path.

Nell could have kissed them all, even the sweaty
blacksmith, the ale-stained innkeeper, and the sancti-
monious prelate, she was so happy to see help coming
up the path. Instead she ordered Redfern, with Chris-

topher's help, to fetch wine and water for the thirsty rescuers as they waited in a close circle for the surgeon's diagnosis.

"He'll live," Mr. Lessiter declared, to cheers and shouts and raised wineglasses. Everyone was celebrating except Alex, who dimly heard the news and chose to disagree with the sawbone's findings. What appeared to be a hundred faces were staring down at him, there in the dirt. If he did not die of the agonizing pain, he would certainly die of embarrassment.

Then the surgeon suggested they might as well put the lord's left arm back in its rightful shoulder socket out here, so the carrying would not hurt so badly. Alex could not imagine how anything could hurt worse, but he looked up, trying to distinguish Nelly's blue eyes. She was beside him, holding his other hand, nodding encouragement, so he gave a nod too.

The blacksmith took one side, the innkeeper the other, while the surgeon pulled and pushed. Alex passed out, the vicar puked, the goose pecked at Kitty Johnstone's red silk petticoats, and everyone cheered again when Lord Carde's arm finally snapped back into place.

"I'll know more once I have him out of his clothes and in a bed," the surgeon told Nell as the men prepared to lift the earl onto the door to carry him upstairs to the largest guest bedchamber. "Of course, I won't know if the head injury's left him with the mind of a mangel-wurzel."

"Oh, no, he knew me," Nell said.

The surgeon looked doubtful. How could this swell know spinsterish Miss Sloane, who never had a London Season? Maybe she was as crackbrained as the rest of her relatives.

Sensing the surgeon's disbelief, Nell added: "Your

patient is Alexander Endicott, the Earl of Carde. My late cousin's stepson. He recognized me, I swear."

"Well, that's all to the good, iffen his lordship has his wits about him. Still, he might have internal injuries that'll flood his bowels with blood, or maybe one of those broken ribs pierced a lung, although I don't hear any rales or whistles in his chest. Or he might have damage to his spine so he'll be a cripple. You never know."

"He'll be fine," Nell vowed as she hurried ahead to turn down the bedclothes and gather extra blankets and towels, and a nightshirt from Phelan's bedchamber. She also vowed to send to London for a more learned physician. And proper servants, who would stay in the house overnight. Young Christopher was making up the fire, but he was already looking over his shoulder, inching toward the door.

Surely Nell and her aunt and old Redfern could not nurse an injured earl on their own. Even now Miss Sloane was ordered to wait outside while the innkeeper helped disrobe the invalid. Oh, dear, she would not have to attend to his personal needs, would she? Nell could not decide who would be more mortified, Lord Carde or herself.

A million thoughts were going through her head, like whom she should notify, and where was her drat-ted brother when she needed him? Would the cook come back to serve an earl, even though it would be sickroom food at first, and where was she to get the money to pay for all this? Her own cache of savings was instantly depleted as she handed coins to all the men who had helped carry the earl upstairs. She paid the surgeon extra to call on the Poseners next, giving him a purse for them to hire what help they needed, to be repaid when the geese were sold. She handed

more to the apothecary's boy to bring back whatever
the surgeon prescribed, and more still to Mr. Ritter,
to fetch his lordship's belongings. With any luck, Lord
Carde would have an extra pair of spectacles in his
bag, or else she would have to find the funds for that,
too. After all, the whole catastrophe was her fault,
hers and that wretched bird's, and Phelan's for leaving
when he must have known the earl was calling.

Phelan was the only one empowered to withdraw
money from the bank. He was the only one with the
combination to the safe in the book room, and the
only one with a key to his desk drawers. Now that
she thought about it, Nell realized the idiocy of that
system, giving the man of the house entire control.
What if he were the one suffering an injury? What if
he never came back from wherever he was? Thinking
of that, she gave the last of the household money to
Redfern, to send riders to Hull and Scarborough in
search of her brother . . . and the money.

A great many of her problems were resolved when
a coach pulled up at the front door. Her brother was
not returned, but this was a more welcome sight. The
elegant carriage carried his lordship's valet, along with
the earl's trunks, his extra spectacles, a heavy purse,
and extra grooms. Now they would manage.

The man's name was Stives, and he had been with
the earl for many years. He was not the least bit fussy
or finicking like Phelan's man, but looked sturdier,
older, more like a former soldier than a dancing master. He appeared to be used to mayhem and making
quick decisions. Thank goodness someone was, Nell
thought.

Stives listened calmly as she reiterated the surgeon's
findings: "His lordship's left shoulder was dislocated,
and Mr. Lessiter says it might never heal properly,

leaving him prone to recurrences in the future. He definitely has three broken ribs, and possibly a concussion. There is a large contusion on his back that might indicate a spinal injury, which might have caused a paralysis, but Mr. Lassiter cannot be sure until the earl is awake. He does not think Lord Carde suffered any internal injuries, but, again, he is not certain. He did not think the wound to the earl's head needed stitching, but if it begins to bleed again, we are to send for him. Otherwise he will return in the morning." Nell could not help the catch in her voice as she concluded, "He says that the next few days will decide Lord Carde's fate."

Stives seemed to take the gloomy litany of ills calmly. "Milord will do."

"Yes, but the surgeon warns a fever might take hold, and that could prove more dangerous yet. He left some powders, but does not think we should administer laudanum for the pain until he assesses the concussion."

The valet bowed at the door of Lord Carde's bedroom, effectively keeping Nell from entering.

She looked in quickly. His lordship was as white as the sheets on the high bed, with a thick bandage wrapped around his head as if someone had started to wind a mummy's shroud then thought better of it. He was not moving, but she could see the sheets were, so he was breathing.

The valet looked back at Nell before shutting the door in her face. "He will do, miss. He's a game 'un, is his lordship."

Nell was heartened by the man's confidence. After all, Stives knew the earl better than anyone, knew his physical condition and his weaknesses. If the gentleman's gentleman said the gentleman would live, well, then Nell would believe him. She could not face any other outcome, anyway.

After seeing that the new servants were housed and fed, thanks to a promised increase in Cook's wages, and a suddenly helpful Redfern sent to rest, Nell could finally change her filthy, blood-, mud- and goose-stained gown and wash her hands. Then she met Aunt Hazel in the drawing room for a welcome cup of tea.

"We need these people," Nell told the old woman. "Desperately. Ace, that is, Lord Carde, needs them here. So please do not frighten them with your tales of long-dead relatives having present-day chats. Do you understand?"

Her aunt added another lump of sugar to her tea. "Just the way André likes it."

"No! Aunt Hazel, listen to me! You must not scare anyone off, especially Stives. We need him."

"We need the earl more. André told me."

CHAPTER SEVEN

He was battered, bruised, and befogged. What battle Alex had fought, he did not know. He was certain he had lost, though.

The first time he awoke in a panic. He could not see anything, not even the blur of being without his spectacles. Great heavens, he was blind! How was he going to conduct the business of the Carde empire when he could not see the properties, read the account ledgers, or look for signs of dishonesty in his employees' eyes?

Then he realized a heavy bandage had slipped down his forehead. He tried to push it off with his left arm. That one seemed pinned to his side, so he used his right one. That worked, and he could see dim outlines of furniture, a fire in the hearth. His eyes were all right, then, or as all right as they had ever been. He would worry why he was trussed like a Christmas goose—there was something about that thought nibbling at his memory, but he did not think he'd missed Christmas—later, when he did not hurt so much.

As he tried to ignore the pain and the worrisome

details such as where he was and how he'd arrived there, Alex thought it would have been a shame to be blind. He wanted to see little Nelly again, to discover if she really had turned into a diamond of the first water. He remembered her, if nothing else. He also remembered his father's story of seeing Lizbeth Ambeaux the first time, and losing his heart to her without knowing her name. She was too young for him, he'd told his heir before the wedding, and not of elevated enough birth for an earl, despite a connection to the French nobility. None of that had mattered, the earl had explained to his elder son. He had seen her, and he had to meet her. Then he had to wed her. It was that simple.

Nothing was that simple, Alex knew. He also knew he had no intention of falling top over tail for a pretty face. That was not how a man selected a wife, unless he was prepared for a lifetime of misery. Besides, beauty faded faster than the ink on the marriage vows. Still, thinking of Nelly's big blue eyes, all filled with concern, for him, took some of the hurting away so he could drift back to sleep.

The second time he awoke, a familiar figure was in the chair by his bedside.

"Stivey!" he said, surprised at his own hoarse voice. "I knew you would come, man."

Stives immediately brought a glass of water to his master's dry lips, as if he had been waiting for just that moment. Which he had, for the last four long, worrisome hours. As the earl drank, his loyal, long-term valet cleared his throat of leftover emotion and said, "Of course I would come. Where else should I be but at milord's side? Of course if you had waited for the coach as I advised instead of tearing out of the house—"

Alex pushed the glass away after drinking half. "Yes, man, you are right, as always. How bad is the damage?"

"Well, your boots are a disgrace. The coat has already been sent to the poor box, although that particular garment is no great loss to milord's wardrobe."

"Cut line, you clunch. What's broken?"

"Ribs. I doubt the local sawbones can count high enough to know how many. Perhaps your brainbox, but I did tell them you were not making a great deal of sense before you set out on this journey."

Alex made a noise in his throat that was almost a growl. Stives set the glass back to his lips.

When he had another sip, Alex asked, "What else?"

"Can you move your legs?"

Alex did, wiggling his toes, bending his ankles, then his knees. He used his unbound hand to check beneath the covers. "All present and in working order."

"Excellent. Then barring fevers, internal hemorrhaging, disordered spleen or cataclysmic heart failure, you should make a full recovery. I am not as sanguine about your coachman, your grooms, or myself, of course, rushing to your side."

Alex ignored the barbs. "If I am so healthy, why do I hurt so much?"

"Because I was instructed not to administer laudanum until I was assured you were not concussed. How many fingers am I holding up?"

"Deuce take it, I can barely see you, much less your fingers."

Stives fit a spare pair of glasses around the earl's head. "Better?"

"Much. And you are not holding up any fingers at all, you miserable makebate. How about some brandy?"

"That is not prescribed." Instead Stives mixed a few

drops of laudanum into a fresh glass of lemonade. While he did so, the concerned valet aired his opinions and grievances, knowing full well he would not get such an opportunity once Lord Carde was asleep, much less when he was back on his feet. "You would not be needing this if you had not gone haring off like the hounds of hell were nipping at your toes. If you had permitted your staff even one day's preparation, we could have had your own riding horses waiting for your convenience. Your secretary could have sent word of your arrival ahead to the residents of this place, who would have called on you, quite properly, instead of forcing you to mount an untrustworthy nag."

"Devil a bit, it wasn't the horse's fault, it was the goose's."

"You were riding a goose?" Stives set the glass of lemonade and laudanum back on the bedside table. "Perhaps we should wait another day before trying the laudanum."

"I was not riding the blasted bird! It spooked my horse."

"And milord fell off?" Stives stirred the drink. "You have not taken a header in all the years of my employ."

Alex had, of course; he simply never mentioned the falls to his valet, rather than suffer the ensuing lectures. Stives was a good man, a good friend, even, but he was a bit solicitous, and stiff-rumped to boot. When he started "milording" Alex, the earl knew he was in for a sermon. He tried to head this one off before Stives could work himself into a well-deserved diatribe. Alex had gone off half-cocked and now he was injured. Old Stivy would see that as divine justice.

"I did not fall from the horse, Stives. I was on the ground, protecting the ladies."

"From the goose?"

"No, from the horse."

Stives shook his head. "I knew there had to be a woman at the bottom of this contretemps. I suppose milord will be fleeing in haste as soon as your shoulder mends." He shook his head again. "Perhaps you will ride in the carriage the next time you make an escape."

"This is not like the other times. Besides, I was not running away. I was making a strategic withdrawal."

Stives snorted his opinion of that interpretation. "You ran like a fox on the first day of hunting season."

"Well, Miss Sloane is not a vulture like those others."

"She does seem a pleasant enough sort. But she is a woman of a certain age, and uncertain means. A dangerous combination for a man in your position."

"What, flat on my back?"

"Unwed and needing an heir."

"Little Nelly does not have designs on my purse or my title, I swear. Why, you'd think she arranged for her goose to attack the horse just so I would be trapped here."

Stives merely raised an eyebrow.

"No such thing, man. Why, she did not know I was coming. She did not even know who I was when she saw me in the carriageway."

Not know the Earl of Carde when the entire village knew of his arrival? Stives raised his eyebrow higher. "The next thing you will be telling me is that the old lady speaks to spirits, as they said at the inn."

"Oh, she speaks to them. I have heard her myself. The question is, do they respond? But little Nelly is shy and sweet." Perhaps he did have a broken head, because he was forgetting the screaming shrew in the driveway. "She's not greedy and grasping like those others."

Stives had seen the lady giving orders like a general. "How long has it been since you have seen 'little Nelly,' milord? I think you will find . . ."

Milord had drifted off, a smile on his lips.

Stives wondered if he should bother unpacking.

The third time Alex awoke, it was to agony that made the previous pain seem like a splinter or a hangnail. He groaned. Someone was trying to pour a foul brew down his throat. Stives, he thought. "Wake up and drink, milord. You need this, for the fever."

Wake up and suffer? No, he'd rather lie here and wait to die. He turned his head away from the glass.

"There's more laudanum, too, for the pain."

Now that was more appealing. Alex sipped and fell back into a stupor, barely knowing whether his body burned with heat or shivered with cold. He could ignore the pain now, but oh, the dreams. They would not be ignored. They could not be endured.

He was being driven off a cliff by a marauding pack of goose-quill pens. Falling, falling . . .

He was waiting at the altar for his beautiful blue-eyed bride . . . to waddle down the aisle.

His father's head, on a long white neck, was hissing: "Promises, promises," which echoed back as "misses, missus, miss us."

The worst nightmare was yet to come. In it, Alex was bound to a bed, immobilized, and there was a woman in the room, a young, unwed, gently bred woman, alone, unchaperoned. He was trapped!

"I will not marry you!" Alex sat up and shouted,

then tried to clutch his head and his shoulder at the same time. He sank back to the pillows with a groan.

"And I shan't marry you either, Lord Carde." Nell set down her sewing and came closer to the bed to feel his forehead for fever. "Besides, I thought we settled that more than a decade ago, when someone commented that we made a charming pair at your father's nuptials."

"Nelly?"

She placed his glasses on his face, as Stives had instructed her, then a cool cloth on his aching forehead. "I much prefer Nell now, or Eleanor. However, Miss Sloane is more proper, my lord."

He winced. "And I much prefer Alex or Carde, if you must be so formal." He raised the cloth to look around the room. The empty room. "Are we, ah, proper?"

She smiled, and he was pleased to see that he was correct: She was a beauty now. She was still too thin, with her gloriously fair hair scraped back into a decorous bun at the nape of her neck. She was dressed in another dull, shapeless gown, not a dressing robe or her night rail, thank goodness. But he saw—and felt, like sunshine on his face—the surpassing sweetness of her lovely smile. Lovely or not, he did not wish to be in such a compromising position, incapacitated or not. "Please tell me your aunt is in some dark corner I cannot see, or she has gone to fetch a pot of tea." With his luck, the relic of a relative had gone to fetch a special license. She might be queer as a two-headed hen, but no woman with a marriageable miss in her charge would miss such an opportunity.

Nell smiled again. "I am sorry, but my aunt has gone to sleep. She is not as young as she once was."

None of them were. That was the problem. They

were not left alone in the nursery while some nanny
took a quick nap.

"Your maid?"

"Oh, the girl who sees to my clothes and Aunt Hazel's never spends the night here. But do not fret.
Your man will be back in an hour or so, the door is
open, and no servants are afoot. No one need know
that I spent part of the night sequestered with you,
although I should think the neighbors would not question your conduct anyway, not after having seen you
carried upstairs on the door."

He still looked disturbed, so Nell added: "Mr. Stives
was falling over on his feet from exhaustion. He worried that he might fall asleep in the chair and not hear
your call or awaken in time for your fever medicine.
I offered to stay with you for a bit so he might get
some rest. It was either me or Redfern."

If the earl saw the butler's sepulchral visage, he'd
think he was facing the Grim Reaper after all. Surely
Nelly—Miss Sloane's face was more pleasant to wake
up to, except . . .

"What about your brother?"

The smile faded from her lips. "If you are worried
that Phelan shall be thundering into your bedroom,
waving his pistols and demanding you do the honorable thing, rest easy. He is still from home."

Nell was not about to discuss with the earl how the
messengers had returned from both Scarborough and
Hull without finding Phelan. She had found the key
to the strongbox in his desk, however, so was in funds.
At least her mind was relieved of one worry.

Alex was frowning. "How long have I been here
anyway?"

"Three days, although you have been out of your
mind for most of them. Your Mr. Stives thinks we

should cut back on the laudanum, but the surgeon says sleep is the best medicine."

"Not with those awful dreams, it isn't. I prefer the pain, I think, and trust Stivey's opinions."

"Then you must ask for a dosage when you require it. I shan't force any down your throat."

"Thank you."

"What, were you so worried I would keep you drugged until I could prop you in front of a parson?"

He was, but told her, "Of course not. A man just likes to know that he is in control, not helpless, at another's command."

Nell thought about the discoveries she had made at the remaining tenant farms. "A woman likes to feel she has her destiny in her own hands, too." She brought him a glass of barley water and raised his head so he might drink. "We seldom do, however."

Now was not the time for Alex to discuss the power women had to make men dance to their tunes. If Miss Sloane was unaware of her beauty, her appeal, he would not tell her. He liked the feel of her hands on his head, and liked the rosewater scent she wore. No, he would not tell her how women ruled the world.

Hell, he was helpless. She could have her wicked way with him—half of him wished she might try—and force him into a situation that could only be resolved with an honorable declaration.

Nell was not like that, no matter what Stives thought. She was not dressed to entice, rubbing against him to arouse, whispering in his ear to excite. She was wiping barley water off his chin, for heaven's sake. She was a lady who would not use his own honor and desires as weapons against him. Miss Eleanor Sloane was still the sweet, shy girl he had known so long ago.

Alex did not know why she was still unwed at such

an advanced age for females—the fellows hereabouts must be as peculiar as the butler and the aunt; perhaps the water was tainted—but he knew she could have trapped any number of them into wedlock if she'd used her feminine wiles. He was safe.

He was a cad, thinking the worst of some poor, innocent woman. He tried to apologize. "I regret if my concerns sounded like suspicions. I am, as you say, still a bit befuddled by the drugs and the fever. I beg your pardon."

"There is nothing to forgive."

"If not for my mistrust, then I must apologize for all the upset to your household, the added burdens."

Having four extra men, an earl, a valet, a coachman, and a groom should indeed have taxed Nell's resources sorely. They did not. "They are as nothing. Your man sees to almost everything. He has wrapped Cook around his competent fingers, so she does his bidding, and now her nieces come by day to keep up the other chores and help your groom serve the sickroom. The maids are considering staying over at night now that the estimable Mr. Stives is here to protect them. We are very comfortable."

Estimable? Comfortable? We? Nell and Stives? "The man does have a way with the ladies."

"Yes, I understand he has the maid servants scurrying to and fro, with smiles upon their faces. I have only seen him in passing, of course, since he spends most of his hours in here with you."

Alex was relieved, for some reason he did not wish to examine. Nell was *his* angel. He'd known her longer. Stives was a fine figure of a man. He was not an acceptable match for a lady, of course, but he was fit for a dalliance, if no gentlemen were handy.

"He seems devoted to you," Nell said, thinking of

how many different valets her brother had employed in the recent years and how the ladies' maids she and her aunt shared never seemed to stay long.

"I saved his life once, many years ago. Now the chap feels he is responsible for mine. Sometimes he acts more like a nursemaid than a valet."

"Well, I, for one, am glad he is so competent in a sickroom, for heaven only knows what we would have done otherwise. You are lucky."

With broken bones and a battered head? Alex did not feel lucky. He felt like something a badger had buried in its burrow to be eaten later. He did not feel like listening to Nelly—Miss Sloane—sing his valet's praises, either. "I am pleased my staff is making the situation less onerous for you."

She nodded, returned to her seat, and picked up her needlework again. She started to light another candle, now that his lordship was awake. "Oh, will the light bother you? I should not wish to injure your eyes or bring on another headache. Or if you wished to sleep . . . ?"

"No, I have had a surfeit of sleep, it seems." He could not really see her well by the shielded candle, but was comforted by her presence, the faint aroma of rosewater. Here was a peaceful, tranquil scene, not one of his horrid nightmares of being chased and strangled and snared.

Soon he would have to ask questions, about her brother, the estate, the carriage accident of so long ago, but not now, when he was too battered, beaten, and bloodied to care. He did care, out of curiosity, of course, why Miss Sloane was still a maiden living at home. Perhaps there had been a fiancé killed in the war, or an unfaithful lover. He'd ask someone, not Nell, about it, some other time when his head did not feel like it had been used for cricket practice. Stives could be counted on to know all the servants' gossip within an hour of arrival. Redfern must have answers, now that he understood where his loyalties should lie. The old lady would know too, if she stopped listening to lost souls long enough to hold a conversation with the living.

That reminded him: "Is Madame Ambeaux well? I trust she took no ill effects from the events of my arrival?"

"She was upset, as were we all, naturally, at your injuries. But a bit of wine and a rest were all she needed to recover."

"And you? Were you hurt? I must apologize yet again, it seems, this time for mauling you about."

"How could you think such a thing? It is I who must apologize for becoming so violent. I was afraid, you see."

"Of me?" Alex could not think of another woman who had ever feared him. He did not like to think that a lady did now, especially not this lady from his childhood.

"I did not know who you were, and had heard stories of a stranger in town. Then when I saw you with my aunt . . ." Her voice trailed off. Aunt Hazel had explained that Lord Carde was kissing her hand in farewell, and taking his sweet time about it, not wrestling with the aged woman to steal her purse or her pearl necklace as Nell had supposed, or worse. "I apologize for my thoroughly outrageous conduct. I am certain no lady of your acquaintance would behave so badly."

Alex could think of a few who would and had, although none of them kept vicious geese as guard dogs. "Think nothing of it."

"How can I not think of it, with profound regret, when my reckless actions caused you so much pain and injury?"

"But I am recovering, as you can see. No permanent harm done." Except for the shoulder that would always be chancy from now on, and the backbone that might give him agony for the rest of his life. "Why do we not both forget the entire incident?"

"Forget the bravest actions I have ever seen? Why, you saved my aunt's life. At least you saved her from grave injury. You protected me from being struck, despite my own idiocy, and you rescued the goose from being trampled. I do not believe I have witnessed a more courageous deed."

His brother Jonathan had always been considered the brave one, the valiant warrior. Alex found he liked being considered a savior. His chest swelled with manly pride until his broken ribs protested. He gasped in pain.

Nell raced to his side, dropping her needlework. "Do you want the laudanum? Shall I awaken Mr. Stives?"

What, seek oblivion after she claimed he was a hero? Alex could suffer like the most stalwart of soldiers, at least until Stives returned. "No, I shall endure."

Nell gathered up her needlework anyway. "It is nearly time for Mr. Stives to come with your fever medicine, so I shall let you rest. He would never forgive me if I caused you more pain or weariness." She stepped toward the door.

"Will you come again?" Alex worried that he did not sound very heroic in his own ears, but more like a sickly child begging for attention. "Please?"

She smiled at him and said, "Of course. And you

need not worry that I might cry compromise or try to inveigle you into parson's mousetrap. I would never cast out lures to any man, much less one already engaged."

"Engaged? I am not engaged!"

"Of course I understand that it is not official yet, but I had it in a letter from the lady herself," Nell said from the doorway. "So I wrote to her as soon as we knew the extent of your injuries. I expect your beloved will arrive within the next day or so. Good night, my lord."

CHAPTER EIGHT

"Wait!" he shouted in a strangled gasp, as if he had been kicked by another horse. "I do not have any—I am not be—Beloved?" He was choking on his tongue, unable to string any coherent thoughts together, much less words. "Holy hell! No!"

She blushed at his language but took a step back into the room. "Do not worry. I will not spoil your surprise by mentioning it to anyone. I had it on strictest confidence from your intended herself and would not go back on my word."

Intended? Alex intended to murder someone at the first opportunity. But who? How the devil had Miss Sloane of Ambiguous Cottage in Humble Nowhere even *heard* of any benighted betrothals? They would not get the scandal sheets here, and the inn's newspapers were three days old.

He frantically tried to recall the three panic-inducing possibilities. What the deuce were their names, anyway?

There was no way on earth Miss Sloane could know Squire Branford's daughter. Daphne was at least seven

years younger, seven times sillier, and had never been
out of Northamphshire except for her London Season.

His former mistress? Alex nearly gagged on the idea
of plain Miss Sloane—she was no longer his old play-
mate Nelly, and no longer lovely, this viper in vapid
dress—in the same room as Mona, Lady Monroe. The
dashing, daring redhead would make this provincial spinster fade into the woodwork, except for her blushes of
shock.

That left the duke's daughter. "Lady Lucinda
Applegate?"

"Of course."

Miss Sloane was looking at him as if he had three
heads, so she must not know about the three fiancées.
At least he was saved that mortification. "Of course,"
he echoed.

"We attended the same school for young ladies, you
see. I realize she is far above my touch, so you need
not look so startled at the connection. We were never
bosom bows, a duke's only daughter and an émigré
Frenchman's ward. But I think Lady Lucinda is happy
to correspond with someone out of her social set,
someone who can be trusted not to repeat her deepest,
most private thoughts."

"If she had such intimate notions, by Harry, then
why did she not simply keep a blasted diary?"

Nell stood taller, although not by much, since she
was never a large woman, not even standing on her
dignity. She certainly did not have the stature—in
inches or in consequence—of his lordship's nobly proportioned noblewoman. She did have her pride, however. "I believe the lady likes me."

Lord Carde had the grace to be embarrassed. "I am
sure she must. I was merely surprised at the distant

friendship." He was surprised that Lady Lucinda had any friends at all, the arrogant, coldhearted cat.

Nell relaxed and admitted, "In truth, I think that all her other friends have married and started their nurseries. She has less in common with enthusiastic young matrons than with an unwed countrywoman of no distinction."

Alex could not believe his damnable luck. "You say you were at school with Lady Lucinda?"

"Yes, the one Lizbeth attended, Mrs. Merton's Select Academy. Many daughters of the Quality were enrolled. Matron prided herself on the peerages she could claim within her walls. Cousin Lizbeth had intended me to attend when I was older, to make acquaintances I might meet again when she presented me in London. My brother generously used part of his inheritance to send me earlier, after all the deaths in the family, since I was too young to remain at home with no one but Aunt Hazel as companion. He was too grief-stricken to deal with a brokenhearted young girl."

Alex would think about Phelan's inheritance, his generosity, and his grief later, after he resolved this latest marrying mess. "So you became friends?" He still had trouble imagining Lady Lucinda befriending anyone who could not further her own interests.

"Lady Lucinda was also motherless," Nell said, as if that explained a great deal.

It did. Alex recalled how his brother and he had grown much closer after losing their father. Even haughty harridans, it seemed, needed someone to cling to. "And you have kept up correspondence after all these years of separation?"

"Infrequently, of course, since the lady has such a

busy social calendar. But she was bursting with her happy news. She wrote to me before the announcement was made public, knowing I would both share her joy and keep her secret."

He sighed. "And so you invited your dear friend here, out of the goodness of your heart?"

"Of course. To be with you through your recuperation."

"What is it they say about the road to hell being paved with good intentions? I suppose I should thank you, which I shall do by mail, as soon as I am gone."

"Gone?"

Alex was already fighting the bedclothes, the bandages, and the unbearable pain of moving his cracked ribs. "Gone."

Nell watched as his bare feet reached for the ground beside the bed. "Good grief, what are you doing? Are you delirious again?"

"No, I am very much in my right mind. I am simply leaving, which should be obvious. If you do not wish to view a gentleman changing into his traveling clothes, I suggest you leave. Or turn your back, at the very least."

"You must be feverish. I'll get Mr. Stives." She tugged on the bellpull near the door.

"Tell him to start packing when you see him." Alex had both feet on the floor now and was standing, wondering where Stivey had stashed his clothes. Then he wondered where he could go to be safe from manipulative women. Perhaps a monastery. There must be one or two in England somewhere. If not, he could always join his brother in the army. How many marriage-minded women could there be in the middle of a war? He started to draw the nightshirt over his head.

"Stop that!" Nell shrieked when the hem reached his knees. She tugged frantically at the bellpull again.

"What, you are still here? Then be a good girl, won't you, and find my boots and breeches."

"No, I will not be party to this idiocy. You are concussed and injured. Further trauma could leave you crippled for life, the surgeon says. You cannot leave."

"Watch me," Alex said, taking five steps toward the door, ready to ride in his altogether if that was all he had. He collapsed at the sixth step, right into Nell's arms. She could not support him, of course, so collapsed onto the floor with his head in her lap.

"I told you no good could come of this jingle-brained journey," Stives grumbled from the doorway, shutting the door behind him lest anyone else see his master's latest fall from grace. "But you wouldn't listen. You had to go trekking halfway across England, just to land in another woman's clutches."

"I am not in Miss Sloane's clutches," Alex said through gritted teeth, trying to keep the room from spinning and his stomach from turning and his back from seizing up. In fact, Nelly's embrace was the only thing keeping him from losing his mind, his lunch, and his will to live altogether.

"His lordship is not in my embrace." Nell almost spit out the words. "I merely caught the clunch when he fell. I would be pleased if you got the thickheaded fool off me. Oh, and he thinks he is leaving."

Stives hauled his master up and half led, half carried him back to the bed. "Pardon me, milord, but you ain't going nowhere but back into that bed." He shoved the earl onto the mattress as if he were a sack of flour. "The sawbones says you could end up in a wheeled chair without proper rest. He might not have an ounce of sense, but I am not taking chances. I do not intend to be wiping your arse until doomsday."

"This is doomsday, and do not say 'arse' in front of a lady, damn it." Alex grabbed for his man's sleeve with his free hand. "She"—he jerked his head toward Nell—"invited Lady Lucinda here."

"The leech?"

"That is right. Dear little Nelly, all smiles and solicitous, is a traitor to the family ties. Blood is not thicker than water in this godforsaken place."

"We do not share any blood, my lord."

He glared at Nell while Stives straightened the covers. "It's all the same, Miss Sloane. You and your goose did not kill me, so you tossed me to the lions, like some doomed infidel gladiator."

"Coming too strong, milord," Stives whispered in his ear with a wink in Nell's direction. "Gladiators wore shields and armor, not their nightshirts and arm slings."

"It is a metaphor, damn it! Or a simile. I do not care which! She turned on me, I say." Alex sighed, happy enough to rest his head back on the soft pillow, although Nell's lap had not been the least uncomfortable. "Women are all the same," he said to his trusted servant. "They might look like angels, all sweet and shy, but they are all alike. Crafty connivers, every one of the miserable menaces. Sweet and shy? Hah!" He jerked his head toward Nell. "An angel? This one is in league with the devil!"

Nell was touched that Lord Carde thought her an angel. Sweet and shy? That had not described her since she was the little girl he remembered. But a limb of Satan? A contriver in collusion? Aiming to murder him?

"I take it you are *not* promised to Lady Lucinda?"

"Not promised, not planning an engagement, not even planning on dancing with the shrew ever again. There is nothing between us but as many miles as I could manage."

Oh, dear. Nell's eyes began to fill with tears of remorse and embarrassment. Stives looked away. Nell raised her chin, though. "Surely you must have led Lady Lucinda to believe—"

"I led her to the terraced gardens. In public, at a ball. One time." He did not mention the kiss. "That does not constitute a declaration. The entire engagement imbroglio was in the woman's mind, and in her dreams of becoming a countess. Lady Lucinda did not want me. I am not half so vain as to think the woman actually liked me. My title and wealth were vastly attractive to her in her desperation to find a suitable husband. I am not he."

"You told her this?"

"In no uncertain terms."

"Then why did she accept my invitation to come here? She sent a messenger, not merely a letter."

"Why? Because *you* told her I was wounded and could not run. Do you know how easy it will be for her to cry compromise in this secluded neighborhood? She'll declare her reputation ruined unless I act the gentleman and restore it with a ring on her finger."

"That is nonsense. You merely have to tell her that there was a misunderstanding. That I sent for her, not you."

"The only one lacking in understanding is you, Miss Sloane. You do not know your so-called friend if you think she will be dissuaded by the simple fact that I do not wish to marry her. She already knows that, yet she is coming anyway. Well, it is your problem now. You get rid of her."

"Me?"

"You invited her, didn't you? So disinvite her when she arrives. I do not care if you have to set your goose on her, just keep the woman away from me. Stives, lock the door. The front door too, not just my bedroom. Let no one in, no one, do you hear? The witch could be hiding in a coal cart. In fact, barricade the carriage drive with trees, then station a guard there. Better make it one of our own men. And tell people in the village that there is a virulent outbreak of some foul disease out here, something dire and disfiguring, to keep her away. Leprosy, perhaps. Not even a countess's tiara would be worth having one's nose fall off. Although Lady Lucinda might think it all right in my case." He rubbed at his own nose. "She said my spectacles were ugly. That's how much she likes me."

"Why, your nose is handsome and—" Nell caught herself before she revealed more of her opinion of his looks than was fitting. Simply noticing the dark chest hairs peeking through the opening of his nightshirt was entirely improper. As was this conversation. "This is absurd. You cannot come here and expect me to be so rude to my invited guest. You cannot demand the whole house be turned upside down on your silly whims, and you cannot give orders as if you owned the place."

Alex set his spectacles more comfortably on his nose. His suddenly handsome nose. "Why not? I do ow—Ow!" he exclaimed, pretending to rub at his not-so-pretended aching head. Alex did not want to discuss ownership of Ambeaux Cottage right now, and not with Nell, ever. He wanted to speak with the solicitor first and see the papers for himself, the wills, the deeds, the settlements. Then he wanted to talk to Phelan, who seemed to have overstepped the boundaries of kinship by a mile.

Alex could imagine Nell's horror to find out that she had been living here at a virtual stranger's sufferance. He was a single stranger, at that, with a newly unsavory reputation, who could evict her at any minute. Not that he would, of course. Her reputation was at stake, and her pride. Alex understood both.

"I apologize," he told her, giving Stives a warning glance to ensure his silence. "I have indeed abused your gracious hospitality, Miss Sloane. It is this business of being an earl, you know. Gives a fellow an inflated opinion of himself and how the world revolves around him. You must do as you see fit about your friend, of course. And I shall do as I see fit about the fiend. The female, that is."

He turned to his valet. "Go into the village and see if a Bath wheeled chair is to be had, one that can be tied to the back of the coach. And if you purchase some extra pillows and blankets, I should do nicely, without any of the dread consequences predicted by the surgeon."

"I knew it would come to this, milord. As soon as I saw the lay of the land, by Jupiter, I just knew you'd be running away again."

"You are . . . running away?" Nell asked.

"As fast as my feet will carry me," Alex cheerfully replied. "Or my horses' feet. As soon as it can be arranged. Craven to the core, that's me."

"Fustian." She stood by the side of his bed now, peering to see if he was flushed with fever.

"No, ask anyone. My brother Jack was always the brave one. Diving into deep water, riding neck or nothing, going off to war. I was always the one who hung back, cautious to a fault. Everyone in London knows it. Carde the Coward, they call me, especially when it comes to women."

"I do not believe you."

"Stives, tell her how I have no backbone. Well, I do have one, all black and blue, but it isn't worth a farthing."

Nell clucked her tongue at his teasing. "As if your man would say one word against your courage. He told me how he was homeless and ill when he returned from the war, and how you fought off ruffians on the streets of London to save him and his meager purse."

Alex frowned at his man for being so talkative. "They were small ruffians, though. Almost children."

"There were four of them, Miss Sloane, and they had knives." Stives was not about to let his employer's modesty mar a good story.

"You see?" the earl asked. "The man was outnumbered. Anyone would have come to his aid."

"But no one did, Mr. Stives told me, only you. Others watched until you came along with nothing but your sword stick and your fists."

"Ah, but I am considered very handy with my fives. And they say I am adequate with a sword, after years of practice sessions with the finest masters in England. I have not fought any duels, naturally, since they are illegal. I am far too lily-livered to break the rules or accept an actual challenge, but I do know how to fence. So there really was no contest. I was never in danger, you must be assured, as long as I did not lose my spectacles. I would have turned tail and fled in that case, of course."

"That is a lie if I ever heard one. You are the bravest man I know. You were absolutely fearless when the horse went wild."

"Ah, but how could I run away without my horse? Tell her, Stivey."

"I can tell her what a pigheaded, flea-brained jackass you are, milord. Thinking to run away from that woman again, and you half dead."

"Again?" Nell echoed. "You have fled Lady Lucinda in the past?"

Alex shrugged, then winced. A man with broken ribs had to be less expressive, he was finding. "Lady Lucinda and others. I seem to be the target of every unattached female in London. That, too, goes with being an earl, I suppose, so it does not feed my vanity. I cannot use my sword or my fists on the ladies, more's the pity, while they use every guile known to womanhood: extortion, entrapment, embarrassment, and, yes, outright lies. So I run. I am sorry if you were painting me the hero, but that is the sad truth. Your hero has feet of clay, to mix the art forms." He wiggled his toes under the covers, making his point but also making certain they still worked after his foray to the floor. "Fiddle-footed, that's me, always running."

Stives was nodding. "Two steps ahead of parson's noose he is. So far."

"And that is why you came so far away from London, to hide from your, um, admirers?"

"Hawks they were," Alex insisted, "circling one poor, trembling mouse of a man. Nothing admirable in any of it. But I did choose your neighborhood as my bolt-hole for other reasons. I should have come ages ago to make your reacquaintance. I have little enough family, as tenuous as the connection is. Now I had some business here with your brother, and a few questions about Lizbeth's death."

"My cousin's death? We do not speak of it. Phelan finds the very mention of the tragedy too distressing."

Now all signs of playfulness left Alex's face. Phelan seemed to find a great many things too distressing to discuss with his sister and his staff. Alex would have his answers, by George. What was the point of having the onus of the earldom without the authority? He took his spectacles off to wipe against the sheet, a gesture calculated to be arrogant, not calculated to cause such pain in his broken ribs. Lud, a chap had a great deal to learn about being an invalid. When he had caught his breath again he said in even, assured tones, "Yet Mr. Sloane shall speak with me, and he shall answer my questions."

No one was more intimidating than Phelan when one of his edicts was being defied or debated. Lord Carde's hauteur was belied by the twinkle in his gentle brown eyes and the laugh lines around his mouth. The man was a great tease, despite his pain, although she knew he was serious about talking with Phelan. After all, he had come all this way to do so when a letter or a mesenger might have sufficed.

Nell did not believe for an instant that the earl had fled London in terror of a troth. She did believe women were chasing him, though. Just look at him, with his head bandaged and his jaw covered in stubble. He was still one of the most attractive men she had ever seen. Granted she had not seen many men of his age and bearing, but Lord Carde was sure to stand out even in the crowded London ballrooms. He was not handsome despite his spectacles and his aquiline features but because of them. Here was a confident man, a manly man, not some prinked and perfumed beau. And his height and weight and breadth of shoulders were all perfect, too, she thought, as if he were a chair being measured for comfort and fitting in a certain corner.

The ladies of the *ton* must have found that Lord Carde would fit their parlors—and their bedchambers—nicely, especially when one added an ancient title and vast wealth. Who would not find him worth a few wiles?

Nell almost wished she had some. Wiles, that is. She had far too many empty corners, in her bed and in her heart.

She also wished he would not confront Phelan, knowing the two would be at outs in an instant, whatever business the earl wanted to discuss. She was waiting to ask about the tenant farmers herself, and that was bad enough to send her brother into one of his rages. Phelan might disappear again, but so would the earl, and that would end the most exciting interval Nell and her neighbors had enjoyed in years.

Not only did Miss Sloane have a peer in her home, but she was expecting a duke's daughter. The last lofty houseguests anyone had entertained were a baronet and his wife whose carriage had broken down outside Kingston Upon Hull. What was a mere sir and his lady to true blue bloods? Why, the duke himself might accompany his daughter! No one could recall a duke in the neighborhood since seventeen aught three. An earl was well and good, far better than the local population had ever dreamed of, but a duke? That was something to tell one's grandchildren about.

Suddenly servants were eager to help get Ambeaux Cottage ready, in hopes of seeing the grand visitors. Perhaps they might win an offer of employment in London, which none of them had ever seen, of course, but dreamed of as paradise.

The vicar called, without an invitation to dinner but in hopes of one when the earl was out of bed.

The local squire kept stopping by, wanting to introduce his two young sons to their first nobleman. The widowed landowner wished his motherless brats to be impressed and influenced by a true aristocrat. It was far too late, in Nell's opinion, to teach the young Pensworth hellions the manners of a gentleman, and Lord Carde was sleeping, besides—every time the man came, conveniently.

The villagers were far more friendly now, wanting to know all the details of his lordship's injuries, and what they could sell her to speed his recovery. The schoolchildren she taught drawing were eager to hear of Lord Carde's derring-do when the goose did not behave, and the church guild ladies invited her to their sewing session in hopes of learning more about his life and love affairs.

The tenants were welcoming now that they'd seen she truly intended to help them. Even Redfern was putting himself out to be accommodating for a change, doting on the bedridden lord, and Aunt Hazel was keeping her conversations private, except when she went to converse with the earl—the current, living earl—for twenty minutes a day.

Nell had someone to talk with and tease and take care of for the first time in her life. How could she not wish this idyll might never end?

Of course she did not wish the earl to continue suffering. But if the nodcock did not insist on getting out of bed for exercise—to be ready for a midnight flight if it proved necessary, he said—then he would not be in so much pain. Nell feared the gudgeon would do himself a worse injury.

She also feared she was falling halfway into love with the foolish man. No, she'd been halfway there when she was a little girl. Now that she realized Alex was a warm, comfortable companion—who was not engaged to Lady Lucinda and never would be—she might even fall the rest of the way. So who was the fool?

How silly for him to think she might try to coerce him into marriage. And how silly of her to wish it were possible.

She was still skinny little Nelly Sloane, with no dowry and no prospects, and he was the Earl of Carde.

CHAPTER NINE

He stayed, of course. Alex had to remain in the neighborhood to speak with Phelan Sloane, Silbiger the solicitor, and the magistrate. Ambeaux Cottage was his most convenient location. Besides, he knew he could not get down the stairs without four men and a plank, so he really had no choice. Everyone else knew it too, but they let him make a bargain, to save his pride.

"I will remain here," he informed his valet, his supposed hostess, and her butler, "on condition that you all swear to protect me with your lives."

Nell was laughing as she held her hand to her heart.

"Miss Sloane," he began, then sighed. "No, it shall have to be 'cousin,' with your permission."

She nodded, although the connection was tenuous at best. She liked that he was wanting to be part of her family, or wanting her to be part of his, which was a far different thing. She made a slight curtsy, acknowledging the honor. "Cousin."

"As I was saying, cousin, you must take my predicament seriously. Think of me as a poor, injured creature at the mercy of ravening beasts. I depend upon you to defend me. When I leave here, I expect to be in the same condition in which I arrived. Not on a plank, of course, but not engaged either."

Nell could not imagine that an earl, especially not this large, commanding peer, could be forced into doing anything he did not wish, despite his pleasant nature. Since he did not seem to wish to be married to Lady Lucinda, he would not be. But she could pretend to protect him, if he chose to pretend to quail and cower. "I shall endeavor to keep Lady Lucinda at bay, my lord—cousin."

"No, that is not good enough. You have to promise, on your honor, to keep her away from me."

"Very well, I shall plan sightseeing excursions, drawing expeditions, and picnics while Lady Lucinda visits, to keep her out of the house. I know the first families of the neighborhood would be delighted to entertain a duke's daughter. Perhaps we might even attend an assembly, if she will deign to go. The company is not what a member of London's elite is used to, but—"

But then he would be all alone. "No, you need not exert yourself to fill every moment of her time. If she is bored, she will leave that much sooner. Just do not leave me unattended with her, is that clear?"

Nell looked from the butler to the valet. "Between us, we can manage that. Now you need your rest, sir, to recover your strength and your courage. I shall leave you in Mr. Stives's capable hands. Good night."

But Alex would not take any more laudanum. He did not want to sleep away any more of his life. He did not want any more of those nightmares, either, nor being all muddled-headed, nor waking with his mouth feeling stuffed with gun-wadding after the pistol had been fired. Besides, he needed all his wits about him if he was to face another skirmish on the matrimonial field. He also decided, between his valet's clucks and warnings, that he needed Miss Sloane, Cousin Nell, about him.

"Make sure you ask her to sit with me a spell so you can sleep and eat and check on the horses for me." And whatever other errands Alex could devise to exchange his nursemaid for a far prettier one. "At least before the harpy arrives. We must have a few days, I estimate, for the lady will not give up her comforts for a flying journey, not even if she hopes to winkle a deathbed betrothal out of me."

Stives shook his head. "No good'll come of it, milord, you mark my words."

"She won't get one, never fear."

"It is not Lady Lucinda that has me worried, milord. That one could land on her feet whichever way she fell."

"Miss Sloane? She knows I am not here to offer marriage."

"There's more than that to go wrong," Stives muttered as he stoppered the laudanum bottle and placed a glass of plain water by his master's bedside.

"Miss Sloane will not be compromised, if that's what you are thinking. Between my injuries and the cousinly connection, the conventions are satisfied, especially with a respectable chaperone in the house."

"There are twenty of them, to hear the old lady speak, but no one can see any of them. But what happens when Miss Sloane finds out about the house? Not being her brother's, and all?"

"She'll most likely set a pig on me, or a goat. I cannot imagine what the brother is about, keeping her in the dark about that matter."

"Can't you? He's been living like the cock of the

walk, with no one the wiser. Why let on that he is a hanger-on, a puffed-up despot beholden to another man for the roof over his head?"

"I suppose that's why he left. It's an untenable situation for anyone, but it must be worse for a woman, who has even less choice. Cousin Nell will not be happy to be in my debt. Lud, if word gets out that she is under my protection, I hate to think what the old tabbies will make of that. Damn Phelan for his lies, and his lying low."

"The word is he's as dicked in the nob as the old woman. Miserly, he is, too, except for his own comforts, and he's bleeding the tenants dry."

Alex's tenants they were, by Jupiter! "But I understood he has his own income from that shipyard Lizbeth's father established."

Stives shrugged. "The staff won't talk much. None have been around long anyway. I've been trying to find what I can from that Redfern, but it's hard going. Queer nabs if I ever saw one, looking like a ghost and all. He gave me quite a start, I can tell you."

"He had me quaking in my boots, too, at first."

The valet chuckled at the earl playacting at timidity. Stives would bet his life that the only thing Lord Carde feared was matrimony. Then he grew serious, shaking his head again. "It's no wonder no young gentlemen come calling on Miss Sloane, between the cork-brained aunt and the clutch-fisted brother and the cadaver at the front door."

"We'll have to fix things for her, won't we?"

Stives grumbled as he prepared to sleep on the cot set up in the adjoining dressing room in case his master suffered a relapse of the fevers or needed the laudanum for the pain. "I should have known you'd get us involved in this mess. There's a woman involved, isn't there? You'll be neck deep in trouble before the cat can lick her ear, milord, see if you won't. Then you'll be flying off to the Antipodes next. And do not say I didn't warn you, either. We should never have come here."

"You are right. I should have come without a nagging manservant. Years ago."

Alex felt guilty—and curious. The estate had waited this long, it could wait a few more days. But what about Nell? Every day a woman of her years went unwed, the closer she was to eternal spinsterhood. It was too bad that he could not come out and ask why she never married while they spoke during the next few days. He still suffered headaches and sharp pangs from his shoulder and ribs when he moved, so he stayed in the sick room. Her visits were welcome, and necessary if he were not to die of boredom. They talked of many things, but nothing as personal as their various marriage prospects. He seemed to have too many; she seemed to have none.

Nell was not beautiful, Alex could see now that he was not concussed or half-blind, being too thin and too plainly dressed, with her pale hair drawn too tightly, too severely off her narrow face. He thought she was lovely, with those blue eyes like a sky a man could soar to, but other men might consider her pale and boney. He found her smile a rare treasure; others might think her dour and gloomy, if not disapproving. Alex thought he detected a slight but shapely figure under her loose gowns, but other men would not be close enough, he thought with odd satisfaction.

The contradiction of wanting to see her happily established and wanting no other man to see her was likely a product of his lingering fever. That's what the earl told himself, anyway.

Alex's eyes could follow the outline of sweet breasts as she leaned over to help him sit up when his servant was out of the room. The local bachelors must be idiots indeed to have missed that enticing sight. They'd fill a man's hands, and what more did any fellow need?

He should not be thinking such things, of course. Nell was an innocent and a dependent, whether she knew it or not. The gentleman's code did not allow Alex to prey on virgins or batten on females who were beholden to him. The first might not understand the consequences; the latter might feel they had no choice. Lord Carde despised men who harassed their female servants, their children's governesses, the unfortunate poor relations in their homes.

Not that Alex wished to batten on Nell. Something about her struck a chord inside him, that was all. Maybe it was the memory of happier times, when his father and Lizbeth were starting their new life together and everything seemed bright to a young boy with no weighty cares on his shoulders. The whole world had smelled of April and May. Nell smelled of rosewater.

Maybe it was how she sat so peacefully with her sewing—an altar cloth, a shirt for the poorhouse, a smocked infant gown for one of the tenant children. Nell seemed content with her lot, not complaining as so many other females did, not whining of her boredom, not needing entertaining. She could converse on books and politics, but she was content to listen when he spoke of plays and concerts she had not seen. She asked about farming, as if she cared, and his duties in Parliament. Unlike most women he met, she was not afraid to disagree with him. Nor was she afraid to beat him at chess.

He idly wondered what she would make of life in

the city. Dress her in the height of fashion, find some high-born hostess to sponsor her, and Nell would be a light in London's sky. Perhaps a minor comet, but a success. Most likely she would lose that serenity he admired, becoming another gadding, restless beauty who was never satisfied unless she was the center of attention. She was a woman, wasn't she?

Speaking of women, Alex told himself, he should be up and exercising. The room seldom spun now when he moved his head, and his ribs and shoulder were healing. As for his spine, he was not ready to try those narrow, steep steps down to the parlor, but he thought a few laps of his room might keep his muscles from growing weaker. That way, he could make a fast getaway when Lady Lucinda arrived.

He wondered if Nell could be convinced to agree to a sham betrothal to convince the leech to unhook her suckers. Lady Lucinda could be told they had a longstanding agreement, promised since childhood. That would be an act of desperation, though, for Nell would be left looking no account when he cried off, or he would look the cad, leaving her unmarried and virtually unmarriageable. If no one would have her now, her negligible appeal would be further diminished when she was cast off by an eligible earl. After he'd spent over a week under her roof. His roof.

He could hear Stives now, muttering his I-told-you-sos when Alex was forced to make a proper offer for Miss Sloane rather than ruin her reputation and her chances. But she did not deserve a forced marriage, and neither did he. No, he would muddle through the coming invasion without taking such drastic measures.

There was always India.

*   *   *

Despite Alex's estimation of the local swains, Miss Sloane suddenly had suitors. No one was more surprised than Nell herself. It seemed as if the earl's spectacles, or the spectacled earl, had opened a few eyes in Kingston Upon Hull.

The vicar called, and called again, even though he was told the earl was too ill for company. The earl was too busy playing cards with Aunt Hazel, too tired for sermonizing, too much on holiday to be polite to a pedantic, sour-faced preacher.

It fell to Nell's lot to entertain the man of the cloth over seemingly endless pots of tea. With his cloth napkin carefully placed on his lap, the Reverend Mr. Chawley paid careful court to Miss Eleanor Sloane.

Mr. Chawley was a man of nearly fifty summers, and Miss Sloane used to be too young for him. Now, at five and twenty, she was at just the proper age for a perfect helpmeet. She was competent, caring, and tireless, despite her fragile appearance. Better yet, this new noble connection just might have a better parish to bestow on his dear cousin and her husband.

Everyone knew she had no dowry, but a grateful, generous earl was certain to see his relation provided for. Perhaps he would donate a new roof for the manse if his cousin were living under it.

As for Miss Sloane, she would be grateful too. At her age, she ought to be thankful for any offer. With her situation and associations, she ought to be on her knees rejoicing that a decent man was willing to take her to his home and hearth. Why, Mr. Chawley had to search his heart and his conscience every time he entered Ambeaux Cottage with its foreigners and freaks. Miss Sloane was the residence's only good Christian, in his opinion, so he would be doing her a favor by taking her away. As his wife, Miss Sloane would have nothing to do with the Papist or the pagans here, as God was his witness.

Chawley supposed he had to wait for the brother's return before making an offer in form, although he found Phelan Sloane no better than a heathen, seldom setting foot in St. Cecilia's church. Still, it would not suit the vicar's standing in the community—or in the spectacled eyes of a wealthy earl—to be thought remiss in the social niceties toward his intended.

He did not intend to court the female. That would have been entirely beneath the vicar's dignity, and beyond his capabilities, if the truth be told. Nor would Miss Sloane expect any ardent wooing, or not so ardent, from a gentleman of the cloth and of a certain age. If she were one of those flighty females demanding flowers and verse, well, then she was not a suitable wife for the parish's prelate.

Miss Sloane was a sensible sort, Mr. Chawley told himself. So he told her about his upcoming sermons, his visits to the homebound, and his plans for Bible study classes. That ought to show his worth far more than any wooing. He did not see where teaching the children to draw or the servants to read was beneficial to their spiritual well-being, but he did not mention his disapproval. Time enough for that later, when he was her husband and could better supervise her activities. Humility was what the lower orders should be taught so they accepted their place, just as Miss Sloane seemed to have accepted hers. He would not have selected her as the future Mrs. Chawley otherwise. He complimented her on her dedication to her family and good deeds, and explained how there were so many other worthy causes she could champion. That counted as flattery, did it not? The old maid ought to be pleased.

Nell was not pleased. The reverend's sermons were bad enough on Sundays. Sitting in her own parlor listening to him spout his nonsense was far worse. She did not need to hear about the needs of the parish; she needed to be out doing something about them. She supposed the vicar was too old to see to all of his own duties, but if he was proposing that she should assume some of them, he was wasting his wheezing breath. She had enough on her dish—he'd eaten the last tea sandwich, so hers was bare—without taking on the entire congregation for him. She had to ready the house for more guests, try to make sense of Phelan's haphazard bookkeeping ledgers, find help for the tenants, and entertain an increasingly restive earl before he reinjured himself. That was besides her regular duties of lessons and Sunday school and household management.

No, despite his rather heavy-handed hints, she was not about to volunteer her efforts so Mr. Chawley could have a longer afternoon nap. Let him hire a young curate if the church made too many demands on his old self. Perhaps the young women in the congregation would pay more attention to the church services then, too.

"Pompous, pedantic prig," Alex declared when Redfern reported on the vicar's frequent visits. Miss Sloane might not know which way the wind blew, but Redfern was a deuced good weather vane, now that he had hopes of a handsome pension. For a promised raise in salary, he could eavesdrop and interpret a caller's intentions as well as any London butler. Redfern's pronouncement was that Mr. Chawley had not pomaded his hair flat to his skull to impress the earl.

"Tell him she's not at home next time, there's a good man. Miss Sloane will thank you for it, although she is too kindly to give the order herself. She does not have time for that braying jackass." Not when Alex was reduced to playing piquet with Madame Ambeaux . . . and her friends, who told her what to discard. The worst part was, they were often right. He owed the old lady a new gown.

Nell did not have time for her next caller either, which did not stop Mr. Pensworth from dropping by a few times a day. The squire said he was checking on the earl's condition, but he never offered to sit with the injured man. He stopped bringing his sons along, though, since those hellions could not encourage a woman to look kindly on his suit.

Pensworth was the largest landowner in the neighborhood, with the largest girth, too. Past his fortieth birthday, he had not been in the market for a wife— he had his heirs and Kitty Johnstone at the inn—but he'd noticed the same quiet air of calm acceptance that both the vicar and the earl had admired in Miss Sloane. He could sorely use some peace and quiet in his house, he had decided.

The first Mrs. Pensworth had been gone for five years now, and the house could use a woman's touch too. Or maybe a mop. Pensworth was more concerned with the conditions of his kennels and his stables. A new wife might let him devote more of his time to his own interests instead of the accounts and the servants. What did he care if the cook served turtle soup or turbot, or if the gardener grew roses or rhododendrons? That was woman's work, by Zeus.

Miss Sloane seemed good at it. Ambeaux Cottage

never appeared unkempt or uncared for, the way his
house did. Of course she didn't have boys and hounds
running through here, dragging in dirt and debris, but
she'd get used to that. A house was for living in, he
always said, not just for company.

With her fancy education, the Sloane woman could
school his boys, too, saving him the expense and
bother of a tutor. The more he thought of it, the more
Pensworth liked Miss Sloane, and liked the idea of
marrying her. He was too caught up in the coming
hunt season to go hunting for a bride. Sloane's sister
was right in the neighborhood, ripe for the plucking
before she withered on the vine.

Ordinarily, Pensworth would not have chosen a filly
from this particular stable, not with that aunt and the
brother. A woman could not be held accountable for
her relatives, though, he supposed. His own sister had
run off with a painter—a house painter at that, not
even one of those artistic portrait daubers either. Besides, Pensworth already had his heirs, so it made no
difference if the mare foaled a runt or a weakling. Her
own birth was respectable anyway, better than his, the
self-made squire admitted. Her grandfather'd been a
duke, they said, although on her mother's side, so
there was no title or money. The father had been gentry, with an adequate income that died when he did.
She had no money, everyone knew that, but Pensworth was looking for an unpaid housekeeper, not a
heavy purse. Of course, if this new noble connection
chose to dower the chit, Pensworth would not refuse
the offer.

It was the earl's presence that had decided Pensworth on his course of courtship. A nobleman's kin
was a far worthier bride than an orphaned old maid.
No need to be ashamed of her at his table, with an

aristocrat at her back. As for his bed, she was too skinny for his tastes, but that was why God created the Kitties of this world. Miss Sloane would suit.

Like the vicar, Pensworth supposed he'd have to wait for the brother to get back so he could ask his permission. A crock of manure that was, between two grown adults, but he'd do the thing up right. Pensworth wouldn't want his wife finding fault with his manners, nor her cousin the earl finding fault either. Still, he smiled at the chit. He had most of his own teeth, didn't he? And he patted her hand so she knew his intentions.

At first Nell thought the man was trying to hire her as a governess to his sons. Then she worried he was trying to wipe his sweaty palms on her skirts. When his true purpose grew clearer—as the tray of macaroons grew emptier—she claimed the earl was waiting to be read to and fled, taking a page from Lord Carde's book, and the last biscuit as well.

"The tub of lard dared to touch her?" Alex raged when Redfern reported what he'd seen through the keyhole. "Next time throw him out!"

Redfern might have half Pensworth's weight and twice his age, but the butler swore to do just that, for another gold piece.

He would not attempt to interfere with her third suitor for any price, Redfern sorrowfully admitted. How could he, when Nell's most ardent swain was General Wellesley, hero of the Peninsula?

That's what she called the goose, anyway.

CHAPTER TEN

Everyone else's names for the belligerent, sharp-beaked bird were less flattering. The goose, which was actually a gander, attacked anyone who came near, refused to be penned, and honked loudly enough to wake whichever of the Ambeaux dead were not currently helping Aunt Hazel cheat at cards.

"How the deuce am I supposed to get my rest," Alex complained, "with that infernal racket outside the window?"

His window was two stories above the carriage drive and closed. In addition, he could see from the sitting room chair that Wellesley was currently being fed handfuls of grain by Nell instead of squawking. What, was she reduced to feeding the livestock now? Alex was offended.

Jealous might also have described his emotional state. And bored, frustrated, and irritated that his—what? Nursemaid? Cousin? Friend?—would rather spend time with a feathered fury than himself.

To be jealous of a goose was absurd; to admit it, even to oneself, was ridiculous, so Alex chose instead to be angry over the additional burden the avian added onto Nell's thin shoulders. She had enough to do, with the added responsibilities of houseguests and a missing host. According to Redfern, she was busy from morning to night, with few minutes to spare for Alex. She had time for the goose, though.

The thing loved her, with the single-minded adoration more often found in puppies and poets. It followed her everywhere it could, cooing like a dove when she stroked its head and neck. Woe betide anyone who got between the bird and its beloved. Nell was constantly smoothing feathers, and not just the goose's. She actually seemed fond of the long-necked nuisance.

"I do not see why that monster is not being served up for Sunday dinner," Alex told her later when she—finally—had a few minutes for the invalid while Stives ate his own supper.

Nell looked at her needlework instead of Alex. The infant gown just might be ready in time for Sophie Posener's baby. "Cook did say she thought he needed fattening up before, ah, cooking." She lowered her voice before saying the last word, as if her new pet could hear her. "But that was before I decided against it."

"Why did you?" he asked, as if he did not know how tenderhearted she was. Teasing Nell, seeing pink embarrassment tinge her cheeks, was the most fun he had these days. This was too good an opportunity to miss. "You serve beef and mutton and pork without a qualm. My compliments to your cook, incidentally. My London chef does not do kidneys half as well. But what is the difference between one farm animal and another?"

She smoothed out the tiny gown before conceding, "I never sat beside one of them in the donkey cart."

"And never gave one of them a name. After that, there was no chance. I suppose they never showed affection, although they might, if you saved them from the butcher. So why rescue the goose?"

"Wellesley is my friend. I cannot, you know, e-a-t an acquaintance."

"What, he can spell?"

"Perhaps he might, someday. I taught the chandler's boy, and he was as dumb as a duck. Wellesley is quite intelligent."

"Intelligent? Look at the size of his brainbox! It's stuffed with feathers, besides. You are just fond of the goose because he dotes on you."

Nell had to acknowledge just how gratifying the goose's affection was. She'd never had a pet, never had a real beau of her own, never felt so special to anyone, even if it was a feathered someone. Of course, she was not going to admit that to the grinning man sitting in the chair next to the window, the sunlight reflecting off his spectacles like angel dust, highlighting his dark hair with gold. *He* must have a hundred friends, scores of people who sought his company. Of course he did. The Earl of Carde was the most appealing, endearing man in the country. Now Nell felt the hot color wash over her face at the direction of her thoughts. She was mortified that Alex might think she was just another female attracted to his title and fortune. She threaded her needle and jabbed it into the fabric, and her thumb. "He is intelligent, and useful, too," she said, when she was done sucking the bleeding finger.

Color rose in Alex's cheeks at the sight. No, he

thought he must have a lingering fever. What were they talking about? Licking? Sucking? Oh, the goose. "I'll, ah, agree that he harried that Chawley fellow onto his horse in a hurry. What other purpose can a goose serve if not to feed your household?"

"He is an excellent watchdog. You might not know it now, with all the coming and going of company, but we live a very quiet, almost isolated life here at the cottage. After you leave, and everyone else, I thought I might feel better about being alone with just Redfern and Aunt Hazel at night if I knew he was patrolling the grounds. Until Phelan returns, of course, although my brother is often away on business." She folded her sewing without having set a stitch. "I know you must think I am silly, being anxious like that."

"Who, me, the world's biggest coward?"

He won a smile from her, just as he meant to. He did not think she was foolish at all, only sadly neglected, like a hidden garden left untended by the gardener, like some poor storybook princess spending days and nights with no company, half afraid of the dark in her haunted castle.

Good grief, was it as bad as that, that a *goose* could give her comfort? A goose, by heaven! Phelan Sloane had a great deal to answer for. Another day or two, the surgeon said, and Alex might be healed enough to safely navigate the stairs. Then he would send for the solicitor. Alex would have some facts, not just fairy tales. And not just about Lizbeth's carriage accident, either.

His quest for the truth about little Lottie, his stepsister, could hold. That was a sacred vow he owed his father, and Alex would fulfill it sooner or later, if it lay within his power. The child could be long dead or irretrievably lost. She could wait.

Nell, though, was a flesh and blood woman, here and now. She was a debt of honor he owed Lizbeth. The young countess had given his father four happy years and a beloved daughter. He owed Nell a chance for that same happiness, a life of her own and a caring family. He was not leaving Kingston Upon Hull without finding it for her, unless he took her off with him to London.

While Alex was debating which connection he might ask to sponsor a Season for a woman who was too old, too poor, too undistinguished of birth, with too many peculiar relations—he would not express it that way, of course—another solution presented itself. A new suitor appeared on Nell's horizon.

Sir Chauncy Gaines arrived at Ambeaux Cottage one morning early in Alex's recovery. An old schoolmate of the earl's and a frequent companion in London at the gentlemen's clubs and the ladies' ballrooms, the baronet was on a visit to his grandmother in Scarborough.

"More like a repairing lease," Lord Carde told Redfern, when the butler asked if his lordship was well enough to welcome visitors. "The fellow is always punting on tick. Overextended, that is," he explained. "He has expectations from the grandmother, so I expect he is hoping she will open her purse sooner rather than later."

Alex thought for a moment of matchmaking, but then rejected the idea. Gaines was a handsome man, he supposed. At least he was sought after as a dance partner, being tall, with blond hair and good teeth. But he was too much the gambler, too much the social gadfly. He'd see Nell established at the outer circles of society, but he'd leave her there, or with his grandmother in Scarborough. No, the baronet would not be an acceptable match for Nell. So Alex instructed he be sent away.

"The man's a rattle. Never shuts his mouth. My poor head could not stand his nattering. Tell him I appreciate the thought, and I shall see him in London soon enough."

Unfortunately, however, Sir Chauncy encountered Wellesley on his way out. Fortunately for the baronet, he had just lifted a sweet roll from the tray Redfern had left unattended in the hall when he went to ask Lord Carde's wishes. Even more fortunately for Sir Chauncy, Nell came along before he was out of crumbs to toss to the goose.

Nell was hurrying from one task to another before leaving for the children's drawing lessons. Her cheeks had color in them, and some of her fair curls had escaped the severe bun she usually wore. Her chip-straw bonnet was hanging by its ribbons down her back, and her blue eyes were sparkling at Cousin Alex's parting words.

In other words, she looked lovely, especially to a bored London gentleman stuck in the countryside. Sir Chauncy bowed and gave his name, claiming the goose was proper enough a chaperone to make the introductions. Nell laughed and curtsied, touched that someone had made the effort to befriend Wellesley.

A relationship developed, like a rash, according to a disgruntled Alex when he heard about it from Redfern, then Stives.

The baronet accompanied Miss Sloane into the village for the students' lessons, his horse trailing behind. He waited at the inn, drinking in Mr. Ritter's excellent ale and the local gossip. Then he walked Nell home and came inside for more refreshments, with Aunt

Hazel supposedly watching to satisfy the conventions. The young people were discussing the scenery, the roads from Hull to Scarborough, and Lord Carde's condition. The old woman was discussing her roses. Heaven only knew—and only heaven knew—with whom.

Since his own grandmother could not distinguish Sir Chauncy from his late father, his later grandfather, or his younger brother, the baronet was not fazed one whit. He was used to old ladies' crochets, and used to ignoring chaperones.

He returned another day with flowers and books. He stayed to luncheon and tea. He carried Miss Sloane's baskets of food and medicines to the tenant families. He paid pretty compliments, according to Redfern, and, worst of all in Alex's mind, he petted the goose.

Of all the cheap, underhanded tricks to win a lady's favor, that was the worst. Alex fumed from his lonely upstairs window.

So he opened the sash, only straining his broken ribs and injured shoulder into minor spasms, not major ones, and called for the man to come upstairs.

"How good to see you up and out of bed!" Gaines exclaimed, pumping Alex's hand into more paroxysms of pain.

Alex was not in the mood for pleasantries. "What are your intentions?" he asked as soon as Stives pulled up another chair for the visitor.

"Intentions? Why, to cheer you up with company. I say, are you well enough for some port? I always feel better with a few glasses of spirits in me. I wouldn't mind—"

"Toward Miss Sloane."

Sir Chauncy blinked. "Sits the wind in that quarter? Sorry, old man, I did not think the woman was in your usual style."

"She is not in my anything. She is my cousin."

"Not from what I hear in the village, but I don't blame you for claiming the connection. A choice morsel, once you get behind that standoffish attitude."

"Nell—Cousin Eleanor—is shy, not standoffish. And she is not a choice morsel." If Alex had two good arms, he'd throw the baronet down two flights of stairs.

"I should hope not, not with your luck. That would make, what, four fiancées? Four of a kind might be good at cards, but it's hell on a fellow's nerves, what?" He shuddered. "Imagine what the scandal sheets would do with another notch on your arrow."

The idea did not bear thinking on, especially not if Nell's name was mentioned. Sir Chauncy Gaines was just the one to mention it to all and sundry once he was back in town. Damnation!

"How long are you staying in the country anyway?"

"Oh, until the dibs are in tune. I say, don't suppose you'd make an old friend a loan, would you?"

Which was worse, sending the gudgeon back to town and the rumor mills, or letting him remain in the neighborhood? Why wasn't there a good press gang when Alex needed one? He decided to keep Gaines nearby, where he could keep an eye on him. Besides, why should he pay for the privilege of having his already blackened name darkened again in the gossip columns? Gaines had never repaid a loan yet that he could remember.

"Sorry, old man. I am on limited funds until I can return to town myself."

"That's all right. Ruralizing ain't half as dull as I expected."

Because he was entertaining himself with Nell? "Unless a few pounds would tide you over?"

"Pounds I can get out of my grandmother. I say, Ace, ain't that the port bottle over there on the side table?"

Gaines poured, brought a glass to Alex, and held his own up in a toast to the earl's recovery. And his pretty hostess.

Alex almost choked on the spirits. "She's not—" he began, intending to set the man straight. Nell was residing in his house, under the protection of his family name.

Gaines misunderstood. "Not pretty in the common way, I agree. Takes a real connoisseur like yourself to spot the beauty and the liveliness under that sober guise. The figure's passable, although I prefer my women to have more meat on their bones."

He could not misunderstand Alex's glass slamming onto the nearby tabletop. "You will not discuss my cousin in those terms, by George, not unless you are asking for her hand in marriage, which, incidentally, I would refuse. You would make a ghastly husband and Nell deserves better."

"Marriage? Who was talking marriage? We cannot all afford a penniless bride, you know. My grandmother is talking up her best friend's goddaughter. Ten thousand pounds."

"And what are *you* talking about? Making Nell your mistress? I'll see you in hell first."

"Thought you just met the woman."

He did not call Nell a lady, Alex noted, and grew angrier. "I have known her for ages."

Sir Chauncy was going on: " 'Sides, there's a brother. If one were going to pay one's addresses in form, that's who ought to receive them."

"He is not here. I am."

"Playing dog in the manger, too, old man. Or are you interested in the gal yourself, despite what you said? Oho, that's it, isn't it? You're too banged up now to win her over, but you don't want any competition, especially when the henhouse has been left unguarded." Alex's former friend slapped his knee. "We'll just see which fox wins the vixen's favors first. Care to lay a wager?"

Alex would wager he could break the man's jaw with one punch. The blow might wreak havoc with his ribs, but it would be worth it. "Get out," he said before he was tempted beyond endurance, "and do not come back. The *lady*," he said with emphasis on the unspoken disrespect-her-and-die syllable, "is not for dalliance, by you, by me, or by the King of Persia. She will be wed to some honest, faithful, loving man of her choice."

Gaines got up, laughing. "Where do you think she'll find that choice? As a poor relation in your house? What man in London is going to believe you have not bedded her? What man is going to take your leavings?"

He stopped laughing when Alex did hit him. Getting up would take too long in his sorry condition, so Alex threw his glass. Too bad the thing was empty, but Sir Chauncy got the point, on the chin.

"Very well," he said on his way out, rubbing his jaw. "Miss Sloane is out of bounds. She is yours for the taking, or the leaving. I shall see you in town, old man, when you are in a better frame of mind."

Alex was not going to be cheerier anytime soon,

worrying about the gossip the gossoon was going to be spreading. He was gloomier still after Nell heard that he had banned her new friend.

"How could you refuse him entry to my house?"

Alex bit his tongue.

"You, sir, are overbearing, arrogant, and rude. You have no right to choose my guests, and so I shall make plain to Sir Chauncy if he ever returns. You have stepped beyond the bounds of—"

"His intentions were not honorable."

"—good manners." Nell took a breath of air. "He had intentions?"

"Of course he had intentions. Every man does, be they for good or for ill."

"Even you?"

"I am not a man; I am a relative. That doesn't count."

"But Sir Chauncy's intentions were dishonorable? Toward me?"

"Precisely. That was why I forbade his entry. For all your years, you are too green to see through a practiced flirt like him."

"But you could?"

"Precisely."

"Because you recognize a kindred spirit? Perhaps that is how poor Lady Lucinda came to such a misunderstanding. I'd wager you were flirting with her and she took your attentions as serious."

"You would lose your bet. I paid Lady Lucinda no attentions, as I told you, dash it, and I had no intentions whatsoever toward her."

"You just said all men do. Do not tell me you are related to Lady Lucinda also."

"Of course I am not related to that shrew."

"Then what about those others Sir Chauncy mentioned?"

Now Alex would murder the maggot for sure, as soon as could hold a pistol steady. He unclenched his fists and his jaw and said, "I had no intentions toward any other woman, either." Except for his former mistress, of course, but those aims were understood. By Alex, at any rate. "Devil take it, this conversation is not about me."

"Well, it is not about me and Sir Chauncy, either. It is about your high-handed, dictatorial demands. I refuse to entertain the notion that he had . . . that kind of thoughts about me."

"There. Do you see how innocent you are? You cannot even say the words. Lascivious. Lustful. Carnal."

She was shaking her head, so he added, "That dirty dish had designs on your virtue! Is that putting it politely enough for your delicate sensibilities to comprehend?"

"I understood your meaning, I simply do not believe you. Men do not have . . . have warm notions about women such as I."

Alex made a rude noise. "That is how much you know." He'd been feeling the heat since she walked into the room in a rage, smelling of roses and bristling with thorns. If he weren't a gentleman, lecturing her about lechery, he'd kiss that prickliness away, turning it into silky flower petals against his lips, his skin, his— Hellfire and damnation! He ought to shoot himself for having such lewd daydreams about Nell. Here he was, claiming to be the woman's cousin! He was no better than Sir Chauncy, except that he never intended to act on those tantalizing imaginings. "They do. Oh, they do."

"Not females of my years," she insisted.

"What, you are too ancient to catch a fellow's eye? You are younger than Lizbeth when my father met and fell in love with her."

"Yes, but I am not like Kitty at the inn." Nell forced herself not to pluck at the neckline of her gown, held up with ties, not with nature's bounty.

"No, thank goodness. And Gaines would not want a woman so easily bought. Your very innocence would have tempted him. Furthermore, you are a lady, with grace and charm and inner beauty as well as good looks."

"Do you?"

His brow lowered. "Do I what?"

"Harbor warm thoughts of me?"

"Great gods, woman, you do not ask that of a man! Didn't they teach you anything at that school?"

"If I do not ask, then how am I to know a gentleman's intentions? I thought Sir Chauncy was being pleasant, out of friendship with you."

Alex snorted again. "He did not bring his posies to decorate my sickroom, did he? He did not pet my goose."

"You do not have a goose."

"That is irrelevant. Discovering a gentleman's intentions is your guardian's duty, your brother's job. Since I am here and Phelan is not, I acted in your interests. You should be thanking me instead of finding fault."

"I see." And Nell saw that he never did answer her question about warm thoughts toward her. He was not in the least attracted to her, just as she suspected and expected. Everything else, the sideways compliments about other gentlemen finding her alluring, was simply Alex being himself, kind and protective, careful of her reputation. She supposed she should thank him for warning off a rake, if that was what Sir Chauncy was.

If Alex was right that the baronet was a dangerous seducer of innocents, then he was not a very effective one, Nell thought. She had absolutely no warm feelings for him whatsoever. She had no thoughts toward Sir Chauncy at all, in fact, and he was not even her cousin.

Alex was wrong, though, for Nell was not half as innocent as the earl thought. She knew all about the Kitty Johnstones of the world, lustful urges, and forbidden fantasies. She was a country girl who read books, who had attended a girls' school where almost nothing else was spoken of after the lights were out. She was five and twenty, for goodness sake. Of course she knew about sex! Just not personally, of course.

Cousin Alex was wrong also about the perils of an experienced womanizer. He himself, with no evil intentions, was proving far more dangerous to her senses than any smooth-talking London buck.

Nell supposed she ought to be grateful to Lord Carde, after all, for reminding her not to dream.

CHAPTER ELEVEN

Lady Lucinda Applegate arrived the next day in grand style. The villagers must have been gratified to see such a sight. Nell was dismayed.

The daughter of the Duke of Apston arrived with the duke, the duke's deaf cousin, and the duke's secretary, in a crested carriage. Nell had expected the old cousin, Lady Haverhill, who was Lady Lucinda's chaperone. She might have considered that the duke would not permit his only child to travel without a male for protection, in addition to the servants, but the secretary? Was His Grace so busy that he had to have his aide at his side at all times?

Her concern must have shown, for Lady Lucinda whispered in Nell's ear after making the introductions. "I brought him for you," she said while she kissed the air near Nell's cheek.

"For me?" It was not even Nell's birthday, not that Lady Lucinda ever remembered the date, and not that a spotty, center-parted secretary was on her wish list. "Why, a new pair of gloves might have been lovely, but what use do I have for a secretary?"

"Silly, he is here so you have a partner for dinner and the local dances." Lady Lucinda kept whispering, loudly, as Mr. Peabody, the secretary, stood waiting for the next coach, the one carrying the servants deemed necessary for a ducal visit. "He is intelligent and well-mannered. Papa says he is ambitious, and your brother must know of a seat in the Commons he can stand for. You can do a great deal worse."

"For a dance partner?"

"For a *parti*. A husband, Eleanor. Do not be a dunce cap. Unless you have decided to put on spinsters' caps already."

Nell took a firm grip on her best chip-straw bonnet, which did not resemble spinsterish lace squares at all, and a firmer grip on her temper. The wind on the carriage drive where she had gone to meet her guests was considerable. So was the provocation; she and Lady Lucinda were of an age.

The duke's daughter was looking more handsome than Nell remembered, if possible. Her black hair was swept up under a fashionable ruched bonnet with cherries peeking over the brim, and her traveling dress was a dark carnelian red, making her fair skin seem more porcelainlike than ever, in contrast. She wore a long, double strand of expensive heirloom pearls and carried a white fur stole. She was tall and shapely, walking with the effortless, assured grace their academy had tried so hard to instill in Nell and failed. Not even a somewhat generous nose could detract from her elegance. All in all, Lucinda Applegate looked precisely what she was: a highborn London lady of means and style, the perfect match for the Earl of Carde.

Nell felt entirely small and frumpish, even in her favorite day gown, which she had donned when word of the entourage's arrival came from the village. Her clothes were old-fashioned and locally made, her only heirloom a plain gold locket from her mother. Her height was puny, her bosom was negligible, her confidence nil. She felt even smaller in spirit when she took enormous satisfaction in whispering back: "You have wasted your time with this journey."

Lady Lucinda clutched the fur to her ample chest. "What? Is Carde dead then? That would be just like the impossible man to up and die before I arrived."

Nell was more sorry than ever that she had invited the woman. A loving fiancée might have inquired about her betrothed's health before checking to see if her baggage had arrived safely. "No, he lives."

"He is not permanently crippled, is he? I could not bear that, you know. Some might think a limp is romantic, but I do not find it at all *comme il fait*. Nothing is more off-putting than all those officers returning from the Peninsula with pinned-back sleeves."

Nell shivered, and not just with the cold. "The surgeon feels Lord Carde's shoulder might remain troublesome, but no longer fears damage to his spine. The earl is recovering nicely."

"With no scars? I worried that Carde might be disfigured, although I am sure a gentleman would hide any gruesome wounds."

How did a soldier hide a saber wound, except by retiring from company? Did that mean no officers should wed? And how could a woman be so cruel? Nell was already wondering how soon her guest might leave, and she was not through the front door yet. "Lord Carde is as handsome as ever."

Lady Lucinda adjusted the tilt of her bonnet. "That's all right, then. The journey will prove worth the inconvenience, despite Papa's complaints the entire trip and Cousin Haverhill's snoring. To say nothing of leaving town before the end of the Season. At least Mr. Peabody was pleasant company. You would do well to try to fix his interest."

The man seemed more interested in his checklists and notes. "No. That is, no, your journey *was* in vain. Although I am delighted to see you, of course." About as delighted as she would have been to see attacking Huns. "His lordship is well, but he does not recognize any engagement."

"What? Are his senses disordered? Your letter did mention a blow to the head, although it was all garbled with something about a goose." The lady's eyes narrowed in speculation. "Of course, if he does not remember our understanding, a gentle reminder will doubtless solve that dilemma."

"His senses and his memory are perfect."

"Oh, then you mean he does not recognize things! What, did those ugly spectacles of his break? No matter. I am certain he can manage. If he concentrates hard enough, he will grow used to getting by without them."

Poor eyesight could be compensated for with determination? That was the first Nell had heard of the theory, but she thought Alex must have tried it. Lord knew he had determination enough. And Lord knew he was going to need every ounce of stubbornness to match Lady Lucinda's obstinance. She took a deep breath. "It is your engagement he does not acknowledge."

"Oh, that. Piffle. When he sees how helpful I can be, how entertaining I can be during his recuperation—you did mention an assembly nearby, did you not?—he will come around. Why, I gave up the Cathcart ball and two of Almack's Wednesday nights. Carde will simply have to recognize my selfless devotion. Besides, Papa's

valet must know just what to do for him, after dealing
with Papa's gout."

That valet stepped out of the second carriage, then
handed out two ladies' maids and a groom, who served
as the secretary's man.

There was still a third carriage, explaining why Lady
Lucinda had taken so long to come to her purported
betrothed's possible deathbed. This one contained
enough bags, boxes, and trunks for a month's stay.
How long did all these people intend to visit Ambeaux
Cottage, and where was Nell to put them?

"Perhaps Mr., ah, Peabody, would prefer to stay at
the inn in the village."

"Oh, he has to be here with Papa. My father has
no head for business, you must know, and there will
be settlements to discuss. That sort of thing."

"Please listen so neither of us is embarrassed later.
There will be no settlements. No engagement. Lord
Carde was very insistent on that score."

The duke's daughter peered down, over her high-
arched nose, at Nell. "You are not trying to snag him
for yourself, are you? It will never do, you know."

Nell gasped. "Of course not. I would never reach
so high. I am well aware that an earl does not merely
select a wife; he chooses a dynasty."

The other woman patted Nell's cheek, all smiles
again. "Good. Then we shall see about that engagement, shan't we? Oh, and be a dear and take Daisy
inside for me, won't you?"

Lady Haverhill's given name must be Daisy. Aunt
Hazel was already escorting the other old woman up
the stairs, asking about the lady's deceased spouse.
"Would you like me to chat with him, or was he one
of those husbands it is better to forget?"

Since Lady Haverhill was nearly deaf, they got along very well. "Ratafia sounds lovely, thank you."

Perhaps Daisy was Lady Lucinda's maid, then. Nell looked around for the girl, who might be carrying jewel cases or bulky hatboxes. Instead, Nell had the white fur wrap pressed into her arms. It squirmed. "Daisy? You wear a live . . . ermine?"

"She is a dog, silly."

Nell could see now that the creature did have the black nose and eyes of a canine, a very small, hairy canine. "You brought your dog along on such a trip?" Unspoken was the thought that she'd carried the animal to Lord Carde's convalescence, unbidden, at someone else's home. And spent days in a closed carriage with it, besides.

"Of course. I never go anywhere without the darling. Oh, but I forgot how out of fashion you are up here. All the ladies in town have taken to carrying their pets everywhere. Mrs. Cholmondley has a monkey dressed in the most cunning little jacket, matching her servants' livery. The Undersecretary's wife walks a large spotted jungle cat on a jeweled leash. And Lady Forbisher has a parrot on her shoulder in the park." Lady Lucinda wrinkled her formidable nose. "And a disgusting streak down her back. I have Daisy. I named her that because of the flower."

Creatures like this grew as common as weeds? Nell doubted it. "Oh, the white color. But what does it do?" So far the animal had hung limply in Lady Lucinda's arms. Now it hung in Nell's, panting. Chances were it had travel sickness, or worse. Nell wondered if the thing were going to be sick on her. Lady Forbisher's parrot did not spend days in a coach. Nell looked around for a servant, but they were all busy with the baggage.

"It is a she, and she does not *do* anything. She simply matches my ensemble. She has collars and ribbons to match each of my gowns, and a tiny blue velvet cape that matches my new pelisse. I had a miniature parasol made to match one of mine, for when we walk in the park, but Daisy refuses to learn to carry it. My maid Browne does, instead, holding it over Daisy's head. You should hear all the delightful compliments we receive. So eye-catching, *n'est-ce-pas*? But of course, you never cared much for being *à la mode*." She wrinkled her nose again, this time at Nell's plain sprigged muslin gown.

Au contraire, Nell thought. For once she was at the height of fashion. "I have a pet, too, one who goes everywhere with me." Perhaps she would find Wellesley a faded ribbon for his neck, to match the one on her bonnet. Of course, if she paraded him in the park he would terrorize the nannies and children, frighten the horses, and overturn carriages. Oh, she would catch everyone's eye, all right.

Wellesley was safely locked in the garden shed, likely decimating Aunt Hazel's seedlings, but where was Nell supposed to put Daisy? Obviously not down in the carriageway where the snowy creature might get dirty.

Better yet, where was she to put all these people? How like Lady Lucinda to consider that everyone lived in a castle or a sprawling London mansion. And how could Nell have forgotten what a self-centered, spoiled girl she had been . . . and still was?

The servants were no problem, since so few of the Ambeaux staff stayed at the cottage at night. They could share the narrow rooms in the attic.

Lord Carde was already installed in the best guest suite, the one with a sitting room, where he could

entertain visitors without navigating the stairs. Nell
would not ask him to move, not even for a duke.

She had assigned the second-best bedroom to Lady
Lucinda. It should have belonged to the mistress of
the house, but Nell had never moved into the spacious
chamber, hoping Phelan might eventually take a wife.
She had placed a cot in the dressing room for Lady
Lucinda's maid.

The duke would have to have the master's suite,
Phelan's rooms. Since Phelan was not here, he could
not complain.

Lady Haverhill could sleep in Nell's room, while
Nell moved in with Aunt Hazel and her incorporeal
companions.

Since there simply were no other suitable rooms,
the secretary would have to take one of the small
chambers in the unused nursery wing. Perhaps he
could take Daisy with him. Some blankets, a bowl
of water . . .

No, there were growls and snarls when Nell tried
to hand over the animal. Daisy did not think much of
the move, either.

Redfern was leading the limping duke up the stairs,
and Lady Lucinda was following the two elderly ladies. Which left Nell holding the dog. She might have
to share a room with Madame Ambeaux's phantasms;
she would not sleep with fleas.

She did put the animal down for a moment so it
could relieve itself outside instead of on the carpets.
Aunt Hazel's blooms were easier to replace than the
Aubussons. Then she carried the creature into Lady
Lucinda's room, in time to hear her demanding that
Browne go find out which was the earl's chamber.

Since the maid's arms were full of gowns and gloves,
Nell said, "You need not bother," winning her a

bobbed curtsy and a quick smile from the harried servant. "It is the one with the footman stationed outside so no one disturbs his rest."

She thought Browne smiled again, but was not sure.

Lady Lucinda took the dog from Nell and placed it on the bed—on the satin coverlet Nell had spent a year embroidering to match the violets on the wallpaper.

Nell took great satisfaction in adding, "The footman is Lord Carde's own man, who is very devoted to the earl and his wishes." In other words, he was not going to be bribed into any relaxation of his master's rules.

Lady Lucinda poured water from the ewer into a delicate porcelain cup, the one with the violets painstakingly painted on it. For a moment Nell feared she was going to offer it to the dog, but she drank it herself, leaving the creature panting.

"I'll have one of the maids bring up a water dish for Daisy."

"She is fond of livers, but will eat minced beef if she must."

Not on the satin coverlet, she would not. "I'll see about it. Oh, and if you were concerned, Stives sleeps on a pallet in the earl's room, in case his lordship requires something in the night."

Lady Lucinda brushed that aside, and a strand of white dog hair that clung to her fingers. "Oh, tomorrow is soon enough to hold a *tête-à-tête* with Carde."

It would not be soon enough, Nell thought, for a woman worried about her beloved's health.

"Besides," Lady Lucinda was going on, "I am too fatigued just now. Travel is so exhausting, you know. Oh, I do not suppose you would know, would you? You really ought to move closer to town, Eleanor."

Nell doubted even a duke's daughter could set up

housekeeping wherever she wanted, but Lady Lucinda seemed to think that all of her desires must be fulfilled. She had merely to express her wishes and someone would grant them.

Hah! She was bound to be sorely disappointed in her quest for the countess's coronet. Nell meant to defend Alex's freedom with her life, if necessary. Why, she would sleep on the floor outside his bedroom door herself rather than let this coldhearted woman attempt to trap him into an offer of marriage. Lady Lucinda might be the epitome of elegant womanhood, the best-connected, most promising potential bride in all of England. Alex deserved better.

The dog deserved better.

"I have set dinner back, to give you time to rest," Nell said now, although the true reason was that the cook needed extra time to prepare for the extra guests.

"Does Carde come down to dine in company?"

"No, the stairs are still considered treacherous for him."

"In that case, I shall have a tray sent to my room. *I* do not care for livers, nor minced beef. A nice slice of veal would do, or perhaps a dish of pork cutlets. With asparagus, if you can purchase them in this part of the country."

Nell frowned as Lady Lucinda surveyed her reflection in the mirror. Where was she to find extra servants to wait on this guest—and her dog—when they were already overburdened carrying the earl's meals?

"I'll fetch my lady's tray," her maid Browne offered. "As soon as I have finished unpacking," she added, with an anxious glance toward her mistress.

"Thank you. I would appreciate that, since we are not prepared for so much company." Nell said the last

for Lady Lucinda's benefit, but she was wasting her breath. The duke's daughter was unwinding her pearls.

Dinner was an odd affair. There was no host, for one thing, and the company had little enough in common, for another. The duke spoke of his gout, Aunt Hazel of ghosts. Lady Haverhill was hard of hearing, and if Mr. Peabody was not, he must be assuming Nell was on a husband hunt. At least the food was good.

Nell thought it might be too good, too rich, for a gentleman with the gout, but His Grace appeared to be enjoying himself, eating heartily, laughing at Madame Ambeaux's comments.

"What, hold a coze with my late wife? By Jupiter, madam, we hardly spoke during twenty years of marriage. Why should we have a conversation now?"

"Did you say you were constipated, Harold?" the duke's cousin asked. "Try the ham with raisin sauce."

"Have you read Donne, Miss Sloane?" Mr. Peabody hurriedly inquired. "He is one of my favorite poets.

"Yes, but—"

Aunt Hazel interrupted. "I spoke with him last week. He is still melancholy."

"Cauliflower? No, I doubt it helps one's bowels. What do you think, Harold?"

"I think I'll see if Carde wants a bit of company after dinner."

"Cards? No, I am too tired, Harold. And you know you are a terrible player."

"Oh, are you, Your Grace? That is, I would not mind a round or two," Aunt Hazel offered, the gleam of avarice in her faded blue eyes.

"I do believe Lord Carde retires early these days, to aid his recovery," Nell told the duke.

"Too bad. I'd like to get this over as soon as possible. No sense beating around the bush. The chap knows why we have come. Every man has to put on leg shackles sooner or later."

Mr. Peabody coughed into his napkin. Nell felt her face go red.

Ever helpful, Aunt Hazel said, "Speaking of leg shackles, I met Dick Turpin last night."

Nell thought that was helpful indeed. The highwayman had been hanged in 1739.

"Turpentine? I never heard of that being a cure for anything but paint stains. You'll poison your innards that way, I do not doubt. Now castor bean oil . . ."

"He wishes he had not committed so many crimes."

"Whist? No, I said I was too tired. Does no one listen anymore?"

The duke blotted gravy from his chin. "It will be a crime, indeed, if Carde breaks my little girl's heart."

At least three pairs of eyes stared incredulously at Apston. The duke thought his daughter was little? He thought she had a heart?

CHAPTER TWELVE

The duke was a dreadful card player, or else his physical ailments were truly bothering him. Aunt Hazel did not have to cheat for her and Peabody to defeat him and Nell. Nell might have contributed to the loss, for her mind was elsewhere. In Alex's bedchamber, to be precise, which had her fanning her rosy cheeks instead of studying the discards.

She was not thinking wanton thoughts—at least not entirely. She was worried that Lady Lucinda would put a sleeping potion in the door-watcher's drink, that she would climb along the outer balcony and creep into Alex's window, that she would somehow suborn Stives out of the room, so she could have her wicked way with the earl.

Nell had been reading too many novels, she told herself. Why, she was not entirely sure what form such wickedness would take, but those conjectures of bare, warm flesh, soft, silky strokes, and whispered endearments were what had her plying her fan.

He was a man, and all men had intentions, he'd said. Appetites, Aunt Hazel had called them, explaining away Phelan's frequent absences. How could Alex resist, in his weakened state, a siren bent on seduction? Nell had a difficult time picturing Lady Lucinda as a temptress, but if the lady would drag her entire household on a long journey, surely she would not cavil at climbing between a gentleman's sheets. Her ploy would work, too.

Where Nell had plums, Lady Lucinda had grapefruits. Where Nell had sharp, angular planes, the duke's daughter had rounded curves. Nell had scant inches; Lucinda had long, lithe limbs. Where Nell's nose turned up slightly at the end, Lady Lucinda's matched Alex's own handsomely proportioned phiz. Alex was not the least attracted to Nell—that was a given—therefore he might find the other woman's opposite attributes infinitely more appealing.

Once he accepted what the lady was offering, the Earl of Carde was lost. Nell knew, with the same inner certainty that she knew her own name, that Alex was an honorable man. He might joke about being a coward and tease about running away, but he would never dishonor a woman. If he stole Lady Lucinda's virtue—or in this case accepted it on a silver platter, in a silk negligee—he would do the honorable thing. If he would bed her, he would wed her.

"I thought I was a poor player, Miss Sloane, but you have me beat to flinders. I doubt you even noticed what cards you were holding." The duke was totaling up his losses. "Good thing this was a friendly game and not for money."

Peabody could not refute his own employer. Aunt Hazel could, until Nell kicked her under the table.

"That's right, Your Grace, and I apologize if my mind went wandering. Perhaps tomorrow Lady Lucinda would partner you. Or Lady Haverhill. Or we might have a musical evening." Now Aunt Hazel kicked Nell under the table. Nell ignored the interruption and the pain. "I recall that Lady Lucinda had a lovely singing voice."

"That might do, but only if Carde can make it down to hear her. Sings like an angel, my gal, but mustn't strain her throat for nothing, eh?"

"I am certain he'll try. But here is Redfern with the tea tray." Thank goodness.

Nell thanked heaven again that no one lingered in the drawing room after the tea and biscuits were finished. She waited until the others had gone up to their bedrooms—far up, in Mr. Peabody's case—helping Redfern gather the cups and saucers so he did not have to bend.

"Is he safe?" she whispered to the old butler.

Redfern understood she did not mean Wellesley, the goose, who had managed to get into the kitchen garden. Cook was proposing paté. Redfern looked over his shoulder to make sure no one was listening, even though they were the only ones in the room. "Her ladyship's maid reported her mistress sleeping like a babe when Browne brought the dog down for a visit with nature."

As long as Daisy did not visit with the rugs, Wellesley, or the stable cats, that was fine. So was the earl.

That was what Hawkins, the footman who sat outside Lord Carde's door, said. He jumped up when Nell passed by.

"No one has tried to bother his lordship, then?" she asked.

"A few made inquiries, miss, just like Mr. Stives warned. But no one got past me."

"Good man. You are not going to sit up there all night, are you? Is someone coming to relieve you, or should I bring you some refreshments?"

"That's very kind of you, miss, but Mr. Stives says as how I can go on back to the rooms over the stables as soon as he's back. No one would get up to any hugger-mugger when he is in the earl's chamber, and he's a light sleeper."

"Mr. Stives is not here now?" Nell worried that Hawkins might be too subservient to refuse a duke admittance, and too young to refuse a duke's daughter.

"He's gone to chat up the company's servants. See what he can find out about any plans afoot. Reconnoitering, he calls it. He and the duke's man will be having a bit of wine Mr. Redfern left out for them, now that His Grace is put to bed. To loosen the man's tongue, he said."

"I see. Better forewarned than sorry. Well, then, good night, and I hope Mr. Stives returns soon, for your sake."

"Thank you, miss. But aren't you going to bid his lordship good night?"

"Me? Go in there?" She tipped her head toward the closed door.

"You weren't on my list to keep out. In fact, his lordship 'specially said you were welcome if you stopped by."

"Oh, but it is late. He is probably asleep."

"No, miss. He were wide awake when Mr. Stives left, writing to his brother what's in the army."

"I shall not disturb him then." She started down the hall, toward her own—no, toward Aunt Hazel's room. Her own was being used by Lady Haverhill.

"He'll be that sorry, miss. Said he was going to start

talking to ghosts soon too, like Madame Ambeaux, if he didn't have any other company." Hawkins looked anxiously up and down the corridor. "He was telling a plumper, wasn't he?"

"Of course he—"

Was suddenly standing in the now open doorway. "I heard voices. Real ones, Hawkins, yours and Miss Sloane's. Good evening, Cousin Nell. Won't you come in?"

He was wearing a dark brown velvet robe with his initials embroidered on the chest. ACE. Alexander Chalfont Endicott. But he did not look at all like the little boy whose brother called him by that pet name. No, he did not look like a boy at all. He wore the same spectacles, with the same serious air, and had the same wavy dark hair he had years ago, but that was where the similarity ended. He was broad and tall now, muscular and manly, even with his arm in a sling, even with a sticking plaster at his temple. Nell tried not to look at the open collar of his robe, where she could see the dark hairs that would trail down his chest toward—

She dragged her gaze lower. No, that was no good. Heavens, he might think she was looking at his—

She decided to stare at the floor. Good grief, his feet were bare. He was bound to take a chill. Nell felt she must already be afflicted, with shivers running up and down her spine.

"Are you all right?" His eyes were full of concern behind the glasses, when she could pull her own eyes from his naked toes.

"Fine. Perfect." Perfectly paralyzed and tongue-tied, while he looked like a demigod in dishabille.

"You do not look fine. In fact, you look tired, poor puss. I suppose the guests ran you ragged. I was hoping you could give me your opinions of the wolf pack. Lady Lucinda and her father, that is. But I can see it shall have to wait for tomorrow morning, after you have rested."

So now she looked fagged and faded, besides frumpish? Nell reminded herself that Sir Chauncy had not found her so entirely unappealing, by Alex's own reckoning. And Mr. Pensworth had hinted about spending the rest of his life looking at her, so she could not be a total antidote. Not that she wished to be the object of any man's base desires, but a small sliver of admiration would not be unwelcome now and again. "I am fine," she said, a bit more snappishly than she intended. "Lady Lucinda is the one who needs her beauty rest."

"A monthlong nap will not improve her disposition, however. But if you are not tired, won't you come in for a moment, just until Stivy gets back? You need not fear for your reputation because Hawkins will stand guard and not let anyone discover you. I really want to hear your impressions."

Of his bare feet? Fascinating. There were dark hairs on his toes, too. But she really had not ought to let him stand out in the drafty corridor. She really had not ought to step over the threshold to his rooms. What, a single lady entering a bachelor's chamber, at night, while he was only partially clothed? She could not claim cousinly concern, nor his incapacitation, for he appeared fit, robust, even. His complexion might be a bit paler than normal, but she had no way of knowing, and a day in the springtime sunshine could cure that anyway, as soon as he could manage the stairs.

No, she had no excuse for visiting Lord Carde in his room, especially without his valet handy. That would be breaking almost every rule concerning the conduct of unwed women. Why, she might as well tie her garter in The King's Arms' taproom. Her reputation would suffer the same fatal blow, if she were found out, in there.

On the other hand, Alex trusted her. Of course he did. He treated her as a relative, half as the little girl he used to know, half as an old maid, so far beneath his touch that any hopes in her flat-breasted chest would be laughable. Even if she cried rape, which she would never do, and ravishment, which he would never do, he would not make her an honorable proposal. He might not even offer her carte blanche, since she was so lacking in experience, appeal, and enthusiasm for the position of his mistress. No, an engagement after a compromise was for gentlemen and their ladies.

Who would believe her, anyway, or care?

The maids might envy Nell for sneaking past Hawkins for a bit of fun. She'd seen the way they peeked at the earl when carrying trays and hot water. They would not believe he seduced her, though, not the stiff and starchy Miss Sloane. Lady Lucinda and her father would certainly never take Nell's word that she had been ruined. Even if they found her bare in bed with Alex, they would turn as blind as Lady Haverhill was deaf. Anything else would destroy their own plans. Nell's own brother had left her alone, knowing a man he distrusted was in the neighborhood, so Phelan could not be counted on to defend her honor.

Still, Alex's friendship was worth a great deal. It was certainly worth jeopardizing her good name if not her virtue, which he was not interested in anyway. He was not afraid she would rip her clothes, throw herself on him, then scream the house down until they were discovered, so she would not fear being alone with him. Even if she ached to rip off her clothes and throw herself at him. He'd only laugh, most likely.

She raised her chin and stepped past him, through the door to his sitting room.

Lud, Alex thought, he was playing with fire. Even if he did not recognize the flames licking at his feet, Stives had warned him. Inviting an unwed woman of marriageable age into his private rooms was foolhardy in the extreme. Inviting one he liked was a great deal stupider.

He could end up engaged. Worse, he could end up giving Nell a disgust of him. He could hardly keep his hands off her now, and all she was doing was walking past him, leaving a hint of roses in the air. Luckily he had one arm in a sling or he'd be more tempted to pull apart that tidy braided bun in the back of her neck, just to see Nell's hair float around her shoulders in glorious waves, like golden sunshine. If he had both hands free he'd unfasten that pink rag she was wearing, to feast his eyes on a starving man's mirage. He would caress those fret lines from between her brows and kiss the sparkle back into her doubt-filled blue eyes. Then he would carry her slight weight into the bedroom. If he had two working arms.

He could manage to carry her as far as the sitting room chair, the devil in Alex's dreams whispered.

No, he could not. Should not. Would not. Nell was his responsibility to protect, not plunder. Nor was he going to embarrass her, or himself, with the evidence of his wayward desires. He thought about Lady Lucinda instead.

That cured the heat in his loins as well as any cold

bath would. By the time Nell was seated, her hands folded demurely in her lap, he did not need to hold the letter to Jack discreetly in his.

"Tea? A glass of wine?" he offered.

She shook her head no and licked her sweet pink lips.

Gads, where was the note to his brother? A blanket? A book? A bitch like Lucinda, that's what he needed. "So, what did you discover about your old schoolmate?"

"She does not love you."

Alex laughed. Trust Nell to amuse him with her quaint notions. "What, did you think she did?"

"I had hoped so, that Lady Lucinda was not so cold and calculating."

"She was trained on the hunting fields of London, though, a cutthroat competition where the winner gets the prize and the losers get to come back another year, if their families can afford the price. Love does not enter into the marriage deliberations at all. Sometimes mere liking is considered a boon, not a necessity."

"I wished Lady Lucinda were different."

"But she was not weeping over my loss, I take it? In a decline that I had not declared myself?"

Nell smiled at his knowing look. "She was complaining at your inconsideration of being injured so far from London."

"I hope that cured you of your romantic daydreams."

Nell shrugged. "I had been hoping for a happy ending for both of you. If she truly wanted to be wed to you, not your title or your wealth, I might have pled her cause."

"I shall be happy enough when she leaves."

"But you shall still need a wife." Perhaps it was the lateness of the hour, or the forbidden intimacy, but Nell dared to bring up a private matter. "A man in your position, needing heirs . . ."

"Do you think I am not aware of that? If I were not, Stives reminds me with great frequency. So do the dowagers, the betting books at White's, and the Prince himself. The damnable coil is that if I dance twice with a woman, her expectations are raised. If I do not spend time in her company, however, how should I discover if we suit?"

"You are right. It is a conundrum, indeed. Yet Aunt Hazel says your father demands it, and soon. I suppose she means your ancestry and your family name demand that you ensure the succession."

"Oh, she means my father, I'd wager. If the gentleman could speak, he'd say precisely that. He was wed to my mother at an early age, in an arranged match."

"But then he wed for love the second time, to Lizbeth. They were so happy at the wedding. Do you recall how merry she looked, smiling all the time? I remember thinking every girl should be as lucky as my cousin."

"To marry an earl?"

"To marry a gentleman worthy of her love, who loved her in return. Your father would want that for you, I am sure."

"He would want grandsons more."

"To be raised by nannies and tutors while their parents lead separate lives?"

"That was how my brother and I were reared. And all the boys at school."

"But not how little Lottie was being brought up. Lizbeth hardly let the child out of her sight, and she said the earl was the same. When she returned here for her father's funeral, one could see how Lizbeth missed Lord Carde and only wanted to get back to him. I remember Phelan urging her to stay because her mother was ill and despondent, but Lizbeth had promised your father to hurry home. She was going to return with him when the Parliamentary session ended and the weather turned better."

"Do you think she might have urged the driver to rush, and that was what caused the accident?"

"Gracious, Lizbeth would not have put her child's life in danger in so foolhardy a manner, much less her own and the servants' lives. She told me she was hoping to be carrying another infant." Nell would not usually discuss such intimate feminine matters with a gentleman, but Alex was different. Here in the hush of the sleeping house, she felt she could speak to him about anything. Well, not about her own private hopes and dreams to have a loving husband and a baby to cherish. Those were too buried in shadow to bring out into the light, even the soft candle glow. Now she was sorry she had mentioned Lizbeth's confidences. Alex looked sad, staring into the fire's dying embers. "I should not have said anything. Phelan will not even permit Lizbeth's name to be spoken in his presence because he finds it too upsetting."

"No, I am glad to know how fond your cousin was of my father. I just never knew about another infant. I don't think my father did, either."

"Lizbeth was not certain. You must know that no one spoke of such things to young girls, but she was explaining to her mother why she could not stay, and I overheard. I cannot imagine your father discussing the unconfirmed possibility with a schoolboy, either, if he suspected."

"I cannot imagine my father permitting Lizbeth to

make the long journey if he did, not even to attend her own father's burial. He would not take such a chance."

"Perhaps that was why she wanted to get back so fast, to tell him, or to consult with an accoucheur. She would never have ordered the driver to race over that hilly cliff road, though, if she thought she was breeding."

"No, and the man was a trusted employee. He would have used his own best judgment as to their speed. I was just looking for reasons for the senseless tragedy, I suppose. It caused so much grief and loss to so many people, without explanation."

"How can anyone ever know what happened that day? The only one who could find out is Aunt Hazel, if you believe her claims to friends in extremely high places."

He smiled again, returning his brown-eyed stare to Nell's face. "Thank you, but I shall live with the uncertainties rather than consult Madame Ambeaux's aberrations. Have you ever wondered whatever happened to the child? Lottie, I mean."

"I do not understand. No one survived the coach accident."

"No one was found alive. There is a difference. They never found the newly hired guard, and they never found Lottie's body. She is not buried in the family vault at Cardington with her parents."

"I remember the servants whispering that she must have wandered to the water," Nell explained. "Again, no one spoke out loud of the terrible events in my presence, and then I was sent away to school when my aunt passed away soon afterward. Phelan was inconsolable and would not talk about it."

"The shoreline was dragged for weeks. They never

found a trace of Lottie. That was the real reason I came here."

Nell could not help shivering at the thought. "To look for her . . . remains after all these years?"

"No, I doubt that would be possible. But to see the place, to talk to the searchers myself if any remain in the vicinity after so long, to try one last time to identify the missing guard."

"Who might have carried the child off?" Nell was shaking her head. "Then why did he not bring her back? I never heard one word that anyone suspected foul play."

"As you said, you were a schoolgirl, and then your brother cast a veil of silence over the accident, if such it was."

"It had to be. Everyone loved Lizbeth. No one would ever have harmed her on purpose."

"Yet my father did not believe that was the case. He never believed little Lottie was dead, either. He bade me look for her."

Nell looked over her shoulder, into the shadows, then tried to laugh. The sound was more a nervous giggle than a mark of humor. "When, before you left London? Never say you are speaking with him, like Aunt Hazel."

Alex was smiling at the way Nell was nearly out of her seat, ready to fly toward the door. "No, he asked me to find my half-sister while he lay dying. That was his last wish, that I bring her home. I promised."

"Then you weren't just running away from Lady Lucinda and the matchmakers?" Nell had never believed Alex's claims to cowardice, so she was glad to have her good opinion of him confirmed. Alex wasn't avoiding his duty, he was performing it. If the search for his lost sister interfered with his search for a bride, well, he was still acting on his family's behalf, obeying his father's wishes.

What a fine, honorable man he was! How could Lady Lucinda not love him? How could any woman?

Oh, dear.

CHAPTER THIRTEEN

Nell would not have thought so highly of Alex if she could read his mind.

What mind? The way she bit her lip in confusion, the way she leaned toward him to listen, how she took his hand, saying she knew he would do his best—Lud, any thoughts of looking for Lottie flew out of his head. What was left was a whirlpool of wanting. Here he was, alone at night with a woman who actually listened to his concerns, who understood family honor and duty, who did not just see a bejeweled title hanging over his head, who had a tempting little body, besides.

This was not the usual itch that his former mistress Mona and her ilk could scratch. That was a simple urge, like needing to blow his nose. He did, it was a relief, it was over. This was more like needing to breathe, he feared, which never went away.

Worse than being aroused—although not much was worse than being aroused, knowing one could not do anything pleasant about it—was the fear that the desire went deeper. He wanted to pleasure Nell, yes, and please her, but he wanted to protect her, too. He wished he could dress her in lace and cover her with jewels, but he also wished he could keep her from disappointment and discouragement and the everyday bothers of everyone's lives. Alex wanted to make her gasp and sigh and moan, but he wanted to see her laugh and smile and simply relax in contentment, with him beside her. Because he was beside her.

He wanted Nell.

He was sunk.

He cleaned his spectacles on a handkerchief while she took a turn staring at the fire. What could Alex say? What could Nell say? Nothing, without destroying the friendship they had between them.

They were both relieved when Stives returned.

The valet opened the door, took one look at the couple sitting across from each other in the matching chairs in front of the hearth, and shook his head. For once he held his tongue. He also held the door for Miss Sloane, after making sure the hallway was clear. No London doyenne of society's dictates could make the point more strongly.

Alex stood. "Stives is right. It is time for you to go." He took Nell's hand in his and started to raise it to his lips, but Stives cleared his throat. Alex squeezed Nell's delicate hand instead, after glaring at his trusted servant. Stivy could be trusted to stick his nose where it did not belong, anyway.

Before she had to leave, Nell warned both the earl and his man that Lady Lucinda intended to pay Alex a visit in the morning.

"Her maid says that milady never rises afore noon," Stives reported. "So we're safe till then."

"Plenty of time to pack the carriage and head out for Scotland, eh?"

Stives groaned, but Nell knew Alex was joking because he winked at her.

The valet scratched his head. "You are not thinking of Gretna Green, are you? I thought you were headed away from parson's mousetrap, not rushing to find a blacksmith to do the job."

Alex had indeed been thinking of flinging Nell over his shoulder and riding north with her. No arguing, no explaining, no asking permission. And no confessing the fire that burned inside him. He'd take nothing but a good horse and a better woman. The scandal would be of epic proportions and Nell would never be accepted in his social circles, but the end results might be worth the outcry.

He would not do it, of course. Nell would think he was crazy, for one thing. She barely knew him, had a houseful of guests, and would not thank him for dragging her out into the cold and damp without a maid or a by-your-leave. Besides, his shoulder would most likely fall out of its socket again if he tried to lift her, light as she was.

"No, I was just thinking of the hunting box," he told Stives. "Not even Lady Lucinda would follow us there."

"His Grace might if you have shooting and fishing," Nell told him, "or if he thought he could ply you with Scotch brew and win an offer for his daughter."

Alex laughed. "The Scotch lochs will all freeze over first. But never fear, I shan't leave you to face the wolves. I shall simply have to bring my courage to the sticking point and make a stand."

"The duke will insist on an interview in the morning," Nell warned, "so you have but a few hours to practice your bravery."

"Unless I decide to pretend I am unconscious."

Stives muttered, "That might work, for a day or two. The leech won't let go that easily."

"But you would only be prolonging the visit." Nell was wondering what she could do with her difficult guests for two days, much less an entire week.

"Very well, you have shamed me into valor. I shall meet with His Grace in the morning, fearing no evil— or engagement. Right is on my side. And you better be at my right hand," he ordered Stives. "You know, I believe I have a thing or two to say to His Grace anyway."

Only then did he release Nell's hand, the one that he'd been holding as long as he could. She looked stunned, as if only now realizing why her fingers were tingling and her toes were wriggling in her slippers. She bobbed a hasty curtsy and left.

Alex wondered if her dreams would be as disordered as his own.

Nell never had the chance to find out. Aunt Hazel mumbled in her sleep all night.

"If you speak with my mama or Lizbeth," Nell whispered in the dark, "ask them to pray for me."

The duke hobbled into Alex's room after breakfast the next morning, leaning heavily on his cane.

"You don't look so bad," he told Alex, who was dressed and shaved and had his left arm out of its sling, testing his shoulder.

"I wish I could say the same for you," Alex said, dragging over a footstool for His Grace to prop up his gouty leg. The man's face was a pasty color, and his eyes had pouches under them.

The duke sighed as he took his considerable weight off the painfully swollen, slippered foot. "Blame Miss

Sloane's cook. My chef at home ain't half the dab hand with the sauces."

His chef at home had not been paid in half a year, Alex would guess. "I take it you ate too much rich food?"

"And drink. The bottles hereabouts never saw an excise label, I'd swear. Far better than what we get in Town. I took a bottle to my bed when my valet was looking the other way."

"Didn't the physicians warn you against over-indulging?"

"Of course they did. Every one of the six I consulted. I was hoping for a different answer, you see. Ignorant fools, they all said the same thing. I could have spouted it myself and still not be cured. So what if they were right anyway, eh? A man's only got so many years to live and he might as well enjoy himself doing it. Not so many pleasures left to a fellow my age."

Alex did not want to think about what pleasures the duke might or might not have left to him at what . . . ? Fifty-five years of age? Sixty? The man looked far older, but that might have been an excess of drink.

"Let that be a lesson to you, lad."

Alex decided against offering His Grace an early toast. "What lesson might that be, Duke?"

"To gather ye rosebuds, of course, or however that nonsense went."

Rosebuds reminded Alex of Nell's scent. The duke could not be meaning Miss Sloane.

He wasn't. "My daughter says you're engaged."

"We are not."

"She says you compromised her."

"I did not."

"She says you kissed her."

"I . . ." She had kissed him. Either way, a gentleman did not discuss a lady's kisses, and certainly not with the lady's father. "She is not compromised," Alex said, wishing he'd poured them glasses of wine after all, and the duke's leg be damned, along with the early hour. "There has been no gossip. Lady Lucinda's spotless reputation"—as an ice maiden, Alex privately thought—"is preserved. In fact, our names would not be linked at all in society's notoriously short memory if you had not followed me here."

"I was afraid of that. But you know my girl. Headstrong."

And desperate. But a gentleman did not say that to a lady's father, either. "Since Lady Lucinda is an old school friend of Miss Sloane's, you can let it be known that the visit was planned, and it was a mere coincidence that I was here. No one will believe you, of course, but then there will be less talk when no engagement announcement is forthcoming."

"Can't convince you to reconsider, eh?"

"I am afraid not."

"Not even if I threaten to call you out over the slight to my daughter?"

"What, I with one arm and you with one leg, taking the field of honor? That would make your daughter a laughingstock. And she would still be unengaged."

"I told her I'd only look no-account challenging a young buck like you. And that's no way to start off with a new son-in-law anyway."

"I am not going to be your son-in-law," Alex said, pronouncing each word carefully, as if the duke were as hard of hearing as his cousin or as hard of understanding as his daughter.

His Grace shifted his leg with a grimace and a groan. "I think you are being too hasty, lad. You'll not find a higher match in all the kingdom, I'd wager. Titled ladies of marriageable age aren't thick on the ground, you know. Doubt you'd be happy with a foreign princess. Look what happened to Prinny."

Alex did not want to think of the unfortunate prince or his unappealing wife. "No, I do not aim for royalty."

"And my Lucy has her fine education, the voice of an angel, connections at all the right homes. Her mother was one of seven children, so you needn't worry she won't be a good childbearer. The duchess and I spent as little time together as possible, which is why we never—"

Alex cleared his throat. If he did not wish to consider the prince's marriage, he surely did not want to contemplate the intimate details of the duke's. "I do not believe one can speculate about a woman's fertility."

"Quite right. They're not brood mares, after all."

Unless one was marrying a female simply to beget sons, Alex thought, which was dismal enough. Then what was she?

"But my girl knows her duty, you can be sure of that."

Which was a more dismal thought, having a wife who looked at conjugal relations as a duty. Going to church was a duty. Serving one's country was a duty. Lovemaking should be a joy.

The duke was going on, enumerating his daughter's fine points as if she were, indeed, a mare on the auction block. Alex wondered if he'd missed mention of her sound teeth and stamina.

"She has exquisite taste. Everyone says so, but you needn't worry about the bills. My Lucy already owns a wardrobe that could bankrupt a nabob and—"

"Your daughter is everything admirable, Your Grace, except for one failing. Not precisely a failing, at that. You see, I do not love her." Alex had already had this conversation with one hopeful parent, Squire Branford, Daphne's father. He held up his left hand before the duke could speak, happy to note that he felt only a minor twinge of pain. "Please do not say that love has no place in marriage, for it does, to me."

"Faugh. Fool notion, that is. I'd wager you fancied yourself in love with any number of females whose names you can hardly remember now."

"No, I never had the good fortune to experience that tender emotion."

"And you may never have. Or you might fall top over teakettle for some pretty gal only to find that the infatuation does not outlast the engagement. But you still need a wife and sons."

Alex bent his head in acknowledgment. His cracked skull no longer pained him, either. "So everyone tells me. Although my brother might yet come home and start filling the Endicott nurseries."

"A soldier? Do not place odds on it."

If Alex were betting, he'd put his money on the chance that this whole conversation was about wagering. And losing. Everyone knew the Duke of Apston was punting on tick, signing his gambling vowels all over town. Alex himself held a considerable stack of His Grace's IOUs.

He was right, as usual.

"The thing is," the duke was saying, staring at his propped-up foot, which was no prettier sight than the future he foresaw, "my gal won't have much of a dowry. She has a good name and the title, of course, but not much gold to go along with it. Except her mother's jewels, but that wouldn't concern a gent like you, with a dragon's hoard of heirlooms of your own. The money wouldn't matter to you, either, from all I hear. You've enough blunt to take a bride from the poorhouse, if you wanted. Not that you would, knowing what's due your own family honor. Wouldn't want your sons called names on account of their mother's low birth. No, you need to take a well-born chit, one whose father would expect a hefty settlement in exchange."

It was true that the family of any female of rank would demand a handsome settlement: generous allowances, widow's benefits, property rights for her unborn children—and a sum of money paid into the family coffers for the pleasure of taking an unwanted woman off their hands.

The duke was counting on that. "Now I might be willing to let my poppet go in return for those trifling gambling debts you hold."

Alex did not think a few thousand pounds was trifling, but he never lost that much in a month, much less at one or two sittings. He straightened his spectacles, as if he were trying to get a better picture of the deal the duke was proposing. "Let me see if I have this straight. You are suggesting I take your daughter, a lovely lady to be sure, but one I am regrettably not enamored of. I would receive . . . what? Lady Lucinda's hand and nothing else. Not only would I have no dowry to set aside for my daughters, but I would lose the money that you currently owe me. Oh, yes, and I could expect to be asked for the occasional loan from my esteemed father-in-law."

"Put like that, it doesn't sound like much of a bargain, does it?" The duke's eyes sunk farther in their folds. Then his whole face brightened. "No, you'd be getting a loving wife, which you wouldn't in many an arranged match. Lucy must love you. She proved it by coming here, didn't she?"

She proved how single-minded and selfish she was, in Alex's opinion. And stupid. He'd no more take that woman to wife than he would Harriett Wilson, the whore. At least one was honest in what she was selling. Lady Lucinda no more loved him than he loved her, which was not at all.

"I do have another proposition, however," he told the disappointed duke. "One that would cancel all of your outstanding debts to me, plus some extra for your efforts, to see you through this spell of, ah, poor luck."

The duke nodded. "The cards are bound to turn soon. What is your offer? I don't have any horses you'd see fit to ride, and all the Apston acres not entailed on a distant cousin have been sold off ages ago. It's nothing underhanded, I say?"

"Not at all. A minor favor, actually. I would like you to take Miss Sloane back to town with you."

"You want me to give the gal a ride, in exchange for two thousand pounds?"

"No, not merely a ride in your carriage. I want you to take her into your home, see that she is invited to parties and such as your houseguest. The Season is not over yet, so she can still meet some important people, see the sights. Her aunt can go along to help Lady Haverhill chaperone, and Lady Lucinda can see that Nell is rigged out in style."

"You want me to get the girl fired off in society?"

"That's right. Coming with a duke's blessings, she will have no trouble being accepted. Her birth is unremarkable but decent. I am sure this estate can provide her a dowry."

The duke pursed his thick lips. "You want my Lucy to become a bear-leader, dragging a skinny nobody around town with her? You must have hit your head harder than anyone realized, Carde."

"Three thousand pounds."

"Damn. Why?"

"Because she is a lovely young woman who never had a chance to enjoy herself. Because she deserves to see something of the world, make some friends, perhaps find a husband—the same reasons every miss comes to town for the Season."

"Why now? You could have foisted her on any number of females when she was a young chit fresh from the schoolroom."

"And I would have, if I had seen the need. I just now realized how long the family has neglected Cousin Eleanor and her future."

"The female is not any cousin of yours, only a distant connection through your father's marriage. Lucy looked it up before we left town."

"She is family," Alex insisted.

"Then see to bringing her out yourself."

"What, a single gentleman sponsoring a marriageable female? How would that look? She would be ruined."

"She'll be ruined from my house too, if anyone learns you were behind it."

"Four thousand pounds."

The duke was pondering the possibilities, and the reasons behind the proposition. "You aren't thinking of polishing Miss Sloane up to be your countess, are you? Lucy would have cat fits."

"I just met the woman last week, after a decade." If Alex did not entirely answer the duke's question, His Grace did not notice. To make sure Apston was satisfied, Alex added, "I owe her a debt of gratitude for her care of me."

"She owes you for not having her arrested. I heard she was the one who set the goose on you."

"It was an accident, nothing more. Will you do it?"

"She'll need a new wardrobe. Can't have her looking like Lucy's maid, you know. Nothing will sink a female faster than looking like a poor relation."

"Five thousand."

"Hm. Lucy has wardrobes filled with gowns she never wears. I suppose they could be cut down and altered without a huge expense. But what about that dowry?" the duke asked about a topic he knew well. "Miss Sloane will never get an offer if she doesn't have a dowry. No title, no lands, no connections, and she's no great beauty, like my gal."

Beauty was definitely in the eye of the beholder. Alex thought Nell far prettier than Lady Lucinda could ever be, despite her elegant clothes and social graces. No, Nell was no hard-as-stone star in London's galaxy, thank goodness. She did not hide her feelings or wear that simpering smile so many misses pasted on their faces, only to wash off at night, he supposed. "A discerning gentleman will see her loveliness."

"He won't give her a second look without that dowry."

"She will be dowered by this estate." If not, Alex would find a way to get the funds secretly channeled from his own account into hers.

The duke was still thinking. "Pretty little thing, if you don't mind the bones. Nice enough manners, and runs a tidy household. Frugal too, I hear. Had the same education as my gal. I suppose she can sing or play, that rot?"

"I believe she has some talent at drawing."

The duke nodded. "The old biddies expect a girl to have some talent. It might do. But instead of saying we found you here by accident, which no one will swallow, we could tell everyone that Lucy came to Miss Sloane's aid. The gal found herself at point *non plus* with an injured earl on her doorstep, so Lucy kindly renewed their friendship. That will look better for both of them."

"That's the ticket! Out of the generosity of her heart"—hah!—"Lady Lucinda invited her friend to enjoy the rest of the Season as her honored guest."

"Very well, I'll do it, take Miss Sloane off your hands for you. How much did you say the dowry was?"

Alex did not like that speculation in the duke's pouchy eyes. In fact, they were opened wide in excitement. No man should look that delighted to have another female under his roof, especially not a stranger.

"I will have to have the solicitor look at the estate books if her brother does not return soon. But why the worry over her portion? Do you already have a young gentleman in mind? Your secretary Peabody will not do."

"I wasn't thinking of him, but I don't see why not."

"Would you let him court Lady Lucinda?"

"Of course not. But my gal is a duke's daughter."

"And Miss Sloane is an earl's—" Damn, what was she? She was too old to be his ward, and she had an older brother, besides. They were not truly related, and he had ignored her existence for more than ten years. "Responsibility. That's it. My father would have insisted she be presented and married well. I can do no less."

His Grace nodded, setting the extra flesh at his eyes and jowls to jiggling. "Then you'll be glad to have me save you from looking any further. There is no call to waste a dowry on Peabody, or go to all that bother of a season. You would not even have to provide the gal a wardrobe, only a wedding dress. I can outfit my own bride from the Applegate attics."

"Yours?" Alex almost fell off his chair.

"Why not? I'm not in my dotage yet. I might be laid low, but that's temporary. And I'd rather have a pretty young thing looking after me than a hired nurse, anyway. Lucy will get married sooner or later. Why should I be alone? Miss Sloane is used to living quietly in the country, which suits me. I'll have a quiet little bride and her dot, your debts canceled, and what did you say, six thousand besides? Who knows, I might even get me a son after all."

"Never!" Alex roared, bringing Stives running from the dressing room. "I'd marry her myself, first."

CHAPTER FOURTEEN

"**I** thought you weren't interested in the girl."

Alex was not interested in seeing Nell tied to a gouty old gambler with a grown daughter, not even if Nell would be a duchess. Apston would go through her dowry and Lady Lucinda would go through histrionics.

Alex sent Stives off for a tea tray. He needed something in his hands, other than the duke's neck.

"After all, your own father took a younger wife. I can't be much older than he was," Apston was saying, "and Miss Sloane can't be much younger than her cousin was. Why would a man of my years want a woman the same age?" He shuddered. "All sagged and shriveled, set in her ways, too. No, a fine young woman to keep me company through the winters, all warm and cozy, that's more like it."

That was more like what Nell had now: an empty life as a drudge in someone else's home. Except at Apston's, she'd have to share the old goat's bed. At Ambeaux Cottage she was only temporarily sharing a mattress with her old aunt and the ghosts.

"I had in mind a love match for her, too," Alex told the duke. "Some lively entertainments at the very least, with other young people. You know, balls and waltz parties, picnics, the maze at Richmond." He pointedly directed his gaze at His Grace's raised leg. The duke could no more dance with a pretty girl than he could fly. Country rambles, tours of cathedrals and museums and art galleries, everything Alex wanted Nell to enjoy, all were beyond the duke.

Apston wiggled his bloated toes, then grimaced. "Peabody can escort her to that nonsense. His birth is good enough to be invited almost everywhere. He already accompanies my Lucy when I cannot. Saves me a lot of boring evenings, too, thank the stars."

Alex was sure the other gamesters were thankful too, to have more chances to win the duke's money. "No, that will not do. Nell—that is, Cousin Eleanor—deserves better."

His Grace pulled at his ear. "Better'n a duke? Seems to me the gal is of an age to make her own choices, anyway."

"She can give her hand where she will," Alex conceded. "But I control her dowry." At least he thought he did. He would send for Silbiger that very afternoon.

Miss Sloane was no longer half as appealing to the duke, cold winter nights or not. Hot bricks were a lot less trouble.

He was no longer eager to explain to his daughter about the addition to their household, either. A young stepmother Lucinda might have accepted and ignored, but another single young woman? That was competition, pure and simple. The duke rubbed at his chin. "I'm not so sure taking Miss Sloane to London is such a good idea after all. What if she doesn't take? My girl will look like a fool, dragging around an old maid antidote who's neither fish nor fowl. Not a relative, not a paid companion."

"Seven thousand. Eight if you keep her away from Peabody. Nine if you forget about courting Miss Sloane altogether."

"Make it an even ten and I'll get her presented at court. I still have some influence there, you know. Cousin Emily used to be one of the Queen's ladies in waiting. Your Miss Sloane will have her choice of eager young bucks, see if she doesn't."

Alex was happy. And worried.

Lady Lucinda was upset.

She was upset the way the Sahara was dry. Her maid ran out of the room. The little dog followed her. Her father wished he could too, but his leg was paining him worse. Of course it was. To hell with the tea Carde's man had brought. His Grace needed three glasses of brandy to get from the earl's sitting room to his daughter's bedchamber. The walk was a mere corridor. The dread was miles wide.

Lady Lucinda was up and dressed, ready for her assault on her groom-to-be. What man could resist her in raspberry silk? She pulled a raven-hued curl of hair forward on her porcelainlike cheek, down her swanlike neck toward her pillowlike bosom, which was barely ladylike in its low-necked gown. She pinched her cheeks, bit her lips, then gave up and resorted to the hare's foot and powders.

She was wearing the Apston ruby between her snowy breasts to remind Carde of her worth. The paste replacement stone was worth a pittance, but the earl did not have to know that. The pendant represented centuries of dignity, generations of breeding, a long history of honor. And it brought attention to her chest.

An unwed woman wearing colored stones, and before nightfall? So what? She was Lady Lucinda Applegate, daughter to a duke, premier belle of London. She made her own rules.

Lady Lucinda was a lady. And she was a lioness stalking her prey. Carde was a mere male, and a not entirely empty-headed one at that. He could not fail to recognize that Lucinda was the perfect wife for him, even if he did have to wear those ugly spectacles to see her.

"He said what?" She ripped the Apston ruby off her neck and threw it at the mirror. Luckily the fake stone shattered instead of the looking glass. Otherwise Lucinda might have had seven more years of bad luck, in addition to the seven since her come-out when her father gambled away their fortune and no worthy gentleman presented himself to her. "Take *whom* to London?"

Her bracelet followed the necklace, inches from her father's head. "To find her a *what*?"

"Now, now, my pet," her father soothed, holding his hands up in peace, or to catch the next flying folderol. "The news is not all bad. Think on it. Carde intends to follow us to town, so you will have him dancing attendance on you both. He would not abandon his cousin to be eaten alive by the tabbies."

"They are not cousins!"

"No, but he is claiming kinship. You know what that means to a straight arrow like Carde: He takes his responsibilities seriously. Very definite about which gentlemen call on her, he is, so he won't leave her to our care. No, he will be looking after the girl, so he'll be looking at you. If you play your cards right—Carde, heh, heh—he'll see you in a better light. You'll be a kind, warmhearted friend to his relation, and he'll be grateful."

"I do not want his gratitude! I want his proposal."

"Give it time, my love. Give it time." The duke sank onto the chaise longue with his leg up, to avoid his daughter's furious pacing. He thought his foot and his face would be safer there, now that she'd stopped throwing things.

She threw the dog's leash, raspberry to match her gown, just to prove him wrong. It landed right on his tender toes. "Yeow!" he screamed.

"What are you upset about? You did not want to pay for an elegant wedding anyway." She resumed her pacing, then paused at her dressing table, a glass jar in her hand.

His Grace cringed and rubbed his foot. "Now, now, my pet, do try to keep calm. You know how the physicians said excitement was not good for my condition."

"If you listened to them in the first place, you might not have any condition," his loving daughter answered. Then she made another angry circuit of the room, still holding the jar.

"You swear he is not courting Eleanor?"

"He says not. Says he is looking for a love match."

"A love match?" she repeated, incredulous, slamming the jar down on the mantel in a cloud of face powder. "That is the most nonsensical idea of all. Lords and ladies do not marry for love, for goodness sake. If they did, everyone would be wed to dairy maids and secretaries!"

Her father ignored the mention of a secretary, out of guilt about the dairy maid. "Carde always did have an odd kick to his gallop, but never worry about Miss

Sloane. How could he love such an insipid little dab of a thing? Besides, we have no choice. I cannot afford another season in town without his blunt."

"A love match?" Lady Lucinda could not believe any titled gentleman could be so careless of what was due his dignity.

"That's right. So go on, poppet, make him love you. I bought you the time. Actually, he bought it, but that's not important. The fact is, if you want him, you'll have to play his game, which is seeing Miss Sloane established in society."

Lucinda frowned, until she remembered that left lines. "Well, I do not see how that is to be accomplished. Eleanor is the most unstylish creature I have ever seen. Her wardrobe is not fit for my maid to wear."

"I thought your maid could cut some of your old gowns down, refurbish them in the current fash—"

"My clothes? Now I am supposed to share my clothes with the twit? First my fiancé, then my house, now my very apparel?" She hefted a china shepherdess from the mantel, not, her father feared, to wipe the powder off it.

"No, no, pet. That was a mere idea to save time and effort." And money. "Carde will see that she has a clothing allowance. Of course, if she does use some of your old gowns, there would be blunt left over to replace them."

Lady Lucinda put the shepherdess down and stopped pacing.

"That's right, Lucy. You always like shopping, so you'll enjoy having your friend with you."

"But everywhere, day and night?"

"Not for long. The social season is almost over, and everyone who matters will be going to their country estates. Who knows, we might get the chit married before then."

"Before me?" Lucinda screeched, snatching up the figurine again.

"Come now, poppet. Remember that you are a lady."

"A single lady. An aging single lady whose father has gambled away most of her dowry."

His Grace felt more guilt about that than about the dairy maid. "But now with Carde forgiving my debt and adding a pot, I'll have a new stake, even after paying off some of the others and a bit to the tradesmen."

"My maid is threatening to leave unless she has her back salary."

"My man, too. There's no loyalty these days, eh? Anyway, with a fresh start and Carde's money, I can win it all back."

The china shepherdess was destined to be forever without her flock. And her head, one arm, and part of her foot. "Hah! The chances of your winning back our fortune are as good as my making Eleanor Sloane into a lady of fashion."

Both chances were still better than Lady Lucinda's odds of getting Carde to love her. The duke knew it. His daughter knew it. Redfern, listening at the door, knew it.

"We both have to try, poppet. It's either take Miss Sloane to London on Carde's credit, or go back to the country without her. Without a marriage prospect, without a chance for next year, without a maid, perhaps."

This time Lady Lucinda threw a crystal vase filled with violets. Nell had picked them to match the room, and had set them on the mantel, bringing the springtime into her guest's room. Now the violets not only matched the wallpaper, they were part of it.

Nell did not know what was happening. First Lady Lucinda's maid went tearing down the hall, then the little mop of a dog, its tail between its legs. Next came loud shouts and louder crashes.

"Is His Grace ill? Has he fallen? Shall I send for the surgeon?"

Redfern took his ear away from the door panel. "I believe you might send for a broom, rather. And your trunks."

Nell was rapping on the door. "My trunks? I—"

Lady Lucinda opened it. Her sour expression suddenly turned into one of honeyed sweetness when she saw who was waiting. "Why, there you are, Eleanor dear. My father and I were just speaking of you."

Perhaps the noises were from Lady Lucinda's being interrupted at her toilette. Nell's guest had not yet put her hair up in an ornate style, nor was she wearing any jewelry. Nell was glad, for she intended to invite Lady Lucinda to walk to the village with her, where intricate fashions and expensive gems would be out of place. The lady's bodice was an inch or two—or three—too low for simple country calls, but she would need a shawl or a pelisse anyway.

Nell was not glad to see a puddle on the floor. "The dog—"

Lady Lucinda waved her hand. "The silly creature knocked over the flower vase, that's all."

From the mantel-top? Nell realized the china shepherdess that always stood there was missing too. She looked around to see the duke on the chaise longue stuffing a violet in his buttonhole. He smiled at her and waved. "Pardon me for not rising, Miss Sloane. Blasted leg."

Nell curtseyed and stepped back, on the broken statue. "Oh, no. This was my Aunt Ambeaux's favorite knickknack. She had it since she was a girl."

Lady Lucinda took the figurine from Nell and stuffed it behind a pillow on the bed. Then she took Nell's hand and pulled her closer to the duke. "Stop worrying over trifles, Eleanor. There are momentous doings afoot."

No, that was the shepherdess's head. "Oh, dear."

"What is one little bit of clay when a whole new life is about to begin?"

"A new life? Sophie Posener is having her baby?" Nell could not imagine how Lady Lucinda had found out before she did, or before Redfern.

"I do not know any Sophie Posie. And ladies do not speak of such delicate matters." Lady Lucinda raised her eyes toward heaven, as if praying for patience. Or praying for help in making this sow's ear into a silk purse.

"It is your life my daughter is speaking of," His Grace told Nell, redirecting her attention, "and the great treat in store for you."

They were leaving today?

No such luck.

Lady Lucinda clapped her hands together. "Isn't it marvelous? You are coming to London with us!"

Nell looked from one to the other. They must both be tired from the journey still, or touched by the sun.

The duke was still smiling at her, reminding Nell of a former prizefighter who had visited the village once. He smiled too, while his keeper led him around on a rope. "Do not worry," he said. "It is all arranged."

"It is? That is, what is arranged? By whom?"

"By the earl, of course," Lucinda took up the tale. "He is so, ah, grateful to you that he wishes you to have a holiday. He asked us, your dear friends, to sponsor your visit to the city. You must know that a single gentleman"—she smirked, as if how long Carde remained in his bachelor state was open to question—"cannot present a young woman to society. Of course yours would not be an official presentation, merely a few introductions and such. Wouldn't you appear foolish at your age garbed all in white like a debutante? And with your sun-bleached hair . . ."

The duke cleared his throat. "He means you to take in the sights, Miss Sloane. The theater, the opera, that kind of thing. A few balls and dinner parties, the museums, the shops."

Now it was Lady Lucinda's turn to clear her throat. "There is no need for dear Eleanor to waste her time with tedious visits to linen drapers and dressmakers, poring over pattern books or being stuck with pins. I have trunks full of discards—that is, clothes I seldom wear. And my maid is a dab hand with a needle. She knows the latest fashions, of course, although she has never had to deal with enhancing a figure, merely displaying it properly." Lucinda puffed up her own attributes in their nearly improper covering.

Her father's brows lowered. "She'll still need shoes and gloves and bonnets. You always do, no matter how many you own."

Lucinda ignored her father, telling Nell, "We will have you rigged out in style before the earl arrives in town. Why, I believe I have a blue gown that will nearly match your eyes. So boring, but what can one do with such nondescript coloring? You must know that blondes are sadly out of fashion." She raised a hand to her own raven-hued locks, then frowned when she realized her hair had become mussed.

"Miss Sloane is a pretty little thing," the duke said as if that pretty little thing were not standing five feet from his chaise longue. "We'll have no trouble finding her a husband, eh, my dear?"

"Please, Your Grace. I do not seek a husband."

"Of course you do. You know, husband, hearth, hordes of infants. That's what all females want. What else is there for you?"

Nell could go into service, or she could stay right here where she had been content with her lot, more or less. She might not have a husband or children, but she did have a comfortable home, also more or less. Marrying a stranger, sharing his bed, moving to a strange place would make her more uncomfortable, less content. "I do not look for a visit to London, either. While a few of the attractions you mentioned do sound appealing, such as the theater, I have never cared for crowds or being constantly on the go. I do thank you for the invitation, however."

"Oh, you cannot refuse, my dear Miss Sloane," His Grace said. "I won't have a groat. That is, I won't hear a word of it."

Lady Lucinda was nodding, not quite as enthusiastically as her father, but encouragingly for all that. "You have to come, Eleanor."

"Why?"

"Why, to get out of this hopeless little hamlet. Father is wrong: There is more for a woman than getting married and getting pregnant."

"I thought ladies did not speak of that?" Nell could not resist asking.

As usual Lady Lucinda ignored anything but her own opinions. "If a woman chooses her mate carefully, she can be a notable political hostess or a patron of the arts. She can travel, she can take up philanthropy"—which Nell thought Lady Lucinda would not recognize if it left hairs on her skirts, like her dog—"or she can become an arbiter of style and manners. None of which is possible to you, here, unwed."

"But I do not wish to become any of those things," Nell protested.

"Then you need not," the duke told her. "You need only spend some time in Town with us, enjoying yourself."

"But why?"

"Ah, I understand your confusion. You wonder why Carde suggested the visit, not that my daughter would not have thought of it herself, to repay your gracious hospitality. Isn't that right, poppet?"

Lady Lucinda looked as if she wanted to throw something out the window. Something like her father. But she pasted another smile on her face and said, "His Grace is correct, as always."

The duke beamed at both of them. "Lord Carde seeks your happiness out of kinship, Miss Sloane."

"But I am not truly related."

The duke also chose to ignore rough spots along his chosen path. "A very important sentiment, that. Why, England's greatness is based on the aristocracy looking out for the lesser people. That is why we have not fallen into chaos like the French. It goes with the title, don't you know, feeling responsible for one's dependents."

"But I am not his—"

"He feels that he has neglected your welfare for too long."

"Do not think that he means anything romantic by

it, Eleanor," Lady Lucinda quickly warned, "for Lord Carde swears otherwise."

"That's right. Wouldn't want to get your hopes up, eh?"

Nell had no hopes there. If Alex cared for her at all, he would not be trying to send her away with people he did not care for himself. "I must admit that I am confused, but not just about Lord Carde's reasons for concocting this mad scheme. I shall speak to him later. But what has me stymied now is why you have invited me. It is not as if we were ever bosom bows, Lady Lucinda, merely correspondents. And you never invited me to your own come-out ball, although you boasted of the sad crush, with nearly a thousand of the beau monde in attendance."

Lady Lucinda waved her manicured hand in the air. "Oh, you were such a quiet, retiring little thing. You would not have known how to go on."

"Yet I am no more experienced in grand society than I was when fresh from the schoolroom, when I might have enjoyed dancing all night. I think I did not fit your definition of Quality then. You have not been here long enough to change your mind now. So I repeat: why?"

The duke *humph*ed a few times while he rubbed his leg and thought, which was in itself a telling statement. At last he said, "To pay you back for the invitation here, of course. And you and my Lucy might not have the same social standing, or the same social acumen, but you are both at your last prayers. That is, you both are on the lookout for a rich, handsome husband, no matter how much you claim otherwise. Lucy will be glad to have the company."

"I am to be Lady Lucinda's . . . companion?"

"A paid employee? Not at all. You'll be our guest. Eager to have you we are, my dear."

Nell was shaking her head.

So was Lady Lucinda. "Cut line, papa. She isn't going to believe you. I wouldn't. He's paying us, Eleanor. Carde has some skewed sense of chivalry toward you, and we are the beneficiaries. He needs to appease his conscience. We need the money. And Lord knows you need a new wardrobe, a dusting of town bronze, and a husband to get you out of this backward borough."

"He is paying you to take me to London?" Nell looked toward His Grace, who had the grace to study his swollen leg.

"Afraid so. But he is paying a lot."

And that was supposed to make Nell feel better?

CHAPTER FIFTEEN

"Fixing this is a forlorn hope."

Whap! The broken shepherdess bounced off Alex's chest, a broad enough target at any rate, but one Nell could not miss from inches away.

"Finding Lizbeth's daughter might be a forlorn hope."

Whap! The figurine's head bounced off his chest.

"But I . . . *I* am not a forlorn hope!" Nell's now empty palm connected with Alex's cheek.

The earl had risen when Nell marched into the room after a brief knock. He'd dropped a fistful of papers onto the desk in his sitting room and adjusted his spectacles on his nose. Now he stepped back behind the desk for safety and straightened the glasses again, once his head stopped ringing.

"I take it you do not wish to go to London?"

"Since when do my wishes matter? Since when has anyone consulted me about what I want?" Nell shook her fist at him, not that she had ever punched anyone in her life, except that day when Lord Carde arrived and she thought he was attacking her aunt. She had never slapped anyone either. She had never been so mad, though. "Since when has anyone treated me as an adult?"

"Children do not get invited to London to partake of balls and the opera."

"Neither do undistinguished country nobodies!"

He picked up the pieces of china from the floor and tried to fit them together. "They do if they have the right connections."

"Like blackmailing dukes with offers of canceling their debts and financing their frivolous lives? That is your connection, not mine."

"You are right."

"How much did you have to pay to—I am right?"

"Yes, I doubt the figurine can be repaired, even if you found the missing arm. I would apologize if I could think how I was at fault for its damage."

"I suspect Lady Lucinda will blame that on the dog, anyway. You are at fault for enough, however. How could you make plans for me with those people as if my future is yours to decide?"

"I thought you liked them. You were the one who invited Apston and his daughter here."

"For you! I thought Lady Lucinda was your future bride."

"So you were making plans for me, were you not, while I was lying in a fevered state?"

"That is not the same and you know it. I was acting in good faith, and you were not conscious enough to tell me otherwise. I did not ride up to your front door like some foreign potentate, then try to take over your affairs. It was you who started giving orders as soon as you were awake, issuing commands, ruling the house as if you owned the place."

"Actually, he does."

Nell spun around to see a small, elderly gentleman standing behind her, next to the door. He was dressed in well-tailored black, and had a shock of snow-white hair and a thick white moustache. If she could have picked a grandfather, he would have looked like this. If she could have picked a stranger to throw a tantrum in front of, he would not have looked so compassionate.

Embarrassed, Nell dropped a hasty curtsy. "My apologies, sir. I did not see you standing there. I don't usually— He what?"

The gentleman bowed, fluttering a sheaf of papers in his hand. "He does own Ambeaux Cottage. The deed was part of the previous Lady Carde's marriage settlements, you see, becoming effective at the death of Gerard Ambeaux, her father."

"My uncle."

The man nodded. "At the countess's death, the property passed into the Endicott family holdings, which now belong to—"

"You snake! You slime! You scurvy sneak!" Nell had turned and was addressing the earl, of course, not the older man. "Why did you never tell me?"

Alex put the shepherdess pieces closer to his side of the desk. To be safe, he moved the inkwell, the penknife, and the decanter of wine, although the latter was looking better by the minute. "The reason I never told you should be self-explanatory, cousin, seeing how angry you are now."

Nell shook her head in disgust. "You truly are a coward, then."

"I never suggested otherwise. But I did want to save you this awkwardness. Ambeaux Cottage is your home, not mine. Besides, I had to speak to Mr. Silbiger to be certain of the facts."

He made the formal introduction to the solicitor, which Nell acknowledged politely enough, considering her world was shattering as badly as the china shepherdess. She gratefully sank onto the chair Mr. Silbiger pulled closer to the desk for her. "You own Ambeaux Cottage?"

"Do not look so stricken. I have owned it any time these past thirteen years, and I never meant to take possession or throw you out. Rightfully the estate should have gone to Lottie anyway, as her mother's heir."

"But she was never found."

"So I left the property in your brother's care, believing he would manage it carefully, in exchange for living here. I was mistaken, it appears."

"Phelan knew?"

"Of course he knew. He was not a child like I was when the wills were read. Your uncle left him the shipyard and its earnings, nothing else. The Ambeaux estate was to provide your aunt for her lifetime, then Lizbeth and her children."

"And your brother sent me reports every year," Mr. Silbiger added, "for the earl's records. Which Mr. Sloane would not do, naturally, if he thought he owned Ambeaux Cottage. I tried to warn his lordship that the estate never seemed to show a proper balance."

"Which I felt was Phelan's affair, not mine. I never expected income from the property, just that it remain self-sufficient. Any profits were always reinvested in the land or used to maintain this house and your comforts. That was what I believed, at any rate. I did not mean to interfere, I tell you. This was your home. It still is."

"But you own it."

"I cannot change that. Nor can I turn the deed over to you, in case my half-sister is ever found."

Mr. Silbiger was shaking his head. "We have looked for over a decade, with nary a clue."

"I am not ready to give up."

Nell rubbed at her forehead. "If you were not claiming the house as yours, why were you ready to send me away?"

"I was not sending you away, dash it. I was—"

Mr. Silbiger cleared his throat. "I'll let you two young people continue this discussion in private. I believe Redfern mentioned luncheon. I shall accept the kind invitation and straighten out these papers at the same time." He bowed and left Alex and Nell alone.

"Why not?" she asked the badly painted picture of Lizbeth on the wall. Nell remembered sitting for the portrait in one of her cousin's old gowns from the attics so Phelan could get the coloring right. "I am already ruined."

"You are not ruined!"

"I have been living in a bachelor's residence for my entire adult life. What do you think people will say?"

"That you were keeping household for your brother, with your aunt in attendance. That you took in a wounded kinsman and cared for him, with your aunt in attendance."

"Everyone knows that Sir Walter Raleigh is in attendance when my aunt is!"

"Nevertheless, your reputation is unblemished. You have the blessings of a duke, for heaven's sake, his titled cousin, and his daughter. They would not deign to accept the invitation of a hostess with suspected scruples."

"They would accept an invitation to skate on the River Styx if they thought you might be there. Which you might well be someday, dastard that you are."

"Dash it, Nell, I did nothing wrong!"

"You never told me I was a charity case! Here I thought my brother scrimped to pay for my education out of his own pocket, but it was you all along."

"No, that was your uncle's money and his wishes. Funds were to be set aside for your schooling. When Mr. Silbiger comes back he can show you Ambeaux's will."

"And a dowry?"

"It was not mentioned, likely because you were so young at the time, and he did not expect to die so soon. He would have expected his wife to provide for you from her own inheritance, since you were her niece. And Lizbeth would have, afterward. The money was there, but now it is not. I shall replace it, of course."

"Never!"

"I must. It was my own intransigence that let the situation evolve. I could not be bothered with looking after yet another piece of property, so I let the trustees and the lawyers and your brother look after this one."

"No," Nell said, finality in her voice. "You must make improvements to the tenant farms, because they are yours. The people have suffered through your neglect, unknowing as it was, but I am not your responsibility. Nor have I ever suffered or wanted for anything. You shall not ease your conscience by paying the duke and his daughter to find me a husband, because I never was your dependent. If I cannot help my brother at the shipyard, I shall go into service."

Alex jumped to his feet and leaned over the desk,

his arms on the papers in front of him. "We have no idea what your brother is doing at that shipyard, and I refuse to allow you to go into trade or find a position."

Nell was not intimidated. "You forget that I am of age. You have no choice."

He did not, but Alex was not going to concede. She was wrong; he was the head of her family whether she acknowledged it or not. As the head, the chieftain of his little clan, everyone connected to the earldom was his responsibility. What, should he let his cousin—his stepmother's cousin, to be precise—go out to be a companion or a governess? Everyone knew how such women were treated, with disrespect and disdain. They were subject to their mistresses' whims and their masters' lechery. Furthermore, they were forever knocking on poverty's door, praying for a pension for their old age. No, he would not see his Nell turned into a subservient, self-effacing menial or stay under her brother's thumb. He was not pleased with the potsherd-tossing termagant, but at least her spirit was not broken.

He might not have control of Nell's destiny, but he did have the upper hand. "What about your Aunt Hazel?" he asked. "Shall she go into service too?"

Nell had no answer to that. Azeline Ambeaux was far too elderly to seek a position, and who would hire her for anything but minding a graveyard? Perhaps Alex would let Aunt Hazel stay on here, but how could Nell leave the old dear alone, with half the village ready to burn her at the stake and the other half ready to lock her up in an asylum?

While Nell was thinking, twisting her handkerchief into a wad, Alex was toying with the pieces of the statue. He kept trying to balance the head on the shepherdess's neck but it kept falling off. Nell could sympathize . . . with the china doll, not the clumsy oaf sitting across from her.

"What's so bad about London, anyway?" he asked. "Most women would leap at the chance to go there."

"I am not most women."

He could swear to that. If she were, his nerves would not be as knotted as her handkerchief. "You do not like to shop?"

"I might, if I had the funds. I might enjoy seeing the famous sights of London, if I had the choosing."

"You would like spending time with your friends there, would you not?"

"Lady Lucinda?" Nell laughed. "She is no friend. Surely you understand that now. I certainly do. Your presence brought her here, and your money brought her to issue the invitation."

"What about your other schoolmates? They would welcome you."

"The ones who became grand London ladies, like Lady Lucinda? Why should they? I do not belong in their society. Most of them tolerated me at school because they had to, nothing more. The girls who were kind to me have married and scattered across the country to raise their families." If Nell was jealous, she kept the envy from her voice. "I have no one in the city I call friend."

"The women in town will accept you. Lady Lucinda can easily see that they do, which is why I thought she was perfect as your sponsor."

"My sponsor for what? For introductions to gentlemen who might wed me for the dowry you shall provide? I would rather find a position at a school than be used so. Or help my brother at the shipyard: I can learn to manage the accounts."

"If his ledgers are anything like the ones for the estate, he needs more than a beginning bookkeeper. But I think you have not given the real reason why you do not want to go to London. Yes, I should have consulted with you first, but the idea arose during my conversation with the duke just this morning, then Mr. Silbiger arrived. And yes, Lady Lucinda is selfish, self-serving, and snobbish. But you could still go and meet people your own age and see the sights. I think you are refusing because you are afraid."

She laughed. "Nay, you are the coward. I live in a haunted house, remember?"

"You do not believe in ghosts any more than I do."

"Yet when André—that is Aunt Hazel's childhood sweetheart, or was—says that it is going to rain, I have the maids bring in the laundry."

"Those are an old woman's aching bones speaking, not spirits from the afterlife. I don't suppose André was a Captain Sharp, was he? A card cheat? Your aunt plays prodigiously well for an elderly lady."

"I believe she learned to deal from the bottom from one of the grooms we used to employ. Few people play cards with her anymore."

"I can well imagine why. But that is all beside the point. I still maintain that it is fear keeping you from the holiday you so richly deserve and the life you would have led if Lizbeth had lived. I think you are worried that you won't find partners at the balls, that the women will turn their backs on you, that your clothes will not be stylish enough or your curtsy not deep enough."

"My curtsy is perfect, thanks to that expensive school for young ladies."

He flashed a quick grin at what she did not rebut. "I think you are afraid of being lost and alone in the metropolis. But you will not be facing the *ton* all alone. Madame Ambeaux can go too."

"What, to meet the mad king and chat about her friend Bess? That is Queen Elizabeth, of course."

Alex set the broken statue to the side of his desk. "I will not leave you to fend for yourself."

"You? The one who runs from women and entanglements? The one who disappears rather than face a confrontation? Who does not admit owning a house if he thinks someone will mind?" Nell snapped her fingers. "So much for your protection. Besides, you let your brother put a frog down my back."

"But not the snake."

"So you have the entire London trip arranged in your mind?"

Alex nodded. He had a great deal more arranged in his mind, once he found out if Nell could adjust to city life, if she could be happy in his world. He was not pressing his luck yet, though. A broken shepherdess was bad enough. Broken dreams . . .

"Let me see." Nell was now pulling at the hem of her handkerchief, unraveling the fabric while she kept her gaze locked on Alex, as if he were a spider about to crawl under the furniture. "You have planned how you will return to London, while still keeping out of Lady Lucinda's net, of course. You will pay my bills, which no one must know lest they think I am your, ah, ladybird. And you will see that I am accepted at the right parties, even if you have to bribe hostesses for the invitations. You will likely beg your friends to dance with me, blackmail some unfortunate gentlemen to drive me to the park, browbeat the duke into hiring a box at the opera. Have I left anything out?"

Not really, except that Alex intended to dance with

her and be the one driving her in the park, and he already owned a box at the opera. "That is not how it will be. As soon as gentlemen see you, they will seek their own introductions, issue their own invitations. And not simply for your dowry. You'll find that not every gentleman, especially in town, needs to wed a wealthy bride. And there are those who do not wish to marry at all but merely like to dance with a pretty girl. There is nothing wrong with simply enjoying oneself, is there? You will. I promise. You have to trust me about that, Nell."

"How can I trust you? You let me live a lie all these years."

"I could not know that Phelan hid the truth about the house and the money! Blame your buffle-headed brother, rather. Find him and ask what the devil he is about."

"That is precisely what I intend to do," Nell said, "as soon as you and your noble guests have left. He never stays away long, and someone must know where he is."

Alex had to revise his plans in a hurry. "If you will not go to London with Lady Lucinda and her father, I am staying too. I wish to speak to Phelan myself. And I shall have to do something about the neglected farms, it seems. Hire a competent land steward at the least."

"The tenants will be glad. And you will be glad to know that you are free of my company. If you do not depart with the ducal party, my aunt and I shall move to the inn rather than jeopardize my reputation any further, or letting anyone think you have compromised it. We shall all be safer that way."

He would be deuced lonely that way. Alex might

have to accept a change in plans, but he would not accept losing Nell's company altogether. "That is absurd. Your aunt is an entirely respectable chaperone."

Nell raised one eyebrow.

"Very well, not entirely respectable, but she does come with enough other, ah, souls to satisfy the highest sticklers. If anyone does have to leave, if there is the slightest whisper of gossip, I will be the one to move into the village until I conclude my business here. And, no, do not rip up at me about this being my home. I told you it is not and never shall be as long as you or your brother or your aunt have need of it."

"My brother has need of me. That is what you left out of your plans for my future. Fear is not keeping me from going to London, my own sense of responsibility is. Phelan has always been troubled. If he is in despair, if he has done something wrong, then he needs his family at his side. You have honor. So do I. You feel you have unpaid debts. So do I. You have a brother."

"For whom I would walk through fire." He nodded. "Very well. We shall both stay to speak to Phelan." He tidied a stack of papers in front of him. "Uh, who gets to tell the duke and his daughter that you won't be accepting their invitation to go to London with them?"

"That you won't be paying them, you mean? That His Grace has to find another way of redeeming his gambling vouchers, and Lady Lucinda has to find another way of clinging to your side? I would guess that the person who made the arrangements has to be the one to shatter their hopes." She smiled sweetly. "Or you could always turn tail and run away again."

"I am not quite that craven."

"I am glad to hear that, for I shall expect you downstairs for dinner this evening. If you are well enough to be busy about my affairs, you are well enough to entertain your guests."

"They are not my—"

"Do you not own the house? Shall you not sit at the head of the table? Are you not the reason these people are here? I might have mistakenly invited them, although I never counted on the duke and his secretary, but they are your guests, all right. Oh, and the vicar is coming to dinner, and a few others who wish to meet you. They will likely ask for a new roof for the church, an additional teacher for the school, your opinions on closing lands for hunting, that kind of thing."

Alex tried not to groan at the idea. Then again, if he groaned loudly enough, perhaps Nell would take pity on him and let him have a tray in his room.

Nell smiled again, maliciously, Alex thought. "Mr. Stives has offered to help Redfern serve, so no one can fetch your dinner upstairs." She stepped toward the door. "We meet in the parlor an hour before dinner. That gives you plenty of time to speak with Lady Lucinda and the duke."

He tipped his head, indicating surrender. "I will speak with His Grace and his gorgon. And I will chat with your local luminaries. I will stay to talk with your brother. But afterward, you and I, Miss Eleanor Sloane of Ambeaux Cottage, will speak about going to London."

Nell took two angry steps closer to the desk and pounded her fist on its surface. "I am not going to London as your act of charity." The head of the shepherdess rolled onto the floor. "Never."

Alex smiled.

CHAPTER SIXTEEN

Nell was *not* running away. She was avoiding unpleasantness, perhaps, but she was walking unhurriedly out of the house. Lord Carde's house.

She even took the time to find Mr. Silbiger in the morning room and invite the solicitor to that evening's dinner. Lord Carde's solicitor.

Before reaching the door, she remembered to tell Redfern to rearrange the seating chart, warn Cook of the added guest, and go to the devil. The sepulchral old butler had known and not told her. Why should he? He was Lord Carde's employee.

They had all conspired against her: family, friend, servant. She had to wonder about Aunt Hazel. Then again, one always had to wonder about Aunt Hazel. Surely she would have known about Uncle Ambeaux's will, since he was her own brother. If he had not told her in life, he might have mentioned it after. Maybe that was why Aunt Hazel and Phelan never seemed to rub along well together. Neither had ever discussed their antipathy, so Nell was unsure.

Aunt Hazel could be forgiven for her lapse. The

old woman was clearly unhampered by truth, logic, or reality. But Phelan? Perhaps he was as irrational as Aunt Hazel, deluding himself as well as Nell and the neighbors, puffing up his own consequence as landed gentry. He must have believed he owned the land, to have treated it and the tenants so cavalierly. Either that or he thought he would never be caught out in the lie, with Alex so far away. Nell did not know her brother's reasoning.

She felt as if she did not know anything anymore, not whom to trust, not what to do. Her world had been small and narrow for so long; now it was the edge of a vast cavern that was waiting to swallow her. Was there such a thing as mental vertigo? Nell felt dizzy and disoriented, teetering on the edge.

Her home was not hers. Her brother was a thief. Her childhood idol had grown into a manipulative liar, and was lily-livered, to boot. He considered her a poor relation to be sent away, married off, foisted onto some other fool. That same man, the one she was more than halfway in love with, did not want her. Oh, no. He might smile at her like a friend, and talk with her like a companion, and hold her hand a bit too long like a lover, but he did not want silly little Nelly Sloane, and he never would. He was ready to bribe a needy lordling into taking her to get her out of his own life. That was how it seemed, anyway.

Well, Nell might have been halfway in love with Alex, more than half, if she was honest—Heaven knew one of them ought to be—but that was before today. Just the memory of his last smile, the sparkle in his eyes, the unspoken request to share the humor, share the warmth, made her want to throw herself into his arms. Yesterday she might have.

She would refuse to love him, that's what she'd do,

the same as she had refused to go to London as his dependent. Of course, choosing to love, or not, was not quite the same as choosing a new gown or one's traveling companions, but she would do it. One only needed willpower and restraint, Nell told herself—that and the fear of having one's heart trampled under his lordship's champagne-polished boots. She and the earl were not equals. Today he'd shown they were not friends. They would never be lovers. Nell would have to be as insane as the rest of her relatives to believe in any other future, in any other dream.

So as soon as she was out of sight of the house, Nell did run. She picked up her skirts and raced as fast as she could, trying to outdistance her despair and disappointment. She ran until she was breathless, to find the only soul she could trust, the one who would love her whether or not she had a dowry, a title, or fine connections, the one who would never lie to her or break her heart.

Honk.

Taking a goose into the village—for any reason other than selling it for someone's supper—was not, perhaps, Nell's wisest decision of the day.

Neither was inviting Sir Chauncy Gaines to the dinner party, but she did that too. Alex did not seem to like his former acquaintance, which was justification enough in Nell's current mood.

Wellesley stood on the driver's bench of the donkey cart as if he were king of the dung heap. Sir Chauncy strutted through Kingston Upon Hull as if he were in Hyde Park. According to Alex, the baronet's pockets were perpetually empty. According to Alex, the town beau was to be forbidden entry to Ambeaux Cottage.

Alex accorded himself altogether too much author-

ity. He owned the house, but had he not said she was
to consider it her home as long as she wished? In that
case she could invite whatever guests pleased her, and
however many it took so she did not have to speak
with the overbearing, underhanded oaf. The oaf, of
course, was the man she would not love, not Sir
Chauncy, whom she could not love. The preening,
posturing baronet was merely a jackadandy, not a
jackal.

Sir Chauncy had been idling in the village awaiting
just such a lucky encounter. He had heard that Apston
and his daughter were visiting at Ambeaux Cottage;
he had not heard that the duke's financial ship was
leaking, much less near to sinking. One would never
guess from Lady Lucinda's wardrobe or bearing, nor
from the duke's lofty attitude. Sir Chauncy never
gamed with the man, not traveling in those highest of
social circles, so he never saw His Grace lose. The
duke's creditors, noblemen like Lord Carde, were not
ones to gossip. As far as the baronet was concerned,
therefore, Lady Lucinda Applegate was a rich plum,
ripe for the picking.

Of course the duke's daughter would not give Sir
Chauncy the time of day in London, but here in the
country, with no elegant company or sophisticated
conversation at hand, she might spare him a glance.
Or a chance.

Sir Chauncy discounted Lord Carde. The man was
injured and uninterested, besides. If the sober-sided
earl had wanted the Applegate heiress, he could have
had her for the asking in town. Rumor had it Carde
could have had any number of willing females. And
what woman would not be willing to become a
wealthy countess?

Lady Lucinda might be here at Ambeaux Cottage,

but Sir Chauncy would wager she was not here at Carde's invitation. In fact, the baronet was betting his health on the earl's lack of interest in the heiress. Carde might be injured now, but he had a steady hand and a deadly aim with his pistols at Manton's shooting gallery. A pursuit of this lady, however, could not be considered poaching on the other man's preserves.

The same could not quite be said for the other reason Sir Chauncy was enjoying the dubious pleasures of Kingston Upon Hull. More than the opportunity to encounter Lady Lucinda in the village, where she was certain to take a look at the paltry shops, was keeping the baronet at The King's Arms inn and out of the pretty barmaid's willing arms. Being turned away from his friend's bedside, away from Ambeaux Cottage, away from Miss Sloane, had piqued the baronet's interest as no rustic miss with no fortune could. She was a taking little thing, and if he could take Carde down a peg or two, so much the better. If he could not win the heiress's favor, perhaps he could win a kiss from the commoner . . . before Carde recovered enough to care.

Forbidden fruit being that much sweeter, Sir Chauncy plucked a raspberry tart from a tray in the inn's common room, where he was seated at the table next to the window. He hurried out and tossed bits of the pastry to the goose, which was terrorizing the nearby horses and deafening passersby.

By the time Miss Sloane came out of the apothecary with a paper sack in her hand, the goose was eating out of his.

"Why, how clever of you!" she said.

Sir Chauncy thought so, too, even if he had to toss

his goose-picked gloves into the dustbin. "Dinner? I would be delighted."

Alex was not ready to give up. Nell deserved a better life, whether she wished it or not, whether he was beside her or not. Her show of temper did not give him a disgust of her, either. Rather, he was glad she was not one of the simpering peahens who agreed with everything a gentleman said. If he wanted an echo, he would buy a parrot.

He wanted a wife he could talk to, listen to, hold a rational conversation with. He wanted a woman who would help him make the myriad decisions an earldom required. He wanted to admire his wife's mind as well as her body.

More and more, he wanted Nell, whose slim body, incidentally, intrigued him far more than his mistress's lush charms ever had.

Of course Nell hated him today—his former mistress likely did also—but that only made things more of a challenge. Now he had only to overcome her fear of the city and society, her devotion to her brother, and her distrust of himself. He was a rich man, an earl, a prize on the marriage market, and a bulldog when he set his mind to something. He could win back Nell's regard.

After he got rid of Lady Lucinda and her father.

"Remember to duck," Stives advised. "You cannot afford any more bumps and bruises. I would tell milord to take his glasses off, but then you could not see what is coming."

"I suggest a stroll in Madame Ambeaux's garden," said Redfern, who never went out of doors. "There is less to throw."

"Rocks and dirt and worse," the valet said in horror, giving a hasty swipe of the polishing cloth to Alex's already gleaming boots. "Think of milord's wardrobe."

Mr. Silbiger, who was back in Alex's sitting room with his files and papers, entered the discussion. "Tell them over tea, with Madame Ambeaux, Lady Haverhill, Mr. Peabody, and the servants present. No lady would so far forget herself as to cause a scene in front of so many people."

Stives nodded. "And His Grace will not cry in public."

In the end, as usual, Alex took the path of least discomfort. He sent a note.

By the time Nell returned to the house, Sir Chauncy incongruously, and hopefully incognito, riding his showy chestnut gelding alongside the humble donkey cart, Lady Lucinda's maid was reduced to whimpers, a carved wooden whatnot box was reduced to splinters, and Mr. Peabody's meticulously parted and pomaded hair was reduced to a tangled thatch as he prepared for departure.

"So soon?" Nell asked Lady Lucinda, after seeing the baronet led off by a disapproving Redfern. Redfern was always disapproving, so Nell ignored his pale-eyed glare. She could not ignore the scattered clothes and opened trunks in Lady Lucinda's chamber, nor the maid cowering in the corner. "But you have just arrived. Why, I thought we would attend the village assembly this Friday, and visit the church and the shops. There is a pretty view of the village from Munch's Hill, where I thought we might go sketching. And Mrs. Mahoney has invited us all to tea tomorrow afternoon."

The look Lady Lucinda gave Nell could have frozen Mrs. Mahoney's tea into a block of ice, and Mrs. Mahoney as well. "Two days in the country is a day and a half too long," the lady declared. "I wished to leave this afternoon, but father insisted we could not reach an acceptable inn before nightfall."

"I am sorry."

"Oh, I'd wager you are. Now you have the earl all to yourself."

Nell glanced at the maid, who took the opportunity to bob a curtsy and flee the room. "I'll fetch some tissue for wrapping, miss," Browne whispered to Nell as she sidled out the door.

Nell picked up a feathered bonnet before Lady Lucinda could step on it in her furious tossing of garments into the cases. "I was hoping he would go with you."

"You expect me to believe that?" Lady Lucinda threw a pair of satin slippers toward the trunk . . . and toward Nell.

Nell caught the shoes and placed them carefully beside the nearest trunk, waiting for the maid to return with the paper, if she ever returned at all. "I expect you shall believe what you wish. But not everyone is set on snaring the poor man, you know."

"Poor man? 'Poor,' did you say? You are even more of a fool than I thought. First you refuse to encourage our Mr. Peabody, who is the most respectable *parti* you can hope for. Then you turn down the chance of a lifetime to go to London. But pitying 'poor' Carde? That is by far the most rattle-brained of all. Why, it is as ridiculous as your setting your sights on him."

Nell folded a shawl that was wadded into a ball in the trunk. "I have not set my sights on him, I tell you. Even if he would deign to notice me, which we both know is indeed absurd, Lord Carde is not what I admire in a gentleman."

"Granted he wears those ugly spectacles and his nose is too large"—Lady Lucinda raised her own in the air—"but what on earth could a woman like you seek in a man that the earl does not possess?" Lady Lucinda stopped pulling clothes from the wardrobe as if she truly wanted to hear Nell's answer.

"He lacks courage." Nell had heard from Redfern about the note Alex had sent rather than confronting the duke and his daughter in person. "And honesty."

Lady Lucinda started emptying her drawers. "Faugh. Those will not buy you jewels or a new carriage. You always were a mousy little thing, Eleanor. I never realized you were a hopeless idealist too. It is you I pity, then." She pulled out a neatly folded pile of lace-edged shifts and tossed them in Nell's direction so they needed to be folded again. "No man is honest, especially if he wants something a woman has." She raised her carefully plucked black eyebrows. "I assume even you know what that is."

At Nell's nod, Lady Lucinda went on: "And all men are cowards when it comes to marriage."

"Surely not, since so many of them enter into wedlock."

"Only when they are forced to it. Or cannot get what they desire otherwise, be it an heir or a quick tumble."

Lucinda scattered clothing onto the floor next to the trunk. Nell wished she could flee like the poor maid rather than listen to the duke's daughter's diatribe, but she could not be so rude. She started to match pairs of gloves and stockings instead, admiring the silky fabric and soft leather if she could not admire her guest's opinions.

Lady Lucinda waved a garter in the air before lobbing it at Nell. "Brave men die young, besides. They go off to the wars, or engage in duels or reckless wagers. The ones who are left are spineless. Of course there is much to be said for finding an older husband, since a wealthy widow has many more options than a single lady. But that is for the future. I have one more night in this desolate place, then I can return to the parties and pleasures of London." She threw the other garter. "I only hope you do not come to regret your lack-witted decision to stay here."

Nell's only regret was that she had to attend the dinner that night. A headache might be in order, but she would not give Alex the satisfaction of thinking she was as cowardly as he was.

Nell's presence really did not matter anyway, for she became invisible. Lady Lucinda wore another low-cut gown, another paste jewel between her breasts, and her chilliest smile. No matter. She was a titled lady, the daughter of a duke who had seats in Parliament to fill, church livings to dole out, and who knew how many thousands of pounds. All of Nell's supposed suitors gathered around Lady Lucinda like ants on a rotten strawberry. The vicar, Mr. Pensworth, Sir Chauncy, even Mr. Peabody jostled each other aside to bring her a glass of wine or a biscuit. And Alex wanted her to go to London in Lady Lucinda's shadow? Nell thought she would disappear altogether then.

He, she noted, was not in the lady's court in the parlor before dinner. He was trying to make conversation with Lady Haverhill, an uphill job if ever there was one.

When they went into the dining room, Nell had the duke on her right hand. He spent the fish course trying to convince her to go to London after all. Then he became despondent, despite the fine meal, when he realized that card parties, masquerades and balls held no allure for Nell. After a glass or two more of wine— far more than he should have had with his condition— His Grace thought he might work on Aunt Hazel, on his other side.

"Think of the fun you could have in town," he told her. "You can visit with your friends there."

"Oh, I do not think my friends can go."

His Grace meant friends among the emigré population, but he was willing to be accommodating, if it won him Carde's money. "Of course your friends can go. We have nothing but room at the town house." And nothing but covers on the wings they could not afford to keep heated. "And we can hire another carriage to get everyone to London."

Aunt Hazel laughed, a high girlish giggle. "Oh, my friends do not take up bedchambers or coach seats." She passed him a platter of eels in aspic. "I think they are happier here. And I know they do not like to travel." She giggled again, so Nell told Redfern to stop filling her aunt's glass, as well as the duke's.

Looking around at her disparate guests, Nell thought that Mrs. Mallory from the village would have been an excellent choice for the vicar, if he could take his eyes from Lady Lucinda's décolletage. Dressed in her finest, which might have been sack cloth for all the notice the gentlemen took of her or her gown, the teachers would make Squire Pensworth a fine wife too, since she was not afraid of his sons. Pensworth was leaning so far across the table to catch Lady Lucinda's eye, though, that his neckcloth trailed through the mock turtle soup.

Sir Chauncy sat beside the duke's Diamond. He

barely touched his meal, offering her morsels and bon mots.

Mr. Peabody did not eat much either. Nell thought the food must not have been to the secretary's taste, for he looked as if he'd swallowed sour milk. He was fastidiously dressed again, but his mouth was pursed as tightly as his hair was parted.

Mr. Silbiger sat next to Lady Haverhill.

"I am a solicitor, madam."

"Yam and asparagus? No thank you. They give me wind."

Alex sat at the head of the table, of course. Nell could not see him around the floral arrangement she had placed on the center of the table for just that reason. She knew he was looking as handsome as the devil himself, with his dark curls combed over the small sticking plaster on his head. Except for the sling made out of black silk, he was dressed as elegantly as any London gentleman, with snowy white linen at his throat and a white marcella waistcoat under his dark jacket. Nell much preferred the earl's somber fashion to Sir Chauncy's more florid one, with yellow embroidered butterflies flapping under his puce-colored coat. The butterflies and the baronet were leaning toward Lady Lucinda, thank goodness. And thank Redfern for bringing the last course, finally.

This had to be the longest meal in memory, Alex thought, forgetting about the endless hours of one of Prinny's feasts. Lady Haverhill made no sense whatsoever, and Lady Lucinda made him ill with her haughty posturing. And he could not see Nell from where he sat, not around the huge centerpiece, damn it.

From gathering in the parlor before dinner, he knew she was looking lovely, almost ethereal in a pink gown trimmed with a bit of white lace to draw the eye to her smooth, softly swelling bosom. Someone, most likely Lady Lucinda's maid, had gathered her hair into a more fashionable topknot, with golden tendrils trailing along her rosy cheeks. Lud, he would skip the meal altogether for the chance to bring a blush to that sun-kissed skin, to touch one of those bright curls, to make Nell smile at him again.

Instead he had to suffer through the dinner, staring at flowers. Afterward, Lady Lucinda offered—hah! She insisted on it, trying to put Nell to shame for her own lack of talent—to entertain the company with a musical presentation. Lady Lucinda sang, exquisitely, while she accompanied herself, expertly, on the pianoforte, endlessly. Alex volunteered to turn her pages rather than see the male guests get into a fistfight over the honor.

The villagers went home, Lady Haverhill went to bed, the duke and Aunt Hazel played at cards, and Nell hid a yawn behind her hand. Sir Chauncy added his baritone in a duet, Mr. Peabody bobbed his head in time with the music, and Alex yawned. He did not try to hide it, not with one hand turning pages and the other in a sling.

Finally Redfern wheeled in the tea tray. Sir Chauncy was forced to leave afterward, but with a promise of a dance at the next ball. Mr. Peabody went to complete the packing, and Aunt Hazel and the duke argued over who cheated whom, on their way up the stairs.

Nell did not know what to do: leave Lady Lucinda and Alex alone, or wait where she was. Lady Lucinda's piercing glance told her she was an unwelcome chaperone, but Nell had promised to protect Alex, so she waited. And waited. Lucinda kept finding one more swallow of tea in her cup, one more piece of music to look over, one more scrap of town gossip to relate to Alex, to exclude Nell.

Finally Lady Lucinda yawned. She gave them both black looks, but gave up and left. She did not throw anything but mental daggers on her way out.

Nell was half asleep, the hour being long past her usual bedtime, after a trying day. "Good night, my lord."

Alex took her hand as she passed him. "Thank you, cousin."

"For what? Not leaving you alone to face Lucinda's wrath?"

"No, for a lovely dinner." His lips twitched. "You have a great career ahead of you as a fine hostess."

"And you might have had a great career ahead of you on the stage if you could say those lines without smiling. It was dreadful."

Alex laughed outright. "The worst I ever sat through."

Nell had to smile too. "*Now* you choose to be honest?"

CHAPTER SEVENTEEN

They were laughing when Lady Lucinda returned to the drawing room. Nell brushed a tear from her eye and Alex clutched his aching ribs.

"I forgot my fan," she said.

They all knew the woman had taken her fan with her, for Alex had handed it to her when she left. She'd hoped to find Alex alone, of course. At the least, she hoped to bring a halt to any tête-à-tête between her hostess and her quarry. Despite all the evidence and all her other admirers, Lady Lucinda still believed Lord Carde was her best match. He would eventually see his way to the right choice, especially if he saw Eleanor for what she was, a drab little nobody.

Nell had worn her best gown that night. That was not saying much: It was pink, with faded ribbons and a lower than modish waistline. She had tried to freshen it up with some lace, incidentally lowering the neckline when she tacked on the trim. She thought her efforts were wasted, like garnishing an ordinary, everyday boiled potato. It was still a plain boiled potato.

She could not know that to Alex she looked like a wild strawberry, sweet and tart and tempting.

Nell thought Lady Lucinda was an exotic delight in smoky-gray silk with a dark green lace overskirt. She was the most beautiful, sophisticated woman ever to grace Ambeaux Cottage, except for Lizbeth, of course. Nell did not blame the gentlemen, or the servants, from ogling the dark-haired diamond.

Alex thought Lucinda looked a poisonous viper in the grass.

Whatever beauty she possessed was destroyed by her curled lip and flared nostrils. "You were wise not to go to London after all," she told Nell. "You would only embarrass yourself and me with such common manners."

"What, by laughing out loud?" Alex asked, instantly coming to Nell's defense. "That is not common at all, I grant you, but the rarest, most precious of things, a woman who truly enjoys herself." Then, before Lady Lucinda could loose more venom, he bowed and said, "I shall bid you farewell this evening, in case I am out when you depart. I have to finish my own business in the neighborhood, which is the reason I came here in the first place. I shall see you in London soon," he offered as a sop. "Unless you find you cannot be in charity with me again."

That was the stick. Lady Lucinda knew that if one word of this visit's events reached the gossip mills, Lord Carde would give her the cut direct. Her matrimonial prospects were dim enough without an eligible earl's disdain.

"Perhaps you will favor me with a waltz when we meet?" he offered. That was the carrot.

Redfern held the door for her as she glided out,

nodding regally as if granting a boon to some lowly petitioner. She ignored Nell entirely.

Redfern stayed by the open door, clearing his throat.

"Go to bed, old man," Alex told him. "We can douse the lights and lock the doors ourselves."

The butler cleared his throat again.

"If you are ill, Redfern, you must certainly get your rest."

The unnaturally pale old man stayed, staring at the portrait of Lizbeth over the mantel, one ghost staring at another.

Alex ignored the unsubtle hint. Instead he stepped closer to Nell and lowered his voice. "Have you found it in your heart to forgive me?"

"No, but I do beg your pardon for my childish behavior."

"What, laughing out loud? It felt good, despite my broken bones protesting."

"No, I apologize for this afternoon, for throwing things and shouting at you like a fishwife. It was not well done of me, and I am embarrassed for my own conduct." Nell looked over at the portrait too. "My cousin would be ashamed. Lizbeth was never other than the perfect lady."

"Perhaps she never faced such provocation. I must apologize also, although my intentions were good. I simply did not wish you to be made unhappy thinking you were dependent upon me."

She tipped her head. "Which I was and am."

"Dependent or unhappy?"

"Both, I suppose. I was used to being my brother's ward, despite reaching my majority. That is simply the way of the world for a single woman, to have her male relatives look after her welfare. I never questioned Phelan's right to that authority. But a near stranger

in control of my destiny? And to find that not only
has my own brother withheld the truth from me all
these years, but you had also? How could I not be
unhappy?"

"That was why I did not wish to tell you, and why
I wanted you to go to town to enjoy yourself. You
deserved it."

"Then you were not trying to marry me off, merely
to get rid of the responsibility for me?"

"Hell, no. That is, I wanted to give you the opportunity to make your own choices. If you chose to wed
some suitable gentleman, I would have rejoiced for
you." About as much as he rejoiced to discover his
shoulder was merely dislocated, not shattered. Then
again, rakes like Sir Chauncy or dodderers like Pensworth were not suitable for her anyway. "If you chose
merely to attend learned lectures and literary soirees,
that, too would have pleased me, if it pleased you."

Nell studied Alex's face now, as if she could find
the truth behind his spectacles. Honesty was never as
discernible as good humor, say, or hauteur, but Alex
did appear sincere. "I thank you, then, although you
must acknowledge that you did not inherit me along
with the house."

He smiled. "I would not have left such a precious
legacy unclaimed."

Nell could not decide if she was being complimented or being considered an heirloom, like Uncle
Ambeaux's watch. "You are not flirting with me, are
you?" she asked, her eyebrows knotted in suspicion.
"For that is as unnecessary as your trying to manage
my future."

Alex held up his good arm. "Heaven forfend," he
said with a grin that was nothing if not flirtatious. "I
am merely seconding your statement that I was not

named your trustee or guardian. And I do admit that I should not have tried to arrange a visit to town for you without your approval. I do think you should reconsider, however, as you truly would enjoy the holiday."

"Thank you. Perhaps I shall go to London someday."

"Pax, then?"

"Pax," she said, offering her hand.

He raised it to his mouth.

Redfern coughed.

Nell snatched her hand back, but not because of the old servant's interruption. "You *are* flirting with me!"

Alex gave her a lopsided smile. "Would that be so bad, then?"

It would be the very worst thing that could happen to Nell, she thought, when he returned to his life in London. He would go back, of course. Without her, unless . . . But he could not be serious, could he? She left.

Alex's hand felt empty without her smaller one in it. The room felt empty without her in it. His life felt empty. He could not go away and leave her here, could he?

Lady Lucinda tried to convince herself to be content with this night's work, despite the pair in the parlor. After seeing all those swains at Lucinda's feet, Lord Carde simply had to reconsider her suitability as his bride. He could not prefer nondescript and nondistinguished little Eleanor Sloane, could he?

Aunt Hazel decided to ask her former beau André about the duke and his intentions. André did not answer her, however. André could not be jealous, could he?

The duke was feeling better than he had in months. That last doctor could not be right about abstinence, could he?

And finally, when they had all tossed and turned in their beds until fitful sleep overtook the residents and guests and ghosts of Ambeaux Cottage, Phelan Sloane, Nell's older brother, made his way home. The Earl of Carde could not still be in the neighborhood after so long, could he?

Phelan had needed more than a few drams of Dutch courage to return to the house, but he needed money more. Carde would have been long gone, he decided. Or he would be at The King's Arms in the village. Phelan thought he could sleep here tonight, in his own bed, open the safe, and pack up everything valuable or salable early in the morning. He would be gone before any London swell had his morning shave.

He worried about Lizbeth, though. No, he worried about Eleanor. He'd take one of Lizbeth's portraits with him. But what about his sister? Phelan shook his head, trying to clear it. He'd already left Eleanor to fend off the earl. He'd have to leave her a little longer, that was all. He refused to think about being caught, being hauled off to prison. No, when he made his way—he knew not where—he'd send for his sister, that was what he would do. She'd manage until then. Liz— No, Nell always did.

When his coachman stopped at the front entrance of Ambeaux Cottage, Phelan staggered out of the carriage. The moonlight was bright enough to show him the steps and the door, so he sent the coach off to the stables and his valet around to the kitchen entrance to start heating hot water. A bath might be out of the question this late at night with so few servants other than the ghoulish Redfern around, but Phelan would not go to bed in all his traveling filth; nor would he let his employees see his inebriated state. Bad enough the coachman and the valet were grumbling about unpaid salaries and uncomfortable conditions. He needed their loyalty, if not their respect, for a few more days.

He waited until the carriage was out of sight, lifted the flask to his lips again, and fumbled for his key.

After a few tries, he unlatched the door. All was quiet. He had another drink, then lit the candle left in the hallway, after the fourth try. He held it up to Lizbeth's portrait. "I'll make it right," he told the painting. "I swear."

A tear rolled down Phelan's lined and ashen cheek as he made his slow way up the stairs, avoiding the creaking treads out of long habit. He staggered as quietly as he could past Nell's door. What, had she taken to snoring now? No, that sounded like a dog growling, which was impossible. He shrugged his thin shoulders and kept going. Aunt Hazel slept like the dead—or with the dead, he thought, snickering to himself—so he did not try to muffle his footsteps as he made his lurching way past the daft old woman's chamber. He tipped the flask up once more, letting the last drops trickle into his mouth. There would be a decanter in his bedroom at least.

The room was warm, the velvet bed hangings were closed, a fire's embers were still glowing in the hearth. Good old Nell must have kept his room ready for him every night, Phelan thought, swallowing the lump in his throat at leaving her behind. He had to. With no money and no home, how could he look after her? Carde would never throw her out. He hadn't in all these years, so she would have a roof over her head, which was more than Phelan could promise.

Perhaps she would wed Pensworth anyway. Yes, Nell would have left him for a home of her own anyway, Phelan decided, so he could stop feeling guilty over her. She would have gone sooner or later, just as Lizbeth had. Damn them all.

He found the decanter but no glass, so he drank out of the bottle, trying to hold his hands steady enough not to spill the brandy down his chin. No matter, his clothing was soiled anyway. He checked in the mirror. Yes, he had spots on his lapels and dust on his sleeves. Long strands of his thinning hair were straggling into his eyes. Worse, he could still smell his new doxy's cheap perfume on his neck cloth. Phelan set the bottle down and tore at the limp knot at his throat. No reminder of that light skirt should follow him here, to Lizbeth's house.

He stripped off his coat and his shirt, then hopped around, struggling to remove his boots. Phelan could not wait for his valet, not one second longer, not tainted with filth this way. Off went his boots, his breeches, his stockings and unmentionables. Where was the cursed man with his hot water, anyway? It was deuced cold in here, now that the fire was nearly out.

The spirits he'd swallowed were not enough to keep him warm, so Phelan finished the decanter, too. Then he decided to pull open the velvet bed hangings to let whatever warmth remained in the room heat the sheets and bedclothes.

"*Eeii!*" he shrieked. One of Aunt Hazel's friends was in his bed! In Uncle Ambeaux's old bed. "Uncle?" he cried, seeing the figure swathed in white, with a long white cap on its head. "Uncle Ambeaux?" He fell to the bed, sobbing, trying to grasp his dead uncle's hand. "Forgive me. Oh, please forgive me!"

The duke was having a lovely dream of soft curves and tender smiles. She reached her hand out to him and—"*Eeow!*" he howled as one of Madame Ambeaux's ghosts grabbed his hand. A bare-assed apparition, besides! She had said they were nearby, not naked! He screamed again and sprang from the bed.

The specter fell back, crying and moaning. His Grace picked up his cane from the nightstand and started beating it around the head. "Get back to your grave, sirrah! Begone, I say!"

"I'm sorry, so sorry!" Phelan moaned, his arms up to protect his head, leaving his bare flanks exposed.

The duke flailed at Phelan's legs and chest, beating the specter back toward the door. "Get out, foul, shroudless spirit! Get out!"

Phelan knelt, sobbing. His Grace, unthinking, hauled back his foot, his swollen, gouty foot, and kicked at the haunt.

"Yiii!" the duke screamed, falling over in excruciating pain, hitting his head on the nightstand.

Somewhere in the depths of Phelan's alcohol-soaked and agony-ridden mind the thought surfaced that ghosts did not have stiff canes or sharp kicks. He'd been terrified by a man, an old man. He looked down. At least he had not wet himself. He looked farther down. The old man, a complete stranger, lay still. Holy hell, now he'd gone and killed someone, on top of his other sins! *"Yiii!"*

He turned and fled. Phelan grabbed up his clothes and his boots but did not stop to put them on. He pulled open the door, hearing calls and queries from down the hall. Phelan had no idea who was in his house or why, only that he had to leave before they hanged him. He ran past doors that were already opening. "I am sorry," he shouted as he went. "Sorry. Sorry. Sorry. So damned sorry."

Then he was sorry he did not see the little furry dog come out of what used to be his aunt's room, what should have been his wife's room. He tripped over the snarling, snapping creature, right at the top of the stairs.

The dog stayed there. Phelan did not. He bounced down the flight of steps on his head and on his hind end, his clothes flying in all directions, along with his arms and legs. *"Sorr—eee!"*

Everyone rushed out of their rooms, except for Lady Haverhill, naturally, since she had not heard a thing. They were all in various states of undress and shock, shrieking (Lady Lucinda), crying (her maid, Browne), swooning (Phelan's valet, coming with the hot water and a candle), and barking (Daisy, the dog).

Nell raced down the stairs while Alex ran to check on the duke.

"Phelan?" Nell called, righting the valet's light before it could go out or set the carpet on fire. The carpet was too wet, actually, from the hot water, but she needed the light to see her brother anyway. His chest was moving, so he lived, thank goodness, but he did not answer her desperate call. "Phelan, talk to me!"

"Turn your head, missy," Aunt Hazel ordered, making a slower way down the stairs. "The fool is no sight for a maiden's eyes."

"He is not dead! Oh, you mean he is undressed." Nell had been too busy making sure he was breathing to care about the rest of him. She wore only her flannel bed gown, though. She had not stopped to grab a robe or a shawl, or slippers, either, she realized, when her feet felt wet. Aunt Hazel also had nothing on but her night rail.

The older woman had not averted *her* eyes, Nell noted, but was shaking her head. "I always told André that Phelan Sloane was a small man, but I had no idea . . . That is, go find a blanket or something, *cherie*."

Lady Lucinda had stopped screaming when no one

came to her aid. She came down the stairs, clutching the dog to her breast, but made no move to offer her green velvet robe with ostrich feather trim—or to look elsewhere.

Then Redfern was there, his face as white as his nightshirt. He slowly removed his tasseled nightcap and carefully placed it where it would do the most to restore Mr. Sloane's dignity.

"He must have broken his head." Nell choked back her tears and her fears. "He will not wake up. Find someone to ride for the surgeon. The man must know his way here in the dark by now."

"If Mr. Sloane and his valet are home, his coachman must be returned," Redfern said. "He can go." By the time Redfern went below to his rooms to dress, then made his way to the stables, Nell could have run to the village. She could not leave her brother here in the hall, though, wearing nothing but a hat.

"I'll go, Miss Sloane," came the welcome offer from the upper stairs. Mr. Peabody had taken the time to put on his coat and trousers, and was patting down his hair with his fingers, as if he was off to attend a session of Parliament. Nell thought of asking for his coat to cover her brother better, but decided Phelan needed a doctor more than he needed his decency.

"Thank you. John Coachman sleeps above the horses. Tell him—"

"His Grace is recovered from his fall," Alex interrupted, coming to the lower hallway. "And back in bed. But he is in a great deal of pain. And the shock could not be good for a man of his years. I rang for his valet, but I think he ought to be seen by a physician." He straightened his glasses and tightened the belt of his hurriedly donned brocade robe.

"His Grace?" Peabody cried. "The duke is injured?"

He went tearing back up the stairs, his errand to the stables forgotten in his worry over his position. That is, worry over his employer.

"This madman attacked my father?" Lady Lucinda saw the earl and an opportunity. She swooned, right into Alex's arms. At least she put the dog down first. Alex wrenched his shoulder again, catching her. He lowered her not inconsiderable weight to the floor as quickly as he could, accidentally letting her head bounce on the wet rug. He knelt by Nell's side.

"He is breathing." Nell had her brother's head in her lap, cushioning him from the cold. "But he will not open his eyes."

The earl found the man's pulse and nodded. He felt Sloane's arms and legs. "Nothing seems to be broken, but I won't chance moving him until the surgeon comes, and more strong men." Alex regretted not donning his own nightshirt this evening, but he had been feeling overheated enough, without the confining garment. Now he had nothing to throw over the other man but his own robe, which was not an option. "But he might catch his death of cold lying here like this."

"No, he won't," Aunt Hazel said, draping a velvet robe over Phelan's body, a green velvet robe with ostrich feather trim. Nell noticed that Alex never even glanced at the duke's daughter in her dishabille, and felt comforted, even as she tucked the heavy fabric around her brother. She herself was more fully covered in her flannel nightgown than she had been in her pink frock at dinner, not that Alex noticed that either.

By this time other servants had gathered—those who had not packed their bags and left, that is, after hearing the commotion. The ghosts were abroad at Ambeaux Cottage that night, and the two newly hired footmen had fled. Alex sent his own man, Stives, to the stables, and Cook back to the pantry for smelling salts.

"But you can just bring a bucket of cold water to toss over Lady Lucinda," he added, which had that lady instantly demanding her quaking maid's assistance back up the stairs, to assess her father's health.

Phelan's valet woke up at the pungent odor; Phelan did not. Nell looked up at Alex, her eyes begging for reassurance.

"He might simply be concussed," Alex tried to tell her. But then he leaned closer and sniffed. "No, I do believe he is foxed, instead. Cup-shot," he added when Madame Ambeaux raised her eyebrows.

"You mean he is drunk?" Nell let her brother's head fall back on the carpet as she quickly stood up. "He caused injury to a duke, disturbed the household's rest, offended everyone's sensibilities, and frightened the life out of me, because he had too much to drink?"

"That is what it appears to me. The surgeon will make certain he has no grievous injuries from the fall. I expect he will have bruises and black and blue marks aplenty, but likely his inebriation kept him from worse damage. I am sorry, Nell."

Phelan groaned. " 'M sorry too, sis. So sorry."

He passed out again before anyone could ask him exactly what it was that he was so sorry about.

CHAPTER EIGHTEEN

No one was leaving. Alex wanted to return to the inn in town so Phelan could have his room, but Nell asked him to stay. He would have ignored a request made out of politeness, but she looked so . . . so alone he could not refuse. She was everything competent, ordering a makeshift bedroom in an unused back parlor for Phelan, rehiring the sheepish footmen who had fled, arranging for nursing and medications and doctors' visits, and trying to manage a house full of invalids. Yet her blue eyes were clouded with concern, and he swore she looked even thinner. She was still softly rounded and graceful, but he could not like the sharper planes at her shoulders and wrists. Alex could not leave her to cope all alone, even though he could not take her burdens onto his own broader shoulders. He could not take her into his arms either, to kiss away her worries, but the thought kept him awake at night. He thought that he might get a better rest at the inn, without the scent of her rosewater in his head, but he stayed, trying to be less of a bother than the other guests.

Lady Lucinda was no help, not even with her own father. She was suffering a crisis of nerves, her maid reported. She was also suffering a surfeit of curiosity. Having seen Mr. Sloane in his undress, she was suddenly interested in how Lord Carde measured up, or even Mr. Peabody. Perhaps there was more to marriage, after all, than the size of a gentleman's purse.

No, the lady decided after a clandestine visit to the art books in the Ambeaux Cottage library, money and influence were still what made a good match. The rest could wait for afterward. Since Lord Carde did not seem to care for her, he would not care where she satisfied her . . . curiosity, once he had his heir. Surely seeing her with pale cheeks, gracefully reclining on a sofa, a lavender-soaked cloth on her poor forehead, he would be moved to pity and proceed to a proposal. She was not defeated, and she was not departing. Her poor maid had to unpack and press everything that had been wadded into the trunks, in addition to fetching teas, tisanes, and talcum to make milady's complexion look more interesting. Nell had to fetch fashion journals and cordials and cold compresses for her ailing guest when she could not provide company. It was her fault Lady Lucinda was in this condition, was it not? Nell commiserated—with the maid. She did not blame Lord Carde for staying as far away from the die-away diamond as possible. He might as well have gone to the inn, but she took comfort in his presence.

The duke could not be moved. His head was too sore, whether from the wine or the wooden nightstand no one knew. Further, his gouty foot and leg were so swollen he could not pull on his trousers, much less his shoes or stockings.

"I am not one for traveling in the buff," he told

Madame Ambeaux, who was keeping his mind off his woes with a game of cards. "Don't know about this younger generation, eh?"

Aunt Hazel agreed they were all slowtops and sluggards. But she was happy for company she could actually see and touch, and chouse out of a few more shillings. She waved Lord Carde off when he would have taken a hand or two, to keep the old gentleman entertained.

Mr. Peabody, of course, could not leave without his employers, nor could Lady Haverhill leave without her cousins. Lucinda's supposed chaperone was delighted to be on vacation from her town duties, sitting on uncomfortable ballroom chairs and drinking endless cups of tea. Now, at least, she got to sit on a comfortable sofa in the morning room drinking endless cups of tea while reading the novels Miss Sloane fetched from the lending library. Lucinda's withering-rose portrayal was as good as an evening at the theater, too. Besides, the local vicar who kept coming to call was used to raising his voice to reach the rear pews. He might be a prosy bore, but he was loud enough to hear. It did not matter that she could not make out Sir Chauncy's blather, for he might be a handsome rogue, but he was too poor to catch Lucinda's interest. Lady Haverhill went back to her books.

Phelan certainly could not leave. He had hardly moved, although he did sip at his broth when Nell fed him spoonfuls. Lady Lucinda's maid even took a turn at feeding him, avoiding her mistress's demands.

Phelan was avoiding everything else, intentionally or not. No one knew which. He did not sit up, and he did not speak. His bruised but unbroken arms and legs moved, and his eyes were often open, but they stared straight ahead, not at anyone. He would not—

or could not—converse. The surgeon diagnosed traumatic catatonia. Mr. Sloane had been shocked into speechlessness, the sawbones declared, a waking coma. Such mental paralysis was not entirely unheard of in high-strung individuals, he added, carefully not using words such as lunatic or Bedlamite in Nell's hearing.

"I'll get the rapscallion to speak quickly enough," His Grace threatened, brandishing his cane. "What was the gudgeon about anyway, I'd like to know, creeping around in the dark without his clothes on? It ain't proper, I say. If a man cannot hold his liquor, he should not drink," the duke said, ignoring his own aching head and swollen foot. "What if he had stumbled into my innocent daughter's room?"

The duke's innocent daughter was wondering how bare she would have to be, and if Carde locked his door at night.

"I am certain that Phelan will speak to us as soon as he has recovered from his fall," Nell said, staunchly defending the nearly indefensible. She would not believe Phelan guilty of more than an overindulgence until she heard it from his own mouth. She had to believe he would speak to her soon or she would go as crazy as they all thought he was. "And he already tried to apologize for his actions, when he was still speaking. I can only keep adding my own regrets for your misfortune, Your Grace."

"Now, now, missy. Ain't your fault. We cannot pick our relations, what? Skeletons in every family's closet, don't you know. Of course, most houses don't trot them out in the altogether, scaring the wits from honest folk, but you ain't to blame. By the by, do you think you could get your cook to make those sweetbreads again? Or what about that steak and kidney pie? I would not mind another bottle of that excellent port your man brought up the other day, either."

After three days of watching Nell run off her feet, growing more and more haggard-looking, Alex insisted he move to the inn. They were at breakfast, the only ones who came to take the meal in the morning room. All of the others required trays in their rooms—yet more work for the limited staff at Ambeaux Cottage. "You cannot need another guest at this time."

"But you are seldom here." Nell tried to keep the complaint and the question out of her voice. She had no right to pry into the earl's business, and no business missing his company. She told herself that seeing him at breakfast, when he was rugged in riding clothes, and dinner, when he was elegant, were enough memories for her to store away. Nell truly thought he was the most appealing-looking man in the world, if not the most handsome.

Any more memories and she might become like Phelan, staring at the portrait of Lizbeth she had carried into his room, hoping for some response. A tear had trailed down his cheek, but he never looked away. Or Nell might turn into a barmy old maid like Aunt Hazel, imagining her lost love could speak with her. Much better to remember Alex as he pretended to read the newspapers while handing scraps to Lady Lucinda's dog, or as he played at charades during dinner with Lady Haverhill, although no one else was in the game. She did not need more time in his company to lose what was left of her heart, or her dignity. Heavens, she might become like Lady Lucinda, prowling about the house after dark, hoping to encounter him in some unlighted hallway. Which reminded her to speak to Redfern about keeping more candles burning, more footmen on duty at night, a closer watch on the master keys.

Alex took another slice of toast. Nell shook her head when he offered her some, but he shoved the plate toward her anyway. "You are growing too thin."

She shook her head. "I had a slice of bread when it was fresh from the oven this morning." And she was never going to have Lady Lucinda's lush form anyway.

Alex pushed the pot of jam in her direction, ignoring her protest. "I have been visiting the tenant farms. Matters are as bad as you and Mr. Silbiger said they were. I have authorized immediate improvements."

"I heard. Sophie Posener is singing your praises for what you have done to get her geese to market. Her husband is much improved now, knowing that his family will not be left destitute. And they are pleased you hired that one-legged handyman they recommended to be land steward."

"Dan Hasgrove seems competent, and he gets around well enough to oversee the new work until I decide what is to be done. I cannot make any permanent decisions until I figure out what happened here. Why get new tenants if the water is poisoned or the land had grown barren? Which means I need to speak to your brother."

"Not as much as I need to speak to him. Do you think that is why he refuses to . . . to wake up, although I know he is not sleeping?"

"I think he knows deuced well that I am here. He cringes when I come into the room."

Nell took a piece of toast but crumbled it onto her plate instead of spreading jam on it. "You wouldn't take the duke's advice, would you, and try to get him to speak by using force?"

"What, beat an injured man? Or do you suppose I

might torture him by sticking pins in his feet to see if he is truly unaware, the way your aunt recommended? When the surgeon pinched him, Phelan did show some response, which makes me doubt the depth of his stupor, but I would not bludgeon him into talking. Could you really think that badly of me, Nell? Cousin Nell," he added for Redfern's benefit, when the butler poured him a fresh cup of coffee.

"No, of course not. But you might be growing impatient."

"I am that, heaven knows. I've also been speaking with the constables and the magistrate and the sheriff about Lizbeth's accident. Half of those involved in the investigation are dead or have no memories that are not in the official report. I need to speak to Phelan about that, too."

"He never talked about the tragedy, even when he was well."

"He will talk about it when he recovers, I swear."

Nell had her doubts, but she kept them to herself. Alex would not fear Phelan's temper or his retribution, so perhaps he might coerce her brother into speaking about the dark days of the accident, which would be another form of torture for poor Phelan. Nell supposed the cruelty was necessary in order for Alex to complete his own quest. The earl's investigation might prove fruitless, but it was a legitimate, necessary search. That much Nell understood. Then he would leave.

"Phelan could not know anything, though," she told him now, around a lump in her throat that felt as if she had actually swallowed some of the dry toast. "If my brother had any idea that Lizbeth's daughter had been alive, he would have brought her back instantly, no matter the cost. He adored Lottie. We all did."

"As did my brother and I. Yet someone must have known something. That new guard appearing just when the old one took ill with stomach pains is too convenient. To say nothing of the man's disappearance afterward. All of the reports mentioned suspicions, but with no proof, the tragedy was considered an accident. My father was not convinced. I am not convinced. I shall not be, until I speak with your brother."

"If you can be certain of one thing, it is that Phelan would never harm Lizbeth. He worshipped her."

Alex set his coffee cup down, as if one swallow had left a bad taste in his mouth. "I noticed. Anyone would, seeing all the portraits of her."

"He wanted to marry her, you know." Nell was not being disloyal. Everyone knew of it. She was surprised Alex had not heard yet, from Redfern or Aunt Hazel or anyone in the village who was free to speak now that Phelan was incapacitated.

"No, I did not know that. How did Lizbeth feel?"

"Oh, she always laughed. She said they were first cousins and first among friends, but nothing more. Her father would never have approved anyway, because of the consanguinity. And Uncle Ambeaux always believed Lizbeth was worthy of the finest gentleman in the land. We all did."

"And my father did too, obviously. Lizbeth was indeed a grand lady, as kind as she was beautiful." Alex pushed his coffee cup aside, thinking. "But Phelan would have inherited Ambeaux Cottage and your uncle's fortune had he eventually convinced your cousin to wed him."

Nell did not like that note of suspicion in Alex's voice. Phelan was most likely involved in some hugger-mugger, but he was still her brother, still her only true family. "But he did not convince Lizbeth.

She married Lord Carde, your father, so whatever hopes Phelan might have had, financial or romantic, died at their marriage. She bore your father a child. The earl and his countess were happy together, and Phelan was happy for her. He would not have harmed either our cousin or her daughter," Nell insisted. "He had nothing to gain from threatening them, rather than waiting for your father to—I am sorry. I should not be saying such things."

"No, you must say whatever you think. Please. I value your opinions, and need all the conjectures I can get, all the information to sift through. And you are right. My father was considerably older than Lizbeth. One could only assume that she would outlive him and be free to remarry. Her second husband could have been from any walk of life, since the countess would have been a wealthy widow. She would have been old enough, and independent enough, not to need her father's permission either, although she might have wished for his blessing." Alex stirred an extra lump of sugar into his coffee. "There would be no rational reason for your brother to plot against Lizbeth. Still, I believe someone meant harm that day."

"But not Phelan."

He kept stirring his coffee, not looking at her. The word "rational" hung in the air between them.

"Why not a robbery gone awry? The highwayman might have fled after the coach overturned."

"With no booty? Lizbeth's jewel case was still in the carriage." He took another sip of the hot brew, not liking it much better than before.

"He was frightened by the chaos he had caused. He ran away. Or . . . or he was injured too and died before he could reach help. Anything might have hap-

pened. We do not know. But I do know that Phelan
was here all along. He was sitting with my aunt when
the messengers came, trying to rally her spirits. She
was ailing, despondent at the death of her husband
and blue-deviled at Lizbeth's leaving with the child.
Phelan or I were always with Aunt Ambeaux when
she was not sleeping. I was in the classroom when the
riders came. I still remember the great commotion,
and how distraught Phelan was."

"I admire your loyalty, and I never once suspected
your brother of actually causing the coach to veer off
the road. No one did, or does. But even you must
admit your brother's behavior afterward was peculiar,
painting all those portraits of his dead cousin, going
into black moods that frightened half the neighborhood, refusing to speak of the tragedy, claiming the
estate as his. And then there is the money. Neither
Redfern nor Mr. Silbiger has any inkling where the
income from the tenant farms went, or why. Lud
knows he never spent it on improvements, or on his
own sister."

"I never needed anything," she quickly said.

"Like a Season, a dowry, pretty clothes?" Alex was
still feeling guilty that Nell had been denied so much
a young lady should rightfully have expected. "And
then he ran away when I finally appeared, only to turn
up as animated as a turnip."

"He was drunk when he arrived. You said so yourself. The fall knocked him senseless."

"But did it?"

Since Nell had her own fears, she could not answer.
Whoever heard of a waking coma? She shredded another piece of toast.

"Your brother's coachman had orders to have the
carriage ready in the morning after Phelan returned.

His valet knew not to unpack. Phelan was not staying, Nell. But where was he going, and why?"

Nell had asked herself those very questions. Phelan had been going to leave her here alone, again. He would have refused to answer her questions again, too. She wondered if he would have invited her to go along this time, but doubted it. The coachman said nothing about orders to pack additional trunks onto the carriage.

Nell pushed the plate of bread crumbs away and straightened her spine. "He will have a good reason for everything. You'll see. In a few days, Phelan will be recovered and you can speak with him yourself."

"Oh, I intend to. Which is another reason I should remove to the inn. I have the feeling that your brother will recuperate considerably faster if he thinks I am gone. I will leave a man behind to see that he does not make any miraculous recoveries in the middle of the night, disappearing by morning."

"No! Phelan would not— Well, he might. I do not know any longer. I do not know anything, it seems, except that you must not go back to the inn." And Kitty Johnstone, the buxom barmaid. "You are the only one in this house who does not require my presence or my attention. And you are the only one with any right to be here."

Alex set down his cup with a clatter. "I told you to ignore that nonsense. This is your house."

"We both know that is not true."

"It is your home," he insisted. "For as long as you wish. And it is time you reclaimed it from your malingering guests."

"Do you think the duke is well enough to travel, then?" Nell asked with a hopeful note in her voice.

"His Grace is as well as your cook's excellent meals

permit him to be. If she fed him gruel, he would be limping toward London before you could say jackrabbit. Now he is too comfortable to move, and too happy to be saving the expense of supporting his own household."

Nell frowned at the waste in front of her and bit her lip. "That is another thing I do not know, where the money is to come from for all these additional outlays. The household account is nearly bare, and Phelan always handled the estate income. Redfern and I have surpassed our credit in the village."

Alex got up and came to sit in the chair beside hers. He took her hand between his—bread crumbs and all. "Please do not fret about such foolish matters, my dear. None of this is your concern. I will speak to Redfern about the finances. You may serve lobster and champagne to the duke if you wish. No, then he will never leave."

"But if you are not claiming the house, why should you carry the costs?"

Because he would carry any burden so that she did not have to, but Alex could not say so, not when she was looking at him with such cousinly concern. Cousinly was not what he wanted, but cousins they had to remain while all the strangers were at Ambeaux Cottage. Some were stranger than others, but he'd see them all gone before he spoke of more personal matters than decades-old mysteries and doddering dukes.

"Do you not remember?" he asked instead. "I am the earl, high-handed and authoritative. You said so yourself. I take charge. The instinct to rule is in my blood, born and bred, you know." He raised his noble nose in the air, winning him the hoped-for smile, until his spectacles slid off and he had to bend down to pick them up. When he got up he reclaimed her hand—how comfortably it rested in his palm—and added, "Along with the need to slay dragons. I shall bear whatever expenses occur, and I shall rid you of the fire-breathing worms. Your unwanted guests, that is. Not that I am declaring Lady Lucinda a dragon, of course."

Her smile was like springtime, blue skies and sunshine. He could not help himself from bringing her hand to his lips and placing a kiss on it. Or turning it over and placing another on the palm. Or—

"Do you, ah, think Lady Lucinda is fit enough to return to town?" Nell asked, to hide the sound of her thunderous heartbeat. No amount of willpower could get her to pull her hand back, though.

Alex did not mention that Lady Lucinda was fit enough to try his doorknob—his securely locked doorknob—in the middle of the night. He did not believe the resident ghosts were trying to come in for a chat, for they would have entered through the walls, and he was too much the realist to hope that Nell had come calling. She had not taken her hand away, which he took as a good sign, so he kissed the tips of her fingers. They trembled in his. He was wondering if he dared lick the crumbs away, or if he could keep himself from not, when Redfern returned.

"More coffee, my lord?" the butler intoned. "Or does Miss Sloane require another napkin?"

Nell hurriedly placed her hands back in her lap. "We were merely discussing slaying dragons. That is, dislodging the guests."

"Shall I find a pry bar in the toolshed?"

"I think I have a better way," Alex said. "You can leave it to me."

Nell was not as confident. "You are not going to pretend to be a ghost, are you? We have trouble enough keeping any servants as it is. And I do not think the duke will be so easily fooled the next time. He might use his pistol. Lady Lucinda will only go into strong hysterics, requiring another week to recover from the fright."

No, Lady Lucinda would cry compromise if she found a man in her room, specter or seducer. "No, this is a better plan."

Nell distrusted his boyish grin. "I remember some of your plans to avoid lessons and escape the nursery during the wedding visit."

"We succeeded, did we not? Outfoxed our tutors and your governess any number of times."

"I also remember how you and your brother convinced me to go wading in the ornamental fountain while the adults were at dinner and no one was looking. Nasty Jack stole my shoes and stockings, so I was found out when I came back to the house without them. I had no pudding for a week."

"But you had fun, did you not?"

Nell recalled laughing and laughing while the boys splashed and cavorted about like puppies. She'd thought Alex a handsome young god even then. "And your plan to get rid of Lady Lucinda and her father, and Lady Haverhill and Mr. Peabody, will be like that?"

"Better. Trust me."

How could she trust him when she could not even trust her own feelings?

CHAPTER NINETEEN

Alex knew of one sure way to roust Lady Lucinda and her father from their comfortable perch at Ambeaux Cottage. Well, he knew that declaring himself bankrupt would send the female vulture flying, and dismissing the cook would have the duke decamping. Other than those actions, and a pistol, very little would work as well as his latest idea. Happily, Alex's plan fell in with his own wishes.

He would flirt with Nell.

He did not intend any teasing kind of dalliance in private, either, but a public onslaught of Nell's senses and sensibilities. And Lady Lucinda's. Once the duke's daughter saw how matters stood, how she was never going to win his affection or his admiration, since both were directed toward Miss Sloane, she would be gone before the cat could lick its ear, dragging her father and the others behind her.

The very notion made Alex smile. Not the leaving part, but the verbal lovemaking part. Under the guise of evicting Nell's unwanted guests, he could treat her like the lovely, enchanting woman she was. Finally.

He was tired of Nell standing in the background while Lady Lucinda held center stage, tired of watching the ever-present Sir Chauncy and Peabody and even the vicar and the surgeon fawn over the supposed heiress while the real treasure went ignored in her own home. And he was tired of not promoting his own plans for Nell's future.

He needed his quiet, retiring Nell to discover what an attractive woman she was, so she would have confidence enough to face London and his world. She might think he was playing a part for the others' sake—otherwise she was liable to set her goose on him for taking liberties—but damn if he would not prove to her that she was Lady Lucinda's equal in everything that mattered.

Her reputation would not suffer, he swore to himself. Neither the duke nor his daughter would bandy about town the fact that Lord Carde preferred an unpolished gem to the reigning diamond. And Alex did still hold His Grace's gambling vouchers.

He started at dinner that night, complimenting Nell's gown, the same pink muslin one she had worn three times since his arrival, but with a nosegay of violets at the neckline tonight. She almost pulled her hand out of his—she almost slapped him for staring at her bosom so long—until he winked and jerked his head in Lady Lucinda's direction, where the beauty's jaw was hanging open in disbelief. Lucinda pulled down the bodice of her own green satin gown and pulled in a deeper breath, but Alex ignored the blatant invitation. Mr. Peabody turned as green as the gown in his efforts to raise his eyes from his lady's assets. The ubiquitous Sir Chauncy did not bother to hide his ogling. Alex almost expected the coxcomb to take out his quizzing glass.

Luckily, Lady Lucinda let out her breath before her entire chest was exposed or the secretary had apoplexy.

Since neither the duke, nor Phelan, of course, came to dine, and Aunt Hazel had declared her intention of keeping His Grace company upstairs, Alex announced that the small gathering need not keep to the usual rigid formality. He quite correctly led Lady Lucinda into the dining parlor, but seated her between Peabody and Sir Chauncy on one long side of the table. He sat next to Nell, with Lady Haverhill on his left, on the other side, leaving no gentleman at the head of the table. Nell was about to argue with him for disordering her arrangement, but he gently kicked her foot under the table.

"Sh. My plan is working."

"This is your plan? To make a laughingstock out of me by making a shambles of my dinner table, as if I did not know proper precedence?"

"No, my plan is to make you the object of my affection."

Nell swallowed a sip of her wine the wrong way. "I would rather go wading barefoot in the fountain again," she said when she stopped choking. "You are insane!"

"Possibly, but this will work. You'll see." And he proceeded to ignore the other diners, except for passing the platters and the salt. He served Nell himself—far more than she ever ate—and made sure her wineglass was kept filled. He offered her the choicest cuts, urged her to sample the tenderest morsels, and outrageously used his own napkin to dab at a bit of gravy on the corner of her mouth.

Nell turned scarlet. Lady Haverhill shouted toward Peabody, "What, is the gel sickening like that crazy brother of hers that she needs feeding and wiping?"

Lady Lucinda appeared to have lost her appetite altogether.

After dinner, Alex refused to sit with Peabody and the baronet over their port. "Why should we deny ourselves the pleasure of the ladies' company?" he asked, staring like a mooncalf in Nell's direction.

"You are overplaying your role," she hissed at him as he walked at her side into the drawing room.

"Well, I am not getting a lot of encouragement from you, my love," he whispered back. "You could smile at me, you know. Our audience will have a hard time believing I am smitten without some reciprocal show of affection from you." Louder, he complimented her on another fine dinner. "But what food would not taste like ambrosia when shared by a goddess?"

"La, sir, you will turn my head with your flattery," she said, batting her eyelashes and giving him what she hoped was a coy smile.

He stopped walking. "What is the matter? Are you going to be ill? Or have you got something in your eye? Do you need my handkerchief?"

So much for Nell's efforts to turn into a flirt. No one would believe Lord Carde was taken with her anyway. Taken leave of his senses, more likely. She looked away, holding herself as stiff as possible as they proceeded down the corridor.

Alex stopped to pluck one of Aunt Hazel's first roses from the arrangement on the hall table and handed it to her with a bow. "A perfect bloom for a perfect beauty."

Nell stuffed it back into the vase before walking on, before the stem dripped water on her gown. "I am not finding this amusing."

"Ah, but I am enjoying the performance immeasurably." He tilted his head closer to hers, for the benefit of those following. "Have I ever told you that I adore the scent you wear? It reminds me of the rarest, most precious rose, like you, my dear."

Nell pinched at his sleeve, where her hand rested on his arm. "It is all the perfume I can afford, you clunch. Aunt Hazel distills it herself from her garden."

"Ah, a romantic to the core. But all roses have thorns. The hint of danger is what makes them so special, you know, the velvet of the petals so close to the pain if not handled delicately. The challenge, of course, is to fill one's senses with the scent and the softness and the stunning colors, without getting pierced. Like courting a beautiful woman."

Peabody was looking at him as if insanity was contagious in this household. Sir Chauncy's brows were furrowed, as if he were wondering if he'd been mistaken about Miss Sloane's prospects. This time he did draw out his quizzing glass on its ribbon to survey her posterior, as if that might explain Carde's sudden infatuation. Perhaps Miss Sloane would become the owner of this handsome property after all, once the odd duck of a brother was locked away in an asylum. What other reason could an intelligent chap like Carde have, the baronet seemed to be asking himself, for preferring the little country hen to the heiress? Of course he, himself, had found Miss Sloane somewhat appealing, in a reserved, subdued way, but that was before Lady Lucinda's arrival. Now Sir Chauncy quickly tucked the looking glass back into his pocket and hurried after the far worthier quarry.

Lady Lucinda had gathered her reserves and was headed for the pianoforte. No one, certainly not silly, soft-spoken Eleanor Sloane in her shabby pink gown, could compete with her there for a gentleman's attention.

"Not tonight," Alex announced, pulling the bench away from the musical instrument before Lady Lucinda could take the seat. "I thought we would ask Miss Sloane to show us her sketchbooks instead. Did you know," he asked the others, "that she is an artist of note in this community, giving lessons to any of the children who show an aptitude? I for one have been dying to see some of Miss Sloane's work. In fact, my dear," he said to Nell, "I took the liberty of asking one of the maids to bring it down where we can all admire your artistic efforts." He gestured toward a neat stack of perhaps twenty matching sketchbooks, and brought the top three toward the music bench to spread out.

Nell was ready to bash him over the head with the sketch pads, she was so mad. "These are not for public viewing," she said.

"Nonsense. Lady Lucinda shows us her talents"— he lowered his gaze to the other woman's breasts before nodding toward the pianoforte—"regularly."

"I used to be a dab hand at drawing myself," Lady Haverhill spoke up. Before Lady Lucinda could protest both the planned entertainment and Lord Carde's defection, the older woman said, "I wouldn't mind a bit of paper and a pencil. Sit, Lucinda, and I'll sketch your portrait."

So Peabody and Sir Chauncy hovered around Lady Haverhill's shoulder, exclaiming over Lady Lucinda's beauty as her relation tried to capture it on paper. Alex and Nell shared the love seat, as close as she permitted him, with the music bench in front of them.

After turning a few pages, Alex said, "You really are good."

"Wouldn't you have been embarrassed if I were not?"

"Not at all. I would have praised the drawings to

the sky nevertheless." He flipped a few more pages. The sketches were of local people, children, a few dogs and sheep, trees, the common sights of country life. They were merely line drawings, but evocative and finely executed.

Nell tried to excuse their simplicity. "I do work in pastel sometimes when I have the time, but those are locked in a trunk where they cannot be smeared, thank goodness."

"I would love to see them, although these are lovely."

"I had started one of Lizbeth and her child, but never finished it. I was young and unschooled then, so you would not recognize either of them. Luckily I had a dedicated drawing mistress at school. Do you remember Madame Journet?" she called over to Lady Lucinda, trying to join the two groups in conversation. Lady Lucinda was looking bored at sitting still, and at the trite compliments her two admirers were uttering.

She frowned. "She was a bent old crow who had little talent and less respect for her betters."

Lady Haverhill's pencil broke. "Bah, now I shall have to start over."

Alex opened a different sketchbook. As his admiration seemed sincere, Nell grew more enthusiastic about showing the pictures. When Mr. Peabody and Sir Chauncy grew tired of watching the old woman drawing—how many times could one praise the curve of Lady Lucinda's jaw or the arch of her eyebrow?— they came nearer the bench. Both of them actually paid Nell compliments on her skill.

Encouraged, Nell found an older book, from her schooldays. She flipped through the pages until she found the one they would be most interested in: Lady Lucinda in her schoolgirl's pinafore, with dark braids trailing down her shoulders.

Lady Lucinda's good humor was restored when her swains exclaimed how stunning she was even in her youth, what promise of beauty she showed, how elegant her carriage at such an early age.

Nell did not tell them she had done the sketch while Lucinda had been giving her usual lecture to the other girls about finding the proper husband.

Mr. Peabody had picked up another book, Nell's most recent drawings, and was turning pages before she could take it from his hands. "I do not feel you wish this one shown, Miss Sloane," he said, his nose wrinkling like a hare's in distaste.

The sketch was of Lord Carde, asleep in his nightshirt.

Nell's cheeks could not get any pinker. "That was when his lordship was ill, when he first arrived and had the incident with the horse. There, you can see the bandage on his head." She knew she was babbling, but, heavens, she did not want anyone to think she made a practice of visiting Alex in his bedchamber, no matter what his plan entailed.

Alex came to her rescue. "I regret that I was unaware of the lady's company for the most part. I did not even know she was drawing while she took turns with my man Stives to see I did not expire in the night. Only a true lady would give up her own comfort and rest to sit by a near stranger's bedside while he slept."

Peabody got the unspoken message: Miss Sloane's virtue was unblemished. He changed the subject. "I've never seen you without spectacles, Lord Carde."

Alex studied the drawing. "You made me look peaceful, and much more handsome than I merit." He glanced over at her and smiled, sighing dramatically, as if only a woman in love could see him in such a way. "Thank you, my dear."

Nell's cheeks were burning again. A woman in love *had* seen him that way! Not that he was not handsome by any light, in anyone's eyes, or that her pencil could create the sense of strength he possessed, even in repose. "The fire must be too high, don't you think?"

He smiled as if she'd made a brilliant suggestion. "Perhaps you'd care for a walk out in the garden?"

"No!" He was dangerous enough sitting at her side, their thighs touching, tingling, tormenting, no matter how she tried to edge toward the end of the love seat. Who knew what he might do out in the dark? "That is, no, thank you, cousin."

"We could all go, so there would be nothing improper in a short stroll, in view of the windows."

"I say, it is too cold for the ladies," Sir Chauncy protested, not wishing to get his evening slippers wet before he had to go back to the inn in the village. "Lady Lucinda was recently afflicted, you know."

"What's that?" Lady Haverhill shouted. "She looks affected? It's the nose. Can't do much about that."

"My lady's nose is perfect!" Peabody hurried from Nell's sketchbooks to where Lady Lucinda was posing. Sir Chauncy was right on his heels. "Quite delightful, full of character."

"As is Lord Carde's," Nell put in, trying to put Alex to the blush in turn. Instead he raised her hand to his mouth. "Thank you, my dear. I shall savor that opinion."

Lady Lucinda did not savor anything about this bothersome evening. She stood up well before Lady Haverhill was finished. "I am weary of sitting still, and my portrait has been painted by the most popular artists in London, anyway. I am sure some ladies take pleasure in amateur scribbles, but I am not one of them. You shall have to learn not to put yourself forward, Eleanor, if you hope to win approval in town."

"Tea? Did I hear you mention tea?" Lady Haverhill asked, casting doubt on her claims of poor hearing. She'd heard enough to interrupt her relation before Lucinda showed any of the gentlemen more of her sharp tongue than was perhaps wise. Nothing was liable to give Lord Carde a disgust of her faster than a spiteful comment to his new pet.

She was proved right when the earl ignored Lucinda altogether when Redfern wheeled in the tea cart. Alex left it to Sir Chauncy and Peabody to hand round the cups Nell filled, and the plates of biscuits and cakes. He sat by her side again, urging her to take another bite of this, another taste of that.

"Like a goose he is fattening up for market," Lady Lucinda was heard to comment as she and Lady Haverhill took their leave shortly afterward, more shortly than usual. Her distinctive nose was in the air, decidedly out of joint.

Alex patted Nell's hand and winked at her again, mouthing the words, "My plan is working."

"Your plan is setting the house on its ear and making me the object of speculation." Nell was upset, both by the false impressions they were giving, and the fact that they were indeed false. How lovely it would be, she thought, to have a fine gentleman like Alex pay her court. Just once, to be wanted, worshipped, whispered sweet words of love to—when it was not a silly charade.

"Lady Lucinda has gone to bed, so you can stop drooling over my hand."

He looked down. "Is that what I was doing? I

thought I was admiring your fine bone structure, the long, elegant fingers of an artist."

She pulled her hand back. "What, do I have pencil smudges on them?"

He sighed. "You are a hard woman to sweet-talk, my girl."

"And you need not do that either, since most of your audience is gone."

Sir Chauncy had left finally, after Alex's not so subtle hints that he still had a long, dark ride ahead of him. Mr. Peabody was warming his hands by the fire, within earshot, if he tried. Alex rubbed the back of his knuckles gently on Nell's cheek. "*Au contraire*, my dear. If Peabody were not here, I would tell you how delightful I find your blushes, and how your smiles can warm me like no fire ever could. I would praise your satin skin and your angel's blue eyes. If I did not think Redfern and a footman would be in soon to clear the tea things, I would pull the pins from your hair, just to see the golden curls tumble around your shoulders. I would—"

"You would perjure your very soul to see Lady Lucinda take her husband-hunting elsewhere."

"That too." He smiled, so the lines around his brown eyes crinkled and tiny gold lights danced behind his spectacles. Despite herself, Nell felt herself warmed—like no fire ever could—from the inside out. She fled before he could say anything else outrageous, or she could start believing it.

"I am going to look in on my brother. So I shall bid you pleasant dreams, cousin, and you too, Mr. Peabody. Thank you for your kind words and encouragement about my 'amateur scribbles.' Good night."

Alex would have followed, but the secretary stopped him. "Ahem. A word, my lord?"

"Of course." Alex had been meaning to speak to Peabody anyway about finding a better position, one where he could support a wife in style. Alex knew any number of cabinet ministers and diplomats who could advance a young man's career, especially one with excellent breeding whose only misfortune was being a second son. With Alex's connections and a duke's sponsorship, who knew how high an ambitious man could reach? Perhaps high enough for Lady Lucinda, if Peabody could winkle a title out of Prinny. Lady Lucinda was born to be a political hostess, and the poor fool obviously adored her, for some reason. Peabody ought to be bettering himself, rather than basking in her sunshine.

Alex had to laugh at himself, playing matchmaker. Before he could put forth his advice and offers, though, the man started speaking.

"My lord, it is a dangerous game you play."

"What game is that? I thought we were eschewing cards this evening."

Peabody's nostrils flared in righteous indignation. "Toying with Miss Sloane's affections the way you have, that is your game."

And Alex had been thinking the blighter was fit for the diplomatic corps? The infantry corps was more like it, facing the French cannon in the front lines. He wished he had his quizzing glass, to depress this insolent mushroom's pretensions. Who did he think he was, passing judgment on the Earl of Carde?

"Forgive me," Alex drawled, "but are you by any chance doubting my honorable intentions toward the young lady?"

Peabody had the sense to edge toward the door. "Miss Sloane is a lovely young woman and I would not wish to see her injured. She is not used to London ways and might not understand."

"Not understand genuine admiration? Not understand sincere affection? I believe those exist in the country as well as in town."

"She . . . she might not understand casual flirtation used to make another woman jealous."

"Good gods, is that what you think I am about?"

Peabody nodded, his Adam's apple bobbing. "That or seduction."

Alex's hands balled into fists. "I could call you out for that remark, you know. Either remark."

The secretary sidled closer to the door. "The lady does not seem to have anyone competent to protect her. I could not have a clear conscience if I did not speak up."

"I admire your courage, then, if not your presumption. Miss Sloane does not need protection. Not from me."

"But she did not appear to believe that you meant your words any more than I did, or Sir Chauncy."

"Then I shall have to try harder to make her believe, shan't I? And you ought to see to your own courtship. And your packing."

CHAPTER TWENTY

Nell could understand why a man in Lord Carde's employ was stationed outside Phelan's door. This one was not to prevent anyone from entering, nor to call for help in an emergency, but to keep her brother from leaving. She could understand it, but she could not like it. This was her house, but her brother was almost under lock and key? It was Lord Carde's house, plain and simple. She could not like this new game Alex was playing either, which was neither plain nor simple.

"Please wake up, Phelan," she told her brother after she closed the door on the guard. "I need you."

He had his lids closed, but Nell could see his eyes moving behind the blue-veined skin, so she thought he might be listening, at any rate. His valet must have bathed him recently, for his hair was damp and he wore a fresh nightshirt. Phelan liked everything to be tidy, so he must feel more the thing. "You look better," she told him, in case he had not seen a mirror recently. "Well enough to say good evening."

He did not, however.

"Please, brother, talk to me, help me understand what is happening. I do not know what I am supposed to do."

He did not tell her. Nell sat on the bed beside him and took Phelan's limp hand in hers. Strange, she could rarely recall holding his hand except when he helped her into a carriage. They were not close physically or as confidantes, perhaps because too many years separated them, but they were family, alone except for Aunt Hazel, who was no blood relation. Now Nell tried to reach her brother with her warm touch, her voice, her love for him, her need.

"You never did speak to me about important matters, did you? I could understand, for I was a child put into your care far too soon. But I have not been a child for years, although I feel like one now, with the adults whispering behind their hands, making decisions about my life. Now I am the one who has to make the decisions, for me and you and Aunt Hazel, but I do not have the knowledge needed to do so. Tell me, Phelan. Tell me what happened and what I can do about it!"

Nothing.

Nell placed her brother's hand back on the bed. She picked up a glass of water by his bedside, raised his head, and held the glass to his lips. He drank, so she knew he was awake and aware of her presence. "Are you hungry? Do you want a bowl of soup or some of the nice poppy seed cake Cook made for you?"

She got no response as she placed the pillows back behind his neck. "Phelan, I know you can hear me. Lord Carde is a reasonable man. If you tell him what trouble you found yourself in, he will help, I know he will. Were you gambling too much? Was that it? You lost all of our money and so had to borrow from the estate? Or were you speculating on 'Change and lost the investment? Heavens, do you have a secret, shameful family somewhere that you cannot bring to Ambeaux Cottage, but are supporting in luxury? Truly, brother, I cannot imagine any of that, but I will try to understand."

When he did not bother to open his eyes or speak, Nell started to grow angry. If he was truly ill, his body healthy but his wits gone begging, then she would beg his pardon tomorrow. Tonight she had suspicions, and no patience. "Perhaps you should be the one to try to understand, for once. You had a life, with work and income and business associates. You even had a mistress no one was supposed to know about in Scarborough. You came and went at your own leisure, on your own whims. I had nothing here in Kingston Upon Hull, Phelan. No friends, no money of my own, no place to go and no way of getting there. You discouraged callers and disapproved of gentlemen courters. You treated the neighbors poorly, so they kept their distance. I never blamed you, because I thought I would have had even fewer advantages without your blessings. I believed I would not have had my schooling or a roof over my head if not for you."

She straightened his covers, none too gently, tucking the blankets around him with enough force to pull them out of the other side of the bed. She walked around, repairing the damage. "I thanked you every day in my prayers for the very food on our table. But I was wrong. I was not indebted to you. According to the earl and the solicitor, Uncle Ambeaux did remember me. He did intend to dower me. He paid for my education, not you. You did not even own the house you claimed. You stole it, Phelan! You stole from the earl and you stole from me, your own sister. You stole the house, the funds, and you stole my trust. Do you not think you owe me an explanation?"

His hand twitched. Nell quickly took it between both of hers again. "Yes, wake up. Tell me. Let me understand, let me help. It is not too late, I swear. I can still have a life of my own. I can go to London and meet gentlemen, or I can ask Lord Carde if one of his mother's connections needs a companion. I can try to find another home for us, somewhere we can make a new start. I just cannot stay here, in his lord-ship's house."

Now her anger gave way to tears as she squeezed her brother's hand. "It is not right for me to remain at Ambeaux Cottage. Surely you can see that. I cannot accept the earl's charity and I cannot withstand his flirting. He came here because every female in London was chasing after him. Soon I will become one of them, I fear, and with less hope for success. I do not want his pity, but that is all he would offer a lovelorn, skinny spinster with no prospects. We all know that Alex has to marry someday, and marry well. He needs a lady of his own circles, suitable for the Queen's drawing room. We all also know I am not that, and the very notion would terrorize me anyway."

She grasped his hand harder, as if she could wring a response from him. When he did not so much as open his eyes, she went on: "The new Lady Carde will want to visit his properties and be mistress of them, as is only right. How could I bear that? I could curtsy to Her Majesty more easily than to Alex's wife. Oh, Phelan, you have to help me! Please, I beg you. Please wake up. If I can face Alex, so can you. He is kind and generous and silly and smart. He laughs at himself and yet he takes his responsibilities seriously. Oh, Phelan, whatever shall I do about my poor heart?"

Wiser men with all their wits about them could not have answered that question. Phelan did not try.

Nell brushed at her eyes. "The devil take you, Phelan Sloane. I would never, ever abandon you. How can you abandon me this way?"

Nothing.

She left, nodding to the guard in the hall, and headed for the stairs. The earl was leaving the parlor at the same time, as if he had been waiting for her before going up to his own bedroom.

"Good night," she murmured, lowering her eyes and turning away so he could not see that she had been weeping. His sympathy would undo her altogether. Besides, Aunt Hazel always said that men hated a woman's sorrow; tears made a gentleman feel helpless. Perhaps that was something all of them should experience, so they'd understand a woman's lot in life.

"He is no better?" he asked, misinterpreting her subdued silence as he kept pace beside her down the corridor.

"I thought his hand twitched, but I might have been mistaken, my own hopes letting me see what is not there. He did not look at me or speak, and when I left he was as limp and inanimate as when I arrived."

"Do you not find that odd? I always thought paralysis left a person frozen in one place, rigid. My godfather could not move his entire right side after suffering a paroxysm of the brain."

"Phelan's injury manifests itself in other ways. The surgeon says this is not unheard of."

"You are convinced, then, that he is not shamming?"

Nell stopped walking to face Alex. "As much as you are convinced that he is."

"But neither of us is sure."

"No, I cannot be positive, and Phelan has been so still for so long. Do you think I should send to London for a more learned physician? Our local doctor is a mere surgeon, who is also the veterinarian."

"Is he? I thought one of my horses was favoring one leg a bit. I shall have to speak to the man when he returns."

"We were speaking of my brother," Nell replied, not pleased with his efforts to lighten the conversation. "I thought I might consider driving Phelan to the medical college in Edinburgh where they study unusual diseases."

"They study, bless them, but they do not cure many. I would wait, especially since your brother does not seem to be in agony. If Phelan suffers a true paralysis, there is naught anyone can do for him. My godfather remained one-sided until he died, years later. If your brother languishes with a scrambled brainbox, I believe there is even less any healer can do for him. None of the experts has been able to help our poor king."

"And some of the treatments they have subjected his majesty to have been appallingly brutal, or so it seems from the newspaper accounts I have read. I would rather leave Phelan as he is than see him treated so cruelly."

"Those experts have been trying to earn their handsome fees by doing something, anything. No, I would wait to see how your brother fares. If his condition worsens, then we shall have to call on the best we can find."

Nell heard the "we" and felt better, that this was not all on her head. "And if he improves?"

"If he improves, then I might knock some sense into him myself."

"You wouldn't—"

"I told you, I shall not harm Sloane, unless he grows dangerous."

"He will not. He has never harmed anyone. I know he did grievous harm to the tenants, but he never physically abused a soul. As for the duke, that was a natural misunderstanding, aggravated by my brother's inebriated state and His Grace's belief in ghosts."

"Then your brother has nothing to fear from me. Deuce take it, I thought you trusted me more than that by now."

"Why should I? Now you are lying to Lady Lucinda and her father."

"All in a good cause, as you well know. And it is not as if that pair has been truthful either. Sir Chauncy stands ready to escort them back to town, hoping to fix an heiress's interest. He cannot know they are aiming to fix the dukedom's dwindling resources with an advantageous marriage."

"A fortune hunter deserves to be thwarted," was Nell's righteous reply. "Such underhanded motives for wooing a lady ought not be rewarded."

"The lady is twice as two-faced. Not only is she allowing Sir Chauncy and everyone else to believe in a nonexistent fortune while she pursues a richer target, but her affections are engaged elsewhere, I believe."

"Mr. Peabody?"

He shrugged. "There is no accounting for tastes. Not that she would accept a lowly secretary, even if his birth and connections are good. Her head's snobbery outweighs whatever affection her heart feels."

"Perhaps you are wrong and her feelings are engaged, with you."

"Hah! I do not think she likes me more than half. She simply wants every man she meets to worship at her feet."

Nell let out a heavy breath. "They all do."

"No, not all." He touched her arm, as if helping her up the stairs she climbed a hundred times a day.

"Alex—Cousin Alex," she started again, adding the title and the distance. "I cannot like this farce you are directing and starring in. I do not like my role in it, either."

"What? I thought we made a perfect pair, my sighs, your blushes." He laughed and patted her arm. "Never mind, one more day ought to see your bothersome guests on their way, and me free of Lady Lucinda's sticky, tangled web. Surely you can put up with my gallantry for that long? I must admit I have never actually wooed a lady, so I apologize if I have been heavy-handed in my suit. Lady Lucinda seems to have believed every bit of the nonsense—"

So he admitted it was all a taradiddle. Not that Nell was surprised. She was not even disappointed, not anymore. "Yes, judging from how she left the parlor in such a hurry this evening, as if the sight of you at my side gave her the headache."

"Exactly. So can you manage to overcome your scruples for just a few hours more, and pretend you hold me in some affection in return?"

"Pretend? That is, I suppose so."

As they reached the head of the stairs, they both heard a door creak open down the corridor in the direction of the guest room, where Lady Lucinda was sleeping. Alex pulled Nell behind a tall potted palm on the landing.

"Ghosts?" He spoke softly, right into her ear.

"Aunt Hazel's friends do not make any noise," Nell whispered back, resisting the urge to rub at her ear, where his whisper almost felt like a feather's tickle. "At least I have never heard any, in all my days at Ambeaux Cottage."

"Ah, then another kind of goblin is on the prowl, one that would suck out a man's soul if he let it."

"Lady Lucinda?"

"And heaven—or hell—only knows where she is going or what she is wearing to get there. I, for one, do not want to find out."

"She could not be going to your room, for Mr. Stives is sleeping there, in precaution for just such eventualities."

Alex had thought of that. "And I doubt she would go upstairs to visit Mr. Peabody until she is certain everyone is abed."

"She would not do so! For all her faults, Lucinda is a lady. And the servants sleep nearby."

Which never mattered to any of the ladies whose bedchambers Alex had visited in his long career. He wisely chose not to mention that fact. "Perhaps she is peeping out to be sure we go to our own rooms."

"Where else would we— Oh." Nell almost squeaked at the idea that someone thought she would be holding a tryst in the hallway. With his valet sleeping in Alex's chamber and Aunt Hazel sharing her room with Nell, they would have to find an empty nook if they were going to . . . to . . . Heavens! They were in an empty nook right now! "Gracious, she might think we are lovers!"

"Which is perfect for our plan."

"It is perfectly horrid! I am not that kind of woman."

"Too bad, but you can learn." Before Nell could protest, he raised his voice to its normal level and said, "Come, my love. Let me see you to your aunt's room. I hate to say good night, but we must."

Nell followed him and his candlelight past Lady Lucinda's door, which was indeed cracked open, although no light shined forth. The dog did not bark, either because Daisy was asleep or she recognized their voices. Alex stopped outside Aunt Hazel's room.

Then he did the most amazing thing. He put his candle down on the hall table, placed one finger over Nell's lips to stifle any complaint, and wrapped his arms around her!

"What are you— Oh."

He brought his lips down to hers.

"You should not be doing . . . mm."

He was doing, and very nicely. She could feel the heat of his lips spread all the way down to her toes, with interesting stops she would have to consider later.

"I have been wanting to do that forever, it seems," he whispered into her partly opened lips.

He was playacting, so Nell could too. "I have been wanting you to do so for longer."

He kissed her again, this time longer, deeper, his tongue parting her lips to lightly touch her tongue, her teeth, the inside of her lips. Now flames coursed through Nell where a gentle warmth had flowed before.

"Ah." So this was what the poets wrote about. How could they, Nell wondered, when her own mind felt too benumbed with the conflagration to put two thoughts together? Why would they compose verses when they could be kissing? "More," she murmured when Alex took his lips away.

"So sweet. So soft. So giving, just as I knew you

would be." He kissed her again, this time letting his tongue skip around her lips before filling her mouth, then coaxing her own tongue into a more glorious dance.

Surely they would catch the wallpaper on fire! Or else Nell would collapse into a melted pool at Alex's feet, her limbs felt so weak. He would never let her fall, though. His arms tightened around her as if he felt her imminent collapse, pulling Nell nearer so his well-muscled chest supported her. One of his hands drifted lower, to the small of her back, pulling her closer yet, until Nell had to realize that Alex was not entirely pretending.

Nell was an innocent, but she was not ignorant. If country living had not educated her, the school for young ladies had, with smuggled art books, salacious French novels, and studiously accurate medical tomes. Nell knew exactly what was pressing against her lower body, her burning, throbbing, dampening lower body.

That rigidity was no sham, no stage prop. Alex truly wanted her! His body was reacting to hers as much as hers was to him. His hand moved to cup her derriere and lift her higher, against his hardness. He wanted her! Of course Nell knew that a gentleman's desires had little to do with a gentleman's affections. Not every wool merchant or peddler passing through Kingston Upon Hull could fall in love with Kitty Johnstone or her ilk, but Alexander Chalfont Endicott, Lord Carde, London's Ace of Hearts, wanted her, skinny little Nelly Sloane.

She wriggled against him, to make sure.

He groaned.

"You want me," she whispered, with smug satisfaction.

"You'll never know how much."

Now Nell forgot about Lady Lucinda and her dog and the ghosts and the portraits on the wall and the insomniac Redfern. Let anyone who wanted to watch see this perfect moment. Alex was kissing her!

He went on kissing her—or was she kissing him? One of them kept asking for more, at any rate. Neither wanted to stop, not even when Lady Lucinda's door slammed shut. And the key turned in the lock. And a slipper hit the wall, and the dog barked.

They did not hear any of it.

"Blasted Stives is in my room," Alex complained with a moan.

"Blasted Lady Haverhill is in mine," Nell complained right back, not pretending to misunderstand his distress and disappointment. "And Aunt Hazel is in hers."

They went back to what they were doing, only more so. More panting, more pulsing, more pressing against each other with tongues and torsos. His hand found her breast; hers found the tiny curls on the back of his neck and the strong sinews of his shoulder and the curve of his ear.

Both of their defenses were about to fall entirely when his glasses fell instead. Alex pulled back, afraid his last pair of spectacles would get stepped on.

"Deuce take it," he gasped, after retrieving the glasses, putting them on, and looking around the dimly lighted corridor. "I cannot take you here, on the bare floor or against the wall."

Against the wall . . . ? Nell straightened her clothing, wondering how and when her gown had become undone in the back, while she tried to catch her breath. "No, Alex," she said when he would have taken her into his arms again, backing instead until her hand was on the doorknob of Aunt Hazel's room. "No, you cannot take me at all. You cannot take me to London, and you cannot take me under your protection. I will not become your mistress."

CHAPTER TWENTY-ONE

"**M**istress?" Alex tried not to shout. "Mistress? A man does not take a woman like you to be his damned mistress!"

Nell should have backed away when he kissed her. She should have slapped his cheek when his hand reached her nether cheek. She should have raised her knee the way Phelan had taught her when Alex raised his hand to her breast. She should have screamed when his tongue licked at her ear. His tongue had been in her ear? Good grief!

She should have done all of those things, but she had not. Now she did. He might as well have called her a skinny old spinster after taking all those liberties. And who knew how many more he would have taken, along with her virtue, if his spectacles had not become dislodged? So she slapped him.

"I might be a . . . a flat-chested frump, as Lady Lucinda says, but I do have a little pride." She pointed to the bulge still apparent in the front of his trousers. "While you have that. Although I suppose a man is more particular about the women he keeps than the women he kisses." She slapped him again, since he was such an easy target, standing there dumbfounded, staring at her as if she had been speaking Swahili.

"Is that you, Nell?" Aunt Hazel called from inside the bedroom. "What are you trying to do, raise the dead?"

"No, that is your venue, Aunt, not mine. I was just putting the foolish dog back where it belongs."

And before Alex could utter one word other than "Ouch," she opened the door, went in, and shut the door in his red-cheeked face. He could not burst into the room. Nor could he pound on the door or shout, demanding admittance. He could not even go to his own room, not in his current condition, not with his vigilant valet likely still awake. So he walked back down the hall, softly past Lady Lucinda's door, and sat on the top step of the staircase, wondering what had gone wrong.

His plan to discourage Lady Lucinda seemed to be working. His plan to woo Nell had seemed to be working too, until he let his lust—and her eager, untested passion—get the better of them.

Deuce take it, how had he let things go so far? He laughed to himself. That was an easy question to answer. Once he'd started kissing Nell, he'd found it hard to stop. Once she responded so sweetly, it was harder. Everything was harder. Then he could not have stopped kissing her, holding her, touching her, inhaling her scent, sharing the very air she breathed, making love to her, no, not if his very life depended on it. Unfortunately, his seeing depended on it. His blasted spectacles got in the way, and brought Nell, at least, to her senses.

His had flown out the window. But how could Nell think he considered her ripe for a slip on the shoulder? He was no rake, despite his recent difficulties with the weaker sex. Weak, hell! His still-tender cheek did not feel as if Nell were any frail female. He had never propositioned an innocent yet, and he was not about to start with the woman he hoped to make his countess.

And what did she mean by a flat-chested frump? Her breasts were the perfect handful, from what he had felt through the fabric of her gown. Just thinking of holding them, naked, made his fingers tingle, and did not do much to help his arousal subside, either. Was it her clothes that concerned her? He did not care if Nell wore silk or a flour sack as long as he could get her out of it. He'd dress her in satin and lace if that was what she wanted. What he wanted was to have her bare, beneath him.

At this rate, he would never be able to face his valet.

A flat-chested frump? Nell was beautiful. Surely she knew that. Had he told her so? Alex had meant to, along with so much more, before his mind turned to mush. He could not recall, but he did remember groaning a few times. Lud, no wonder she'd taken him in disgust for acting like a rutting beast.

He knew better than to treat Nell like a dockside doxy, so why the devil had he rushed his fences like that? Why? Because he'd been lectured by a slick-haired secretary, who might have been right. Because Lady Lucinda was peeking from behind her door. Because he was tired of being the dull and dignified, responsible earl and wanted to revisit, just for a moment, his carefree youth of pranks and play. And because he wanted to make love to Nell with all his heart and soul.

He might as well sleep on the steps.

*   *   *

The ducal cavalcade was leaving the following afternoon, despite Nell's polite urging of them to stay. Lady Lucinda missed the parties and pastimes of London, she said. Her father missed his own physician, he said. Lady Haverhill missed the word to start packing, or they would have left in the morning. Peabody did not miss an opportunity to thank Alex again and again for the letters of introduction in his hand.

Sir Chauncy was to accompany the lead carriage on his horse. Feeling magnanimous now that the husband-hunting party was moving to more fertile ground, Alex took the baronet aside to warn him that his chances of winning the raven-haired heiress's hand were slim. And her fortune was slimmer.

Sir Chauncy was looking at Nell with regret, at Lady Lucinda with repugnance, and at his empty pockets with resignation.

Then Alex told him about a lovely young miss whose father was a congenial sportsman with a lucrative estate next to Alex's own, and no male heirs to leave the place to. Miss Daphne Branford would make the baronet a charming wife. And Alex would make him a deadly enemy if Sir Chauncy played fast and loose with his young neighbor's affections.

Sir Chauncy brightened instantly. "An unentailed estate, you say?"

"And a pretty girl. Of the untouched, malleable sort. If you want the other kind, I can easily arrange an introduction to Mona, Lady Monroe, if you think you can afford to court her."

"No, no, I am quite taken with the notion of being your neighbor. Besides, I'd just as soon know I fathered my own heirs, rather than the next chap to catch Lady Monroe's eye. And if I am forced to marry money, I realized, I'd rather be the one with the higher title. Lady Lucinda's airs would have grown stale before the honeymoon. A fellow has his pride, you know."

Sir Chauncy had too much pride to get an honest job, it seemed to Alex, but Squire Branford and his daughter would be happy with a handsome baronet, since they could not get an earl.

Satisfied with his matchmaking efforts, Alex decided to promote his own cause. Unfortunately, he never found Nell alone until they were on the steps of Ambeaux Cottage seeing the guests off. He had been ready to explain at breakfast, apologize at midday, grovel at tea, but he never got the chance, not even to beg once. She was helping Lady Lucinda with the packing, since the maid Browne had pleaded for a position at Ambeaux Cottage rather than returning to London with the duke and his daughter. Or she was helping her aunt mix potions to relieve the duke's pain. Or else she was with her brother, who still did not speak, although he seemed to appreciate the attentions of Browne, who was hiding in Phelan's bedroom rather than face her former mistress.

Nell inclined her head to Alex with chilly politeness as they watched Peabody direct the loading of trunks onto the duke's crested carriage and baggage wagon. She looked as tired as he felt. Alex knew he'd slept too briefly, too restlessly, thinking of the kisses and caresses they had shared, and all they had not shared. He wondered if she suffered unsatisfied urges too, or if she thought of him at all.

She had obviously been thinking of her reputation. While the duke's valet tried to make sense of Aunt Hazel's directions for the various elixirs and effusions, Nell asked Alex, "Do you think Lady Lucinda will tell anyone of what she heard or saw last night? I do not wish my name blackened further. Not that I care about London gossip, but the rumor grapevine eventually finds its way to the countryside. Families already hesitate about letting their children attend my drawing classes. None of the students would come if I were considered fast, besides everything else."

She waved her hand to encompass the surroundings, where Madame Ambeaux was conversing with the duke's valet after consulting with some physician who had been dead for twenty years. Nell included the servants tripping over one another and the bags, because her butler could not go outside in the afternoon sunshine to bring order to the chaotic scene. She did not even need to mention her comatose—or cunning—brother.

"If I am to live here, I would not have my name besmirched."

"It shall not be. I spoke with Lady Lucinda. She will not whisper a hint of any impropriety to anyone. I made sure of that by mentioning a tender love scene I had accidentally witnessed in the conservatory. She and Peabody were behaving far more scandalously among the oranges and ferns."

"They were? That is, that is blackmail."

"With which Lady Lucinda is also intimately acquainted. She will not speak, though, because I also said I'd find a position for the poor bastard—er, blighter. One with both income and importance, possibly with the Home Secretary. Who knows, with the lady's ambition and her father's influence, Peabody might become a cabinet minister someday. It's not an earl, but politics will suit Lady Lucinda like a glove. Peabody might even find himself with a title if he rises

far enough, or if the duke's fortune is restored suffi-
ciently to pay some of Prinny's bills. And his firstborn
son might be duke, if His Grace petitions the college
of arms to let the title devolve on his grandchild, if
some old cousin passes on first. I doubt Peabody
would mind changing his name to Applegate for such
a worthwhile cause."

"I see you have been busy this morning, too. All I
have had to do was listen to Lady Lucinda thanking
heaven that I am not accompanying her back to London, and Aunt Hazel lamenting that I am not going."

"She wishes you to leave?"

"I believe she wishes to see more of His Grace. At
first I thought she just wanted to win more of his
coins, but now . . ." Now Nell worried that her relative
had shared more than a few rounds of cards with the
duke. "André is still not speaking with her, it seems,
and she fears being lonely here."

"What did you tell her?"

"I said I would reconsider a visit, when Phelan
recovers."

"And if he does not?"

"Then how could I leave him?"

That was Alex's worst fear, but he did not say so.
Now was not the time, with servants bustling back and
forth, and the duke hobbling toward his coach, Madame Ambeaux on one side, his valet on the other.
Lady Lucinda was berating the new maid assigned to
accompany her, and the dog was barking at all the
commotion. The lady wore a green striped carriage
dress, and the furry dog had a matching green bow in
its topknot.

Alex pointed toward where his man, Stives, was
packing bags into his own coach, farther down the

carriage drive. "I have also been busy making arrangements to move to the inn in the village after all. That way there will be no possibility of any gossip."

"But you said Lady Lucinda would not carry tales."

"Nor shall she. But with her gone, and Lady Haverhill too, I am afraid you require a more vigilant chaperone than your aunt Hazel. She is not known for her, ah . . ."

"Sanity?"

"For paying attention to the physical world rather than the fantastical. And your brother is known to be incapacitated. People will talk."

Nell could not say she did not care, right after claiming she worried about her neighbors' opinions. "I think you are making too much of local interest. No one concerns themself with us."

"I am concerned, however, lest there be a repeat of my brutish behavior of last night. There is less likelihood with me sleeping at The King's Arms." And more chance of him sleeping, period.

Nell clutched his arm in dismay. "Oh, no, you cannot let what happened last night put you out of the house. The playacting for Lady Lucinda's benefit simply got out of hand. I was to blame too, for not protesting sooner."

He patted her hand. "You are to blame for nothing. I am the experienced one who should have known better than to play with fire. I do know better than to take advantage of an innocent woman, leading her to believe that my intentions were dishonorable."

"They weren't?"

"Of course not, silly. You are a lady. I respect you far too much to offer you carte blanche. I respect your powerful right arm now, too. I cannot guarantee that it will not happen again, however, not with less chaperonage, not with you so near to hand, looking so lovely."

"Your plan worked and Lady Lucinda is already leaving, so you do not need to hand me Spanish coin."

"Looking so lovely," he insisted. "Nigh irresistible."

"Do not be absurd. I did not sleep at all and have shadows under my eyes. I spilled one of aunt's decoctions on my gown, which was old and unstylish to start with. I smell like an apothecary shop and my hair is all undone."

"Now you are being even more foolish. Loveliness has nothing to do with your gown or your hair." He tucked one golden curl back off her face. "If no one was around I would show you why you need a chaperone, and why I need to go to the inn."

"You would? Even though you are safe from Lady Lucinda?"

He tipped her chin up so that he could look into her blue eyes. "Lady Lucinda can go to London, or she can go to Hades. You look beautiful to me, Nell."

"I do?"

He nodded, and touched her cheek with his fingers. "You do."

Unfortunately, she looked beautiful to the goose, too.

Nell's devoted pet had been content in the pen fashioned for him at the rear of the kitchen garden, complete with a little shed, a water trough, and a lady goose purchased from Mrs. Posener. He preened and he strutted, and he waited for Nell to come with crumbs from breakfast, tidbits from luncheon, biscuits from tea. She had not come at all today. Wellesley was not content.

Nell did not see him coming around the side of the house, because she was too bemused to notice anything but the tiny amber flecks in Alex's eyes, and how his mouth curled at the corners, for her.

He thought she was beautiful. He thought she was a lady. And he respected her. One was a treat, two were a treasure, three were a trove to be hoarded away, taken out on rainy afternoons to brighten the gloom. They were to be cherished and held in one's heart forever after.

Whatever else happened—and she would not think past this moment—the finest gentleman of her experience admired her. Of course he was driving her insane, with emotions that varied with the hour, from agony to anger to ecstasy and euphoria, with indecision and despair and desire thrown in the mix. She felt like one of Cook's leftover pots, with a little of this and a bit of that, till no one knew precisely what they were eating. Nell hardly knew who she was anymore. But Alex thought she was beautiful. She wished he'd say it again.

Instead, he said, "Oh, hell."

Wellesley waddled into view.

"Oh, dear, and I do not have any food for him."

The big bird did not want food. He wanted his beloved Nell safe from the marauders: the strangers, the horses and . . . the barking dog.

Wellesley set off at a flying run, wings outstretched, long neck extended, yellow beak open and hissing.

Lady Lucinda shrieked and threw herself into Peabody's arms. Aunt Hazel leaped into the duke's carriage, pulling him behind her and slamming the door shut, narrowly missing his gouty foot. The valet scrambled to the roof of the coach, along with two other menservants who had not moved as fast in years. Sir Chauncy was attempting to control his bucking horse and stay on its back, while the new lady's maid was trying to hold two hatboxes, a jewel case, and her own satchel as she ran back into the house. And the dog kept barking.

So what if the mop-haired creature was the smallest of the intruders? It was the noisiest. The goose aimed right at the shaggy four-legged beast, who doggedly—or dunderheadedly—stood her ground.

"No, Daisy!" Nell called. "Run!"

Nell was too far away to get between the bird and the brave little animal who thought she was protecting her own mistress from a flying fury. That mistress was in Peabody's embrace, which seemed less protective than possessive. Neither the woman nor the secretary looked at the dog.

Daisy snapped and snarled; the goose kept coming. Nell started down the steps. Alex was right behind her.

The goose struck first. Pluck went the green bow, with some of Daisy's hair. Daisy yelped. Pluck went another tuft of long white hair. Daisy screamed. Nell screamed. Lady Lucinda screamed and dragged Peabody behind the baggage wagon where no one could see them.

Pluck. Pluck. Pluck. The little dog, half the goose's size although with heavier bones, was yowling, high-pitched barks of pain and rage. Daisy still did not run, and she still kept getting attacked. She could spin and she could leap, but she could not launch herself off the ground.

Daisy managed to get a mouthful of feathers, which she had to spit out before she could return to the fray. Wellesley had no gentlemanly instincts whatsoever, no sense of fair play or calling a truce. While the dog was choking, the goose snagged her tail. For a moment Daisy was half suspended in the air, then the goose looked like he was carrying a barrister's wig, and poor little Daisy looked like a rat in a fur cape.

Alex's man, Stives, was racing up the drive, brandishing a pistol.

"Put that away, man," Alex shouted as he ran. "You are liable to shoot one of us before you hit the goose."

Shoot the goose? Nell was almost near enough to grab her pet—and get bitten herself, most likely—when Alex's coat went sailing past her. The expensive dark blue superfine garment fluttered, then fell in the dirt, right on top of Wellesley.

"Good throw!" Nell called, rushing to gather up the bird, Alex's coat, and a good portion of the graveled driveway.

"That animal is a menace," he said with a growl, going to the dog, who had no more growls left. Daisy was trembling and whimpering and looking for her mistress, who had not come back from behind the baggage wagon. Alex picked her up and held her close, whispering soothing sounds to the bedraggled little beast.

Nell had uncovered Wellesley's head so he could breathe, but she held him tightly, her back to Alex and the dog so he would calm. Redfern handed her a dish of comfits to feed the goose before the old butler hurried back into the house, one hand over his pale, weak eyes.

Lady Lucinda had her hand over her eyes too, so she would not have to see the results of the melee. Her other hand clutched Peabody's arm as she finally came out into the others' view.

"This is the most dreadful visit of my life!" she said to her companion, ignoring Alex and Nell, who was wiping her fingers on Alex's coat while the goose ate, still in her arms and still tightly wrapped in the fabric. "I cannot wait another instant to be gone from this awful place. Help me into the carriage, Peabody, and get in right now or I shall go without you. Lady Haverhill and that fumble-fingered maid can come later with the rest of the baggage."

Lady Lucinda nearly shoved Aunt Hazel out of the coach, taking the seat next to her father where the older woman had been. "Go," she ordered the driver, before Mr. Peabody had a chance to hand down Madame Ambeaux and get in himself. The other servants were still climbing to the ground from the carriage roof, so the driver ignored Lady Lucinda's shouted orders.

"But what about your dog?" Alex wanted to know, holding out the poor shivering creature.

Lady Lucinda took one look out the window at her pet, at the bald spots and the red, raw patches where silky white hair had been, and pounded on the roof for the coach to start moving. "What would I want with an ugly animal like that? Driver, move!"

Aunt Hazel handed Alex her shawl to wrap around poor Daisy, who licked the earl's chin as the carriages drove off, Sir Chauncy and his lathered mount behind them.

"It appears you own a dog now, my lord."

Alex's valet looked at the sorry excuse for a dog, already shedding what was left of its white hair onto Alex's maroon waistcoat. Then Stives looked at Nell, with milord's best Bath superfine being used as a swaddling cloth for a berserk goose. Then he looked at the pistol in his hand.

No one would know just what Stives was going to aim at, the fowl, the fur, the female, his feckless employer, or his own forehead.

"I'll save you, Lizbeth," Phelan shouted from the doorway of the house, his white nightshirt flapping in the breeze, a fireplace poker raised above his head. "Don't move, I'll save you."

CHAPTER TWENTY-TWO

"**D**o not shoot!"

Nell had the goose, Alex had the dog. Stives had the gun, but he could not shoot a lunatic, even before Nell's plea. It was up to Aunt Hazel to throw gravel from the drive at poker-brandishing Phelan, trying to stop his assault on the valet by blinding him. "That is Nell, not Lizbeth, you crazy cabbagehead."

Browne came running out of the house, crying. "I went to see what was causing the commotion, and Mr. Sloane ran past me. I am so sorry, miss. I could not catch him."

Alex thrust Daisy into the maid's arms. By the time he could reach his man, Stives had fended off three blows from the fireplace poker with his upflung arms, but had taken two. It was a miracle the carriage pistol had not exploded or fallen. Worse, it might have fallen into Sloane's hands.

Alex did not want to hurt him, knowing Nell would never forgive him, and he needed to speak to the skitter-witted Sloane, besides. He could not let the barefoot berserker injure anyone else, though. He tried to grab him from behind, but Sloane swung the poker over his head. Then he tried to pull Sloane to the ground by his flowing nightshirt, but the man, if not the fabric, was stronger than Alex thought. He held a fistful of white cotton; Sloane still held the poker.

"No, leave me be!" he shouted. "I have to stop him!"

"No, he will not hurt her. Put down the poker."

"It is all right, brother. No one is trying to hurt anyone. Mr. Stives is the earl's man, that's all. Please stop."

Sloane did not stop or set down his weapon. He turned it on Alex instead, catching the earl a glancing blow on his bad shoulder. The pain made Alex not quite as sympathetic. Sloane owed him for that, and for upsetting his sister, too. He swung his good fist, but missed. Gentleman Jackson would not be proud, but the boxing master was not facing a madman with a metal rod. Alex had to duck and skip back, without the chance to aim another punch that could have ended the fight.

While Sloane's back was to Stives, though, the valet took his own advantageous opportunity. He turned the pistol around and bashed Nell's brother on the head. Stives had no reason to feel sorry for the make-bate, not after having his arm almost broken from the man's blows, so he hit hard enough to knock Phelan unconscious, and then some.

Nell cried out and dropped the goose. The maid ran inside with the dog. Aunt Hazel picked up the poker. "One step closer and I'll stick this up your tail so you are ready for the spit." She was speaking to the goose, not Phelan. Wellesley was more interested in the fallen comfits than further conflict.

Alex was more interested in the pistol, scooping it

up and wondering why it had not discharged after so much mishandling, although he was thankful for the lucky escape.

"It's not loaded, milord."

"Why the devil not?"

Stives was a valet, not a bodyguard. Offended, he rubbed at his sore arm. "There was no time. And which should I have shot, milord, the bird or the Bedlamite?"

The goose was picking at crumbs, the madman was unconscious. Nell was kneeling on the ground at her brother's side. Alex handed the pistol back to Stives, saying, "Find some cold cloths for your arm, and then get help to unpack the coach."

"We are staying? I thought milord decided the wiser course would be to—"

"I cannot leave Nell, Miss Sloane, alone now. She'll need help with the injured man, or protection from him—if he is not pretending again."

Phelan was not pretending. He needed eight stitches to close the gash on his head. The surgeon shook his own head. Years had gone by without a message from Ambeaux Cottage; now he was sent for almost daily, it seemed. Bad luck haunted the place, besides the ghosts of past residents, but it was good fortune and a heavy purse for him and the apothecary in town.

Phelan stayed still, his eyes closed, not speaking. At least he was in his own chamber, with a different, larger portrait of Lizbeth facing his larger bed. The only other difference between this week and last week was the white bandage around his head and the new lock on the door.

Phelan's valet packed up and left, refusing to work for a gentleman who kept appearing out in public without his proper attire, to say nothing of being out of his proper mind. So Stives and the footmen had to look after Phelan's personal needs, while Nell fed him and read to him and prayed over him. Browne helped. Alex paced.

He felt guilty. Not because Phelan was injured, but because he wished the man had been injured worse. They would all be better off if Sloane died, as cold and cruel as that notion was. The estate books were a mess, but they proved Phelan had been systematically bleeding the place dry while his own comforts were secured. The shipyard's books were worse, showing near bankruptcy. Phelan was a thief, at the least, and Alex refused to forgive his neglect of the tenants, and of Nell. If he recovered, Alex would have to bring charges against Phelan, for the man was too dangerous to be allowed to simply walk away. Wasn't that a fine way to prove one's interest and affection for a lady? Or he could send him to some asylum for the insane, to live the rest of his days locked behind bars. Nell would never hear of that. Alex had a property in Jamaica that might be far enough away, if he could get Nell to agree, and if Phelan stayed there.

Phelan could stay as he was, and stay right here, Alex supposed, with guards and keepers and attendants. Alex could easily afford the cost in money: What he could not afford was the cost to Nell. He knew her now, and knew she would not want to leave her brother to servants' care. He admired her loyalty, but dedication was deuced inconvenient at times.

Alex did not want the man in England. In the ground would be far better. Not that he intended to help matters along, of course, but Alex could not help hoping. He went again to see Phelan's condition for himself that evening.

There was Nell, as usual, sewing more infant clothes for one of the tenants by lamplight. A pad and pencil was on the table beside her so she could draw when her eyes tired of setting tiny stitches while her brother slept on, or whatever the surgeon called his supposed comatose state.

"Doesn't he look better to you?" Nell asked, setting aside her needlework.

Better than what, a maggot? "He does appear to have more color in his complexion," Alex conceded.

"The surgeon hopes for a full recovery."

So much for Alex's hopes. "Wonderful."

Nell could tell from Alex's tone that he was not pleased with Phelan. "He will wake up soon and explain everything. You can ask about the estate monies, and you can ask about Lizbeth, too. Now that he has spoken, he is sure to come back to us again."

She was whispering, as if Phelan could hear her. If the dastard could hear, he could talk, Alex would swear. He swore now, but too low for Nell to make out the words.

"He will not like it, but Phelan owes you answers to your questions. You have been so patient, and I know you have been providing all the extra servants and luxuries we are enjoying."

"No, the additional staff is for the additional work my presence causes. You must not consider the cost of anything you need."

"You are the most generous man I have ever met, and I will make certain my brother knows that. I am sure he will cooperate then."

Alex was sure of nothing except how much he

wanted to kiss her again. He had been keeping his distance, to keep his hands off her. Besides, it had not seemed fitting to dally while her brother lay at death's door.

Tonight, though, Phelan was recovering, damn him, and Nell was temptation on a tea tray. Her hair was loosely braided, then gathered behind her neck with a few artful curls left trailing, begging for a man to wind them around his fingers or tuck them behind her ear. They were most likely that maid Browne's handiwork, who would know the latest town styles. Alex made a note to increase the woman's wages so Browne would stay in Nell's employ. Then again, after Lady Lucinda as a mistress, the woman appeared as if she would be happy to work for Miss Sloane for free.

Nell was still wearing the same gown she had worn to dinner tonight, with the vicar and Madame Ambeaux passing opinions on the afterlife along with the peas and potatoes. The gown was pale blue muslin, with tiny blue flowers embroidered here and there on the fabric. Forget-me-nots, Alex thought, as if he could forget the feel of her against his chest. If the brother could not hear or see . . .

No, Alex might wish the man dead, but he could not forget his presence. Alex stared at the still figure on the bed rather than the lithe figure in the chair. "Let us hope Phelan feels as cooperative when he awakens. I have no one else to ask for answers."

"I thought you were going to Hull and Scarborough to find out what Phelan had been involved in?"

"I did. I took the sketch of your brother that you gave me and showed it to innkeepers and hostlers. It was an excellent likeness, by the way."

"Thank you, but I have still not forgiven you for dragging my sketchbooks out into public that way."

"You have been hiding your light under a barrel too long. No one had any trouble identifying your brother by the drawing."

"And what did they say?"

"That he visited both towns regularly, but he kept mostly to himself. The shipyard in Hull is derelict, and has been closed for three years. He still did a little banking in each place, however, and a great deal of drinking. The banks will not reveal his private business, although Mr. Silbiger feels we may be able to subpoena the records if it comes to that."

Nell's face lost some of its color. "You mean if he is accused of pilfering from the estate?"

"No, I mean if he does not recover his wits. Someone will have to be appointed to stand as legal guardian and trustee of his finances. But let us not worry about that until we have to."

Nell was worrying about nothing else. What was going to happen to them if Phelan stayed lost in his coma? She could not expect Alex to keep paying her brother's bills, especially not when Phelan had stolen from him. She picked up her pad and pencil rather than wring her hands or throw herself at Alex and beg for his mercy . . . or just throw herself at Alex, period.

He looked so very, very good to her tonight, with his hair in damp curls from his bath and a spotted kerchief tied around his neck. Another silk kerchief was carefully wrapped around the small white dog that sat at his feet, to cover the goose-inflicted bald spots. Holes had been cut in the kerchief for Daisy's legs and tail, and a belt of sorts had been fashioned from what looked like a striped watch fob ribbon.

Nell thought she would ask Aunt Hazel to knit the little dog a better coat, to make up for the goose's malice. Aunt Hazel was doing nothing but pine for her lost love anyway, although whether that was the disappearing André or the departed duke, Nell did not know. Aunt Hazel believed Phelan was feigning illness, other than the head wound, and refused to make him tonics or tisanes from her stillroom. The least she could do was knit a little garment to keep the dog warm—and unembarrassed—until her hair grew back.

Meanwhile, Daisy was gazing up at her rescuer as if she would never let Alex out of her sight again. Nell could understand the dog's adoration.

She started to draw both of them, an endearing picture to add to the memories indelibly etched in her heart. How many other men would suffer a silly pup with bare patches, and dressed like a miniature jockey, besides? As she drew, she smiled, thinking that here was the essence of the Earl of Carde, and why she loved him. She truly loved him? The pencil fell from her fingers. She picked it up and quickly asked, "What else did you discover?"

"That everyone knew the direction of your brother's last, ah, lady friend. He made no effort to hide the connection."

"She was his mistress. You might as well use the word. I did. I am no milk and water miss afraid to hear the words, you know, or unwilling to acknowledge the existence of such women."

"No, but the rules of polite society do not permit ladybirds to be discussed in front of a lady."

"I am not a member of polite society, remember? And if you were so concerned about the rules London lives by, then you should not be alone with me, here in Phelan's bedchamber, after dinner. I doubt an unconscious man counts as chaperone."

"Ah, but exceptions are made for sickroom duties."
If not, they ought to be, Alex decided. "Anyway, the
woman's name is Helen. I called on her, hoping she
might know what he did with the money."

"I admit I am curious about that, too. And her."

"Do not be. She has not seen your brother in two
years. Even then, she was not strictly in his keeping.
He never bought a house for her, as she had one from
her deceased husband, and she saw other gentlemen
there. In fact, she ran her home as a, ah, boarding
establishment for male guests."

"A brothel? Goodness, I have never known anyone
who—" She stopped. Now it seemed she knew two,
from Alex's sudden bending to pet the dog. "That is,
I never would have thought Phelan comfortable in
such a place."

"He was not. Your brother stopped there occasionally for years, since about the time of Lizbeth's marriage to my father, from what Helen recalls. He
seldom stayed at her house long. He was never generous, either, she told me, so he was not spending his
blunt, my blunt, on her."

The overweight, overpainted, overaged for her line
of work woman had also told Alex that Phelan was
never much interested in intimacy. After she tucked
the earl's folded banknote between her drooping
breasts, she confided that Phelan had seemed half
ashamed of his body's needs, and totally uninterested
in *her* body's needs. She'd winked at Alex, as if she
could tell that the handsome young earl knew more
about pleasuring a lady. Alex had asked another question, quickly.

It seemed Phelan always hurried off to wash as soon
as he finished what he'd come for. Then he'd taken

to drinking, as if to wash the rest of the sinning away. None of which was suitable for Nell's ears, no matter how liberal-minded she considered herself.

"He mostly used her house as a place to get drunk."

Nell glanced up from her pad to look at her brother. "I knew he imbibed, but I never thought more so than any other gentleman. I never saw him more than a bit on the go until he returned here last week."

Alex took the dog on his lap, the better to scratch its ears. "He hid a great many things from his family, it seems. According to Helen, he stayed foxed for days on end. Sometimes he turned maudlin, other times mean, so she was happy enough to see the last of him, especially when he started complaining about her prices. She had no idea what he did at the bank, or if he had any odd sums of money. If Phelan was indeed stealing from the estate, he was not spending it there."

Nell went back to her drawing. "I am sorry. I know you were hoping for more information, but in a way I am glad. I hadn't liked thinking that Phelan had an unsanctioned relationship, possibly illegitimate children tucked away. Or the idea that he might bring them here eventually."

"If he did have another family, or even another paramour, he never visited her that anyone knew, aside from a few calls on local, ah, ladies of the night in the past years. Helen recalls him saying he was going to London once or twice for brief visits, but not regularly."

"London? He never told me." Nell could have gone along, to see a play or visit the shops. She felt even more betrayed.

"Well, a man would not take his sister along if he were up to no good. He never called on me there, for that matter, and I never saw him at any of the clubs or sporting events or horse auctions. I just wish I knew what he was involved in." He stood up and walked over to the bed, staring down at Phelan, wishing he could shake some answers out of him. The man did seem improved, so Alex supposed he would recover. He made a sound of disgust. The dog in his arms growled.

So did Nell. "I am not finished with the drawing yet."

Alex went back to the hard chair and tried to reposition the dog on his lap. "I got nowhere looking into Lizbeth's death, either."

"After all these years, I am not surprised."

Which only made Alex feel worse, that he had let his own investigation wait so long. "I doubt I could have discovered anything Mr. Silbiger had not, anyway. The man is nothing if not efficient."

"And a gentleman. I wonder if he would come to dinner this week, and perhaps take Aunt Hazel's mind off the past."

Poor Mr. Silbiger, Alex thought, but he said, "He spoke highly of your cook. At any rate, I was able to go back over every one of his reports for the last decade, since he had copies of each document. I could then locate the last living witnesses to the coach's departure, and as many of the search party as were still alive and within reach. I interviewed constables and sheriff's assistants and magistrate's clerks, and checked every parish record for miles, looking for unclaimed bodies, arrests of strangers, anything that might give some hint as to the unknown guard's identity."

"You still think he might have taken Lottie with him when he left?"

"I think he is my only hope."

"But you discovered nothing?"

"Nothing that we have not known all along: that he was an average-looking man whose name might have been Fred or not, that he spoke to no one at the posting house, and that his only noticeable mark was a gold tooth. Do you know how many men have gold teeth?"

"Redfern has one in the back of his mouth. I saw it once, but— Wait!"

Nell jumped up, tossed her pad and pencil onto Phelan's bed, and rushed out of the room.

"They are all attics to let here, Daisy," Alex told the little dog, who had been startled out of her nap. She looked around for the nightmarish goose, then barked. Alex thought Phelan might have winced at the noise, but he supposed an unconscious man could have some of his senses.

Then Nell came back, hair flying, bright color in her cheeks, her eyes shining. She thrust one of her old sketch pads at him.

"Here, this is what I recalled. I went through my earliest books after you brought them down, the ones from before I went away to school, the ones I would not let anyone see, remember?"

He nodded, catching her excitement. "And?"

"And I remembered this one!" She flipped through a few pages, then stopped at a rough pencil sketch of two men in a stable, with a badly drawn horse looking over its stall door. Even at her young age Nell had shown talent, Alex thought with pride, for one man was instantly recognizable as her brother, more like the Phelan Sloane Alex recalled from his father's wedding than the wan invalid in the bed, with his deeply etched wrinkles and receding hairline. But the other man . . .

"He has a gold tooth!"

"It looks as if I tried to show how it gleamed in the light," Nell said, looking over his shoulder.

"And you did! He has deep-set eyes and a weak chin and light-colored hair. And if this was done before you went to school, it was at just the right time. Now maybe someone will recognize him and tell us his name! You did it, my precious girl, you gave us the clue we need!"

Nell glowed under his approval, but she could not help warning, "But that is not saying it will lead to Lottie, you know."

"Of course not, but now we are one step closer. Why did no one ask you before? Everyone was looking for a man with a gold tooth."

"I was just a girl, with tragedy all around. Who thinks of a child at a time like that? And then I went off to school."

"And you might never have remembered this particular drawing if no one asked about it."

Nell was staring at the page, biting her lip. "In a way I am sorry I remembered it now. It proves Phelan knew the man and never spoke up, doesn't it? They are playing dice together."

Alex could not lie to her, so he turned and kissed her cheek instead. "We still have a million questions. But now we have one more answer than we have had for a decade. Thanks to you."

He put the drawing pad down, picked Nell up, and twirled her around in a joyous circle, this time kissing her full on the mouth, and staying there. She was beautiful. She was brilliant. She was the best thing he had ever held.

The dog growled.

Or was that Phelan?

CHAPTER TWENTY-THREE

Aunt Hazel could not give the man a name, but she knew she had seen him somewhere. No, not in the stable with Phelan, but here in the house.

Alive or dead, that was the question.

And no, no one had ever asked her about him before, not that she could remember. Since no one had thought to question her about the man with the gold tooth, Alex decided to ask Aunt Hazel about Lottie. "Did you ever wonder what happened to her?"

"*Mais, oui.* Of course I did. She was such a pretty child, and so well behaved. I was hoping to help raise her when she was found, since both her parents and grandparents were all dead. Eleanor was too young, of course, and you were naught but a schoolboy. Phelan? Faugh. What kind of parent would he be to a near infant when he could not do right by his own sister? Little Charlotte might have been the child I never had."

"But you never saw her after the mishap?"

"How could I? She disappeared. I thought that was why you came."

"Yes, it was. But if she was dead . . . ?"

"Then you would not have come at all, would you?"

Alex did not want to address the criticism implicit in the old woman's query. He should have been here as soon as he reached his majority, seeking his half-sister or not. The property was his, along with the responsibility for his stepmother's relatives, and they both knew it. He was the head of the family, no matter how tenuous the connection. He was the earl.

"I am here now," he replied. "And asking if you would have . . . seen Lottie if she were dead." He removed his spectacles to polish them and give himself a mental shake. Lud, had he really asked if the attics-to-let auntie had spoken to a ghost? Kissing Nell must have rattled his own brains more than he thought. The memory made him smile.

Aunt Hazel clapped her hands. "Oh, you do believe me! I always thought you were a lovely boy. Much more intelligent than the other one."

"I am keeping an open— That is, you have not spoken to my brother recently, have you?" Alex asked in a hurry, just in case the feather-headed French-woman did have some way of communicating with the departed. "Jack isn't . . . ?"

"He is not putting spiders in my bed, if that is what you mean, and I do believe he would, were he on the Other Side."

Alex was annoyed at himself for being relieved. He did not believe in ghosts, or gray-haired ladies exchanging gossip with them. Still, it would not hurt to ask: "What about Lottie, Lizbeth's little girl?"

"Oh, baby Charlotte was much too sweet a child for that kind of nonsense. But, no, I have not spoken with the dear girl since she waved farewell with her tiny hand, all those years ago. Now that you mention it, I suppose she would have visited with Lizbeth if they were together now, wouldn't she?"

Alex was getting a headache. Half of him wanted to ask Aunt Hazel to question Lizbeth about Lottie's whereabouts and to tell his father that he was trying his best to fulfill his promise. The other half of him wanted to lock Nell's rattle-brained relative away, like Phelan.

There were no ghosts. There was no way of making amends or making friends with the deceased. One could talk to one's dear departed as much as one wanted, he supposed, but it would be a cold day in hell indeed before they replied. That was what he firmly believed. Then why did he now also believe, in his heart if not in his head, that Lottie was alive?

He could not answer that question, but he felt the truth of it: Lottie was alive. And he was going to find her. Now he had a way to do so, thanks to Nell.

Nell seemed to believe it too, for she was busy making copies of her sketch. Alex intended to show the picture of the gold-toothed man to everyone in the surrounding counties and send a copy on to London for the Bow Street Runners. He would have posters printed and reward notices placed in the newspapers again. The portrait was old and the man would have aged, but surely someone would know his name and direction.

No one in Kingston Upon Hull did, nor Upper Kingston. Mr. Silbiger kept apologizing for not questioning Miss Sloane himself after the tragedy, but he did not know the man in the drawing. Nor did the magistrate, his bailiff, the constable, the sheriff's assistant, or the owners of any posting inn or pub within two hours of Ambeaux Cottage.

"I shall have to go farther afield, to the taverns and

inns Phelan frequented. He must have met the man there, since no one nearby recognizes him. I doubt I will be back for a day or two."

"You are going to call on that woman, Helen?"

"She would be the most logical, owning a boarding house and all."

Nell knew the "and all" meant the scores of men passing through the woman's doors, if not her bedroom door. "I wish you would not."

Alex studied her downcast eyes, then he raised her chin and placed a kiss on her nose, smiling. "If I did not know better, I would say you were jealous."

Nell did know better, and she was. "I . . . That is, she . . ."

"She is five and forty if she is a day, and she is fat, with sagging chins and—and bleached hair. Do you think that is what I want?"

"But she knows how to please a man, and you might . . ."

"But I won't. You are the only woman I want, Nell. The only woman I will ever want."

She believed that as much as she believed in Aunt Hazel's ghosts, but oh, how nice if it were true. "Hurry home, then," she told him.

"I can see your doubts, sweetings, and I would stay to disprove them, but I really must be off."

"Of course you must. You have come so far, after so long, and you have tried so hard. Now that you are closer to a solution, you should not wait another instant. Lottie might be waiting around the next corner for her big brother to bring her home."

"She is nearly sixteen years of age by now. I wonder if she will even wish to return to us. She could be planning her wedding to a Gypsy, for all I know."

She could be in a workhouse, or a house like Helen's, or in the home of whatever beloved family had taken her in all those years ago. They had no way of knowing. Nell thought about Lottie's homecoming if, indeed, Alex succeeded in bringing her back. No matter where the child had been, or with whom, she would not have had the advantages of the daughter of a nobleman, the life she was entitled to. She would not know the rules of polite society or have the education of a lady. Why, she might not be able to read! How could she fit in with the debutantes? How would she fare with the dowagers? Likely as poorly as Nell herself would. Charlotte's life might get easier in some respects, but far harder in others.

"If she is happy," she told Alex, "that is all that matters. Now go, find out."

So Alex rode off on Phelan's horse, leaving Stives behind to keep Nell safe and Phelan secured. Both of his saddlebags were bulging. One held food for his ride, bread and cheese and raspberry tarts and a jar of ale. Nell had also tucked in a bit of clover for luck, and one of Aunt Hazel's new roses, to remind him of her. The other saddlebag held Daisy, her newly shorn head peeping out of the leather, her tongue lolling in joy to be at Alex's side.

Nell wished she could go too.

Nell kept busy so she would not think of Alex, except for every other minute. Had he found the man with the gold tooth? Had he found Lottie? Had he stayed at Helen's house? She spilled soup down Phelan's clean nightshirt.

Would Alex come back tonight, and what should she wear? She cut the flower stems too short for the vase she was filling.

Could he truly want her? Nell twirled in a circle,

and almost toppled poor Redfern as he brought in the post.

But she would not think about Alex.

She spent the afternoon with Sophie Posener and her new baby, instead. Sophie wept at the stack of little garments Nell presented to her—minus one knitted sweater that had been altered for the dog. Nell wept too, at the miracle of little Alexander. Sophie and her husband had named the boy after the earl, their landlord and benefactor, so it was impossible for Nell not to think of him and his kind, generous heart, not to think of holding a baby to her breast the way Sophie was holding hers.

The new mother was staring down at the infant, totally besotted, a silly smile on her face, and Nell could understand why. The babe was still red and swollen from the birth and bald, but he was perfect. Nell's arms ached to hold a tiny boy of her own, but hers would have dark curly hair. And spectacles.

"If it had been a girl," Sophie was saying as she held the infant against her shoulder for him to burp, "we would have called her Eleanor, with your permission, of course, Miss Sloane."

"I would have been honored."

"Maybe next time," Sophie said.

Or maybe Nell would never get the chance to have a child of her own. She could never wed another man than Alex, not after experiencing Alex's kisses, so she might never know this great bond between mother and baby. She might not even know what came after kisses, if he did not come back.

He would come back, of course. His manservant was at Ambeaux Cottage, as were his coach and his clothes and his boxes of papers about the search. He would come back, but he might not be returning to

Nell. A night away, with who knew what temptations, was sure to bring the earl to his senses. He was an earl, for heaven's sake! He had to marry well, and Nell was not a suitable bride.

But she would not think about him.

Alex did come back, and he had a name. He laughed and hugged Nell, then he hugged Aunt Hazel. Redfern stepped back into the shadows.

"Helen knew the man in your drawing. For many years he had stayed at her place between coaching positions. That was what he said, anyway. She suspected he might have taken to the high toby when jobs were scarce because he always had money to pay his shot and never looked for work that she knew of. Oh, a fellow on the high toby is a highwayman," Alex explained as he accepted a glass of wine from Redfern, who was unabashedly eavesdropping now that the exuberant homecoming had been duly celebrated. Alex drank quickly, since he had ridden home so fast he had not stopped for refreshments, only to rest the horse.

"In other words," he said, "Helen thought he might be a thief, a criminal, as we suspected from his suspicious actions. He stopped coming to her place, but she could not remember when. He definitely knew Phelan. They drank together in her parlor."

Nell was quick to insist, "That does not prove that this man or my brother caused the tragedy."

Aunt Hazel made a snorting noise in disbelief.

Alex tried harder not to condemn Phelan without evidence. "No, but why did Dennis Godfrey, which is his name, incidentally, not come forth after the mishap if he had nothing to hide? And why did your brother not give Godfrey's name when the officials were looking for a gold-toothed man? I do not suppose your brother woke up and started jabbering, did he?"

"Faugh," Aunt Hazel said, expressing her opinion of Phelan, as well as of his physical and mental state.

"Phelan is still, ah, still," Nell said. "He does not speak or move a great deal, although he does eat more than any unconscious man I ever heard of."

"Devil take it, he could tell us so much if only he would." Alex set the glass down hard, in frustration. He had a name: Dennis Godfrey. Phelan had the rest of the story, Alex believed.

Aunt Hazel believed she could find out if this Dennis Godfrey was alive or dead. Alex did not want to ask how, but he did say that he would appreciate any help. He also appreciated being left alone with Nell after sending Redfern for a platter of cold meat and bread when Aunt Hazel wandered away to consult her incorporeal friends.

"Did you miss me, my sweet Nell?"

Of course she did, or there was no excuse for the brain-fogged bumbling she'd exhibited in his absence. While Nell was trying to choose her words, to be honest without sounding forward, to be encouraging without being overeager, Alex spoke up:

"I missed you like the very devil."

"You did?"

"I did, and thought of you constantly."

"I did, too."

"Thought of me, or thought of the prettiest, sweetest woman in the kingdom?"

He was smiling, feathering kisses on her shoulder, on her neck, so that she shivered in expectation of a real kiss, which did not come until she admitted, "I missed you."

"Good."

Oh, it was very good indeed. The kiss was almost worth the wait. Nell kissed Alex back and wrapped her fingers in his windblown hair the way she had been longing to—and which she had sworn not to do. This was foolish and improper and dangerous, and she never wanted to stop.

Neither did Alex, but his stomach grumbled and so did his conscience. He stepped back.

He could not keep kissing Nell this way. Or any other way, for that matter, not without a proper declaration. Of course he was too cowardly to make that declaration, not knowing her answer. On the other hand, the one aching to reach for the softness of her breast, if she said yes, he could do more than kiss her.

No. It was too soon, their lives were too different, she still did not trust him or her own worth.

He could teach her, though, teach her how a woman could be cherished, teach her how much he valued her.

No. Nell was a lady, and the lady he wanted as his countess, as the mother of his children, as his lifemate and lover. He'd had two days to think about it, and had struggled with the facts: He could not be happy without having Nell in his life, and he could not have Nell without a wedding ring. There was only one possible conclusion. Well, there were two: now or later. He'd chosen later.

He might not be ready to make a proposal—Lud, he hadn't been ready in twenty-seven years!—but neither was he willing to keep stepping away. A gentleman had only so much fortitude, after all. After that, he was all for throwing caution and honor to the wind, and tossing his woman over his shoulder like a barbarian. Alex wanted Nell, and he wanted her by his side, now, tomorrow, the next day.

"I do not want to miss you again."

"So you will stay here, with us?" Nell could not keep the hope from her voice, the joy from her radiant smile. "You will hire investigators to pursue the search?"

Alex had to destroy what he wanted most to preserve. "I will hire a battalion of Bow Street Runners, but I cannot stay. I need to hire clerks to pore through morgue records, hospital records, arrest records. I have to find ship agents to sift through a decade of passenger sailing lists, and I have to threaten or bribe the Admiralty officials for the navy's impressment rolls. The man will be found if he is anywhere on the face of the earth, but I have to take Dennis Godfrey's name to London and lead the search."

"Of course you do. I should never have thought otherwise." She lowered her eyes so he could not see the disappointment.

"Come with me, Nell." He tipped her chin up. "I do not want to spend another day—or another hour—without seeing your blue eyes. Come with me, dear Nell, come help me find Dennis Godfrey and Lottie."

"Oh, Alex, do not ask that of me. You know I cannot. I cannot leave my brother. Surely you can see that."

Alex could not see past those same blue eyes, glistening with sudden tears. He kissed one away from her cheek. "He does not need you as much as I do."

"He has no one."

"He has Redfern and that maid Browne, and a hundred servants I can hire to see to his every want and need."

"But that is not family."

He handed her his handkerchief to wipe her eyes, because kissing the tears away would only lead to kiss-

ing his honorable intentions away. "What about me?
My closest family is fighting a war, by Jupiter. Do you
think that does not make me terrified that I might
lose my only brother? But I live my life."

"As Jack lives his. Phelan cannot. Until he is
recovered . . ."

Alex was losing patience. The dastard might never
recover. Was Alex supposed to wait decades to claim
Nell? He wanted sons, not someone else's aged nursemaid. "Deuce take it, the man is guilty of some crime
or other. That's why he turned to drink, I would
wager. He has ruined your life. Perhaps he helped end
your cousin's, and contributed to my father's death.
He might have been the reason we lost Lottie. How
can you stand by him?"

"Because we do not know. And because he is my
brother."

"But he stole your dowry. Would you now let him
steal your future? Our future? I will not let you—
or him."

"We do not have to let that happen. I . . . I have
decided that I will become your mistress after all. I had
time to think about it, and, yes, miss you. I can stay
here, where I belong, and wait for you. No one will
question the arrangement, since the house and property
are yours. We are not so far from London or your country seat, so you can come whenever you wish."

"Is that how little you esteem yourself, that you
would become a rich man's convenient? Is that what
you think of me, of my honor? What about my sons'
honor? Or did you forget that I have a heritage to
preserve? Would you be happy if I took another
woman to wife, to give me legitimate sons, while I
had you in my keeping in the country?"

He might have struck a knife through her heart, the way Nell gasped.

"I suppose that is answer enough," he nearly shouted at her. "You are as feather-brained as your goose if you think I will agree to an affair. I want you in my bed, Nell, make no error about that, but lovemaking is not enough." After finally finding the woman he wanted, Alex was not going to waste any more time. He was so angry, he forgot all his own doubts and excuses to delay. "Come."

He took her hand and pulled her toward Phelan's bedroom. "Go," he told the footman in the hall. "Stay," he ordered the little dog when they reached the door. "Out," he told the maid sitting by the bedside with a lap full of mending. "Wake up!" he yelled at the lifeless figure in the bed when Browne had left.

"Alex, shouting will not have any effect," Nell protested. "We tried. He cannot help his condition."

"And I cannot wait. Sloane, if you hear me, I have come to ask permission to pay my addresses to your sister."

Nell would have tripped over her own foot if Alex had not been holding her up. "You cannot mean that!"

"I do mean it, and a great deal more that is none of your brother's concern. As the head of your family, he is supposed to ask about my ability to support you in comfort. Consider it asked. I can buy my Nell the moon if it is for sale, Sloane, and yes, I can keep your sorry, selfish soul housed and fed without feeling the pinch. And Aunt Hazel, and all her haunts. Do you have any more questions?"

Phelan had not moved.

"Good. I intend to make your sister my wife," Alex

told him, "with or without your blessing. If she will have me, of course. Will you, sweet Nell?"

Nell was shaking her head. "I . . . I . . ."

"'Am overcome with gladness,' are you not, my love? As am I. You have made me the happiest of men, and the most fortunate. But please do not make me wait for the banns to be read, my darling Nell. I can purchase a special license as soon as we arrive in town and we can be married the next day." He turned back to the sleeping Sloane. "I don't think your sister would like a huge social wedding, St. George's, all the trimmings, the crowds of gawkers, the Prince."

Nell took in so much air she coughed. Alex squeezed her hand, still talking to Phelan. "Whatever she wishes, Nell will have, as long as she does not postpone the nuptials too long. So what do you say, Sloane? I am not asking for her dowry, nor what you did with it. I will find out about Lottie one way or another when I find Dennis Godfrey. Which I will, never doubt that. But for now, just nod so Nell can leave you to rot on this bed if that is what you want. She deserves better."

Phelan did not move so much as a finger. One eyelid did seem to twitch. "Ah, so you do give your consent," Alex decided. "Good. Now I can kiss the bride."

Before Nell could catch her breath from Alex's startling announcements, he pulled her closer and bent her slightly back over his arm, to make sure Phelan could see. He kissed her loudly, so Phelan could hear. He kissed her with all his heart, all his hopes, but that was for Nell's sake, and his.

"Arrghh!"

No, Nell was not choking from being held upside down with his tongue in her mouth. Phelan was shouting, leaping from his bed, launching himself at Alex's back, trying to wrap his hands around Alex's neck.

"Oh, no, this time I am ready." Alex spun around, giving Nell a push away, and put his own hands at Phelan's throat.

Phelan gasped. "No! No, you bloody bastard, you will not steal my sister like your father did Lizbeth! No, I say."

Alex was younger, heavier, stronger, far more physically fit. He was easily able to shake off the other man's hands, and fasten his own more securely. He lifted Phelan off his feet and shook him. "And I say you will give your permission, and give us the truth about what happened all those years ago."

Nell cried, "Please, no, Alex!"

"Please do not hurt him for leading to so many deaths? For withholding the facts about Dennis Godfrey? Or for stealing from me?" He shook Phelan again, like a suit of clothes needing an airing. "What did you do with the money, you maggot? Where did you spend Nell's dowry?"

Phelan stopped struggling. Now Alex was holding him up, rather than holding him off the ground. Tears started falling, and his chin was trembling. "On blackmail," he said with a whimper. "I was paying Dennis Godfrey blood money to keep Lottie alive."

CHAPTER TWENTY-FOUR

Alex shoved Phelan into a chair, purposely not back into the bed where he might hide in his covers or his coma. "Talk," he said.

Phelan could not, he was crying so hard. Nell found him a handkerchief and a glass of water.

Impatient, embarrassed at the man's sobbing, Alex pulled the draperies open wider. The sun was finally going to shine on this mess or he'd toss Sloane out the window, Nell's brother or not. "You knew Lottie was alive and you never told anyone? You let some kidnapper keep my sister for thirteen blasted years?"

"I . . . I had no choice!" Phelan blubbered. "He said he would kill her if I told anyone, and then he would tell the authorities that I hired him to wreck the carriage."

"Did you?"

"No, not for that! I only wanted him to damage a wheel or something, so they would have to turn back."

"Why, man? Why?"

"So I could have her for another few days. She might have listened then."

"Listened to what?"

"To me, and how much I loved her. A few more days and she would have seen that I could make her happier than that old man she married."

"That old man was my father, by Jupiter."

Phelan ignored Alex. "We could have fled to Ireland."

"But Lizbeth loved her earl, brother. She would never have left him."

"No, she loved me! She always did!"

"As a cousin."

"No!" Phelan clutched one of Nell's hands and pleaded with her. "She loved me! And I loved her. Tell him I would never have hurt her. I only wanted her to stay for another few days."

Alex felt like crying himself. Nell was silently weeping, still holding her brother's hand. All the deaths, all the sorrow, for one man's foolish infatuation. "You mean it was all a mistake?"

"I do not know."

"Deuce take it, you know more than anyone else! What happened?"

Phelan shook his head. "Godfrey never said. He wrote a note, saying he had the child."

"So why did you not pay her ransom and get her back? My father would have paid everything he had."

"Godfrey's message said he could not bring her back yet. He'd been shot, so everyone would know there was no accident. And she could identify him and describe what happened."

"She was a three-year-old baby! She would not have understood. He could have left her at a church with a note and her name."

"But he did not. He did not say where he was, or how I was to bring him the money. Only that he would kill her if anyone tried to find him."

"She might have been dead, for all you knew."

"He sent a lock of her hair. I burned it so no one would know."

"Oh, Phelan, how could you?" Nell's voice was hushed, quavering.

Alex was so angry he kicked at a log in the fireplace until sparks flew. The log rolled and there was nothing he could do but kick it back, since the poker had been removed. "What happened then?"

Phelan blew his nose. "Nothing. For a fortnight. I kept searching. That was all I could do, until another note arrived. When it came it gave the address of a bank in London, and a sum to be deposited there twice a year, under my name, if I ever wanted to see Charlotte again." He held up his hand before Alex could speak. "I know you are going to ask why I did not go to the bank officers then. I did, but they would not reveal the name of the account holder."

"They would have revealed it to an earl, you idiot!"

"Your father had succumbed to his illness by then. You were a schoolboy, a helpless child yourself."

"My guardians were not helpless. My trustees were all sworn to move heaven and earth to get Lottie back."

"But they would have sent me to prison if I had confessed then. What would have happened to my own sister? And Dennis Godfrey had said he'd kill Charlotte, too."

"Damn, damn, damn!" was all Alex could say.

"But you tried at the bank?" Nell asked.

"Over and over. I brought the money and waited to see who came for it. I wrapped the money in notes, begging for word of Charlotte. I pleaded with the bank manager. In the end I could only keep sending the money, even though there were no more messages from Godfrey."

"For thirteen years, without knowing if Lottie was alive or dead?"

Phelan started weeping again. "How could I take the chance? And if she was alive, then she would need food and clothing and books and pretty ribbons for her hair. Lizbeth would have wanted me to provide for her daughter."

Alex had heard enough. He pulled the sniveling Sloane to his feet by the front of his nightshirt. "Do not dare to excuse your actions by speculating what Lizbeth would want. The countess would want to be alive, at my father's side, watching their beloved child grow up in their tender care. But let me guess. You ran out of money, didn't you? Your own inheritance and income could only support your own comfortable life, not the cost of extortion. So you started stealing from the estate."

Phelan sniffed. "Times were bad. The shipyard failed."

Alex threw Phelan from him in disgust. "So you used your own sister's dowry."

"You would have done the same, would you not, Eleanor? You would not have let Lizbeth's daughter go hungry, would you?"

"Of course not, but surely you could have found another way. When Alex reached his majority, you could have gone to him. You could have told me, let me help."

"There was nothing to be done, I say! The money was always withdrawn. The bank told me that much. I was going to stop paying next year when Charlotte would be seventeen, old enough to go out to work, or wed, or look for us if she wished. Once I stopped sending money to Dennis Godfrey I was going to put the funds back into the farms. I swear!"

"It would have been too late for the tenants, you fool. Half of them have already left, before their roofs fell in on them."

Phelan was rocking back and forth in his chair, his arms folded across his narrow chest. "I had to do it. For Lizbeth."

"You did not have to do any of it, from the beginning. Now you could hang for the memory of a woman who was another man's wife."

"No, Alex, please, no!" Nell cried.

He ran his fingers through his hair. "Lud, Nell, I do not know what crimes your brother can be charged with, but he is as guilty as the devil." He headed toward the bedroom door. "I am leaving before I am tempted beyond endurance to take justice into my own hands. I would kill that pitiful, puling wretch as soon as look at him."

Nell had no answer, for she understood his anger.

Phelan had no answer, for he just kept rocking, his eyes closed.

"I will do it, I swear," Alex threatened, "if he feigns some illness again. I need him to answer more questions when I am not so furious. The name of the bank, Dennis Godfrey's last address, that kind of thing."

"He will answer. I promise. Go now, have your supper. I shall speak with you later, after I make sure Phelan is back in bed."

"An hour, that is all your time I am willing to give him. I need you, Nell."

An hour later, Alex repeated his words. "I need you, Nell. Please say you will come to London with me. You know I have to go, more urgently than ever. I can force the bank to divulge names and addresses, since we know there was criminal activity. I can consult with a barrister I trust about what formal charges might be brought against your brother by the Crown before we make anything public or decide what to do with him. I have to find Dennis Godfrey and shake the truth, and your money, out of him. Mostly, I have to find my sister."

"I need you too, my dearest Alex." Nell was already taking comfort from his embrace. "But I cannot leave Phelan now, in this state."

"What, you would defend him?" He rubbed her back, easing the tense muscles of her neck and shoulders.

"No, I would stand by him. I cannot turn my back on my brother, no matter what crimes he has committed. Would you stop loving Jack if he became a traitor?"

Alex was offended enough that he stopped massaging her back, but not enough to let her out of his arms. "My brother would never betray his country!"

"And I thought mine would never betray Lizbeth, but he did. Phelan needs me now, to make sure he does not slip back into that suspended state of brain paralysis where he does not have to face his sins."

"What of my need?"

"I think you need time to reconsider your words."

"What, about murdering that imbecilic brother of yours? You must know I would not, much as I might wish he would disappear. And I shall do all in my power to keep him from arrest and scandal, for your sake."

Nell showed her gratitude with a kiss. Alex started his hands moving again, but now they were not rubbing her back. Nell inhaled sharply when his fingers touched her breast, then she stopped breathing altogether when he untied the fastenings of her gown to touch her bare flesh. "Oh."

"Oh, yes, my love. Let me show you how I need you, and you need me."

She was ready to burst from the need—or the lack of air. Nell pulled back, at least an inch. "No, I did not mean you need to think about my brother, but about what you told him. About seeking my hand, getting a special license. Or was that all for Phelan's benefit?"

He placed butterfly kisses on her neck, and down to the gaping front of her gown. Between kisses and feather-touch tastes, he said, "Not a syllable of it was for him alone. I know I should have done the thing properly, on my knees and all, but there was no chance. I do want to marry you, Nell, more than I have ever wanted anything in my life. Well, except for my first horse when I was five. But I did not know any better then. Now I do."

"No, you are still thinking like a boy, wanting what you immediately desire, whether it is right for you or not. You cannot want a wife who will not be accepted into your world, who will not know how to go on in your social circles."

"I have never heard of a countess, a wealthy one at that, who was not accepted, except Lady Grimshaw, who was her husband's housekeeper before marrying him. Besides, you are beautiful and talented and every inch a lady. No one can help but be charmed by you. And if a few high-sticklers do not send us invitations to their boring dinner parties, so what? We shall have balls of our own, or live quietly in the country. My friends will welcome you, once they get over wishing they had found you first."

He kissed her again, to prove his point. What he proved was that they could not kiss and touch and fondle and unfasten while standing up. So he ended on his knees after all, with Nell in his arms. That quickly grew uncomfortable, so they slid to the floor.

While she could still think, Nell protested, not the position, but the proposal. "No, you are thinking with this"—which she touched gingerly, curiously, yet with great effect—"instead of this," which was now between her breasts, nuzzling and nipping, with great effect.

He raised his head, affronted. "Do you think I am merely infatuated, then? Or lusting after a pretty wench? Well, you are pretty and I am obviously lusting. You can feel that between us." He did not mean the electricity; he meant the erection. "In fact, if you touch it once more, I will leave evidence for the maids to find in the morning so everyone knows how much I want you."

Nell quickly moved her hand. She moved it to his chest, though, unknotting his neckcloth so she could open the collar of his shirt. He was touching her bare skin; she wanted no less.

He sighed with pleasure, that his Nell was no ice maiden. Chilly? He was burning. "I do want to make love to you, my sweet, oh, how I want to, right here, right now, although I know we must not. More than that, though, I want to make love *with* you for the rest of our lives. What is that if not love?"

"I do not know, for I have never felt love before."

"If it means not wanting to be apart, not wanting to think of anything but your glorious eyes, not wanting any other man to look at you? Wanting to keep you safe and smiling and satiated all the days of our lives?"

"I do not know, but I feel that way too."

"Then come with me, dearheart, marry me in London."

"No. You have to be sure. Go do what you have to with the bank and Dennis Godfrey. Then come back with the license."

He pulled her skirts back down before his hand, and his arousal, could reach the point of no stopping. "You are afraid I will change my mind, aren't you?"

"I want you to know your own mind. I would die if you discovered next year or the year after that you'd rather have a beau monde belle like Lady Lucinda."

"I would not discover that in ninety years. I would have been wed ages ago if I wanted an empty, polite, social match. I want passion and pride and springtime, for ninety years, at least. I want a marriage based on love that will last even longer, like your aunt's for her André."

"He is not speaking to her."

"Well, it might be hard for a dead chap to stay constant while his beloved flirts with a duke. But I would."

"And I would not flirt with anyone. Except you."

"Promise?"

"I promise. And I shall gladly swear to it on our wedding day, if we have one." She started fastening her gown back together.

"If? Devil take it, you just said you loved me!"

"Yes, but I have to know that you are sure."

"No, you are not thinking of me, you are thinking of your own fears. You are afraid I do not mean any of my clumsy words of love, that I will change my mind and not purchase that special license, not wish to marry you once we are in London among the primped and polished beauties. You are nothing but a coward, my love, and that will never do. Two lily-livered cravens in one family—make that three, if you include your spineless brother—are far too many. Our children will be afraid of their shadows."

"Are we going to have children, then?"

"As many as you want, as soon as I can convince you." He stood up. "How can I prove my love to you, though? If my words are not enough, and my kisses are not enough, what will it take for you to make me the happiest of men instead of the most despondent and confused?"

Nell rubbed her palm along his jaw, feeling the new bristles growing there while she stared into his brown eyes. "You can go and then come back. If you do not return, I will understand that you had second thoughts. My heart will be broken, but I will understand that it was for the best, and better now than years later."

So he went. What else could he have done?

He could have taken Aunt Hazel along, besides his dog.

The old woman was outraged that Nell had turned down her best chance for happiness, to say nothing of a fortune and a title. As soon as she heard that Nell was sending the Earl of Carde on his way, she started to shout. Life was too uncertain, Aunt Hazel ranted, and love too precious not to grab hold of with both hands and never let go. Look at her and her André, the old lady declared. She had lost her lover, but she had known a grand passion. Nell was liable to end up a shriveled old prune, without so much as a warm memory through the cold nights of her barren spinsterhood. Worst of all, Nell had tossed aside her own future for the felonious Phelan.

Besides, Aunt Hazel wanted to go to London herself. "Things are dull around here now that the guests are all gone and André is not speaking to me. Phelan never was much for conversation, and I do not wish to speak to that dirty dish, knowing what he has done. I cannot find Dennis Godfrey, which means either the scoundrel is not dead or he is too far away to answer my call. Perhaps he went straight to hell instead of staying around to chat. Why should he talk to me anyway, when I would only give him a piece of my mind?"

And her aunt had so few pieces to spare, Nell thought, setting aside the vase of flowers she was arranging for Phelan's room, to cheer him up. Nothing was going to raise her own spirits, certainly not Aunt Hazel's lectures about the decades-dead Frenchman or conversations with a kidnapper. Nell was lonely enough herself without Alex; she did not need reminding that he had begged her to go with him.

She picked up a stem of irises to add to the ferns. "What would you do in London, Aunt Hazel? You said you had no friends there."

"That was then. This is now. I might just try my luck with Apston. His Grace was fond of me. He said so himself, hinting about how he'd like a companion in his old age, when his daughter was out of the house. And one of us has to be thinking ahead, my girl. Who knows what will become of us if they cart your brother away? If you do not marry Carde, some other female is bound to, and she will not want us around. We could find ourselves out in the street, and I am too old for the poorhouse."

"But the duke is poor. You heard Alex say so. He cannot afford an indigent wife, much less her equally poor relation." The iris fell to the floor. "You cannot be thinking of becoming His Grace's ah, light of love, can you?"

"At my age? Do not be more of a fool than you have already been today. But who says we are insolvent? I have my dowry."

Nell's cutting shears fell to the floor. "You have a dowry?" Uncle Ambeaux's sister had to be sixty. And poor.

"Of course I do. My father did not leave me impoverished, no more than yours did. But my brother trusted me enough—and trusted I would never find another sweetheart after André—to leave the money in my hands. I never let that shifty brother of yours get wind of it, or he would have found some way to steal it. I have invested wisely over the years, so now there is quite a nice little sum, ample enough to interest even a duke, I do believe."

Nell thought of the darned gloves and turned cuffs on their gowns. "Why did you never spend any of your funds if they were earning interest?"

Aunt Hazel straightened her shoulders. "It was for my marriage, of course, nothing else. I thought I might give it to you, for yours, when you found the proper husband, since your makebate brother had spent your dowry. If you are going to marry the earl, though, you will not need it. If you are going to refuse a nonpareil like him, you do not deserve it."

Nell agreed.

A tear fell to the floor.

CHAPTER TWENTY-FIVE

The coach traveled slowly, weighted down with second thoughts. Alex tried to sleep on the road south, but his regrets kept him awake. So did his valet.

Stives was sniffing his disfavor. *Snort* as he expressed his opinion of the hasty departure. *Snort* as he made known his disapproval that milord had taken the dog along with them instead of the cook, who not only made the flakiest pastries, but who was not averse to a bit of cuddling in the kitchen. *Snort* as Stives picked white dog hairs off his somber black suit.

"If you are coming down with a chill, Stivy, I can set you down at the next inn we come to."

Snort for the sarcasm.

The only one in the carriage who was happy to be there was Daisy, who would follow the earl anywhere, unlike some females Alex could name but would not—his mood was black enough already. He should be elated at finally finding the perfect woman for his countess, the only woman who could make him eager to forget every other woman. Instead he was miserable, wretched, and angry besides. Yes, he was spoiled, and yes, he was arrogant. He was the earl, wasn't he? But no female had ever refused his attentions before. No female had ever been so pigheaded before either.

Alex worried that she would find another excuse when he returned with the special license, she would have some other reason not to leave Ambeaux Cottage. This time it was the brother; next time it might be the aunt, or the tenants, or the blasted goose. One would think he was asking her to go to the Antipodes with him, not to London, where she could dance and shop and go sightseeing and take in the theater and galleries and museums and bookstores. She would adore the metropolis, he knew, and his friends would welcome her warmly. It was not as if he was asking her to spend the rest of her life in the sooty city, either. He had to continue the search for Lottie there now, but later they only had to spend a few months in town when he was required in Parliament. The rest of the year she would have all of Cardington to ramble in, to draw the new vistas, to fill Carde Hall with love and laughter and children.

The thought of those children, tiny tots with golden ringlets and blue eyes—and hopefully tiny noses—pulled at his heartstrings. The thought of begetting the little darlings pulled at his privates. Lud, how could he live without Nell? He was barely surviving this first hour.

He should have argued more. What kind of spineless jellyfish was he, anyway, to give in so easily? No wonder Nell doubted his sincerity if he did not fight for his love. Besides, what kind of marriage would it be if he let his bride have her way in everything, before the ring was even on her finger? He'd be wearing

one through his nose soon enough, that was what kind.
Of course, he could think of very little he would rather
do than please Nell, but she was wrong now, damn it.

What he should have done was give her no choice.
He should have packed them all up, bags, baggage,
batty aunt, and bedeviled brother, and carted them off
to London with him. No choices, no excuses. No
goose, no matter what Nell said.

He had the right to take Phelan into custody, and
the duty to find him a better doctor or the best barrister. The rest of them were his responsibility, too. He
owned the house, he had been paying their bills, he
was the only competent male to look after Nell and
the aunt. Nell would have had to come with them, on
his terms. That was what he should have done, instead
of sitting miserable in a carriage with a snooty valet
and a sweatered lapdog. That was what he would have
done, if he had any ba—

"Back. Stives, tell the driver to turn around. We are
going back."

The valet did as ordered, but he shook his head.
"That's what comes of milord staying at that cottage.
Mad as a March hare, like all the rest of them."

Alex had to agree, when they pulled up the carriage
drive in front of the house. Everyone, Nell and her
aunt, the maid, the indoor servants, a gardener, and
the cook, were all outside, staring at the rain falling
from the sky. Even Redfern was out of doors, since
the day was overcast.

"What the . . . ?" Then Alex looked up. They were
not gazing at the rain; they were looking at Phelan in
his nightshirt, up on the narrow third story balcony
that gave access to the roof for chimney cleaning.
"Oh, hell."

Stives gave his unsolicited opinion, as usual. "He

would have done it already, milord, if he were going to."

Then Nell was running toward Alex. He could not tell if those were tears on her face or raindrops, but he opened his arms to her.

"You came back! Thank God. Phelan ran past me when I was pouring his tea, and now he says he is going to jump. You have to do something!"

Like what? Give the dastard a shove?

Alex rubbed her back while he studied the situation. He did not have a ladder or a hot air balloon to get up to Phelan's perch, or enough mattresses to cushion a fall from that height. What he did have was a weeping woman who expected him to perform miracles, and centuries of authority bred into his blood.

"Sloane," he shouted with all the command he possessed, "get down this instant. I insist."

"No," Phelan called back. "And you cannot make me."

So much for the voice of authority. He tried reason. "Killing yourself is no answer to anything."

"It is for me. This way I will not have to face prison or exile or hanging or my own shame."

He was right. Alex tried tender emotions next. "But think of your sister, and the sorrow you will bring. You are frightening her now and upsetting the servants."

"They will be better without me."

Well, Phelan was right about that, too. Still Nell was clutching Alex's arm. "Nonsense. Killing yourself is no solution. In the eyes of the church it is a worse sin than anything you have committed."

"But I have nothing to live for."

"Your sister is something. My sister is something. Don't you wish to be around to see Lottie restored to her family? Don't you want to see Lizbeth's little girl all grown up? Don't you want to see that dastard Dennis Godfrey brought to justice?"

"No, I cannot stand the guilt anymore."

"Then atone for your crimes by helping us right the wrongs." Alex's throat was getting sore from shouting and his neck was aching from looking up. "Get back inside, damn you, before you slip on the wet tiles."

"No, blast you, Carde. You and your father have ruined everything. You will not ruin this." Phelan stepped away from the house and put his hands on the balcony railing, as if he were going to climb it. One of the maids screamed. Redfern sank down on the gravel driveway, praying.

Alex sighed, then he called up to Phelan, "Well, if you must, you must. But you do owe me a favor, old man, for the money and the aggravation. Gentleman's honor and all that."

Phelan must still consider himself a gentleman. "A favor?"

"Yes. If you are going to dive off the balcony, at least wait for me to leave. I can't stand the sight of blood, you see." Without looking to see if Phelan was watching, he headed back to his carriage, Stives at his side.

"You are going?" Nell ran after him, looking at him in disbelief.

"Yes, I am going to try to save that imbecile's life, although I do not know why I should bother. You keep him talking." He pressed a quick kiss on her lips and got into the coach, loudly ordering the driver to head toward the stables. As soon as they were out of sight of the front of the house, he stopped the carriage and leaped out, minus his tightly fitting coat. He climbed to the roof of the vehicle and directed his driver to pull closer to the house, and the drainpipe.

"I hope that thing holds. Damn, I hate heights."

Stives held the coat and the dog. "What if there had been no drainpipe?"

"Then I would have found a rope or some ivy to climb."

"I do not suppose milord would consider using the back door?"

Alex was already partway up the side of the house.

Nell kept talking, and when her throat ran dry, Aunt Hazel took over. "You'd better not come back to haunt me, you miserable, mange-ridden maw worm, or I will have my friends make your next life wretched too. If you think this one was hellish, wait until you meet Attila the Hun."

"That is not helpful, Aunt Hazel!" Nell went back to pleading, and telling Phelan that she loved him, no matter what he had done in the past. She promised to stay with him as long as he needed her.

Alex would have stopped climbing if he'd heard that and let the fool jump, but he was nearly to the roof by now. The muscles in his arms were burning and his legs were going numb from clenching around the narrow pipe, and his neck was aching because he had to keep looking up instead of at the ground. He would not be surprised if his shoulder became dislocated again, or his ribs burst with his pounding heart. Or if he cast up his accounts altogether.

Then he was scrabbling up over the edge of the roof, panting. He bent down and scuttled toward the front side of the house, trying to catch his breath before the worst part: trying to take Phelan by surprise without looking down.

He thought he heard gasps from the watchers below when he reached the side of the roof that overlooked the drive. He looked down at them for an instant, so he could estimate Phelan's position. Then he had to swallow the bile that rose in his throat. He considered taking off his spectacles so everything was a blur, but he was liable to fall off the roof instead of rescuing the rotter. He got down on his belly. He crept forward as quietly as he could. Then he had to look over, to gauge the distance. Lud, it was a good thing he had not stopped for refreshments on the road. He took a deep breath, and hoped Redfern was still praying. Then he jumped.

Phelan shrieked so loudly that Alex barely heard the screams from the ground as he landed on Sloane's back, knocking him to the balcony landing.

"Let me go! Let me die!" Phelan pawed and clawed his way back toward the railing, kicking and biting and punching. Alex held on.

"I deserve to die!"

"You'll get no argument from me there, but you will not do it in front of your sister, and not before you tell me the name of that damned bank."

Finally Alex had enough leverage and enough room to swing his fist. It was over. Phelan lay still. Gasping, Alex hoisted him up and over the windowsill, where two footmen were waiting.

They carried Phelan back to his bedroom. Nell raced in, followed by half the household, it seemed.

"Is he dead?" she cried, seeing her brother so lifeless on the bed. "Or back in his coma?"

Alex was still panting, rubbing at his sore shoulder, his neck, his knuckles. "No, he is merely unconscious this time. I had to strike him to keep him from struggling. Otherwise both of us would have gone over the edge. And I am sorry, my dear, but I have to admit that I enjoyed hitting him. And if the gudgeon gets up in the next half hour, I fully intend to hit him again. I hate heights."

Nell drew her arm back and punched him right in the nose.

"Blast, woman, the thing is big enough as is!" Alex took the handkerchief the efficient Stives handed him, in case his nose was bleeding. "What if you'd broken the deuced beak? Besides, what was that for? I had no choice but to hit your brother, and I did say I was sorry."

"That was not for Phelan, it was for lying to me. You said you were a coward and I expected you to be a coward. Your brother is the reckless, hey-go-mad one, not you, Alexander Chalfont Endicott. Not you! If you ever do such a crazy thing again, I swear I shall push you off the roof myself! I thought I would die, seeing you leap from the roof. Why did you do such a foolhardy thing?"

"Because he is your brother."

Then she was in his arms, and he forgot about the other people in the room. "Because I love you."

"Oh, Alex, I love you so. And I will never forgive Phelan for almost costing me your life. I think I no longer care what becomes of him, he has made us all so miserable. And I would follow you anywhere."

"Even to London ballrooms?"

"Even to court, if you still wish."

"Still wish?" he echoed. "Do you think I climb roofs for just any old woman? Of course I still want you by my side, forever and ever. In London, traveling the continent when it becomes safe, visiting the properties in Jamaica, but mostly at home at Carde Hall."

Redfern was still praying when he finally wheezed

his way up to Phelan's bedroom. "Hallelujah!" He poured wine from the liquor cabinet for everyone—everyone but Phelan, that is. Nell and Alex had to share a glass. Stives drank out of the bottle.

"But what are you going to do with the dregs?" Aunt Hazel wanted to know, so Stives poured the last drop of wine into a dish for the dog. "No, not those dregs. That one," she said, pointing at Phelan, where one of the footmen was tying his wrist to the headboard of the bed, on Alex's orders. He was not going back onto that roof.

"You cannot leave him here when we go to London," Aunt Hazel was saying. "I am not staying behind to look after him, and Redfern is too old."

A lunatic asylum was a death sentence, and prison was a disgrace on Nell's name. Alex rubbed his sore nose.

The maid Browne stepped forward, ducking a hasty curtsy. "Pardon, my lord, Miss Sloane, but I might know of a place where he'll be safe. My pa has an inn outside London, but the new toll road stole all its business so half the rooms are empty and not much traffic passes by. It's nothing fancy, but it's clean. And one story only."

"But Phelan could simply walk away. Heaven knows what trouble he could get into then."

"Not with my four brothers what work there and on the bit of a farm that goes with it. They could watch after Mr. Sloane and keep him safe. My family could use the money, ma'am. That's why I had to go into service, but I would be happier off home, tending to the poor gentleman. I've grown right fond of him, I have, and would be glad to keep him with us."

"That might serve, Nell, having him where you could visit."

"And he might recover sooner away from this place, with all of his own ghosts haunting his mind."

"And it could not cost more than a fancy hospital would," Aunt Hazel added, ignoring the reference to her erstwhile associates.

"I'll gladly pay whatever it takes," Alex said, "if you agree, Nell."

She nodded, for this was truly the best solution she could hope for for her troubled sibling. Phelan might even find some peace and happiness with Browne and her family. "Thank you, Alex, for your generosity."

Generosity? He'd pay half his fortune to be rid of the man. In fact, while he was at it, Alex told the maid, "I'll pay double if you take the goose, too."

Then they were alone, while everyone started packing, hiring extra coaches, sending messages to the tenants and neighbors and Mr. Silbiger. They would leave tomorrow. "And no one shares our carriage," Alex firmly told Nell, determined to be the master of his marriage.

"Not even the dog?"

"Well, if Daisy promises not to look. I do not intend to wait until I have that special license in my hand to have my hands on you. I deserve the time alone, after what I went through."

"You deserve the world, my love." Nell reached out to touch his red, swollen nose, and Alex tried not to wince. She bit her lip in regret and he tried not to put his own lips and tongue and teeth there instead.

Nell apologized. "I am sorry, that was poor reward for such bravery."

"Bravery? It was no such thing. I was quaking the entire time."

"I do not believe you. That was the most courageous, most selfless act I have ever seen in my life, even if it was the most witless. You were a true hero."

"Silly, that is my brother's job, remember? I just did what had to be done. If I had stopped to think about it, I would have fainted. And I did almost lose the contents of my stomach. A fine sight that would have been for the servants."

She smiled, not accepting a word of his denial. "You were dauntless, while I was afraid, Alex, so afraid that I could lose you and Phelan both."

"Sh, my love," he whispered, forgetting his aching arms as he wrapped them tightly around her. "The thing I feared most was losing your love."

"Never. I do not think I could stop loving you until I drew my last breath. And then I would try to stay near you, like Aunt Hazel's André. I belong here."

Here was not Ambeaux Cottage, here was in Alex's arms. "Wherever you are, Alex, that is where I want to be."

"Good, because I shall never let you go again."

Their kiss of promise turned into one of passion, and they might have shared their wedding night at least two days early, right there in Phelan's bedchamber, except he groaned.

"Deuce take it, I should have hit him harder."

"Tomorrow, my love."

"I can hit him again tomorrow?"

"No, tomorrow we will be together."

"Wrong, my precious Nell. We will be together forever."

EPILOGUE

They did not find Lottie. They found Dennis Godfrey's grave, marked the same year as her disappearance. The records showed he had died of a bullet wound turned septic.

They did find out that the bank account was in the name of Mrs. Dennis Godfrey, although the money had not been withdrawn in two years. They made regular deposits anyway, with the bank on notice to apprehend Mrs. Godfrey. Her marriage had never been registered in any parish the scores of hired clerks could find. Godfrey did have a sister, however, a seamstress at Drury Lane who had disappeared over a decade ago. Breeding, she must have been, an old actor recalled, for he'd heard she had a child soon afterward.

Alex and Nell did not find Molly Godfrey, or whatever name she was using, despite all the reward notices and broadsides Alex had printed, all the sketches Nell drew from her drawings of the child, all the Bow Street Runners and private investigators they hired.

What they did find was love: companionship that

shared the disappointment, joy that kept growing along with their young family, and passion that never waned.

For two years, while Nell learned to be a countess and Alex learned to be her hero, they never stopped trying to find Lizbeth's daughter and they never gave up hope. When Jack came back from the wars, maybe he could bring Lottie home. . . .

BARBARA METZGER

"Barbara Metzger deliciously mixes love
and laughter." —*Romantic Times*

Wedded Bliss
0-451-20859-5

A Perfect Gentleman
0-451-21041-7

The Duel
0-451-21389-0

Available wherever books are sold or at
penguin.com

Also by
BARBARA METZGER

Two holiday stories in one book!
Father Christmas and Christmas Wishes
0-451-21352-1

*Barbara Metzger and four other beloved
Regency authors with a collection of five
stories of wedding-day romance.*
Wedding Belles
0-451-21189-8

Coming October 2005:
Five new novellas of holiday romance.
Regency Christmas Courtship

Available wherever books are sold or at
penguin.com

S027/Metzger

All your favorite romance writers are
coming together.

SIGNET ECLIPSE